Edge of Oblivion

PAINTING THE MISTS, BOOK 9

PATRICK G. LAPLANTE

Published by: Patrick G. Laplante
Editing and Interior Design by: Crystal Watanabe
Cover Illustration and Design by: Samuel Alves
First edition, 2020
ISBN: 978-1-989578-14-8

Other Painting the Mists Books:

Clear Sky

Blood Moon

Light in the Darkness

Pure Jade

Corrupted Crimson

Kindling

Shattered Lands

Edge of Oblivion

Words of Creation (forthcoming)

Dedication

To those who are overwhelmed. Hang in there.
You can make it.

Author's Note and Acknowledgments

I try to keep a positive note in my writing (aside from the obvious satire in my prologues), so I hesitate to talk much about current affairs. Recent events, however, dictate that I should take a stance on some key issues. I don't do this lightly—political opinions can cost authors their career. So I'll keep it simple and straightforward, focusing on issues I think shouldn't be (but somehow are) divisive.

First: Black lives matter. There is obvious systemic racism in the US and in my home country, Canada. While I don't believe I've perpetuated racism, and I don't consider myself racist, I know now that I may have said or done things that make things worse without realizing it. If I have done so, I apologize. That was not my intention, and I will try to be more self-critical and do better.

Second: COVID-19 is a seriously huge problem. Wear masks. Practice social distancing. Work together to keep everyone safe.

That's it. I'm not going to comment on anything else. Now back to personal updates.

As I write this note, I'm approaching the 75% mark on a secret project, which is not-so-secretly another book. I'm going to finish it, then sit on it before publishing. I don't want a repeat of Violet Fate. For those of you who don't know it, I published a Painting the Mists side story about Cha Ming's disciples. But when I sat down to write the second part of the duology, I realized the first part wasn't up to my increasing standards. So instead of writing the second part, I unpublished it. I don't plan on rewriting it. My apologies to anyone affected.

Writing is a journey, and I can only try improving with every book. I have two goals in mind every time I write: your enjoyment and my own. I especially hope you'll enjoy Edge of Oblivion, as it finishes off the first arc of Painting the Mists, Angels and Devils.

Before moving on, I'd like to finish with some words of thanks. Thank you to my wife, Xing Wen, for your continued support. Thank you to my parents, my brothers, and my sister for being there for me.

I'd like to thank this book's beta readers: Dave Yeung, Aljoscha Volk, Drew Kennedy, John Wilson, and Ardash. Your feedback was a great help in improving the story.

Many thanks to Crystal Watanabe for her excellent editing support. My writing continues to improve with her help, so I'm glad to have her on board. Thank you to Samuel Alves for the great cover—I didn't know how painting a Taotie would turn out, and he didn't disappoint.

Last, but not least, thank you to my readers. I write to tell people stories, and a story is worth nothing if it isn't shared. I hope you enjoy reading this book as much as I enjoyed writing it.

Cheers,
Patrick G. Laplante

Previously in Painting the Mists

To repay a life debt to Wang Jun, Cha Ming journeys to the Southern Lands to instigate a blood feud between the Wang family and the Spirit Temple.

Blending in proves surprisingly easy. Through clever use of his Seventy-Two Transformations Technique, mind-skimming techniques, and the Monkey King's direct interference, he forges a false identity as Pai Xiao, a prodigal spiritual blacksmith. War is brewing, however. He barely creates the first part of his disguise before getting dragged into a fight with a Blood Master Monastery. Tens of thousands die, and though he destroys the monastery, he is only able to save a single life, a girl named Mo Ling.

In order to bolster his disguise and facilitate his infiltration of the Wang family, Cha Ming travels to Ashes, taking the helpless Mo Ling with him. By crafting a few key weapons and forging a false history, he catches the eye of Director Wang Yong, who asks him to work for him in Bastion, the capital of the Ji Kingdom. Cha Ming accepts but is forced to alter Mo Ling's memories and leave her behind. He dares not risk her safety by pulling her closer to Zhou Li's pet project.

Cha Ming works hard to gain the favor of the Blackthorn Conglomerate, the Wang family's secret Southern business. His efforts pay off. Through carefully concealed ingenuity, he manages to join the special weapons development division. Their goal? A weapon called the Breaker. It is a treasure meant to destroy the defense of the Song Kingdom, Southhaven Wall.

Instigation is a delicate art. His first attempts gain him the enmity of Bastion's Blood Master Monastery. He is forced to go mining north of Bastion Wall in the Shattered Lands, where a life-leaching aura makes it impossible for all but the strongest to function. Through a series of adventures, he discovers the source of this supposed curse—a powerful demon monarch guarding the Leyline of Gold. He first breaks through to half-step rune carving to protect himself from the aura. Then, by speaking to the Life-Leaching Monarch, he discovers that the last remaining component for his body cultivation, the Gold Source Marrow, has been taken by the Wang family.

Upon returning to Bastion, Cha Ming discovers that things are moving quickly in the Southern Alliance. Due to a rapidly moving deadline, he is approached by the crown prince of the Ji Kingdom to betray the Blackthorn Conglomerate and join the Ji Kingdom in earnest. Only he can develop the Breaker on time, and they know it. Cha Ming accepts, knowing full well that his betrayal will greatly damage the Wang family's reputation.

The next few months are a mad rush. By using his increasing importance, Cha Ming gains access to the vault. He secretly steals the Gold Source Marrow and breaks through to half-step blood awakening. Then, after witnessing Mo Ling giving birth, he discovers his own meaning of life and imbues it into his Living Talisman.

With his power at an all-time high and a dreaded Taotie heading to Bastion courtesy of Feng Ming and Gong Xuandi, Cha Ming begins a chain reaction. He slays the three Northern traitors in the Blackthorn Conglomerate, steals the Breaker prototype and data, and raids the vault. He then gives a defective Breaker to the crown prince. As he destroys Bastion's Blood Master Monastery and Spirit Temple, Feng Ming and Gong Xuandi wreak havoc in the city. Concurrently, the Taotie attacks. Bastion's wall is broken, leaving the city defenseless against the Life-Leaching Monarch and her army of skeletal spiders.

Cha Ming escapes the chaos by joining forces with Feng Ming

and Gong Xuandi. They leave just as the Taotie is sealed by the South's transcendent forces. Though he achieved his goal, it came at a great personal cost. Overusing his newly obtained Spirit-Banishing Eyes has blinded him, and guilt at the deaths of millions of innocents is overwhelming.

While Cha Ming does his part in the South, Wang Jun wages a different war in Gold Leaf City. He resorts to darker methods, using the powers of shadow and fate to forge documents and karma and recover long-lost secrets. That and the resulting assassinations prove too much for Wang Jun. Hong Xin tries to reassure him while waging her own battle with the Icy Heart Pavilion. Though their means aren't ideal, these rogue members are far from criminal. She strives to unite their respective factions, a difficult task given her possession of the Frozen Heart Oath Stone.

Circumstances force her hand. The Spirit Temple's assassins begin slaying members of the Icy Heart Pavilion. She takes advantage of the opportunity to combine their factions, resigning and destroying the Frozen Heart Oath Stone to accomplish this. Free of her karmic obligations to the Red Dust Pavilion, she vows to join Wang Jun and help him sort out his family issues. Unfortunately, Wang Jun's family has other ideas. They capture her, cripple her cultivation, and force Wang Jun into submission just as he's about to win.

As humans struggle on the continent, Huxian walks his own path. His four friends are busy condensing their initiation marks, and he must do the same. To do so, he enters a secret realm hidden in the Silverwing Mountain Range. The realm is cursed with a sun that never sets. The first place he visits is filled with ghosts that are trapped in the moment, forced to relive the last few minutes of their lives in perpetuity. Upon receiving a mysterious gold jade fragment, he decides to free these ghosts. To that end, he journeys to the east, where monks reside.

The monks have not been reduced to ghosts. Instead, there are cursed to relive their entire lives endlessly. They are chained to the mountain's shadow, which never disappears due to the shackled sun. Huxian escapes by obtaining a second jade fragment. He follows a deceased monk's advice and journeys to the west. There, after chasing the scorching sun for what seems like an eternity, he obtains the Spirit-Banishing Scripture and its corresponding eye technique. He uses it to solve the curse of the realm, freeing millions of souls to be reincarnated.

Cha Ming and Feng Ming journey to the Eastern Desert. Cha Ming is blind and ridden with guilt. Wang Jun, helpless due to Hong Xin's imprisonment, submits to his brother Wang Ling and Patriarch Wuling. Meanwhile, Huxian's meddling in the Candle Dragon's realm has caught the Godbeast's attention. Huxian accepts the Candle Dragon's trial because he, more than anyone else, knows what they must face: a fiendish demon unlike any other; a world-ending calamity made flesh.

*C*lank. *Clank. Clank.*

VOID-X3CX-R04 turned his head sharply toward the sound of metal on the bars of his cage. It was a delicious sound, he decided; every sound had a taste, and every sight had a flavor, adding color to his otherwise dreary existence. Meaning could also be savored. The clanking was a distraction, a simple attempt by simple beings at catching his attention. They were treating him like a two-day-old kitten, an insult if he knew one, but something far preferable to being sealed again, cut off from all sources of sustenance in a place where time lost all meaning.

Though he preferred this result to the alternative, it didn't take away from the fact that every single one of these humans was an annoying gnat. The first thing he would do when he broke out of his cage would be to consume whoever was doing the clanging. But then again, what didn't he want to eat? Alas, the bars imprisoning him, the only things within his reach, were inedible. Their ochre glow reeked of delicious transcendent might, and while he instinctively knew its flavor and its corresponding value, he could only stare at it with a wide, drooling mouth not powerful enough to savor it.

Clank. Clank. Clank.

He drank in the sounds, annoyed. Did they think he was a child? Did they think he was mentally incapable? He was smarter than the lot of them, that annoying gnat of a seer included. Sure, he was slow to respond. Who wouldn't be with a gnawing hunger like his, forever urging him onward, everything in sight just another tasty morsel to fill the endless pit in his stomach? It was a wonder he could even function, let alone recognize each of their delicious scents with everything he had going on in the background.

But that didn't stop them from being annoying. The gnat was back, it seemed. This time, however, he brought something tasty. Bones, delicious bones of a peak-core-formation demon were pushed through the bars of his cage. He immediately grabbed them with his horned tentacles, stuffing them into his torso, where his main mouth appeared and bit down on them.

Bliss. Pure bliss.

Every time he ate something significant, he felt a sense of raw, untamed happiness. And for a moment, he could even forget the gnawing hunger and that wretched unfilled void that egged him on, telling him to destroy, when really, all things considered, all he wanted to do was paint. He'd tasted many paintings, and he appreciated their colors, their emotion, and their tasty ink. How nice would it be to sit down, sated, and paint on a blank canvas with all the colors that he knew?

Alas, that would never be his lot in life. He was never meant to create, only to destroy; his master had seen to that, wherever he was. Without him, he could only do what he could to fill his stomach. Right now, that meant pandering to that pesky seer. VOID-X3CX-R04 contorted his face. Was this the kind of response the gnat was looking for? The seer shook his head, so VOID-X3CX-R04 changed his posture—it had worked last time. The seer seemed unimpressed.

Drat, VOID-X3CX-R04 thought. If he couldn't please the seer, how could he get more food? He panicked and tried many simple yet energy-efficient gestures. The second platter waited outside his cage, taunting him. The tasty demon-beast meat on it had been shaved off the bones he'd just eaten. He heard a sound coming from the seer but ignored it. What could be more important than the literal feast waiting just outside his cage? After all, that might be the one, the last bit of energy that would finally propel him to the half-step-initiation realm by forming his World-Ending Calamity Mark.

The seer continued talking, and VOID-X3CX-R04 tasted more buzzing. He scratched his head. He held up a claw. He stood on his head. Nothing seemed to work. So, unsure how to proceed, he did a little dance, though he doubted the seer would understand its subtle intricacies, the emotion behind it, and its significance to his people's heritage. A lonely people, they'd been forced to come up with a style only they could understand, an amazing development given there were usually only two or three of them in existence at any given moment. The dance failed, predictably. The seer facepalmed and let out more annoying sounds.

Maybe I should actually listen to what he's saying, a small piece of VOID-X3CX-R04's mind said, *if only to get more sustenance.* He waited, and the seer repeated himself. Instead of immediately sucking in the sounds like he usually did, he savored them, savored their meaning. Then he looked to the seer in confusion. *Just that? You just want me to nod if I understand you?* So, he did. Immediately afterward, or as immediately as mere ants could make happen, the tray of beast meat entered the cage. He ate it ravenously, and when he was done, he discovered another tray had appeared. The seer spoke again.

This time, VOID-X3CX-R04 listened. The seer said words—a silly thing like "stand on one leg and put your hands behind your head, flailing three tentacles." He did just that, and he was rewarded with another delicious tray. Another tray appeared, and he listened to instructions. He lay flat on his back, propelling his humanlike feet like he was riding a bicycle—a pastime he would enjoy, he was sure, if only he didn't have to spend every waking moment foraging for food. He finished another tray, and just as he looked to the seer for more instructions, he noticed the man was gone. Everyone but his guards had vanished, and there was no food to be seen.

VOID-X3CX-R04 howled the song of his people. He'd been played with, given the illusion of endless food, only to have it snatched away. Illusions were tasty but not at all that filling. His stomach let out a soundless growl as it returned to its normal state—empty.

He sang for what seemed like hours. Likely, it was only a few minutes. Time was subjective that way, especially when you were hungry. No one came. No one cared about him or his plight. He waited. To conserve energy, he lay down in his cage, his tentacles licking at the delicious transcendent bars he couldn't eat. The time would come, he was sure. But by then, even the entire plane wouldn't be enough to satisfy his endless hunger or slake his infinite thirst.

People hollered and screamed outside Town Hall, waving signs and doing everything they could to voice their support for their chosen candidate. Thousands of ballot stations were accepting votes near Town Hall itself, and millions did the same, scattered across the massive metropolis known as Diyu. Spirits, ghosts, and buddhas alike waited in line to submit their votes. After all, this single Underworld day would determine the next ten thousand years of mayorship. Oh, and the counselors, but no one seemed to pay attention to those, even though it was them, in the end, that held pretty much all the power.

"Down with the devils!" one supporter shouted.

"Tax the rich!" another shouted.

"Regressive tax!" yet another said. That last one was one of Judah's supporters. The regressive tax, a cornerstone of his electoral platform, was predictably only popular among the top twenty or so percent. In effect, the poor would get taxed a higher percentage than the rich, driving them out of the city if they couldn't push their way to the top.

"Look at all of them," Judah said, a glass of ghost wine in his hand. Made from ghost grapes, it had an ethereal flavor only spirits could truly appreciate. "So many people, riled up to vote." He shook his head. "On my home plane—the one I lived on before dying and coming to Diyu—it was amazing if forty percent of the general population showed up. But here, it seems like every person wants a say. It's truly an outstanding sight to behold."

His electoral team shifted uncomfortably at his words. His closest confidants, Usama being one of them, coughed lightly. One of the key counselors up for reelection stepped up to answer the unasked question.

"It's more like six or seven percent, sir," the tall graying woman in a black skirt and bright-pink blouse said. Mary was not only one of his most fervent and level-minded supporters, but she helped fill in many knowledge gaps whenever she could. "Spirits used to care, but then the elections got so polarizing that only a minority bothers to vote anymore. All of them are crazy, without exception."

Yama, who'd been brooding beside the window, nodded. "We tried to fix the system many times. With proportional representation, it got worse somehow. Even more fringe parties were introduced, and believe me, a government with literally thirty different parties arguing on how to get things done can only be a bad thing. Plus, campaigning was confusing.

"We experimented between first-past-the-post and preferential ballot. The first led to the most liked candidate being elected, but everyone grumbled unhappily for the next ten thousand years. The preferential ballots were, on the other hand, a smashing success. While most people didn't get who they liked in power, they got to be smug about picking the winner as their second or third choice. It also narrowed down the playing field so that no more than four or five candidates ever participated in one election."

"Huh," Judah said. "Whoever thought democracy could be so universal? I said forty percent, but it was on a downward trend."

"It happens in every mortal plane," Mary said understandingly. "At first, they're super enthusiastic, but then it wanes, leaving only the crazies with enough energy to stand up for what they believe in. Then, one of two things happen: A civil war splits the country apart, leading to two competing dictatorships, or you get a situation much like ours. The advantage in the second case is that no one has the energy to mount a revolution, because not enough people care."

"Do some places trend one way or another?" Judah asked, curious. "We had a pseudo-democracy in Rome, but then it eventually imploded. Some people say it had something to do with lead in the water."

"By and large, it seems to depend on the level of technology or cultivation," Mary explained. "When you reach the point where 99.99 percent of the population could theoretically be wiped out by the most powerful democracy in the span of a day, people tend to call the situation good enough, and no one bothers with a revolution. Eventually, it merges with other countries around it and forms one massive mega government where no one can really do anything. Most people think that's just rosy."

Usama, who'd been chatting with a business associate at the back, walked up. "Hey, buddy!" he said, shaking Judah's hand. "I just wanted to wish you congratulations in advance."

"Isn't that bad luck?" Judah asked. "I hear all of the other candidates are way more popular than I am. It'll be a miracle if I win."

"And who's saying that?" Usama asked with a twinkle in his eye.

"The news?" Judah answered uncertainly.

Yama hmphed, drawing glances. "The news wouldn't know what's going on if it hit them upside the head with a spirit-sealing brick. They're all mouthpieces for one candidate or another, spewing crazy rhetoric as though it were fact. There are a few sane media outlets out there, but they don't fare very well on election years. It takes them a few decades to recover after each election."

"He's right," Mary said, shaking her head in disgust. "You mostly don't have to worry about the news and reporters, though it really would have helped if you'd spoken out against Ragthor the Bloodied. That devil-worshipping psycho deserves every bit of bad press he gets. I mean, come on! Bringing back spirit sacrifices? Bicentenary wars to cull our population?"

"He's very popular with the middle class," Yama pointed out. "We didn't want to alienate them. They think very highly of their odds of survival in the bicentennial wars, given their better resources. Since our regressive tax policies already attracted the rich, it was wiser to remain silent."

"I'm just not sure how people can take these guys seriously," Judah said, shaking his head. "Here I am, trying to keep a clean election, but there's Elsa of the Hive Mind here saying every spirit should be connected to a hive matrix to operate more efficiently, and everyone should get equal resources. She literally wants to enslave the entire population. Then, she weakens her case and admits it should be done slowly, first subduing ten percent of the population by random lottery to see how it works out."

"Instantly creating a hive mind is tricky," Usama chimed in. "We tried it once at my evil research and development company. It didn't work out so well."

"And then there's the sanest of the lot, Galahad the Brave," Judah said. "He's all about honor and justice. Going over the entire law with a fine-tooth comb, doubling our police force, and increasing standards for judges. He's got all this good stuff going for him, but then he wants to do unnecessary things like fine people for shaking off after peeing in the urinal."

"He's always been a bit of a puritan," Yama muttered. "Runs in every election, and he always seems to get about twenty-five percent of the vote. His base is very strong and self-righteous. Still, you're polling behind him by six percentage points. The other two are neck and neck at twenty-eight percent."

"Are you kidding me?" Judah exclaimed. "Elsa of the Hive Mind and Ragthor the Bloodied? Are these people crazy?"

"I *did* say that," Mary said dryly. "They have personal appeal. Unfortunately, the people you're appealing to just don't care enough." She sighed.

Yama sighed too. As he looked over the crowds, his consciousness reached out to the Yellow River. It was surging again, and his employees were having trouble keeping up. The shark squad was working double overtime, and their newest invention, sin-purifying nanoweave, was barely holding off sin from corrupting the reincarnation pool. Which wasn't a bad thing, per se, since that time was coming. He just had to hold it off for a few more millennia before letting it loose.

This election was the key to getting him the labor he needed, at a price he could afford. With those things in hand, he could keep the universe running in good order and avoid a Second Great Apocalypse. Not that most people knew there had been another, but the lack of public embarrassment didn't make it any easier for Yama, especially since the Jade Emperor and the Curse Sovereign were privy to that information.

Unfortunately, they were losing. Without a miracle, most of the universe was doomed.

Chapter 1:
The Eastern Desert

In the Southern Lands, three cultivators were waiting atop tall cliffs. Cha Ming, Feng Ming, and Gong Xuandi looked over the dunes below, whose red sands were speckled with small black stones. This was the Eastern Desert, a wasteland that ran both north and south of the great wall that ran between them. Just north of them, a wide canyon exposed a large gap in the otherwise impenetrable barrier between the only two deserts on the continent.

Legends said that the two deserts used to be the lushest of lands. It was for that reason that the South had invaded centuries ago. They'd sought to breach the wall and claim the fertile land as their own. Ultimately, they were rebuffed. By destroying the wall, a wind had started blowing, and that wind had eroded the rich lands to the north and south, covering them in sand and silt and blowing away water, leaving nothing but a desert behind.

Since then, the wind had helped the North. All defensive structures took it into account. The North had bunkers near the canyon's entrance, with cutting edges facing the gusts and gales, and long tails of sand tapered away from their stable surfaces. Likewise, the north-facing edge of the dunes to the south were jagged and distorted. Their south-facing tails were smooth and tapered like carefully crafted wine flutes. The group of them resembled a school of fish heading into an open river from a lake.

How about now? Cha Ming asked Feng Ming, who stood on a nearby cliff, waiting. He'd asked many times over the past hour.

Not yet, Feng Ming said. *The best time to dive into a battle is when you're needed.*

He didn't seem inclined to explain, and Gong Xuandi, the other military man, didn't either, so Cha Ming waited. As he did, he admired the canyon walls. Like the sands, they were red, though many layers of strata could be seen on their tall surfaces, which reached a mile high in some instances. They provided a beautiful backdrop to the grim scene that was unfolding below, and though blind, Cha Ming could see faint shadows of that beauty through the eyes of his soul. He could also see Southern armies that were assembling between those speckled dunes; they now seemed like enemy ships or mounts more than anything else. Northern forces stood firm near the canyon entrance, where the bunkers protected their flanks.

What Cha Ming couldn't see was the wind, which was the crux of the problem. It wasn't his bad eyesight that hid it from him, but rather the fact that there was no wind in the windy canyon. A sickening stillness had replaced it. As such, all the usual defenses were useless, and the Northern forces were now greatly outnumbered in an indefensible position.

Troops continued to move, but suddenly, a horn sounded. Then many horns joined in. Northern troops began shifting their defensive lines. Both armies marshalled with surprising speed, and soon, the South was charging.

The North joined in large shielding formations to protect themselves against enemy attacks while archers shot qi-piercing arrows from the back. They felled many Southern forces, but eventually, their enemies reached their defenses. Blood splashed across the red sand, leaving one to wonder if it was naturally red or if war had made it that way.

Such a waste of lives, Cha Ming said, shaking his head. Many soldiers fell in the first wave, though the South had taken the brunt of the damage.

It's how the South fights, Feng Ming said. *That's just the prelude.*

The South always liked sending expendable troops as fodder. As he spoke, troops that were much better equipped followed. A few among them wore the familiar red robes of blood masters. They sucked in the blood from their fallen comrades and fearlessly charged into the Northern army, ignoring severe wounds that regenerated instantly due to their fierce blood vitality.

The North, apparently, was ready for this. They assigned elite troops to contain these blood masters, throwing out chains and talismans to constrict them before using fire and lightning to drain them. The battle continued. Ground was lost, and ground was gained. Still, they did nothing. Despite the lack of wind, the bunkers played a crucial role. Whenever the South tried to encroach on their flanks, the massive buildings lit up with wind and fire, annihilating anything that dared come close to them. Moreover, they were physical obstructions. Both sides might have core-formation cultivators, but most were reserves, ready to be deployed at a moment's notice.

Back and forth. The currents of battle were confusing to Cha Ming. Someone had once told him that many generals played *Angels and Devils* to keep their minds sharp for battle. Yet despite his significant skill in the game, he saw none of it. Only chaos.

There, Feng Ming suddenly said, pointing toward the western flank. Without Feng Ming's warning, Cha Ming would have missed the unspoken cue. Southern troops crashed through a hole in their defenses, forcing through it, expanding it. Swords, sabers, and spears clashed and took lives, and bursts of all five elements filled the battlefield.

Though Cha Ming was unprepared, the Northern forces had clearly been waiting for this moment. Their reserves had already been on their way to reinforce. Core-formation cultivators dove in, killing dozens of blood masters where they went. Southern core-formation cultivators joined in to aid them.

A mistake, Feng Ming said, shaking his head.

Are you sure? asked Gong Xuandi.

Feng Ming nodded and pointed just east of the center of the Northern army, where fighting suddenly intensified. Hidden core-formation cultivators suddenly emerged in the opposing army and began viciously slaughtering nearby troops. One group of men resisted the attack. They were clearly outnumbered, however.

That's where we go. They flew, and as they did, Feng Ming explained. *It's difficult to sense the flow of battle accurately, so commanders often stay hidden among their own forces in the guise of a lesser commanders. It makes them more difficult to target and makes it easier to control the army. Unfortunately, it's a double-edged sword.*

It seemed the Northern commander had somehow been spotted. Though Southern forces did their best to strive for a quick kill, their group was faster. Cha Ming used creation qi, along with 1,080 combat sigils to create wind and lightning combat formations. Their speed doubled, and they crashed into enemy forces. Feng Ming moved to defend the enemy commander, while Gong Xuandi dove right into his opponents, ignoring blows as he wielded his mighty trident.

Cha Ming summoned his pseudo-domain, coating the Clear Sky Staff in a frigid blue light as it grew to the size of a massive pillar. He smashed it across dozens of enemy troops with all his strength. It should have been more than enough to kill a few of them, but to his surprise, they resisted. The twelve of them combined their strength and knocked his staff aside. They dove in, clearing the staff and lunging at Cha Ming's defenseless body. He quickly evaluated their strength, sensing a certain *wrongness* he couldn't quite pinpoint.

One of them, a half-step marrow-refining blood master, rushed at him with a wicked serrated blade. The others unleashed fire, water, wood, earth, and metal. All five elements surged toward his exposed body. Cha Ming was surprised by the sudden assault but not worried. He grinned. Then he opened his eyes.

"Argh!" Three of his opponents shivered visibly, nearly dropping their weapons as their movements slowed. Cha Ming couldn't see any better with his eyes open, but that didn't stop the air from being suffused with thick Devil-Sealing, Demon-Subduing, Spirit-Banishing Intents. His eyes were the antithesis of devils, and their hatred need not be targeted. The quick burst of power got him the opening he needed.

Cha Ming formed rapid hand seals, faster than anyone could see. His combat sigils turned golden and swung with the might of a thousand and eighty blades toward the wood-aligned cultivator. Based on his reaction, Cha Ming now knew he was a devil. As an apex cultivator, the man didn't disappoint. He transformed, surpassing his limits and burning excess vitality to promote himself one sub realm to half-step blood awakening. The swords of metal qi bit into the devil's body, and though they caused little damage, they diverted the man's attention. The Clear Sky Staff disappeared and reappeared in Cha Ming's right hand. He swung down with the longer, thinner staff, crashing down on the beleaguered devil, who held up a large half-step-transcendent truncheon to deflect it.

The staff sheared right through the truncheon, cutting the devil in two and crashing into the sand below. It wasn't enough to kill the creature, but Cha Ming acted quickly and changed his formation. The thousand and eighty swords became a thousand and eighty grinding blades. He infused Devil-Sealing Intent into them, and they ate away at its writhing body.

Three, two, one... Just as he was about to finish the creature, he abandoned his target, immediately terminated his formation, and threw up an icy defensive formation. His Clear Sky Staff swung up in an arc, deflecting three thick blades that had just cut through his qi shield. The wood devil scampered off, badly wounded despite being a body cultivator. The others moved to contain Cha Ming instead of trying to kill him, prioritizing their own lives over his. Individual. Selfish. Out for their own interests. These were the dominant values promoted by the Southern Alliance.

How are you doing? Cha Ming asked Feng Ming, who was fighting nearby.

Almost safe, Feng Ming said. *You wouldn't happen to be able to break out and join me, would you?*

I can try, Cha Ming sent. His staff was a blur, deflecting dozens of blows per second as he mobilized his combat formations to deflect elemental techniques. He scored several hits on his opponents, but they also scored some on him. They added to his existing injuries, which hadn't yet healed from his battle in the Ji Kingdom. His opponents rotated as they were injured, retreating and regenerating before coming right back at him, keeping up the containment. Gong Xuandi had also been boxed in, leaving poor Feng Ming to defend three survivors from their assailants.

Why do I make these if not to use them? Cha Ming thought. He summoned five sheets of colored paper and threw them out. These simple-looking papers were half-step-transcendent talismans, one for each of the five elements. The first, Matter-Suppressing Seal, summoned a massive column that increased the gravity in the area. The second, Life-Suppressing Seal, greatly decreased the regeneration of surrounding cultivators. Shape-Suppressing Seal, Energy-Suppressing Seal, and Flow-Suppressing Seal similarly dulled his opponent's weapons, dampened their attacks, and slowed their movements. Moreover, the appearance of all five seals formed a black star that began disintegrating those within the impromptu formation's boundaries.

The sudden development took his opponents by surprise. Cha Ming used that surprise to send out a ball of metal and flame to a nearby cultivator, grinding him into meat paste. As his body regenerated, Cha Ming swung out with Splitting Heaven and Earth, forcing his opponents to defend against the blur of white lest they be cut in half. This bought him just enough time to finish off his beleaguered opponent. He then kicked off another's chest, summoning his staff and executing a sideways Crushing Chaos. This time, the staff struck true, killing a peak-core-formation cultivator before he could land a blow with his poisoned short swords.

Almost there, Cha Ming thought. His opponents tried their best to close the gap, but they were too slow. Moreover, their movements had exposed some of their more vulnerable core-formation cultivators. He grasped his staff with both hands and lunged toward them, pouring five-element qi into it and executing Origin Strike. A lone opponent burst into a cloud of gray mist, leaving a convenient gap for Cha Ming to leave the encirclement. He flew like the wind itself to Feng Ming's aid, just in time to see a lethal strike heading toward his friend's back. A frozen shield appeared just in time to deflect it as Cha Ming struck the attacker with a destruction-qi-laden palm to the back, reducing his body to smoke and ashes.

Tired but thrilled to be fighting again, Cha Ming turned around to face his opponents and defend Feng Ming. It was only then that he realized no one remained to fight him. They were already retreating at their commander's instructions. Even Gong Xuandi, who'd been boxed in since the beginning, had been released by the retreating attackers.

"You have my thanks," said one of the three men, who was evidently the Northern commander. The man flipped out a yellow fan and swept it toward the ground. Blood splashed off the peak-core treasure, which had evidently seen better days. After cleaning the fan, he put it away and wiped off his bloodied golden longsword. His blue robes were covered in cuts and burns, and much of his own blood leaked out from beneath his armor.

"Heavens, if I'd known it was you, I'd have left you to die," Feng Ming said, putting away his lucky spear.

"We don't all get to choose our allies," the commander said, grinning. "But I, Jiao Ming, chief marshal of the Desert Wind Kingdom, thank you from the bottom of my heart. A few seconds later, and you'd have seen the Southern army pouring into the North."

Chapter 2: Mark of Wind

"A lthough the battle was intense, we actually lost much fewer men than you'd expect," Jiao Ming said as he paced around the map in his command tent. Several other generals, each wearing different colors, nodded in agreement. "We lost ten percent of our forces while the South lost twenty percent, mostly due to the untimely demise of a few of their peak-core-formation cultivators." He nodded to Cha Ming. "If not for your timely intervention, the consequences would have been disastrous."

"It seems like your forces are a little on the slim side," Feng Ming said. Though he'd mostly been sitting by the side of their table quietly, he'd been studying the map the entire time. "If you don't gain reinforcements soon, you'll lose."

Instead of the scowls Cha Ming expected, the generals and marshals instantly began muttering and arguing amongst themselves. Jiao Ming looked toward Cha Ming and Feng Ming and sent them a mental message. *It would be best not to irk them so. I am a patient man, but our current alliance is tenuous. We are not friends protecting a collective border here, but enemies. North of the Windswept Canyons, we are spilling each other's blood.*

The war hasn't changed that? Feng Ming asked.

Cha Ming was also surprised. Wasn't it best to put aside petty grievances when a common enemy was knocking at your door?

What better time? Jiao Ming sent bitterly. *The Eastern Desert is an undesirable land, and the chaos of war is the best opportunity to struggle for power.* He shrugged. *It's a wonder none of them have betrayed us yet. I expect that to happen anytime now.*

On cue, an older, gray-bearded man spoke. "I, for one, don't even think we should be defending this place," he said. "My Lei Clan has always maintained that it's a waste of resources to hold it. We're only here because we don't want to be the odd one out."

Many voices muttered in agreement.

"How can you say that?" another man said. Though he seemed bold and upright, there was something about him that screamed politician. "We're defending our homes, and every year, the rest of the Northern Alliance sends us a tithe to keep us supplied. Our Lan Clan is grateful for their support and proud to defend our border."

"Of course you're grateful," a slender woman with a deep scar that ran across the right side of her face said. According to Feng Ming, she had red hair, a rare color on the continent. "The fact that you take a disproportionately large cut of that tithe hasn't escaped the rest of us."

The bickering turned into clamoring, and soon, all of them were arguing again. Jiao Ming let it continue for some time before raising his hands and releasing his cultivation. He was one of the stronger cultivators among them, so this act immediately attracted everyone's attention. They slowly quieted down, though it was uncertain whether they'd actually stopped or had just switched to mental communication.

"Everyone here has problems," Jiao Ming said. "And everyone here has grudges. I myself confess that the Jiao Clan didn't come by our leadership honestly. We got there by hook or by crook, just like everyone else."

His audience frowned but didn't interrupt him.

"As leaders, it is our responsibility to protect our people. If not for our countrymen and the other desert dwellers, we do it for our clans. And I assure you that the South is avaricious. You think we have it hard now, but their lands are just as barren as ours. What we would call a tiny oasis, they could call a lake. What we would call a farmable plot of land, they would call a bountiful one. If they cross this line in the sand, they won't ignore us for richer lands like you think they will. If we fall, our kingdoms are over. Our neighbors to the South will take everything away from us, leaving not an outpost contested. Do you want that to happen? Good. Now tell me, how many forces can each of you offer?"

"A thousand more foundation-establishment equivalents at most," the man from the Lei Clan muttered. "Armed."

"The Lan Clan?" Jiao Ming asked, turning to the upright gentleman.

The man coughed, then looked to the glaring red-haired woman. "Since the tithes have been so generous to us, two thousand."

"We've sent all the troops we can," the red-haired woman said, attracting glares from the others. "Don't look at me like that. We lost three cities in the past two weeks." She hesitated, then shook her head. "We have some geomancers and storm wards we can spare. Maybe they can make up for a part of the wind that's lacking."

The others seemed to lighten up at her mention of the storm wards, a strange profession that controlled the weather for a living. Normally, they would be used to grow crops on a massive scale or protect the people against storms. It seemed that in the Eastern Desert, they also had military applications.

"The wind," Cha Ming suddenly said, drawing their attention. "It's of demonic origin. I couldn't tell earlier, because the energy is stale. But when I opened my eyes in battle, I felt a strangeness in the air. What happened among the demons recently?"

A wild-looking man wearing a leather vest replied. "Others might not know this, but us beast tamers have been hit pretty hard by a strange demon tide. These demons are strong, and their eyes glow ochre. They've been attacking the slopes of Burning Wind, the demonic mountain near the canyon."

"Fiendish demons," Cha Ming said. "Perhaps this is what's causing the anomaly in the wind patterns."

"Maybe," the beast tamer said, shrugging. "All I know is that it's getting harder to tame demons, so I can't replenish my forces. Which is annoying, given that many of them can control wind and sand."

"What of the local demon monarch?" Cha Ming asked. "Who is it? What kind of demon is it?"

"I don't know why you care so much," the beast tamer said reluctantly. "But since you helped us out, I'll tell you. Last thing I knew, it was the Swiftwind Monarch, a wind-aligned fox that's very difficult to see. That might have changed recently, but be warned—no one's seen her in fifty years. It was my master who told me about her."

Cha Ming turned to Feng Ming and Gong Xuandi. "Since the lack of wind is what's making defending this canyon difficult, I'll try to solve that problem. I have a few friends in high places in the demon world, so I might be able to get us more information. With any luck, we'll get the wind back, and defending the Eastern Desert won't be a problem."

Feng Ming nodded. "Since the defenses here are lacking, it's my duty as a member of the Northern Alliance to contribute to its defense. Gong Xuandi and I will remain here and work with Marshal Jiao Ming. I might not be as strong as Gong Xuandi is, but I guarantee you that with me here, luck will be on our side." His declaration obtained a mixed reception. Some perked up, while others groaned.

"I'm very thankful for any help you can provide," Jiao Ming said, then turned to Cha Ming. "When will you leave?"

"As soon as I build something," Cha Ming said, looking northward. "I might not be great with the wind element, but I'll try to make up for it with a formation. Does anyone here have any formation flags or spirit stones?" No one volunteered. "I didn't think so. Well, I'll build it first, and if you want it to last any longer than a day, you'll need to feed it spirit stones. My generosity only goes so far."

Though he wanted to help out more, he'd burned through much of his wealth causing chaos in Bastion. A much greater war was breaking out, and he'd need all the resources he had at his disposal.

Cha Ming flew away from his newly crafted masterwork a thousand and eighty flags short, much liquified elemental essence depleted, and many spirit stones lighter. A strong wind began blowing southward through the north mouth of the canyon. There, it could draw as much air in as it wanted through the desert to the north, pressurizing it and blasting it through the narrow canyon.

Though the effect was mediocre, the formation gave Cha Ming clarity on the situation. The impossibly strong wind currents of the Windswept Canyon weren't possible with only two gaps in the wall generating a current. After all, there were oceans all around them, and wind could always travel upward. It stood to reason that something else was responsible for the current. That reason, he decided, was demonic.

A mile up, the sharp canyon walls gave way to a barren plateau. Demons roamed these lands, though most of them were of the reptilian variety that absorbed demonic energy from the scorching sun. There were also many birds that preyed on the weaker reptiles and took shelter from the sun in short spires that dotted the lands.

He traveled several miles before the plateau began to slope up toward a tall but sharp mountain peak. Oddly enough, it, too, had a north-facing blade that cut into winds that came from the north. It tapered slowly to the south, leading down into rocky forests and a thriving valley. There, demons went about their daily lives. They fed, they fought, and they protected their honor.

Several birds flitted by him as he flew, blowing sharp gusts of wind across his skin that almost drew blood. He ignored them, proceeding not toward the mountain itself but toward the valley at its base. He heard clashing there and sensed violence. Demons were fighting, and the ferocity of their struggle left little doubt that the aggressors were of the fiendish variety.

A tree broke beside Cha Ming as he landed, destroyed by a large demonic cat batted away by an approaching aberration. He looked at the thing, noticing that it seemed like a cross between a pig and a dog, with horns jutting out of a nose that it used to impale enemies as it charged. It moved in for the kill, but Cha Ming swept out with a strike of his staff. It cut through the demon's core, completely negating any chances it had of regenerating.

The large cat, which Cha Ming noticed was a bobcat, got back on its paws and stared at Cha Ming warily. *Why are you here, human?* it asked.

I'm looking for the Swiftwind Monarch, Cha Ming said. Best to be direct with demons. They didn't like dancing around when they talked like humans did.

The bobcat's eyes narrowed. *A mere human, no matter how powerful, does not possess the right to meet such an exalted individual.* Sighing, Cha Ming opened his eyes slightly. The Demon-Subduing Intent that leaked out caused the bobcat to cower in fear. *But if an exalted one such as yourself went to the battlefield, she would surely welcome you.*

Many thanks, Cha Ming said, speeding toward the fighting.

In the middle of the forest, tens of thousands of powerful demons clashed in a war of attrition. Enough blood fell to the ground to fill barrels, soaking the land in a sludgy layer of red and violet. The trees, most of which were also demons and elementals, could hardly keep up with such a massive influx of energy. They did what they could, drawing nutrients from the earth and clearing the battlefield of corpses. They avoided drawing in black blood, however. The baleful substance, which even Cha Ming in his blind state could identify, corrupted everything it touched. Dead and dying demons stirred as it brought life to them, coercing them to join the much smaller but more powerful ranks of the fiendish demons. Meanwhile, the forest blackened. It started at the roots and worked its way up to the trunks and leaves. Vines were no exceptions. Even the most resistant weed could only give in to the corruption.

Cha Ming flew north to where the most powerful figures were

fighting. Five monstrosities, each a cross between a wolverine and a serpent, had surrounded an airborne group of three demons. The two birds—an eagle and an owl—struggled to find an opening while another figure, barely visible to both the naked eye and Cha Ming's transcendent force, attacked the invaders with swift, biting strikes.

The rapid creature was none other than the Swiftwind Monarch. The white fox's claws and teeth were sharp and bloodied, and its single white tail flailed so quickly it looked like four separate appendages. It was covered in blood, though any black blood that landed on the white tail was swiftly thrown off by its sharp whipping motions. All three of the demons were peak-core-formation demons of excellent bloodlines. Unfortunately, the fiends seemed to hold a distinctive advantage. The three beleaguered demons could barely hold on as their forces below were overrun.

Cha Ming was no tactician, but going for the enemy leadership seemed like a no-brainer. Air whirled around him as he forced his way into battle. He first used his Clear Sky Staff to deflect a claw strike that would have wounded the Swiftwind Monarch, then stabbed at the creature with an Origin Strike. To his surprise, however, the beast met his blow head-on and pushed him back.

Right, he thought. Demons were already far stronger than human body cultivators, but when in their own territory, that difference grew especially exaggerated. Fiendish demons brought a devilish strength along with their powers, making them far stronger than normal demons.

Left with no other choice, Cha Ming opened his eyes once again. Subduing and sealing intents gushed out uncontrolled. As he couldn't direct them any longer, his powers suppressed not only the five fiends but the three demons they were attacking. Luckily, the fiends had a dual nature that gave them both devilish heritage and demonic heritage; his eyes seemed to loathe them twice as much as the demon monarchs. With their opponents suppressed, the fight turned in their favor. The demons began mounting their counterattack.

The eagle, the one who'd been most heavily damaged by the

fiends, let out a sharp, piercing cry. The ears of the fiends bled, and the cries paralyzed them. The eagle gave them no time to recover and dove in to attack with its beak and talons. Cha Ming struck with Crushing Chaos at the paralyzed beasts, though surprisingly, he could only cut deep gashes into the creatures instead of bisecting them. Further, any wounds he inflicted swiftly regenerated despite being caused by destruction qi. The energy of the land seemed to gush into them, reinforcing them against invaders.

We need to strike decisively at a single target, the Swiftwind Monarch said, running up beside him. She jumped on the demon Cha Ming had wounded with his staff and began lashing it with her tail. Barrels of black blood poured onto the ground as the bladelike tail cut many gashes half as deep as Cha Ming's staff strike.

Cha Ming, hardly the expert on fighting fiends, went along with the fox's instructions. He unleashed one Crushing Chaos after another, infusing his staff with a pseudo fire domain, boosting his attacks. Golden combat sigils cut away at its thick hide, though they barely did any damage before the wounds were healed.

Beside them, the owl defended. It didn't harness the offensive power of wind, but its blunt impact. It blew back the demons, pushing them away as they tried to aid their companion. Unaided and isolated, the fiend grew weaker and weaker until finally, the Swiftwind Monarch bit into its head and pulled out a black core. It didn't swallow it like Huxian often did but bit down on it, shattering it. An evil black aura evaporated from the broken core. At the same time, much of the black blood on the battlefield receded. So, too, did some of the corruption in the forest.

The four remaining fiends, which the owl had held back, followed the winds and ran away. They turned back toward the southern end of the battlefield and rejoined a figure clothed in black leathers. To Cha Ming's surprise, it was a human. Yet the savageness the man bore was no joke. The moment the fiends returned to his side, their presence soared. They immediately entered the battlefield and began sowing chaos, and the eagle and owl chased after them, joined by a few other more powerful demons for support.

What is it you want, human? the Swiftwind Monarch asked, exhausted. *Humans never do anything except out of greed. Even those eyes don't make you an exception.* Her deep wounds were finally healing, though they seemed to take extra long, as her body first had to expel the black blood that had contaminated them.

I'm from the canyon, Cha Ming said. *It's being invaded by forces from the South. Normally, that wouldn't be a problem, but the winds died down. I was wondering if you knew anything about its disappearance.*

I see, the Swiftwind Monarch said. *I used to control the winds. No longer. Someone else took my crown, though it's currently being contested. The winds won't blow until there is a clear winner. As to whether it blows north or south, that will depend on the victor.*

Cha Ming frowned. *Are you not the monarch of this mountain?*

I was, the Swiftwind Monarch said. *Now, I am only a lesser monarch. The Silverwing Monarch took my crown. He began condensing a mark right away, drawing demonic power away from the valley. That was when the fiends came. They used this moment of weakness to launch an assault and wrest power away from the demons on the mountain.*

The Silverwing Monarch? Cha Ming asked. *A small silver falcon? Likes small things? He strikes with his sharp wings and razor claws and has a tool on his claws that attracts escaping prey?*

The very same, the Swiftwind Monarch said, her eyes narrowing. *It was that tool which allowed him to catch me in our match. I take it you are acquaintances.*

Friends, Cha Ming said. *And it sounds like he's in trouble.* He took in a deep breath and looked toward the South, where the attack was intensifying. *What help does he need?*

He only needs time, the Swiftwind Monarch said. *We're fighting to win every second we can. Unfortunately, the fiends are corrupting the mountain and drawing power from it. This is slowing the process. And if they manage to take over at least half of the demonic energy on the mountain, he will fail.*

To make matters worse, there is a powerful human helping them.

We call him a fiend whisperer. With his presence, the fiends grow stronger and ignore their natural destructive impulses to rally behind him. It won't be long before we are overrun.

Then I'll have to help, Cha Ming said.

You, a human, will do this? the Swiftwind Monarch asked. *I don't trust you.*

Cha Ming turned his closed eyes toward the battlefield, where fiendish forces were snowballing. The black portion of the forest was significantly larger than before, as the encroachment had continued on while he and the Swiftwind Monarch spoke. *It seems to me that you don't have much of a choice in the matter,* Cha Ming said. He then flew toward the battlefield. The Swiftwind Monarch followed alongside him.

The wind howled as they charged. They felled smaller fiendish demons on the way, spilling their black blood onto the forest floor. Cha Ming used fire qi to destroy whatever black blood he could, though in doing so, he also destroyed much of the forest's demonic energy.

Can they be saved? he asked the Swiftwind Monarch. It wasn't just trees that were corrupted, but sentient demons and elementals.

No, the Swiftwind Monarch replied. *Corrupted trees and demons are beyond redemption. We must uproot every last one of them.*

Cha Ming nodded. He and the Swiftwind Monarch dashed through the corrupted trees, cutting down their trunks and setting them ablaze. Black blood hissed and oozed as it was burned away, reducing the influence of the fiends in the land. Unsurprisingly, that drew the attention of the four fiends, and this time, the fiend whisperer appeared. The owl was busy holding back the tide, leaving them with only the help of the eagle.

Storm clouds formed on Cha Ming's feet, and to his surprise, the peak Stormchaser Formation came much more easily than it usually did. It boosted his movements as he dove in and slashed three times with Splitting Heaven and Earth. The white windy blade cut into the fiends with surprising effect. He wondered if creation-aligned techniques were much more effective against the creatures or if it was the wind-aligned mountain lending him strength.

Cha Ming opened his eyes again, and the fiends weakened greatly. The fox jumped onto one of those he'd wounded, and Cha Ming moved to protect it from the others as the eagle screeched and joined in. He threw up 5,040 sigils, setting up a half-step-transcendent combat formation that summoned an icy box, trapping two of the fiends. He then threw out an earth-aligned talisman. An illusory mountain appeared where it landed, suppressing the movements of the remaining fiend and the fiend whisperer.

Both recovered quickly—not surprising because one was a peak-core-formation fiend and another a half-step blood-awakening cultivator. They managed to block Cha Ming's follow-up Origin Strike and close in on him, cutting a deep gash into his chest. He took it in stride, however, using the attack as an opening. He closed in and struck out with a fist of destruction qi that obliterated a large section of the fiend's chest. Before Cha Ming could press the advantage, however, the fiend whisperer hummed. The two trapped demons writhed violently, and the sudden burst of energy blew apart his combat formation, hitting Cha Ming with a strong backlash.

We can't keep fighting with them, the Swiftwind Monarch sent.

Cha Ming scanned the rest of the battlefield and discovered she was right. While they were busy here, the fiendish tide was snowballing. They would win the battle but lose the war. Gritting his teeth, Cha Ming kicked off one of the two fiends charging at him and summoned his pseudo-domain. He channeled metal and slapped a gold-aligned talisman on his staff, boosting its power even further.

"Origin Strike!" he yelled, unleashing one of the most devastating attacks he'd ever executed. A Myriad Truths Diagram materialized as he struck down and poured all five elements into a single point, striking the prone fiend that was being attacked by his two demon companions straight in the chest. Its entire upper body disintegrated in a gray mist tinged with five elements, and its head fell to the ground. It began reattaching to its body, but with its defenses gone, the Swiftwind Monarch appeared beside it and retrieved its core, crushing it.

Go! the Swiftwind Monarch yelled. *We'll hold them off.*

Four against two were poor odds for anyone, but Cha Ming did as instructed. He threw out three talismans on each of them, one for regeneration, one for defense, and another for offense. He didn't boost their speed—they had that in spades. They used their swift movements and newfound abilities to constrain the four as Cha Ming flew out and crashed into the ever-expanding fiendish tide.

He swept out with his staff, using Splitting Heaven and Earth and imbuing it with fire. Entire swaths of blackened forest burned down. By now, forty percent of the forest at the base of the mountain had already been converted. That one strike might have destroyed a large portion, but in that time, the black tide had grown by twice as much. According to the Swiftwind Monarch, the fiends would need to take over seventy percent of the forest to gain a fifty percent share of the mountain's demonic energy.

Cha Ming sent several combat formations to the south, east, and west as he ran north. They burned what fiends and corrupted wood they could with flames infused with Devil-Sealing and Demon-Subduing Intents. Even the lakes of black blood that had been shed in the battle were evaporated as he made his way toward the advancing demon horde. Core-formation fiends lunged at him as he finally reached their ranks, but he batted them away with his staff, its pillar form destroying dozens with every blow.

Fifty percent. The count was increasing faster than Cha Ming could destroy. And though he could reclaim territory by destroying fiendish blood, the land was lifeless and was a poorer contributor to the overall power balance. Another wave, more combat formations, and even more destruction. Fifty-five percent. Sixty percent. Sixty-five percent.

"Silverwing!" Cha Ming shouted. "You'd better not fail to get your mark, or even Lei Jiang and Gua will mock you until the end of your days!"

Sixty-six, sixty-seven. He felt it through his eyes. Just a little more, and the mountain range would reach a tipping point. Its ownership would shift and become a nest of evil. It reached the sixty-nine percent mark, then finally shifted to seventy. He braced himself for disaster.

Fortunately, disaster didn't come. Neither did the mass conversion to fiendish lands he'd expected. Instead, the corruption moved back. A wind suddenly started blowing from north of the mountain. At first, it was only a gentle breeze. Then it became a gale. Finally, twin tornadoes began to form just south of the mountain, on two barren patches south of the bladelike protrusion. From the looks of it, the wind was back to normal.

I dare you to say that again! a voice boomed within his mind. A silver falcon with massive wings rose up from the peak of the mountain. He seemed the same as before, save for one key difference—a mark had appeared on his forehead, a rune for wind. His bladelike appendages sent two swift strikes to the retreating fiends, devastating their ranks, far outstripping what Cha Ming could achieve. He'd never known a half-step-initiation demon or witnessed what they were capable of. Perhaps farther away from his dominion it might be different, but near this mountain, Silverwing seemed invincible.

As if to prove his point, Silverwing dove down, crashing against the remaining three fiends and the fiend whisperer. The whisperer bit his tongue and burned his blood essence, separating himself from his tamed pets. Silverwing ignored the three large creatures and dove straight for the human. His claws extended, with wind funneled toward the fiend whisperer, bringing him into his outstretched talons. Just as he was about to crush the man, however, a gray light appeared. His claws caught only empty air.

He just had to have a Spatial Talisman, Cha Ming thought. Since his quarry had escaped, Silverwing unleashed his pent-up anger on the fiends, beating on them with the entire power of the mountain. With their death, their black blood, which should have killed everything it touched, evaporated to nothingness. Some of the trees it had infected, though weak, were still alive. Some of the demons that had been corrupted, though limping, could still stand. Some, but not all. Most of them became black smoke that drifted away in the wind.

I'll make them pay, Silverwing said, glaring southward.

I don't doubt you will, Cha Ming said. *But we have an urgent problem.*

The stupid humans? Silverwing asked.

The stupid humans, Cha Ming admitted.

Fine, Silverwing said. *It's time for this big daddy to teach them how it's done.* He spread his wings and flew.

Chapter 3: Fierce Opponent

Shields up!" Jiao Ming yelled just as the enemy nocked their arrows. There was a slight delay after the order, but he'd predicted such a thing. Runic shields came up, defending the tender troops below from a rain of arrows. Men fell, some dying, some wounded, and some not knowing what the hell was happening.

The casualties, however, were much lower than they otherwise would have been. Why else would Feng Ming be called the Lucky Marshal? Black spear in hand, he fought alongside their brave troops, pushing back enemies as they forced their way around bunker fortifications. The enemy general, seeing that he couldn't pierce through this section, called for a tactical retreat. His troops first pulled back then combined with another army, who'd seemingly predicted this outcome. They swooped toward the west flank, not far from where Feng Ming stood, frowning as he realized how precise the maneuver had been.

The west flank should be fine, Feng Ming thought, pulling closer toward the center. There, another blood master blitz was happening. It was a tactic he'd grown familiar with. Blood masters, except for elites that supported normal troops, were by and large reserve forces. They were crack troops that waited for mounting casualties, then struck at tired and wounded enemies.

Feng Ming rushed in to block a sickle congealed from the blood of friend and foe alike, dispersing it with a wall of burning sand. The blood master, surprised at his sudden appearance, didn't fare any better than the ones before him. Feng Ming cut him down like a fresh sapling that just didn't belong. Then, he called out orders, and a dozen elites joined him in pushing back the intense assault. Normal troops pulled back—they'd only get in the way if they stayed. They reinforced other groups, pushing back the overwhelming Southern armies, and Feng Ming did what he did best—win. His spear scored hit after hit, spilling a seemingly endless amount of blood on the ground below.

Still, his opponents were body cultivators, and blood masters at that. Even barrels of blood meant nothing to them. But he kept them distracted long enough for reinforcements to come. Three other elites joined him before he finally felled one.

Twenty more seconds, Feng Ming thought, fighting with everything he had. That, he predicted, was how much time the blood masters had until the blood dried up. Despite the wounds he'd dealt them, and the fresh bleeding corpses on the ground, what used to be a slurry a few inches deep was now just a single inch of slick red gore. When it was gone, the blood masters would lose the source of their power and regeneration, and they could easily destroy them with an overwhelming offensive.

Ten more seconds remained. He continued attacking, but at the five-second mark, Feng Ming felt a stab of fear. He looked to the east and noticed Gong Xuandi diving into a melee, his trident crashing against another dozen elites, breaking open flesh and shattering bones.

Wasn't he supposed to be on the western flank? How did he get so far east? He looked to the west and noticed that all was calm. Likely, Jiao Ming had sent the man to take care of more pressing matters. Still, that empty gap worried Feng Ming.

"Think you can daydream in battle?" he heard, just before throwing up his spear to block a deadly battle-axe. The blow caused the ground beneath him to give way slightly, sinking him a few inches into the bloody mud as his bones creaked and his breath left him.

Where had *that* come from? He'd been fighting blood masters, but none of them were half-step-blood-awakening cultivators like the man attacking him was. Gritting his teeth, he pulled out a defensive talisman Cha Ming had given him and slapped it on his chest. He blocked another blow, and the brown runes from the talisman were the only thing that stopped his arms from breaking under the strain.

Another order. Six more elites joined him. Together, they forced back the battle-axe-wielding blood master.

But where did those troops come from? he wondered. He knew the answer already: They were from the west. Always from the west. He hoped their enemies wouldn't notice the weakness, but at this point, it was only wishful thinking. At that moment, a battle horn sounded. Hurried orders were called out. Loud cracking noises filled the air as explosions went off.

One of the bunkers, the fortified structures they used as anchors, had been breached. Large chunks of fortified rock fell onto friend and foe alike. Everyone scrambled to protect themselves, but their desperate actions only brought chaos to the previously stable defensive line.

At the same time, a reserve force struck the western front, which Jiao Ming was commanding from. He brought his own reserve troops in, but they were behind by a few seconds, allowing the enemy to wedge deeper into their formation. Another squad of elite crack troops, usually reserved for places with extra-high casualties, suddenly struck the forces near Jiao Ming, who'd just joined the battle.

Elites flew from the center, forcing others from the east to fill in the gaps. Feng Ming cursed and handed off his opponent to others as he dove in to rescue Jiao Ming. Sensing his intent, luck flowed from the rest of the battlefield toward the marshal's position. Troops began slipping or not hearing orders. Swords broke, buying him enough time to come to the marshal's defense.

"Thanks!" Jiao Ming yelled, cutting down with his golden sword. Metal and qi surged and decapitated three foes. He continued spinning counterclockwise, using the momentum to sweep out his yellow fan, sending wind blades where enemy troops were more concentrated. Cries of agony rang out as he swung with his sword again, lopping limbs off the lucky foes he didn't outright kill.

As much as Feng Ming didn't like the man, Jiao Ming was a great fighter and a fierce general. The western flank soon regained stability, but the dread Feng Ming felt hadn't receded. Instead, he looked to the east again, which had been weakened to respond to the attack. During their maneuvering east and west, their troops had been spread too thinly.

Then, something unexpected happened. General Lan, who'd been fighting alongside Gong Xuandi, yelled out an order. His troops turned around and cut down their former allies and grouped up with the South. The about-face happened faster than anyone could respond to, and their actions were swift and decisive. Southern troops crashed into where Gong Xuandi was fighting and attacked him with everything they had. Though he cut down man after man, and though he was a half-step-blood-awakening cultivator, Sea God bloodline included, he was only one man. Troops flooded around him, cutting down surprised Northern forces.

"We need to retreat," Feng Ming said to Jiao Ming. "Abandon the bunkers and regroup. If we keep fighting here, we'll lose."

Jiao Ming grimaced, but he was a competent commander. "Ungrateful traitor," he spat, glaring at where General Lan now fought alongside their enemies. Horns blew out all over the battlefield, calling for a tactical retreat. Troops fled from the bunkers, which blew up only a few seconds after their departure in a rain of stone and fire. These might be Northern fortifications, but it was better to destroy them than let them fall to their enemies. If they took back this land, they could always rebuild.

Run. Fight. Run. They ran and fought for three miles before the enemy finally relented, allowing them to muster whatever forces they had. Jiao Ming cursed when they finally stopped.

"What now?" Feng Ming asked, dreading the answer.

"They knew where our trap line was," Jiao Ming said softly.

"That's not surprising," Feng Ming said, wiping blood from his spear. "If General Lan betrayed us, he likely gave them all sorts of information."

"Yes," Jiao Ming said. "Except General Lan wasn't privy to the information."

Feng Ming's expression fell. "What now, then?" Hot wind blew from behind their backs, pushing at enemy forces and reducing their visibility. It was better than nothing—hell, it probably reduced the enemy's effectiveness by ten percent or more. Unfortunately, they were outnumbered. Moreover, they'd lost their strongest line of defense. Temporary enemy fortifications sprang up one after another. Thick metal plates appeared from out of nowhere and wedged themselves into the ground. They assembled into a "V" shape, giving shelter to their most tender troops while their earth-aligned cultivators formed their own small shelters for the remaining members of their army.

"We can't attack them, not with so few forces," Jiao Ming said. "Fortunately, they only know about this trap line. There are others out here I've told no one about." He said this out loud and out in the open, where everyone could hear. More likely than not, it was the truth, but sometimes the truth was more effective when revealed. Their enemies would be extra cautious and would likely think twice before attacking them.

"Enter the hideouts!" Jiao Ming yelled. His troops hurried to comply. They pressed depressions on the cliffs, which slid open and revealed passageways. Feng Ming followed Jiao Ming into one of them and noticed there were several holes from which to fire arrows, as well as a large stockpile of bolts and crossbows. There were also reinforced mechanisms that could launch much thicker bolts out of larger holes. These holes, though a small weakness in the walls, were much easier to shoot out of than into. Combined with the smaller defensive bunkers their forces unearthed from the sand, they could put up a reasonable defense against their invaders.

Endless minutes passed as they waited for the inevitable push. Cultivators were mortals like any others, but their recovery time was much shorter. Further, spirit doctors and spirit medicine were involved. After half an hour, their opponents began moving about.

A half hour after that, they formed up battle lines again. The metal plates, which they'd placed as defensive shields, were pulled back. Metal and fire qi filled the air as the South welded the plates together, effectively forming a massive portable wind break.

Horns sounded, and they marched forward as predicted. General Lan, the traitor, stepped up and shot a flaming arrow from a green bow. He fired three more, and where they landed, explosions rang out. Metal wire, arrows, and all sorts of traps were disarmed in an instant. Then, he pulled back behind the large moving shield wall.

Jiao Ming didn't order his troops to fire right away. He held a core-transmission jade, ready to give the signal at any moment. Enemy troops advanced, encroaching on their small bunkers, forcing Northern troops back as their bunkers were plowed through.

"Now!" Jiao Ming shouted after three bunkers fell. Golden crossbow bolts soared out from the canyon walls, some from above, some from the side. They pelted Southern troops, who raised shields, expecting this. The shields blocked around three quarters of the bolts, but another quarter found their marks. Most of them left wounds, but a lucky few killed their foes.

Round after round fired into enemy forces, who now began sending out raiding parties to clear out bunkers. Some even moved forward, accidentally detonating traps but saving the rest of the army from the impact. As they advanced, they sent out troops to openings on the wall. Though locked, the doors were weaknesses in the canyon. They first destroyed the mechanisms, then pried the false stone walls open, then sent small armed crack troops inside to slaughter the defenders within.

"How long will we hold out?" Feng Ming asked.

"As long as we can," Jiao Ming said somberly. "We can keep retreating, but the moment we leave the canyon, the South will gain the most defensible foothold they can ask for, escaping the wind, if it ever starts up again. They'll have full access to the Eastern Desert through the canyon, and we won't be able to do anything about it."

Feng Ming nodded. As Southern forces advanced, he and Jiao Ming kept retreating. Gong Xuandi did the same on the other side. They evacuated their troops in a leapfrog manner. Given the precision of their movements and the practiced ease with which they did so, they'd likely trained for such a scenario. That, or such a breach had happened in the past. They'd been forced to learn such tricks for their very survival.

"Anytime now," Jiao Ming muttered.

Feng Ming didn't press him. Yet, as Southern troops advanced, the back of his neck tingled. "Look out!" he yelled, grabbing Jiao Ming by the arm and pulling him forward. They moved just in time for a large crossbow bolt, propelled from a contraption among the South's forces, to pierce the wall, slamming where they'd stood.

"How did they—" Jiao Ming said.

And then they heard it. Wailing and screaming. Their forces, which held defensible positions within the tunnels of the canyon walls, began killing themselves. They weren't part of any specific side—these cases sprang up evenly. Out of the corner of his eye, Feng Ming could see crimson veins covering their bodies.

"It's possession!" Feng Ming yelled. "The Spirit Temple is here!"

"Damn it all," Jiao Ming spat. Their forces were spread out too thinly to deal with ghosts. If they were in an army formation, at least it would be easy to cut down traitors. Here, however, a single possessed cultivator could kill three other surprised ones before being overwhelmed.

"Order a retreat out of the walls," Feng Ming said. "They can take the walls, but the slits are oriented southward. No matter how hard they try, they won't be able to use them against us."

Jiao Ming nodded slowly. He held a jade orb and sent out a command. Troops began pouring out of the canyon walls. They assembled with those near the bunkers, forming a slow but steady defensive line. With the wind at their backs, they could hold out for some time.

"If they want a quick victory, we'll make them pay dearly," Jiao Ming said.

Feng Ming nodded. Gong Xuandi, who'd just joined them, did so as well. Though he'd been wounded many times, he was a body refiner, after all. Traps went off as the South advanced, but death and wounds did little to stop the approaching metal leviathan. They braced themselves for the inevitable conflict, hoping to the heavens above for a miracle.

And then, the wind died down. They looked back toward the mouth of the canyon and realized that Cha Ming's formation had stopped working. The enemy had known about it, and they'd already planted traitors to deactivate it. They'd lost their only advantage.

A horn blew. The approaching metal shield dropped, and enemy troops poured out from behind it. Jiao Ming called out orders, and Feng Ming did so as well. Troops charged and clashed, and their elites, headed by Gong Xuandi, dove into their opponents. Luck was on their side. Their opponents miscalculated, misfired, or failed to spot something. Old injuries played up at the last moment. Unfortunately, all the luck in the world couldn't save them from these devastating odds. They were losing, and there was nothing anyone here could do about it.

Is this the end? Feng Ming wondered. He might be able to survive, but if the Eastern Desert fell, the North would fall soon after. He thought about his family—his son, his newborn daughter—and held his spear tightly. For them, he could *not* let that happen. He bellowed, charging into enemy forces. His spear, though flailing wildly, struck true and downed weaker core-formation cultivators that had been about to unleash a deadly technique on Jiao Ming. A horn sounded, but he barely heard it. He had only two things in mind: kill as many of them as possible and don't let them take a single step out of the canyon.

The battlefield was a mess, and suddenly, he noticed fur and feathers. *Did the enemy bring beast tamers?* he thought. Theirs had all been killed in the first few assaults. *No, wait.* He looked back and saw what was happening. Demons, core-formation ones, flying through the air, and purification-realm ones running down cliff walls, joining their forces and attacking the South's vulnerable flanks. In the back, he saw Cha Ming waving about his ridiculously huge pillar of a staff and sending out combat formations, incinerating vulnerable enemy troops at the rear.

Then, the winds started. The South struggled to retreat to their shield, but the tempest came too hard and too fast. The gale gently caressed the Northern forces before forming tornadoes of hot sand that blasted away at skin and sinew and wore away at Southern armor. A massive bird with an azure mark on its forehead flew above the mouth of the canyon. It flapped its wings, sending out bursts of sand one after another.

The North, invigorated by this development, charged. Facing the storm was difficult, but running downwind was easy. And catching routed enemy forces? Even easier. They roared as they cut down retreating troops, making up for lost ground. They passed the metal windbreak, cutting down the strong porters that had carried it. They passed the traplines the South had sprung, killing every man they could while still maintaining their brisk pace. They did so until they reached the exit of the canyon, where large tornadoes crashed into their opponent's reserve forces.

"You could have come sooner," Feng Ming muttered as Cha Ming landed beside him. Feng Ming was clutching a wound on his left shoulder, which caused his arm to hang limply to the side.

"I did what I could," Cha Ming said, placing a glowing green hand on Feng Ming's arm. His skin began to reknit, and tendons began to heal. "Now that Silverwing has condensed his initiation mark, it'll be impossible for them to take the winds back."

Feng Ming nodded. Already, Jiao Ming was barking orders, getting his geomancers to repair windbreaks and bunkers.

In the distance, he could see two figures floating above their troops. They were tall, regal, and oozed power and malice. One wore black armor, with a massive sword affixed to his back, while the other wore black leathers. The black-armored man, clearly the enemy marshal, saluted. Then he turned around to organize his routed forces.

Chapter 4:
The Candle Dragon's Hourglass

Huxian's paws landed on dry cracked earth as the gray portal disappeared behind him. He looked around warily, carefully checking his surroundings for traps. Though the Candle Dragon was likely a benevolent demon emperor, it was best to be careful during inheritance trials. For some demons, preparedness and reaction speed were key characteristics they looked for in those who picked up their mantle. For others, it was caution and patience. Given that the Candle Dragon presided over time, both seemed especially fitting.

The earth beneath Huxian's feet was made of a reddish-brown rock and extended a full ten thousand feet in every direction, forming a perfect circle. In its center was a crystal hourglass covered in golden patterns of dragons, stars, and shining suns. Unlike normal hourglasses, however, it didn't contain a single grain of sand. Instead, it stood empty, as though time was lost to this place.

The rocky red land might be familiar to Huxian, but the sky didn't remotely meet his expectations. Its starless expanse was pitch black like the darkest void, and in the distance stood a single bright sun. It illuminated the plateau, exposing every nook and cranny that sought to hide, but no matter how bright the sun might be, it did not expose the sky that hid behind it. Platform, hourglass, and sky aside, there was also a transparent bridge that led from this platform to the next. The bridge was short, wide, and imperceptibly thin. It led to a red stone platform just as wide and circular as the one he stood on.

Was he meant to go to the next plateau right away? Or was he meant to wait for instructions? He hesitated. These tests could be tricky, and caution was usually advised. Often, the administrator of the test would leave hints at the beginning for worthy descendants. Unless it was a test of speed, of course, in which case he was missing out on precious seconds that could make or break the inheritance.

"No need to panic," the Candle Dragon said, appearing in the black sky. The moment he did, the sun shone a little bit brighter, and the patterns on the hourglass hummed with excitement. The Candle Dragon wasn't one of those belly-dragging dragons with wings but a large, coiling creature, whose opening eyes brought dawn and whose closing eyes brought dusk. "The hourglass is something I made on a whim many aeons ago. Unfortunately, it's rather useless. It is made of my scales and my blood essence, and only my inheritors can use it. Each of them has either outgrown its usefulness or died trying. Such is life. Time waits for no one."

Huxian took gulped deeply and did his best to put on a brave face. *You spoke of an inheritance trial earlier,* he said. *And fixing my eyes.* He couldn't speak like the Candle Dragon could. That would change once he reached the initiation realm and escaped the shackles of mortality, but for now, he was limited to mental speech. And a normal, foxy form.

"These two things are part and parcel," the Candle Dragon said, his voice low and rumbling, like thundering clouds. "By completing this inheritance, you will gain two things: the Candle Dragon's initiation mark, and the Candle Dragon's Time-Torching Eyes. Many people think my strong body and sharp claws are my greatest weapons. They *are* great weapons, which I use proudly, but those fools are mistaken; my eyes control the rising and setting of the sun. They control the rising tides and vanishing waves. They control time as it affects all things, and so their power is both immense and devastating. Normally, only my descendants would have a chance at inheriting this great gift. But for you, I've decided to make an exception. After all, you've been gifted a very good template to build from."

"Template?" Huxian asked, thinking of what the dragon could mean. "The three-eye techniques I cultivate can be used as a template?"

"No," the Candle Dragon replied. "The scriptures are useless, as they are in conflict. They destroy your eyes as we speak. These techniques are perfect on their own but cannot work together. Rather than form a good template, they've ruined each other. They've left your eyes filled with hate, and your eyes see too much. This dual burden, unless rectified, will lead to blindness at the very least."

Then... Huxian said.

"You will have to rid yourself of one thing or another—hate or truth," the Candle Dragon said, grinning. His enormous body, which floated in the air, had never ceased its continuous coiling movements. "Fortunately, time hates all things. Time is the greatest killer. It ravages creation, bringing it further and further into destruction. It is the hatred your eyes contain that we will use as a template, and by inheriting my technique, you'll discard the three intents to pursue a greater truth. I trust that this is acceptable?"

Huxian nodded. He rather liked seeing things, and what the Candle Dragon said rang true. Time had a taste, like it had been dosed with a spice called odium that permeated anything it affected. "So how does this work?" he asked, looking to the bridge that led to the next platform.

"This hourglass used to contain sands of time," the Candle Dragon said. "But it got bored, so I decided to create this independent plane for it to play around in. It lurks on these plateaus, with the weakest pile staying on the first platform and the strongest pile staying on the farthest. Your job is to collect it. By doing so, you will prove your strength as my inheritor, and by collecting the sand, you will refine the Time-Torching Eyes. You will use these eyes as the basis to condense your Candle Dragon initiation mark."

"That's it?" Huxian asked. He'd expected more. Trials were usually complex affairs that tested many different attributes.

"That is all that I require for inheritance," the Candle Dragon said. "I don't care for riddles, only strength. If you are strong enough, you will succeed, and if you are weak, you will fail. Just remember, however: The path only goes one way. The moment you leave one platform, the sun will rise on the next. And the bridges you take will not allow you to backtrack. Forward is their only direction.

"You will have a day to recover the sand on each platform, after which it will hide from you, unobtainable. The day is your ally, the sun is your friend. Beware the night, for it is not the Candle Dragon's domain." As he spoke the last words, the dragon cackled, and his massive body faded into the empty sky. Without his presence, the sun grew dimmer, and the hourglass now resembled a dull piece of glass and metal.

All this for presentation, Huxian thought, sighing. Despite all his talk about hating riddles, he was awfully cryptic. After sniffing around for a while for extra clues and finding none, he walked away from the hourglass toward the edge of the platform. The crystal bridge connecting it to the next one was only a few hundred feet long, and a little narrower. It resembled a giant transparent playing card that could fall down at any moment. Huxian took a deep breath and stepped across it. True to the Candle Dragon's words, he felt a force behind him, preventing him from taking a step back. He crossed it, and the moment he set foot on the next platform, the sun blinked out of existence and began rising from the platform's circular edge.

Let's see what this sand thing is all about, Huxian thought. He walked to the center of the platform where he saw, to his surprise, a small rat. It was a peak-core-formation demon beast, but a low-grade one. And all around the rat were broken rocks and rubble, some of which looked like they were pieces of the platform and others that looked to be from elsewhere. Each one was covered in years' worth of ratty tooth marks. If the Candle Dragon was trying to convey a facet of time in the display, he'd succeeded. Rats were synonymous with decay and pestilence, with erosion and corruption.

The rat seemed quite at home in the broken and ruined display. It looked up cheerfully and curiously at Huxian. *I don't suppose you know where this sand that I'm trying to collect is, would you?*

The rat, who'd been lounging on its back as though satisfied at having eaten a huge pile of trash, sprang up, alert. He looked around in surprise and glared at Huxian accusingly. Then, to the fox's surprise, he ran away.

Oh no, you don't, Huxian sent. He chased after the rat, who was awfully fast despite its grade. The air warped around it as it ran with its tiny paws, darting through the rubble and through holes in abandoned walls on the platform. Fortunately, Huxian was a Godbeast. Whatever rubble or ruin he tried to crawl into was quickly smashed to bits by massive paws or powerful jaws. Still, it took the better part of a minute for him to catch up with the rat. And when he did, it broke off in another direction before he could capture it. He didn't want to hurt the poor thing, after all, even if he *did* need answers. So they continued their merry chase for a few minutes, during which Huxian noticed the sun was already at its highest position, directly above them. The days here were shorter, it seemed. He didn't have a real day, but rather, a day according to the rising and setting of the sun. It seemed he had no choice. No more Mr. Nice Guy.

The air around Huxian warped. He used time acceleration, a useful skill he'd gleaned from the time essence in the Sea God Clock Tower, quickly surpassing the surprised rat. It tried to dodge the blur of a fox, who suddenly grew greatly in size and smacked his mighty paw down on it. Demon beasts were tough, after all. Yet, to his dismay, the rat didn't grow at all like peak-core-formation demon beasts should. Instead, he simply lay there, barely breathing.

Did I kill it? Huxian wondered. He hadn't thought it would be so weak.

As the rat's breathing grew shallower, Huxian thought of all sorts of excuses he could repeat to the Candle Dragon. *I'm sorry I hurt your pet, but he was grossly incompetent.* No. Too snarky. *I'm sorry I hurt your rodent, but the thing wouldn't cooperate.* Too dodgy. The rat's breathing continued to grow shallower until finally, its body vanished. It faded away, joining the void, but where its tail once lay was a small pile of golden sand. The sand shot into Huxian's eyes, and the moment it did, his eyes began to glow golden. The Devil-Sealing, Demon-Subduing, and Spirit-Banishing Intents began to merge into something different.

Well, that was easy, Huxian thought. He'd thought the platform would be a riddle, something with a deeper meaning. Well, he supposed there was a deep meaning. The moment the sand hit his eyes, he became aware of a subtle essence the rat embodied, of decay, of disease, but also of enduring tenacity. The sand wasn't just a magical currency to purchase the technique he wanted, but a lesson separated into bite-sized pieces.

The lesson faded quickly, and as it did, Huxian looked up at the sun in the empty sky. The chase on the platform hadn't taken long, and he had plenty of time left. But there was no point in waiting any longer. He hadn't exhausted himself, and he had no time to spare. So, he trotted over to the edge of the platform, hoping there was a bonus for rapid completion.

The bridge connecting this platform, and the next was the same as before. The same thinness. The same transparency. It refused to let him walk back, but the moment his paws touched it, he felt something unusual he couldn't quite put a claw on. He looked back at the platform and sensed a lingering presence, a sinister aura he actually feared. Whatever it was he felt, however, he couldn't see. Nor had it come out when he'd fought the rat. So, he simply shrugged and finished crossing the bridge. There, he saw two rats instead of one.

Who would have thought the Candle Dragon would have such a soft spot for rats? he thought. The ruin and decay on this stage was much more pronounced. Larger sections of buildings covered the place, and there was spoiled food the rats had been fighting over.

Time to get this over with. He shook his head and ran. Both rats immediately darted in opposite directions, doing their best to avoid him. They didn't last very long, however. Now that he knew they were mere piles of hourglass sand, there was no need to hesitate.

Rats scattered as Huxian landed on the platform, his body expanding fifty-fold. Buildings crackled and crumbled under his weight as his paws crashed down on the innocent creatures, causing them to immediately abandon their peace-loving ways. Their eyes glowed bright yellow as their hairs bristled, and their claws gleamed with dangerous light. They jumped onto Huxian as a group, digging deep into his flesh like it was carrion or a pile of rubbish, and drawing blood as he batted his back with his tails and rolled to throw them off, crushing pillars and tooth-marked stones in the process.

These rats were smart, and their numbers too great. He couldn't just use brute force against them, so his body disappeared in a puff of smoke, only to be replaced by 256 copies of himself, one for each of the rats he was fighting. Each of his clones wasn't nearly as strong as his main body, but these rats weren't very strong either. Their battle continued for half a minute, during which a third of his own clones were destroyed, but a third of the rats also perished, a fair exchange. He amalgamated into one fox and took in a deep breath. The sand the rats had left behind in neat little piles flew into his mouth and drifted to his eyes, which grew much brighter with the surge in energy.

As Huxian had learned in previous rounds, rats did not take kindly to the death of their comrades. The moment he breathed in the sand, their eyes lit up, and they began chattering maddeningly, and their movements became frenzied and unrelenting as they joined together in small packs and began attacking. Huxian's shadow and light domains expanded, purifying and devouring the creatures. They hastened their assault, the battlefield becoming a war of attrition. The landscape around them crumbled, as his domains didn't spare the terrain, and the rats and their tiny paws seemed to resonate with the ruins, accelerating their breaking and crumbling.

The sun was only a third of the way to completing its cycle, but the rats, he knew, would get craftier. One moment, they fought viciously before quickly relenting. Now, they fled. Likely, they knew the rules of the game—they didn't have to defeat him to live; they only had to survive a single day. The fight with the rats had been an annoying exchange, a hunt where he could easily become the hunted.

Why are these rats so troublesome? Huxian thought. When a dragon offered you a chance to prove your strength, you expected to fight something fierce, like a bear, or better yet, a dragon. The Candle Dragon had lost the memo, apparently, and had opted to go for quantity instead of quality. Huxian zipped to one group and bit down, crushing three in a single chomp. He sped to another, killing four more. Two hundred and fifty-six rats might not seem like a lot, but when you only had a few minutes to get rid of them, it was more than most could handle.

They fled as he attacked, not putting up the tiniest shred of resistance. They fell like flies, and for a moment, he felt like a fox in a chicken coop. Then a dozen of them launched a blitz attack on his right thigh, their sharp claws digging deep into his demonic flesh. Though his vitality surged to regenerate the wound, blood oozed onto the platform, pooling into a small pond.

Not again, he thought. It was a meaningless wound, but the blood meant everything against these thirsty creatures. The moment they saw it, their eyes glowed red. They doubled in size, and so did their teeth and fangs. Huxian gulped and paused his assault. He was in for a world of hurt.

He shrank down and dodged as the rats, which had been fleeing until now, went for his jugular. He used time acceleration to target individual rats, devouring each one in a single gulp. The others were trapped by a time dilation zone he left behind with his tails, but despite their slowed movements, they still gave it everything they had to sink their sharp teeth into his beautiful neck. Even the time dilation seemed to follow in the footsteps of the crumbling landscape, its intricate framework breaking down into nothingness and allowing them to escape its stubborn confines.

The battle took until the sun started sinking over the horizon.

Their bloodlust was temporary, and he had to repeat the cycle a few times before finally succeeding in his extermination. The sand migrated into his eyes, and he knew intuitively that he'd reached a landmark in the first quarter of the technique. It wasn't enough to achieve an embryonic form of the Time-Torching Eyes, but his three conflicting intents seemed a little more reconciled. They weren't competing any longer but cooperated in their hatred.

As they gained focus, however, Huxian found that the slight violet glow on the platform was fading. The vivid violet aura he usually saw surrounding demonic things had faded to a deep mauve. Hatred, it seemed, was blinding. It didn't see friend or foe, fact or fiction. Still, the loss of supernatural sight was a small price to pay. The Candle Dragon was a Godbeast, so his inheritance would be worth it.

Weary, Huxian looked around the platform. His blood was swiftly evaporating from the rubble-filled stage. As the sun set, the ruin on the platform accelerated, and the rubble soon became nothing more than powdery dust. At the same time, the deep wounds he'd suffered from the rats were healing. He'd fought long and hard to get to the ninth plateau. For the first time, the rats had actually posed a challenge to him. It was time to rest, and it was also time to see the night the dragon spoke of.

As the last sliver of sunlight fled over the platform's circular horizon, a new body of light took its place on the opposite edge. It glowed a subdued white, and its light painted the platform light blue. It was a cool and refreshing light, and the air grew chilly, a nice change of pace considering the plane he'd been on before had been scorching hot, and this trial wasn't any different. With the sun gone and the moon rising, he could finally relax.

He yawned and stretched out, relaxing outwardly but remaining inwardly vigilant. He took the Candle Dragon's words of warning to heart. Godbeasts didn't lie, as it was both dishonorable and out of character. As his wounds healed, he watched.

The platform, it turned out, was very boring. Save a light sprinkling of snow that appeared on it, he saw, heard, and smelled nothing dangerous about it. By the time the moon reached the halfway point, he'd fully recovered from his injuries. Yet he couldn't help but worry as he looked around. There was an edge in the air, a feeling he could almost taste.

Time passed more slowly at night. As he regenerated, he waited for the inevitable ambush or invasion, but it never came. Before long, he was fully recovered. Confused, Huxian looked around one more time before shrugging and walking toward the exit. So much for that. He hadn't pegged the Candle Dragon for a liar, but facts spoke much louder than words, even if those words were uttered by a gigantic coiling dragon that controlled time itself.

He was halfway from the center when his hair rose on end. The dusting of snow around him suddenly swirled, and he felt a sharp pain on his right thigh. To his surprise, a glass shard had appeared there somehow, its sharp surface embedded deeply in muscle and bone. Moreover, the glass was so sharp that it had completely ignored his natural defenses. His eyes flickered to catch the assailant, but it was nowhere to be found. Fear unlike anything he'd ever felt before completely overwhelmed him. Where was his enemy? Where would it strike?

He peered in the dark sky and only sensed faint distortions all around him, each one a potential attack point, a point of entry. He had no idea what was happening or what to expect, or when to expect it. Keeping his guard up, Huxian continued his journey toward the crystal bridge. He only took three steps this time before a familiar feeling of crisis filled his body. He used time acceleration to speed up and dodge a glass shard that would have otherwise stabbed into his neck but instead glanced off his back. It cut a deep laceration in his muscles and ribs, mercifully missing his spine, which was harder to heal. Once again, he didn't see what had caused the cut. The only trace of the assailant was yet another glass shard protruding from the wound. The first one had already dissolved into nothingness, leaving a gushing, bloody hole where immaculate fur had once been.

I can't keep taking my time, Huxian thought. *At this rate, I'll be too weak to face the next trial.* He activated his time acceleration ability, using it to boost his speed, and ran in a zigzag pattern. As expected, the attacks resumed. He was able to avoid them, and out of the corner of his eyes, he caught glimpses of a creature. It was a gray-purple bird with glowing blue eyes, the kind you normally saw while sitting on a park bench.

A pigeon? Huxian thought, frowning. What was a pigeon doing on the platform? Why did its eyes glow pale blue, and when did it learn to summon spatial shards as daggers? The glass shards, he'd decided, were spatial shards. No other material could cut through his hide so neatly and without resistance. He also realized that the pigeon didn't just hide its presence. Instead, it flitted through wrinkles in space, instantly appearing and disappearing whenever it liked. It was an enemy unlike any Huxian had ever faced, and it was out for his blood and his life. The moment he slipped up, it would all be over, and his mangled corpse would be left on this silent platform covered in snow.

Huxian silently thanked the Candle Dragon for his warning. If not for that, he'd already be dead, a spatial shard protruding from his heart or his head, or worse, his core. Fortunately, there was only a single pigeon, not 256 of them like the rats. He used his time acceleration in conjunction with the time deceleration trailing from his tail to stall his enemy. He threw purifying light and devouring darkness at several possible positions, but neither of them seemed to affect it at all, as it could simply pass through them like they were empty air.

Instead, only the power of time seemed to constrain it. Even then, just barely so. The death pigeon's strikes became more practiced and focused, like a child learning something for the first time. And as its experience mounted, it began to predict Huxian's movements, which had a clear goal in mind: the exit. He'd been told a new day would start if he left the platform, and since the pigeon had come with the night, perhaps it would disappear with a new dawn. He wanted nothing more than this night of insane killer pigeons to end, so he ran as quickly as his legs would let him.

Just a little more, he thought, racking his brains for a plan. To close the distance, he'd need deception. Out of options and desperate, he split into two clones of himself, each one possessing half of his power. Both dove toward the bridge, which was surprisingly wide, all things considered. As he suspected, two spatial shards appeared to intercept them, one after another: The pigeon couldn't be in several places at once, it seemed, so he had each clone split in two to avoid the daggers, and as new strikes came, they split apart. Soon, a veritable army of Huxians barreled through the exit, each one looking harried and worn out.

Who would have thought a bunch of pigeons could teach me a lesson? Huxian thought as he trotted through the barrier. Night immediately ended, and the sun began rising on the new platform's horizon. The killer pigeon was gone. But he was bleeding, exhausted, and it hurt to breathe. *Time to get me some rats.* But there were no rats to be seen. Instead, he saw a lone ox, its eyes glowing and its horns shining with golden light. They let off a stubborn aura, an unyielding aura, one that would not diminish no matter how much time passed. Its eyes glowed bright like the sun, covering Huxian in a light that wouldn't allow his wounds to heal. In fact, they only got worse. His muscles burned. His eyes grew irritated. His soul began burning away as a relentless heat ate away at it.

Annoyed, Huxian grew to his full size of 330 feet long. The ox did the same, and both mighty beasts clashed head-on. Fortunately for Huxian, he wasn't just any demon. He immediately got the upper hand, though not without paying a price. The ox gored him before getting flung down on its back, Huxian's teeth biting into its tender underside.

Golden blood spilled onto the stage, most of it evaporating under the sun, but part of it remained in the form of golden sand that joined the sand that came from its horns and eyes. All of it migrated into Huxian as the golden aura faded, finally allowing his wounds to heal. The pounding bruises he'd suffered from the horns and hooves began to disappear as time's merciless grasp on its surroundings returned.

First rats, now oxen? Huxian thought, looking up at the sun, which was slowly setting. Fortunately, this portion of the trial had finished quickly, and he could use his remaining time to regenerate. Though he could technically try to heal during the night, that definitely wasn't something he wanted to try for the time being.

Time passed, and when he was three quarters healed, the sun finally set. He hesitated, looking at the last sliver of sun as it disappeared before walking across the one-way bridge to the next platform. Though he wanted to fight the pigeon again, he needed to be prepared. He needed an edge, something to tilt the scales in his favor. The first stage of the Time-Torching Eyes seemed like just the thing to hurt it.

Decision made, Huxian looked to the center of the newest platform and noticed two oxen instead of one. *Great. Just great.* They charged, and he charged straight back at them.

Chapter 5: Cessation

Wang Jun stared at an empty mirror, his hands moving mechanically as he brushed his long blond hair. The strands of white in it had multiplied of late, nearly half of it from obscuring the Wang family's secrets. In more real terms, that meant he'd spent around half his lifespan, 250 years, should he fail to reach rune carving.

The loss of lifespan was the least of his worries today, however. He had a simple assignment to carry out: betraying the North. It wasn't an overt task, but neither was it under the radar. It was a carefully chosen mission given to him by the Patriarch and Wang Ling, one that only he, with his trade connections and way with words, could accomplish. Or so they said.

He saw through their obvious lies just as everyone else would. The task was more a test of loyalty than anything else. By accomplishing it, he would show the world where he stood and draw hatred from every country in the Northern Alliance.

There was a gentle knock at the door. Wang Jun adjusted his robes before answering. "Enter," he said, and it opened, revealing Wang Bing and Elder Bai. "I thought I told you two to liquidate your family assets and flee while you still could."

Though they were the best assistants a man could hope for, it would break his heart to have them tangled up in this mess. The game before had been one of money and lies, but this new one would thrive on crisis and fear.

"Nonsense," Wang Bing said, pushing her way into his suite. "I couldn't get a good price for my assets, so I decided to stay. I figured that by working for you, I'd get to maintain a bit of control over my fate. Besides, you of all people should know that one does not simply *quit* a family."

Which was true, especially in their particular family. Their leadership was known to go to great lengths to punish and make an example out of deserters. It would cost her much more than the steep family discount she would have to give when selling her property. If she handled the situation poorly, or they were feeling sufficiently spiteful, it could even cost her poor life.

"I accept that," Wang Jun said, then turned to Elder Bai. "You, however, are not bound by such things. You are not technically a member of the Wang family. Not by blood, anyway."

The older man simply smiled and waved his hand. "This old bag of bones has been tied to the family longer than you've been alive," Elder Bai said. "I've had the pleasure of serving you since you were a babe. How could I abandon you now when things have gotten difficult? It's like asking a mother to abandon her newborn."

Wang Jun smiled a rare smile. "You haven't the slightest clue about what's happening. You know I've given up my bid for the family leadership, given up the struggle of my lifetime, but you don't know why I've done it, or the dark underlying secrets that have pushed me. So let me tell you this now: run. Run while you still can, while your involvement is still at a minimum."

"Run?" Elder Bai said, cocking his head. "Run where? My family is long dead, and I've spent centuries serving this household. Consider me an adopted member of the family, a stray picked up with nowhere else to go."

"I'm afraid that if you stay, you'll be forced to act against your principles," Wang Jun said. "There's no avoiding it."

"Then all the more important that I'm there," Elder Bai said. "To steer you in the right direction when you *think* you have no other options."

"A boat blown by fierce winds can only go one direction," Wang Jun said, shaking his head.

"But a clever lookout can spot rocks beneath the ocean waves, pointing them out so the captain can avoid them," Elder Bai said, still smiling.

"And whatever you're doing, you'll want to keep well dressed," Wang Bing added. "I'm sure you'll now have a much larger budget for my new fashion line now that you're in charge of so much of the family's finances."

Wang Jun chuckled. "I'll make it happen. It's the least I can do for anything I drag you into." He said it and meant it, but he was sure that whatever he did wouldn't cut it. They just didn't know how bad things had gotten. How could they, when even *he* hadn't suspected it?

"Where will we be going today, young master?" Elder Bai asked, packing up Wang Jun's things for him in a small briefcase on the table. The caring man had already anticipated his intention to travel. He'd always been good like that. "I see trade association materials. A declaration about quality control. An official warning. This is going to be fun."

"We're going to make a grand announcement," Wang Jun said, holding his hand to his chest. "I, the prime director of the Wang Family and personal whipping boy of the Patriarch and Junior Patriarch, will personally make life difficult for the entire Golden Kingdom, if not the entire Northern Alliance."

"You could use a little glamour to give it more impact," Wang Bing said, pursing her lips. She took out some bottles and powders from her storage ring, and before Wang Jun could object, she'd pushed him to the wall and begun drawing on his face. A brush here, a flick there. Before he knew what was happening, he looked in the mirror and saw that he was indeed much more handsome. He could tell because his shadow had returned; it stood in the mirror, perfectly imitating his appearance.

"Good work," Wang Jun said. "Whoever said men couldn't wear makeup."

"Important figures always do," Wang Bing said with a sniff. "Even if just to make them look even more a curmudgeon."

"Let's go. We're late," Wang Jun said. He grabbed the packed briefcase and flicked his sleeve for dramatic effect. They walked out of his room and were followed by two new personal bodyguards: wicked-looking men with more than a few scars to their name. People moved out of their way as they proceeded down the corridor toward the entrance to the mansion, where Wang Ling, the person he despised most in the world, was waiting.

"I take it everything is in order?" Wang Ling said, glancing at Wang Bing and Elder Bai but saying nothing.

"I've organized all the necessary paperwork and prepared speeches for all contingencies," Wang Jun replied. "Have no worries, your will shall be done. I will perform my duties to the highest standard of excellence."

"Good," Wang Ling said. "We're counting on you."

Wang Jun stifled the urge to stab the man in the eye and walked out the front door. If it wasn't for Hong Xin's life being dependent on Wang Ling's continued existence, he'd risk it all for even the slightest chance at murdering him. Alas, that was all in the past. His hands were tied now. He'd have to outgrow his hatred for his new master, if only for the life of the beautiful woman that hung in the balance.

It was a bright and sunny day outside. Their small procession walked out of the Jade Bamboo Pavilion, passing customers and entering Gold Leaf Square in all its natural splendor. The leaves only had two colors; it was summer, so red had yet to appear on them. It was also the weekend, so families were out playing with their children in the park. They were happy, if only because they were oblivious to the storm that was quickly approaching.

Then again, he thought, *their fate isn't set in stone.* Despite the likely fall of the city, one did not simply claim economic territory and destroy its inhabitants. Every person here was a contributor to the city's output, and disturbing them too much would degrade the city's value. Their fate would likely be much better than his.

From the Jade Bamboo Pavilion, they traveled east to a large building downtown. The tall, angular building with odd shapes for windows was the Gold Leaf Association. There, every single relevant trade in the city was represented. It also housed the standards for all professions on the continent, for while other cities were better at crafting—Haijing, Blacksteel, and Quicksilver, to name a few—they weren't nearly so dominant in trade. After all, it wasn't the producers that set the standards, but the buyers and resellers.

The Jade Bamboo Conglomerate enjoyed a special position in the Gold Leaf Association. As the single largest corporation north of the wall, they happened to buy a huge portion of every product imaginable. As such, they had considerable influence with its many members, as well as a seat at the table for every important meeting.

They were welcomed at the entrance of the building by a small crowd standing before a strange open door. The door was made of wood and stone and enhanced by metal runes seared into its surface. It was a mosaic depicting many colors and symbols, joined by jagged patterns. It symbolized all allied trades and was there to send an important message: No matter what, no matter the situation, these craftsmen would stand united. Their founding principle was that they would always negotiate as a single, immovable body.

"Welcome, Prime Director Wang," their leader, a short man with a long beard said, bowing lightly. "Please follow us. Our members are anxiously waiting for your grand announcement."

Wang Jun nodded and followed the man without much fanfare. He'd arrived late, and on purpose at that. He wanted them to sweat a little before he stabbed and twisted the knife.

They made their way up a multicolored glass staircase that wound around an enormous crystal chandelier. It hung from the ceiling at the center of the building, hanging a mere twenty feet above the tiled floor. It was a work of art, and every lit crystal hanging on it was unique. And the higher they climbed, the more beautiful it got, and on every crystal was a runic pattern.

They soon reached the second to the last floor and proceeded into a conference room that overlooked the city. A few empty seats sat by the door—those for Wang Jun and his entourage. There were fifty men and women seated at the U-shaped table, which opened up toward a single pane of glass that allowed everyone a look at the entire city, Gold Leaf Square included. It was, in Wang Jun's humble opinion, the best view within a thousand miles.

"I can't say I've had the pleasure of seeing this before," Wang Jun said, motioning at the window. "It's marvelous, truly beautiful. Whoever picked the location for the association headquarters was gifted with great foresight."

"Pardon me for saying this, but you've never had the status to enter this room in the past," said the man who'd led him inside. "As prime director of the Jade Bamboo Conglomerate, however, you now have the right to table meetings here once per month. Please don't abuse the privilege, as meetings are a terrible waste of time."

Wang Jun nodded but took his time to enjoy the view. His entourage and his escort took a seat—the shorter man was a tinker, someone who made mechanical contraptions of high quality. Wang Jun didn't sit but remained standing with his arms folded behind his back for dramatic effect.

"I have come," Wang Jun said finally, dragging out every word as long as he could, "to make an announcement." He let his words hang over them like a guillotine, or like a noose around their neck before the hangman pulled the lever. "It is a difficult time for the North, but a prosperous one for trade. Recent reports have come in from border countries. The South is mounting large-scale attacks on the wall, and orders are coming in from every nation. What a wonderful time for business." He grinned, and the people at the table nodded. This knowledge was a day old, and in business circles, that was considered ancient.

"As prime director of the Jade Bamboo Conglomerate," Wang Jun continued, "I have noticed some discrepancies in orders."

"Discrepancies?" Lao Fa, the tinker, asked.

"Discrepancies," Wang Jun repeated. "We buy and resell a large chunk of what you produce—thirty percent, by my count, including affiliated producers. And we've found discrepancies. Many of them, in fact."

The audience gulped, waiting for more, but he said nothing.

"These discrepancies..." Ya Ning, a graying lady with long, flowing hair eventually said. She wore the badge of an alchemist but fortunately didn't carry their usual arrogance. "Could you please elaborate? I'm afraid your words are a little vague, and leave too much to the imagination."

"It is difficult to elaborate," Wang Jun said, "for the discrepancies are rampant. But to illustrate my point, I will make an observation. By my count, there are at least seven standards for even the most common goods in each profession, which is confusing, to say the least. Then, these numerous standards get mixed up in our orders— very large orders, might I add—leading to confused and dissatisfied customers, who grumble and bicker with us, the innocent resellers. As a result of this grumbling and bickering, we see a corresponding increase in requests for refunds and discounts, many of which we can't talk ourselves out of due to agreements with our clients. You can see how this would be both annoying and expensive."

"I can see that, yes," Ya Ning admitted.

"Well, unfortunately, this has come to the attention of our family's leadership," Wang Jun said. "With business spiking, the amount of errors is increasing exponentially. They've decided that enough is enough. This has to stop. Immediately." There were more confused frowns and reluctant stares.

"Stop?" the stout tinker Lao Fa said. Though he'd greeted Wang Jun at the entrance, his standing amongst his peers was quite high. He was one of the three vice chairs of the board, which, for some symbolic reason had no actual chair. "What do you mean, stop?"

"What I mean," Wang Jun said, "is that until this problem is resolved—until there are uniform standards across the board, and these standards lead to a corresponding reduction in errors and liability for errors on our part—our trade will stop." These words silenced the room of any mutterings, and soon, only ragged and confused breaths could be heard. "We've had it with the chaos in this marketplace, the disorganization covered up by the thin guise of unity. Until we have proper regulations for consistency in the products we buy, we will not only cease trading, but we will actively hinder trade until this gets resolved. This conflict has only revealed what we've known for a long time, and we will *not* be going through this crisis by getting fleeced at every opportunity."

Jaws dropped. Silence reigned in the room. Many even ceased breathing. It would be one thing for one of their association heads to say something like this—strikes for increased compensation or benefits were common—but the Jade Bamboo Conglomerate saying this, and during a war of all times, was akin to the sky crashing down on their large communal heads. It wasn't an exaggeration to say that their very existence depended on the Wang family. It was for that reason that the Wang family's prime director was also a vice chair of the board.

It took a full minute for anyone to say anything openly. Even Wang Bing and Elder Bai, who were used to his sweeping and bold speeches, didn't know what to say. They simply averted their eyes and awkwardly coughed or fidgeted as the board members took in the sudden and spiteful information.

"Your proposal is, of course, taken very seriously by our members," Lao Fa finally said. "We will consult and see what we can do to remedy this situation."

"I'm afraid it wasn't a proposal," Wang Jun said apologetically. "It was a statement. From now on, we *will* cease trade until standards are agreed upon. We will hold daily meetings to discuss progress and headway, and we expect your full cooperation. End of story."

"That's madness!" said Ya Ning the alchemist, slamming her bony hands on the hard wooden table. "You can't just stop trade! It's wartime. Countries are involved, not just our organizations. And as the major trading hub for the entire Northern Alliance, it is our duty to do what we can."

Wang Jun laughed lightly, as though he'd heard the funniest joke in the world. "I'm afraid I can, and I will," he said, looking at her almost pityingly. "You've gotten away with this for far too long, especially you alchemists. I will *not* be bullied under the pretence of Northern unity. Our Wang family values profit above all else, which you should know very well by now."

That was the straw that broke the camel's back, the stone that started the landslide. The room erupted into heated discussions, and the word traitor popped up every so often. But those who said such words were quickly told to shut the hell up, or else, since after all, one did not simply denounce their greatest buyer, especially since individual actions could easily drive each of their associations into insolvency. They weren't like the Wang family, whose vault could let them ride the currents for decades without the need to actually do business. They were representatives of real people and businesses with real expenses and real needs.

It took some time for everything to quiet down, an entire quarter hour by Wang Jun's count. Finally, Lao Fa and the last vice chair, Cheng Gang, stood up. "I see that there is no dissuading you," Cheng Gang said to Wang Jun. He was a calm middle-aged man with streaks of gray on in his hair. He was strong, and rightly so given that he represented blacksmiths, the hardiest of professions. "Since you've made your announcement, I'm sure you have a list of demands and a plan to move forward as quickly as possible. We wouldn't want to waste any time on such an important priority."

"I do," Wang Jun said, placing his briefcase on the table. He pushed it all the way across the U-shaped surface and was pleased that the unnecessary container—storage rings were much more convenient—brought about the appropriate dramatic effect. The man unclasped the suitcase and pulled out a few pieces of paper, which he quickly fingered through.

"Very extensive," Cheng Gang said. "And difficult. We will not argue about these things now. I will assign teams to go over each item to resolve them as soon as possible, and I expect that as the initiator, you will be ready to discuss things as early as possible." He then began calling out names and assigning duties like he'd said. He didn't look up at Wang Jun during this time, a clear soft dismissal.

Not even Lao Fa, who'd escorted him in, paid him any attention anymore.

"Let's go," Wang Jun said to Wang Bing, Elder Bai, and the guards. They made their way out of the building and into Gold Leaf City's streets. Not much time had passed during the meeting, and the bright sun still filled the city with warmth. Despite the heat, however, Wang Jun could only feel cold. He'd finally done it, his first act of defiance against the Golden Kingdom's defense efforts.

"Bold," Wang Bing said as they left the square in front of the association headquarters. "Though I don't see how this will improve our family's profitability. The profits we'll lose on stalling trade are astronomical, and our competitors will likely leap on this and try to establish alternative trade agreements within a few hours."

"And they'll find very aggressive legal teams and stacked courts blocking them," Wang Jun said. "They'll find their suppliers, in turn, not cooperating, for fear of going bankrupt. My dear lady, it's official: trade has stalled in the North."

"This will get political very quickly," Elder Bai warned. "Expect visits from princes and kings, lords and ladies. Even the clergy will want to speak with you, despite your obvious heresy against their church and goddess."

"By all means, let them get tangled up in this as well," Wang Jun said. "There are many political allies involved that will make their lives difficult. Any effort at untangling this knot will find the string pulled ever tighter, ever more difficult to undo."

"This isn't about making money, is it?" Wang Bing said softly. She'd finally begun to grasp the gravity of the situation.

"I'm afraid it isn't," Wang Jun said. "Now I'll ask you one last time, do you still want to stay? It will only get worse from here on in."

They continued their walk back, and by the time they entered the Jade Bamboo Pavilion again, neither of them had given him any sign of wanting to leave. It was both relieving and worrying. They were his greatest allies, his greatest friends. And unfortunately, they were now with him to the bitter end.

Hong Xin looked down caringly at Wang Jun, who lay down on her prison couch with his head on her lap. He'd done something awful today—she could tell from the look on his beautiful face, as much as the glamour sought to hide it. Though her cultivation was crippled and her soul force was sealed by the collar on her neck, she could still see past the amateurish brush strokes. The slight paleness in his complexion. The way his jaw clenched slightly. The slight movements in his neck as his eyes darted left and right, as his mind imagined things that had come, would come, and what could be.

"Do you want to talk about it?" Hong Xin asked, not expecting an answer. She already knew everything thanks to a tiny pin Hong Yinyue had given her and concealed on her clothes. The powerful artifact was practically impossible to detect—it fed her a constant stream of information from the world outside her cell. Trade in the Golden Kingdom had been disrupted, and its effects were expanding to nearby kingdoms. The one responsible for all this was none other than the ambitious new prime director of the Jade Bamboo Conglomerate, Wang Jun. The North was incensed, and monarchs were angry, but there was nothing they could do as they beat back their eternal enemies.

"I did something today," Wang Jun finally said. He paused a while before continuing. "It was something that didn't have any outward consequences but that will undoubtedly have many implications. There were no deaths, no murders. No laws were broken. There were a few lies, but those were seen through. It was practically as honest as I've ever been, but I've never felt so crooked and deceitful."

"What could be so bad about lies?" Hong Xin asked, encouraging him to elaborate. "The Red Dust Pavilion thrived on lies, and the truths we often gleaned from them."

Wang Jun sighed and opened his eyes to look at her. Those

beautiful eyes, ones that, now that she thought about it, were darker than night itself. She could get lost in those eyes and the void within them, the endless abyss that the love of her life represented. "What I did will have a greater impact than killing millions," he said. "So, on the morality scale, I might not technically be a murderer, but I'm definitely a terrible traitor. What's worse is that what I did was perfectly legal, so no authorities will punish me. Tell me, these lies, aren't they as bad as they get?"

"Something to do with money and contracts, then?" Hong Xin asked, unsure of how to get him to elaborate further.

"Something like that," Wang Jun mumbled, groaning as she dug into his shoulders. Hong Xin hadn't been idle as they talked. She did her best to release what tension she could from her awkward sideways position. Doing anything while someone was lying on your lap was extremely difficult, even more so when you couldn't use qi or soul force to facilitate it.

What I wouldn't give for my dousing powers, Hong Xin thought. *I'd use them to soothe his worries and ease his pain. And with my kindling powers, I would light up a flame in his heart, sewing a bright seed of hope that would flourish in an instant.*

Unfortunately, she could no longer do such a thing. The patriarch of the Wang family, Wang Wuling, had seen to that. Where her Dantian used to be was just an empty blip in space, a shattered remnant of a once-rich cultivation. She could no longer cultivate, nor could she manipulate qi. Her meridians and qi pathways had all dried up. And no medicine in the world could change that, or even gift her a short burst of power if she needed it. "I hope you can find a way to do the right thing, Wang Jun," Hong Xin said softly. "The man I committed my life to wouldn't give up so easily."

"And how can I do that?" Wang Jun said, closing his eyes again. "My orders are explicit and very detailed."

"In my experience, when you can't solve a big problem, you can still solve small parts," Hong Xin said. "Isn't that what you always said? When you were in the Song Kingdom, you managed with what little funds were available to you. You didn't care about the bigger picture, because you weren't qualified to play in the bigger game. Isn't your situation now the same? Now that you report to Wang Ling and the Patriarch, there are some things you can't help. But still, they can't micromanage you, or they'll greatly diminish your effectiveness. And even when they do, can't these games be played both ways? If they restrain your spirit with words, you can follow their words to the letter but not to the spirit."

Wang Jun got up slowly, letting out a deep sigh. "You're right. I'll do what I can. But I'm afraid it won't be much. It won't be nearly enough for what's to come."

Hong Xin smiled and wrapped her arms around him. A foot shorter than he was, she rested her head on his chest. "If it's not enough, and you think it's worth it, there's always one thing you can do. There's one freedom they can never take away from you, no matter how hard they persist."

"And what's that, my love?" Wang Jun asked, running his hand through her soft hair.

She wished they could do more, but under the leering eyes of her jailors, she didn't dare push further. Instead, she pulled away from him and looked him in the eyes. She stared into their blackness, into the blackness of his soul, and past it to the spark of light that still existed. "You can always let me go and do what needs to be done. I don't matter so much any longer. You're a powerful man, with much to live for. But more importantly, there are many others you can live for."

His expression grew serious, and he put his fingers to her lips. "Never say those words again, my love," he said. "I already lost you once, and it almost broke me."

She didn't need her cultivation or her soul force to see that pushing him further would do no good, so she remained silent and embraced him. Time trickled by, every minute of it precious. Then, a short while later, the guards separated them. Their time was over, and they wouldn't budge on that limit even by a minute.

They led Wang Jun up the stairs and away from her. Once a day, he could see her. Once a day, she could do what she could to steer him in the right direction and sow seeds for a better future. There were many ways to go about this, many things she could say. But one thing was certain and couldn't be avoided: her life was worthless, and the greatest push she could give him was ending it.

Chapter 6: Hostilities

"The state of the union," Jiao Ming said, pausing for appropriate dramatic effect before finishing his sentence, "isn't good at all."

They were seated at a round table, and on the round table was a large map covered in exquisite pieces that represented Northern and Southern armies. Some key individuals, such as Feng Ming and Cha Ming, had their own little pieces. Cha Ming's was carved from a perfect piece of stone, while Feng Ming's was cast out of dull metal, his features too difficult to make out.

"War is intensifying everywhere. No country in the North has been spared. Whether cults or bandits or outright rebellion, even the coastal kingdoms are seeing their fair share of destruction.

"Aside from our battle here, which we won by the skin of our teeth, there are three other major battles taking place on the continent. The Phoenix Cry Empire has called out for help just west of here. On the other side of the continent, the Evergreen Battlefield is seeing intensified skirmishes and troop movements."

"The Southaven Battlefield is as calm as it can be given the circumstances," Feng Ming said, nodding. "Troops are amassing there, but Quicksilver is supporting us. Fortunately, the South hasn't used any major weapons like those cannons from years ago. Though what they have against our specific section of the wall, I'll never guess." The only thing he could think of was that it had something to do with Gong Lan and her pestering insistence about the importance of her monastery, an isolated place in the middle of the mountains somewhere between the Song Kingdom and the Quicksilver Empire.

"Meanwhile," Jiao Ming continued, "countries near the coast are refusing to aid us. All save True North Country, who we bled for dearly."

"They have honor," an elder at the table said. "We paid blood for them, and so it is blood they are repaying."

"For the Evergreen Battlefield," a middle-aged man muttered.

"For the North," Jiao Ming said sternly, quieting them. "And in case you've forgotten, it was my brother who died there. If I'm not complaining about it, what gives you that right?"

His words shut the middle-aged man down, and he uttered not another word. Some others shuffled uncomfortably, but since their recent victory and General Lan's defection, many of the seats at the table had been shuffled in Jiao Ming's favor. He was the de facto head of the Eastern Desert, and they could do little but follow his lead.

"I realize this might be a little insensitive given the recent battle and betrayal, but what exactly are your plans?" Feng Ming asked. "With the Windswept Canyon now secure, and the enemy marshal gone to tend to another battlefield, there doesn't seem to be much to worry about here. Will you at least entertain my request to aid in other battles?"

"I'm not sure I'm willing," Jiao Ming said, shaking his head. "We suffered a devastating blow near Beihai, and though we won the battle in the canyon, we paid a steeper price than we can bear. We may seem orderly, Marshal Feng, but the Eastern Desert is ever shifting. Our armies fight each other as we speak."

There were nine others at the table, each one the head of their respective kingdom. Though their clan property was smaller than Jiao Ming's three large cities, they still held significant sway in the turbulent Eastern Desert. "Besides, I'm not sure how honorable these ladies and gentlemen are. We all saw what happened to the most recent example, General Lan."

"Don't compare us to that traitor," the middle-aged man Jiao

Ming had scolded before spat. His name was Xiaohou Deng. A mighty warrior back in his day, his thick frame carried a broad belly covered in a thick layer of fat. His wicked curved greatsword, and the chain it was attached to, had once instilled fear in the Eastern Desert, enough that no one ever dared try taking his city.

"You and I both know there's a standing offer out there for betrayal," Jiao Ming said bitterly. No one contradicted him. "Should any of us give in, they'll leave our paltry land untouched. Moreover, they'll give us a portion of the land belonging to those who didn't. Open intrigue at its finest." Temptation, even public, could only unnerve everyone involved. It could drive a wedge between the best of friends, who never knew when the price would increase enough to actually be tempting.

Cha Ming, who'd been silent the entire time, stood up and pointed at a dark spot on the board within the borders of the Quicksilver Kingdom. There were hundreds of similar spots all across the map. "What are these?" he asked, placing his finger on it.

"Mostly devil cults and bandits causing chaos in their respective kingdoms," Jiao Ming said offhandedly. "There are too many to stamp out, and they're good at hiding. Those that are large have major figures like transcendents backing them."

"And this?" Cha Ming asked, pointing to a paler spot near the wall, where a large mountain lay. The map was topographical, giving the reader a rough idea of respective elevations.

"That," Feng Ming said, "is Mount Tai. It's the largest mountain at the very center of the continent. It's considered one of the happiest places in the kingdom, and it's far from any of the battlefields." It was also one of the poorest and most difficult kingdoms to cross, which meant it had been left largely ignored for the better part of three centuries.

"There are reports of chaos in the wilderness," Jiao Ming explained. "Fiendish demons are sprouting just like those you reported. I'm worried they're taking over the demons there, who live peacefully with humans."

"How did they get North of the wall?" Cha Ming asked.

"The wall isn't impassable," Feng Ming said, shaking his head. "It's difficult, but doable. They will almost certainly alert us when they do. The reason there are battlefields is because core-formation cultivators can't hold ground like foundation-establishment cultivators and qi-condensation cultivators can. After all, if you conquer a place, you can't just kill people until the rest of them listen. It's not efficient. Other than that, they're outnumbered north of the wall. But in a secluded place like Mount Tai…" His words hung over them uncomfortably.

"None of us will defect like General Lan did," a woman with red hair said, bringing the conversation back to the previous topic. Though she was older, three centuries old by Feng Ming's estimation, she had a youthful vigor about her. She resembled the scarred lady they'd fought beside in the Windswept Canyon, but with many more pages of battle accomplishments. "We are all men and women of the desert. We've had hard lives. We're not like General Lan, who simply raked in wealth and farmed his arable land while the rest of us paid in blood and sweat to make a living."

Jiao Ming nodded and looked to Feng Ming. "I never did trust General Lan, and I only put up with him for the sake of a united front. But I've fought with and beside these men and women, and I can attest to their honor. I was only joking when I mentioned further betrayal."

"I know you can't make promises, but please do what you can," Feng Ming said. "In three days, we'll leave for Quicksilver, where the next Northern Alliance meeting is being held." And then there would be meetings. Lots of them. Feng Ming hated meetings and did everything he could to avoid them.

"Can't we just attend remotely?" Jiao Ming asked, echoing his sentiment.

"Do you dare call in at such an important time?" Feng Ming asked. "Some things are best said in person. During such trying times, some of the softer kingdoms will get cold feet. We need to be there to remind them that danger exists, and that even those who bicker at every meeting can stand together when the times require."

No one argued more than he and Jiao Ming did at those meetings. Not even half as much. Their coordinated message should shut up at least a quarter of them.

We need to go to the mountain, a voice suddenly said. Silverwing, Cha Ming's little falcon demon friend who'd saved the day, flew from the windowsill and landed at the center of the map on the table. *That place is a powerful well of mountainous energy. With it, it's possible for fiendish demons to destroy a section of the wall.*

Heavens, demons complicated things.

Cha Ming frowned. "There's more to this, isn't there?"

The small bird nodded. *Mr. Mountain is there, condensing an initiation mark like I did near the canyon. If we aid him in condensing the mark, he'll be of great help in reinforcing the wall. There's a reason the wall was built right beside it—mountains are the mightiest of demonic energy sources.*

So there was both a vulnerability and an advantage to claiming it. Feng Ming added it to his growing to-do list, things that took priority over everything else, including Gong Lan's repeated calls for help.

"But who do we send?" Feng Ming said, tapping his jaw as he looked at the map in concern. "You and I can't go." What he wouldn't give for another two or three powerhouses who were easy to deploy like Cha Ming was.

"We experienced firsthand how a fiendish invasion can weaken us," Jiao Ming said. "But you're right; it's necessary that we go to this meeting together. Otherwise, they'll balk and do nothing like they always do."

Cha Ming looked to Feng Ming and shrugged. "It looks like I'll have to go. I'm lucky enough to not have an entire kingdom resting on my shoulders. But what about the Evergreen Battlefield? Isn't that also a priority?" According to what he'd said before, Huxian's friend Gua was also condensing an initiation mark in the poisonous swamps near that farther battlefield. As for Lei Jiang, the angry mouse, no one had any idea where he'd gone.

"The situation is stable in the west," Feng Ming said with a sigh.

"During times of war, it's important to prioritize things. There are battles you want to fight that would strengthen your position, and battles you *have* to fight. Rallying the North's united troops is a must. So is securing that mountain. If Silverwing words are correct, we don't have much of a choice in the matter."

Cha Ming nodded. "Especially if their fiend whisperer is there." According to his report, the man in black leathers was a half-step-blood-awakening cultivator that could set off a storm in any demonic territory.

I'll accompany him, Silverwing said, flying onto his shoulder. *I'm not needed to guard the mountain. The mountain will guard the pass and itself.*

Thank heaven for that, Feng Ming thought. "Good luck, my friend," he said to Cha Ming. "I just hope we're not too late. Our alliance was strong during times of peace, but that's always the case, isn't it?"

The man and the falcon left the room, leaving Feng Ming to brood with the others. Then they turned their attention back to the board and its many game pieces. In particular, they focused on the territories in the Eastern Desert. The enemy marshal might be gone, but he could return at any minute. And this battle had taught them an important lesson: the canyon might be safe from most invasions, but there were tactics they'd never thought to defend against.

"What first? Ghosts?"

"Ghosts." Jiao Ming nodded, and the others agreed. Before long, they were amending battle plans and deciding on drills and strategies and writing up contingencies. Like Feng Ming, these men and women lived and breathed battles, though they brought centuries of experience the younger man didn't. Working with them would be a pleasant stroll in the park compared to the diplomatic meetings he would soon be attending.

Chapter 7: Mountain

Cha Ming landed with a thump, and Silverwing landed on his shoulder. They'd traveled a long way before finally arriving in the peaceful village known as Taishan. Despite being called a village, it consisted of buildings sprawled over the entire mountain, small pockets of civilization dotting the wild woodlands. According to Feng Ming, the people here lived in harmony with demons. There were no boundaries separating humans from the potentially savage beings on the mountain. They worked together, ate together, and traveled between their respective domiciles without restriction, never needing things like guards to protect their way of life.

But that was not what Cha Ming saw. What should have been a peaceful, happy village was instead a veritable ghost town. Shops were closed, doors barricaded, and the occasional wall caved in from what was clearly a brawl involving demons. All around him, he could sense people holing up indoors, as though their stone and wooden walls could protect them from the inhuman forces at work here. The demons that would normally have roamed the streets were gone, preferring the company of trees to suffocating isolation.

There's a wrongness in the air, Silverwing said from atop his shoulder, his wings quivering slightly. Cha Ming nodded as he walked north to a building that was larger and more ornate than the others. He couldn't make out the bright colors in the otherwise plain design, but he could tell at a glance that it was his destination.

"What tipped you off?" Cha Ming muttered. "Was it the deserted streets or the bleak atmosphere?"

Those aren't normal? Silverwing asked. He seemed earnest in his curiosity, so Cha Ming shook his head. *Well, I didn't know. I don't pay attention to the doings of you humans. What I was talking about was the thick miasma floating in the air. It's an eerie brown cloud that clings to everything, choking out demonic energy it meets and swallowing it up like a snack before bed.*

"I hadn't noticed it," Cha Ming said. How could he? Before, he'd have been able to see many things, even the tiniest details, thanks to his strong eyes. Now, he could only see vague outlines of buildings but couldn't make out the details that made them beautiful. He couldn't sense the strong primal energy of the mountain, for that wasn't something a human soul could sense. His ability to see merit or sin had also disappeared. The only thing his eyes could see was a fuzzy world of black, white, and gray. And things he hated.

Cha Ming knocked three times on the manor's oak door. There were no walls surrounding it, as would be standard in normal human cities. This surprised Cha Ming. Despite having been told they were a peaceful lot that knew little of crime, he would have thought that those living with demons, who dueled if someone so much as sneezed in the wrong direction, would prioritize safety. There were footsteps, and someone opened the door—a woman with curly dark hair and a light-colored outfit. She was strong, surprisingly so. Her late-core-formation cultivation would be the cream of the crop in any kingdom.

"Can I help you?" the woman asked, pushing back her curly hair with the hand not holding the half-open door.

"My name is Cha Ming," Cha Ming replied. "I'm here on behalf of the Northern Alliance, under instruction from Marshal Feng Ming." He proffered a token Feng Ming had given him prior to his departure. She inspected it for a moment before handing it back.

"Who would have thought help would come so soon?" she said, sighing in relief. "Come inside. I'll take you to the village chief." She opened the door and led him through the main hallway. It opened into a garden courtyard in the center of the building that contained a wild assortment of shrubs, trees, rocks, and water features. There were many men and women in the courtyard, all of them powerful. They drank tea and ate snacks as other, smaller animals did the same. Birds drank out of communal baths, and bear cubs struggled to eat whole cakes with their paws. Tiny wolf pups ate tiny pieces of cooked meat that had been roasted and spiced to perfection.

"They're powerful," Silverwing said solemnly. "Not as strong as I am, but not far off."

"Village chief," the woman said, leading Cha Ming to a squirrel the size of a large badger. Its rust-red fur looked surprisingly soft, as though he'd applied a great deal of shampoo and conditioner. "This is Cha Ming, from the Northern Alliance."

The squirrel wrinkled his nose. *They send a single blind man, who reeks of demon-subduing energy and a bird I've never heard of?* His eyes flickered to Silverwing, then widened. *My pardons, half-initiate. Please call me Sir Nutcracking Monarch. I'm sure you can forgive this one's irritation given the situation in the surrounding area.*

The many small demons around squirmed uncomfortably at the squirrel's words. They looked to Silverwing and gave him short, curt bows or gestures of submission.

"We came straight from the Eastern Desert, where there was a similar problem with fiendish demons," Cha Ming said. "I might be blind, but I'm especially effective in fighting those creatures. Silvering is also a potent fighter." He then looked to the peak of the mountain, where he sensed… something. "I am told that our friend Mr. Mountain is currently condensing his initiation mark here."

Ah, that fellow, the Nutcracking Monarch said in a very human fashion. He used his tiny clawed hands to grasp a small teacup and saucer and took a sip. All things considered, he was very dexterous despite the clear limitations of his form. *Please get our guests some tea, Lin Yue.* The woman in curls who'd seen them inside nodded and did just that. She seated them on stumps near the important-looking squirrel. A few human cultivators—one of them at half-step rune carving and two more at the peak core formation, pulled their stumps up beside them.

I'm not sure what there is to say, the Nutcracking Monarch said, sighing. *We asked for assistance because we are helpless. Flesh and blood enemies can be fought, but how can we fight that which we cannot see? I'm sure your friend Silverwing has described what invades us.*

"A mist or miasma," Cha Ming said, nodding solemnly. "Intangible and strange."

It offends all our senses, the squirrel confirmed. *It is also likely the cause of the outbreaks we've been seeing. Every once in a while, one of our demons goes crazy. He transforms into a fiend, rampages, and has to be put down by the council. Sometimes, we aren't quick enough, and the creature kills a few humans and demons and runs down the mountain where its dark brethren accumulate.*

"And you haven't tried attacking where they gather?" Cha Ming asked.

It is difficult, the squirrel said. *We've tried attacking, but in their territory, we cannot draw on demonic energy. Meanwhile, they can draw on the fiendish miasma. The humans accompanying us aren't powerful enough to support an attack, and I doubt you can make that difference.*

"So the solution is…" Cha Ming asked.

Waiting, the squirrel said nonchalantly.

"We attack and kill any fiendish demons that pop up to buy him the time he needs," an older man with a gray mustache said. He had thin gray lines streaking his head of long hair and wore elegant robes one might wear at a dinner party. "In the end, it's a competition. Sir Nutcracking Monarch has made it quite clear that mountainous demonic energy is difficult to attune to. He's been trying for a thousand years with no success. A mountain mark simply isn't compatible with most demons. When Mr. Mountain came, we were overjoyed at the prospect of finally having a half-initiate to defend us. Unfortunately, he's proven to be a little…" He made a painful grimace as he searched for a polite word to use.

"Dense?" Cha Ming asked.

Slow? Silverwing added.

Slow is most appropriate, Sir Nutcracking Monarch said, setting down his teacup. *He's been at it for a nearly a year, and though we've urged him to speed up the process—we're seeing progress by the day— it's just not going to be fast enough given the growth rate of the miasma. And as Elder Long Bo has been kind enough to point out, all we can do is kill fiends that pop up. We've ordered civilians indoors and beasts to isolate themselves to reduce casualties. As you might know, fiends multiply through contamination, and those they kill and wound join them.*

In the end, we can only hope that dense lump of rock can pull through before their numbers grow to the point they can overwhelm us. And that could be any day. We— He cut himself off, and his tiny eyes narrowed. A crow, which had been perching in a corner, suddenly twitched and grew. It spread its massive wings, destroying pillars and walls within the beautiful courtyard. Granite broke like the porcelain teacups they were drinking from as guests increased in size, Sir Nutcracking Monarch at their head. Cultivators summoned swords and looked to Sir Nutcracking Monarch. The demon held up his clawed hand in the universal gesture to stand down.

Sir Crow Monarch? Sir Nutcracking Monarch said gravely. *How are you feeling?*

Fine, Sir Crow Monarch said, his head twitching, his feathers ruffling like a swarm of angry moths disturbed during their daily slumber.

You don't look fine, Sir Nutcracking Monarch said cautiously. *And I've noticed you've closed off your demonic senses and sealed off your demonic core. We're a team, Sir Crow. And as a team, we need to be able to keep an eye on each other. To make sure we're all healthy.*

I don't want to, Sir Crow Monarch said stubbornly. *And you can't make me.* His head twitched again, and his feathers began to warp. In the light, they now looked like lustrous scales on a dark dragon in a moonlit sea.

"We don't need any more proof," Long Bo said, holding up his sword. "He's clearly one of them." The other humans, and even some demons, murmured in agreement.

Give him time, Sir Nutcracking Monarch pleaded. *He might pull through.*

"He has ten seconds," Long Bo said.

The squirrel sighed and nodded. Endless moments passed as the transformation grew more vivid. A set of extra wings sprouted, and the crow's beak sharpened. Each mutation was stranger than the last. However, there was also movement in the opposite direction; his scales became normal black feathers, and his talons, which had become lethal blades good for nothing more than tearing and destroying, returned to healthy limbs meant for grasping prey.

These ten seconds were some of the longest in Cha Ming's memories. Perhaps it was the strangeness, or simply the consequence of the uncontrollable outcome. Finally, slowly but surely, the extra wings receded. The beak turned back to its normal orange hue, sharp but well suited to a crow's anatomy. The cultivators sheathed their swords, and the demons retracted their claws.

Well, that was close, Sir Nutcracking Monarch said jovially, hopping up beside the crow. *I knew you'd pull through, my dear friend.*

Thanks, the crow said. They moved to return to teatime and clear debris, but Silverwing suddenly let out a piercing caw and dove toward the crow faster than sound could travel. A sonic boom followed him, shattering all the glass in the courtyard.

Cries of shock ensued, but the reason Silverwing had done so was quickly apparent. The crow, which they'd assumed had recovered, suddenly exploded in a symphony of black strangeness. His feathers became sharp metallic scales, and two more pairs of wings sprouted from his body. His claws transformed, and he even sprouted a third talon in the middle of them. His neck became snakelike, and his body grew a strange, carnivorous mouth. Black flames surrounded what was clearly a fiend and exploded outward, burning the greenery in the garden and many innocent bystanders that hadn't yet fled.

Sir Nutcracking Monarch was the second to act. Not only was he right beside the crow, but he'd clearly not let his guard down. His body grew and lengthened, and his prominent teeth bit deep into the crow's neck, spilling black blood all over their broken furniture.

Swords slashed at the creature. Cha Ming summoned his combat formations and formed a shield in their immediate surroundings, boxing them in to protect civilians inside and outside the mansion. He threw his staff like a spear, and it stabbed into the crow. Then, jumping up, he summoned it again and slammed down with the staff in pillar form using Origin Strike, infusing it with Devil-Sealing and Demon-Subduing Intents. The demons trembled at the outburst of subduing energy, but the crow let out a bloodcurdling shriek as it met its nemesis. The Clear Sky Staff smashed into its head, striking a solid core where his fiendish energy lay. Gray Grandmist energy and the two intents surrounded the core in an angry bubble, then little by little, the core cracked, and the energy inside it was absorbed into the voracious staff, before even the pieces broke into small dustlike particles, rushing into the gray weapon and leaving behind only void emptiness.

Everyone fell silent. A few of the weaker human cultivators regained their wits and went about healing the wounded, and others began fixing up the mess. Surprisingly, with the help of cultivators and demons, it didn't take long to bring things back to normal. Only Long Bo left as they cleaned up, apparently to put down a weaker fiend that had sprouted during a separate event.

We thought only the weaker ones would be affected, Sir Nutcracking Monarch said with teary eyes. *Sir Crow Monarch was always strange, but… we thought… we thought…* His unsaid words spoke volumes. Any demon, whether weak or strong, could turn against them.

"With the miasma so strong as to affect even Sir Crow Monarch," one of the human elders said, "I think it won't be long before they launch their assault."

You're right, Sir Nutcracking Monarch said. *The time is nigh. Unfortunately, nothing we've tried has hastened Mr. Mountain's progress. In fact, sometimes it has stalled it.*

"We'll give it a try," said Cha Ming, who'd just finished repairing a broken pillar with earth-aligned formation arts. "He can be stubborn, but we have experience dealing with him. Silverwing especially."

Silverwing squawked, then landed on his shoulder. *He may be dense, but being dense is part of what being a mountain is all about.*

"Where is he?" Cha Ming asked.

Near the peak, Sir Nutcracking Monarch said, looking up toward the cloudy mountaintop. *The peak is where the demonic energy here is densest. The moment we led him there, he turned into a violet mist and began harmonizing with the environment. We go there sometimes to speak to him, but he rarely ever answers. It's like he's in a world of his own, cut off from the words and worries of mortals.*

"We'll see what we can do," Cha Ming said. "He's our friend, and we don't want him dying any more than you do." He and Silverwing flew out of the courtyard and of the now-fixed mansion and headed up the steep slope of the massive mountain.

The air grew chilly as they flew up the rocky slope, passing miles and miles of untended forests that eventually gave way to a rocky, snowy peak that jutted above the clouds. There, it became difficult to breathe. Even the toughest plants didn't dare take root here, and mere mortals would last no more than a day at such a high elevation. There was snow here on the mountaintop, thick and crusted, as it had been there for hundreds if not thousands of years with minimal disturbance. All save a path that led through the snows, though it had been some time since someone had passed to clear it.

The snows persisted as they left the wet clouds that brought them, though not much farther. A mile past the clouds, the snow all but ended, and what remained of the mountain was a sharp, conical peak that resembled a smaller version of the mountain. Clouds blanketed the earth like soft white grass, giving the impression that the world above and below were distinct and separate.

At the very top of the mountain was a dense purple mist. It

snaked down around the slopes, feeling and probing. Cha Ming and Silverwing followed a small path that led to a shrine at the top. There, they found an onyx statue in the shape of a large cone. There were braziers in front of it where incense still burned.

To their surprise, a familiar figure sat cross-legged near the cone, speaking softly to it. The mist at the peak stirred around the black object, trying to harmonize with it. *That's likely the core of the mountain,* Cha Ming thought. *But what is* he *doing here?*

The man was none other than Bear One, a chance acquaintance Cha Ming had met south of the wall in the Shattered Lands. The bare-chested man still wore his usual open vest and short pants, despite the chilly weather. That wasn't surprising—body cultivators were hardly affected by these worldly temperatures. His looks, his voice, and his demeanor were similarly unchanged. He grinned when he saw Cha Ming and Silverwing walking up the steps.

"Like I was saying," Bear One said to the black cone. "Strength is built upon many layers. Even this mountain took many millions of years to form. It was forced up bit by bit from the center of the earth. You rush, but in so doing, you work against what nature has told you. By rushing, you go slower. Or at least, that is my limited interpretation as a mere mortal man who has spent much time surrounded by rock and metal."

The violet mist that was Mr. Mountain seemed to consider his words. Then, it shook and dissipated, floating about the cone and probing like moments before.

"Ah, Bear Six," Bear One said, looking to Cha Ming. "Or is it Pai Xiao this time, perhaps?"

"I go by Cha Ming in the North," Cha Ming said, smiling. "Though I wonder, after all this time, I still don't know your name."

Bear One grinned. "Call me Ivan Vladimirovich. Or Yiwan for short, if you like. People from around here find my real name difficult to pronounce." It was definitely a strange name on the continent, and it hinted at something akin to Russian from Earth in Cha Ming's prior life. And yes, it would definitely be difficult for most people to pronounce.

"I can't say I've heard of any language that matches your name around here, Ivan," Cha Ming said. He made sure to pronounce it Eevaan, like the man had said it. "The name must have quite the story behind it."

"It doesn't," Ivan said. "The people that made the language have quite the story, but perhaps that is a story for another time." He looked to the shrine where the black cone sat and back to Cha Ming. "Come here to pray, have you? I didn't take you for a religious man."

"Hardly," Cha Ming said. "And I take it you haven't either." He sat down cross-legged before the man, who, surprisingly, lit up an incense stick and replaced the one that had just burnt out. The flame burned slow and steady, despite the shortage of oxygen at these elevations. Likely, the stick had a magical origin. Silverwing, who'd been standing on Cha Ming's shoulder, flapped his wings and landed beside the cone and began to peck at it.

You're really making them sweat down there, Silverwing said, pecking again. *You'd better speed it up, Mr. Mountain, or there'll be a lot of deaths to answer for.*

Ivan shook his head. "I don't know if this is the best way to do things. Perhaps provoking him would be counterproductive."

"I'm no expert, but Silverwing *is* a demon," Cha Ming said. "Humans and demons often see things differently. One could argue that your stories might confuse him."

"Perhaps," Ivan said, grinning. "Though, I do not think it is possible to confuse him. You need to think fast to be confused." He rubbed his hands for warmth, though he didn't seem uncomfortable. His vest buttons were undone and his arms bare. "I was merely attempting, with my limited knowledge, to give him tidbits he might seize and understand. I believe humans and demons are not so different. To progress, this violet mist will need to discover the deeper secrets that reflect who he truly is."

Hmph, Silverwing said, growing slightly and landing upon a stone perch on the altar. *Humans are all alike. Think they know everything. When I condensed my mark of wind, I focused on doing it as quickly as possible. It worked out just fine for me.*

"Like I said, I am human, and my experience limited," Ivan said, shaking his head. "Forbid this lowly one from imparting improper knowledge. Who am I to interfere when a bird wishes to teach a mountain to fly?" Silverwing ruffled his feathers. "I mean no disrespect to one so exalted; that is just the way I see it. The wind is fast. The wind cuts to the chase. It tears apart all obstacles and blows them apart like the vicious creature it is. But a mountain is strong, steadfast, and stubborn. It is not people who move mountains but people who move around a mountain."

"Are you saying that to condense a mountain mark, Mr. Mountain must learn to become *more* of a mountain?" Cha Ming said, frowning. He'd never dwelled too much on the advancement of demons.

"Humans become better humans by becoming more like themselves," Ivan said, shrugging. "I often find the world is strange and varied but filled with similarities. Who knows?" He looked down toward the clouds and frowned. "I only regret the time constraints we have been dealt. I was looking forward to many months of tedious conversation to determine the truth of the matter."

"To what end?" Cha Ming asked, still suspicious of the man's motives. "When we were in the Shattered Lands, you were gathering rare ores."

"And here is the same," Bear One said. "I am looking for something special: mountain essence iron. Unfortunately, there's only a little of it spread out throughout the entire mountain. Rather than go about this the hard way—destroying the nearest ten miles to obtain it—I figured I'd settle on a softer, less violent approach."

Was it possible to destroy an entire mountain? Cha Ming wondered. How long would that even take? To even consider such a thing, Ivan definitely wasn't as weak as he pretended to be—a peak-marrow-refining cultivator, by the looks of it. And though Cha Ming had lost his sight, he could still feel the man's clear blue eyes on him. They bypassed his defenses, inspecting his very strong soul.

"You've had quite a few experiences during our short time

apart," the man said softly. "When we were hunting for ore, you could definitely see."

"A price I had to pay, I suppose," Cha Ming said. "Killing evil spirits is tricky."

"Perhaps," Ivan said. "It just feels sad to look into your eyes. They were curious once, but within them, I see only hatred now." He didn't elaborate, and simply let the observation hang there.

"Maybe it's difficult for these eyes of mine to remain curious after witnessing so much violence," Cha Ming finally said. "I used to see things as complicated, but it seems that, more and more, I'm forced to split things into black and white, destroying one side while helping the other."

"I sense regret," Ivan said. "Great regret, hidden deeply."

"No," Cha Ming said, perhaps a little too quickly. "Maybe. But I did what needed to be done. Nothing can change that." His actions in Bastion might have killed millions, but he was sure his actions had also saved many others. Besides, were those men and women in Bastion truly innocent? Were they not supporting the very enemies that were invading the North to begin with? He didn't know anymore. But the more he thought about it, the more he realized that he was making justifications in hindsight for the actions he'd committed. When had he started being so judgmental?

"I have a story to share, if you care to listen," Ivan said, still rubbing his hands and blowing on them with breath that misted the moment it left him. He lit up another incense stick, as the one he'd lit earlier had already burned out, and Mr. Mountain coiled around the fresh offering, as though wondering if it was intended for him. "In my youth, I was a brash man. I was not a simple prospector like I am now, but a vigorous man out to prove himself."

"A common trait among young men," Cha Ming said.

"I was maybe two hundred," Ivan said, prompting a cough from Cha Ming. "A very young man indeed. Back in those days, I liked to drink, a drink called vodka. There was a similar drink for mortals, but what I drank was stronger. Body cultivators being what they are, I had a very large capacity. And when I drank, I fought." His eyes darkened. "One night, I killed a man. He was a larger fellow no one seemed to care much about, and I was much aggrieved about it. Our argument was silly, and he didn't deserve such a harsh punishment."

"What did you do?" Cha Ming asked.

"What any proper man should do," Ivan said. "I went looking for his family, only to find that he had no one. And I went looking for his friends and found that no one wanted to be known as his associate. It took me much time and money to finally discover that he was actually a local thug who extorted money from families and businesses. He'd even killed over a dozen people, so he was universally reviled. So I convinced myself that I'd done the world a favor, and that I'd done nothing wrong after all."

"That seems legitimate," Cha Ming said. "And consistent."

"Yes, it is very consistent," Ivan said. "It was only many years later that I found myself dwelling on this in the middle of a breakthrough. It was a breakthrough in soul, and during these breakthroughs, it is important to not have doubts in yourself or your actions. Both good and evil men alike can progress.

"Therefore, it is interesting that, of all things, I found myself stuck on this very particular case. I'd done terrible things in the past, and they haunted me in nightmares. In fact, I would often see within them faces of loved ones I couldn't save, and innocents that had accidentally been caught in my line of fire. So why this man?

"I pondered on it for a long time before I finally realized the crux of the matter. It wasn't that my reasoning was incorrect, but that it was incomplete. I'd done the world a great favor, but at the same time, I'd intentionally killed someone I thought innocent. I was both guilty of a sin and responsible for great merit all at one time. The results and intentions both matter." Ivan chuckled. "After that, many knots were undone inside my heart. I realized that I'd painted the world in black and white. So, little by little, I resolved to see the world in its many shades of gray. And Cha Ming, my eyes changed that day, and I could see so much further than I'd ever dared dream." His piercing crystal-blue eyes seemed to bore even further into Cha Ming's soul, to the point that he almost asked for Sun Wukong's help.

But then, their intensity was retracted, and Ivan smiled, patting the cross-legged Cha Ming on a shoulder.

"No need to dwell on this story too much," Ivan said. "But I insist on hearing a story from you, if only to pass the time."

"A story," Cha Ming said. "What kind of story are you looking for? I have many."

Ivan looked up to the black cone, which Silverwing had been pecking and goading the entire time. "Since our goals are both to nudge this mountain along, why don't you share a story of strength and stability?"

Cha Ming chuckled. "Strength? Stability? Is that what you see with those eyes of yours?"

"I see a strong man, filled with vitality," Ivan said. "I see a man who always stands up for what is right. Perhaps there are other layers I am unaware of?"

"Too many to count," Cha Ming said, picking up a rock from the ground and manipulating it in his fingers. He crushed it, reducing it to a pile of sand. "Ironically, if I were to pick a time that reflects strength most, I would pick the time where I was weakest. I washed up in Crystal Falls. I was a lowly qi-condensation cultivator then. I had faced a lightning tribulation and succeeded—with help—but unfortunately, I had to flee with a Spatial Transference Talisman. It left me wounded and crippled, my qi pathways torn up and destroyed. I had weeks left to live if everything went well."

"That's a harsh blow to any cultivator," Ivan said. "How did you pull through?"

Cha Ming grimaced. "Through grit and determination. I was broken. I had nothing left to lose. I put up with one painful night after another, using destruction qi to destroy my qi pathways. As a body cultivator, I'm sure you understand pain, but I assure you, there's nothing more agonizing than having your insides destroyed by black lightning as a tiny mortal. I purged out everything broken and rotten, and then I forged new ones out of the purest creation qi. These pathways ended up being stronger than my originals, and through them, I recovered my health cultivation."

He motioned with his hand, and the pieces of the crumbled stone flew together like a puzzle. Cha Ming poured a bit of his domain-infused qi into it, and the cracks sealed up. He tossed the rock back to Ivan. "Does this rock look the same to you?"

"It does," Ivan said. "From the outside, it seems indistinguishable. It's only…" He frowned. "The inside is completely different."

"The cracks couldn't seal completely," Cha Ming said, shaking his head. "A pity."

"Yet if I try to break it again, the effect is not the same," Ivan said, looking at the rock with interest. He squeezed his fingers, and a few chunks fell off. "The leftover weakness actually makes it difficult to crush. I can't crack the entire stone without substantially more effort. If this weren't a rock, but metal instead, the effects would be even more profound. The metal would gain strength, and pieces would not fall like they do here. It would be a proper weapon, ready for battle."

"Some people are like stones, and others are like metal," Cha Ming said. "They sometimes break, and when you put them back together again, some, not all, are stronger for it. Many are crushed by life, but a few see the hardship as opportunity." Just like he had, in hindsight. Yes, it was always in hindsight. Just like he tried to paint the suffering of Bastion white, he was looking at his adversity through rose-colored glasses. He hadn't tried to heal himself because he'd seen opportunity. He'd tried because he was desperate. That he'd succeeded didn't change his original intention in the slightest.

"I see that our friend liked your story very much," Ivan said, pointing up to the black cone where the violet mist was not swirling quickly. It began to take on a violet glow that matched the rich color of Mr. Mountain's illusory mist.

It's working! Silverwing cried out. *All my pecking worked! I told you rotten humans your ways were trash.*

Cha Ming coughed lightly but didn't contradict him.

"It will still take time," Ivan warned, getting up and stretching. He looked down through the clouds toward the base of the mountain. "Unfortunately, I do not think we have enough of it."

"What can you see that I can't?" Cha Ming asked, worried. "What Silverwing can't."

The bird, who was looking in the same direction, wore a puzzled expression.

"You don't need to see it to know what is happening," Ivan said gravely. "You can hear it."

Cha Ming heard it then. One roar after another, bestial and carnal. They were filled with rage and hostility, anger and resentment. Fiends were awakening. And this time, it wasn't just one of them. The entire mountain trembled at their coming.

Chapter 8:
Death

"I do not know what it is that you hope to accomplish," Ivan said as they flew out of the clouds and toward the base of the mountain where chaos had erupted. Cha Ming sensed fiends everywhere. They were sprouting up like tiny weeds in a spring garden, attacking friend and foe alike. Most were weak, simple spirit beasts that never had any hope at becoming purification-realm demons, but some were strong, though not as strong as the Crow Monarch from earlier. But overall, the horde was enormous, and it covered the mountain like a suffocating blanket.

It was a tide, an oozing black sea that inched its way up the single island of land for the nearest thousand miles. The fiends that had escaped to the woods down below now emerged in full force, attacking everything in sight, using their black blood to taint any living demon or elemental in sight. As for the humans? They simply killed them, feeding them to the writhing mass below, the uniting presence that gave them their unnatural powers.

"What's the status?" Cha Ming asked, appearing beside Sir Nutcracking Monarch. The elder was medium sized now, as large as a horse. Cha Ming joined him in suppressing a middle-core-formation fiend that was terrorizing a neighborhood. It fell to the ground, dead, bisected by his staff while Sir Nutcracking Monarch extracted and broke its fiendish core like it would an acorn from a frightening demonic tree. Unfortunately, there was little they could do to prevent its blood from spilling on pavement, plant life, houses, and the many humans and demons that inhabited them. Cha Ming used combat sigils to summon flames and evaporate what blood he could, but they were forced to put down some weaker demons that had been converted by it.

Chaos and the miasma grew hand in hand. A group of allied humans fought every fiend they saw but occasionally caught innocent demons in the crossfire. It was as though they didn't care whether it was demons or fiends they killed—every demon on the mountain was a potential adversary.

"Send everyone up the mountain, away from the miasma," Cha Ming said. "We'll try to buy you time."

He and Silverwing flew, and Ivan followed them. They crashed into a stampede of strange bulls with a murky brown aura, whose horns were twisted serpents and whose hooves were made of crimson glass. As Cha Ming swept out with Splitting Heaven and Earth, Ivan slapped his hands to the ground. The mountain heaved, sending a wave of tectonic energy through the herd, swallowing some in the rocky tide and breaking much of the rest. Silverwing swooped in to snipe them off, destroying their cores as Cha Ming burned their remnants. But their efforts seemed akin to a single log trying to block a river, and there were endless fiends urgently rushing past them.

"They're fast," Cha Ming said, bashing into another group of fiends. "Faster than the last time we fought them."

"Perhaps your enemy has learned the value of adequate preparation," Ivan said. "Sometimes it is better to wait until you are certain to reach your target before rushing to the finish line."

"Thanks for pointing out the obvious," Cha Ming grunted. Combat sigils burned everywhere he could reach, setting fire to portions of the black mountain and the miasma that accompanied it. As he did so, the beasts that came at him became stronger and stronger, some reaching middle core formation or higher. He pierced his staff toward one such being—a giant wolf with feathers on its body and talon-like claws. His staff split the fiend's head in two, but to his surprise, it healed in the middle, transforming the creature into a two-headed monstrosity.

Cha Ming cursed. He advanced on the creature, punching it with a fist laced with destruction qi. The two-headed wolf's body split apart in a million places, covering him in a shower of black blood. He summoned his pseudo-domain and covered his hands with an aura of gold and used them to rip the beast in half in an effort to expose its core, which he couldn't sense despite his wide-open eyes, which burned the fiendish miasma along with the abominations it supported.

Finally, when it seemed like the fiendish wolf had truly died, he looked for its core but came back empty-handed. Instead, it wriggled again, and the miasma fed it even more fiendish energy. It split apart, and within seconds, two new two-headed wolves appeared. They rushed at him with bared teeth, and Cha Ming batted with his staff but discovered that their physical strength was now equal to his, and their teeth and claws were as strong as transcended treasures.

What's happening? Cha Ming asked, retreating. He slapped a golden talisman on his staff and pierced at one of the wolves, obliterating half its body with an empowered Origin Strike. The gap quickly filled up, restoring the lost flesh, and the wolf resumed its assault as though nothing had happened.

They're channeling fiendish energies, much like demons can channel demonic energies, Silverwing said. *They're pooling their powers to face us as the rest of the tide takes over the mountain.*

Cha Ming looked up in horror. Silverwing's words had been insufficient to convey the cruel reality. Now, over half of the mountain was covered by a darkness deeper than the blackest night, and its edges nipped at the fleeing demons and humans that escaped the carnage under the leadership of Sir Nutcracking Monarch and a human elder, who protected their rear.

Meanwhile, the other elders were doing everything they could to destroy fiends and the miasma that accompanied them. Their efforts, though valorous and effective, simply weren't enough to stall the dreadful horde. It kept creeping up by hundreds of feet every minute, only slowing slightly when one of the mightier fiends was slain.

Silverwing and Ivan were particularly effective. One used his mark of wind to summon tornadoes of lethal energy. Though he was not this mountain's initiate, his power still far outstripped the average fiend or demon, and his authority over demonic energy was far greater. He drew on the mountain's strength to obliterate anything they passed through, shattering cores and claws like they were nothing. Ivan, on the other hand, used more insidious methods. He overturned land and summoned spikes that seemed to pierce exactly where they needed to, shattering thousands of fiendish cores with every wave.

But what did thousands mean when ten thousand more were created? As the miasma grew, so, too, did the power of their opponents. Their ability to kill them slowed, and soon they were forced to retreat up the mountain along with the refugees. It was only just before disappearing behind the clouds that Cha Ming finally saw the fiend whisperer, his arms crossed, mocking, safe behind the fiendish lines, taunting him to attack him where he had a home advantage.

For the mountain was *his* territory now, and he owned every piece of it. The clouds turned a sickening yellow color as they passed through with brown miasma at their heels. Their wetness became a damp blanket that began to suffocate everyone within. When all seemed lost, they broke through the clouds and onto the rocky mountain peak and were overjoyed to find that it was still pristine and unoccupied. But their relief was short-lived. Mr. Mountain, who was almost fully incorporated into the black cone, suddenly came to a halt. Another force invaded the cone and began turning it sickly brown.

Come on, you stupid mountain! Silverwing said. *You're almost there!*

The violet on the cone began to recede, and the fiendish brown took over the remaining area. And then, it began to devour the violet mist. Mr. Mountain roared in agony as the miasma took over, and the violet mist diminished in density.

I am a mountain! Mr. Mountain said in protest, struggling against the brown coloring with everything it had. The color of the cone began to alternate. It shifted between violet and brown, demonic and fiendish. Then it paused. For a brief moment, Cha Ming held on to a faint hope that things would reverse and everything would be all right, just like the time in the Eastern Desert where Silverwing had been the one gaining his mark. But that hope was short-lived, as the cone suddenly turned completely brown, expelling the violet mist that was Mr. Mountain and blowing it outward, scattering it to the nine winds as it dissipated to nothingness.

"Mr. Mountain!" Cha Ming cried out.

"Mr. Mountain!" Silverwing cried out as well. He took to the skies, looking around for any signs of his friend but not finding a single trace of him.

"What will I tell Huxian?" Cha Ming whispered. The little fox might have been arrogant and uncaring at one time, but he'd grown very close to each of his friends. They teased each other and bullied each other, but they were still brothers, sharing life and death.

Ivan looked around with a grave expression. "It is as though he has been dispersed across the entire mountain, spread too thinly for most to notice. Is it death, or simply joining with nature? Illusory demons are rare, so who can tell what has happened?"

The mountaintop was crowded with a few hundred thousand people and demons, a far cry from the tens of millions that had once inhabited its peaceful slopes. It had only taken less than an hour for their entire nation to crumble, reducing them to a rabble of refugees.

No, refugees wasn't accurate. They were trapped on a mountaintop, with only a few core-formation cultivators that could help them escape, while roars echoed up the slope and through the mist. Black ooze was climbing up the peak, making its way toward the core, and once there, it would put a nail in their coffins.

People made way as a single line of corruption climbed. Cha Ming threw flame and staff strikes at it, but all to no avail. The black line wasn't on the surface of the mountain; it ran deep within its body of rock and metal.

"Why?" Cha Ming wondered aloud. "Why are some creatures born to destroy, Ivan?"

"Why are some born to create?" Ivan asked softly. "The world was painted in black and white, Cha Ming. It is a saying that holds true across continents and planes."

But Cha Ming saw no white, nor any shades of gray. Now, he only saw creeping blackness. And in that blackness, he saw the death and chaos he'd sown in Bastion, and the destruction his interference had brought about. He saw the death of the North's forces in the Eastern Desert, and the routing of their enemies near the end.

He saw the death of the demons near the Windswept Canyon, and now he saw the deaths of the people and demons of Mount Tai. Their death was so quick, and their lives so fragile. It pained him that they died, but what could he do about it? He could only accept the senseless loss of life. And with acceptance came understanding, and with understanding, words came to mind.

Dying leaves carpet the forest floor;
Man is left pondering his demise.

Men and demons were pitiful in their final moments, and in the end, they could only serve as food for various decomposers. No matter how impressive their lives, in that moment they were worth no more than leaves shed by trees at the first hint of cold. Some still struggled to hold on, but they, too, would fall. For was that not the fate of every living thing? Dying like those before them?

Cha Ming held up his hand, and a half-step-transcendent talisman materialized out of thin air, draining the requisite wood essence from the Clear Sky Brush to fuel the creation. By realizing the words to this poetic talisman, he had touched something amazing. A deep well of power, a hidden ability he couldn't yet draw on.

But he didn't care about this. He didn't care about enlightenment or power. He waited for the first of the fiends to cross the cloudy threshold, and for Silverwing to flap his wings, forcing it all away, revealing a massive army that glowed with a sickening brown color. Cha Ming clenched his jaw as they appeared and threw the talisman onto them, pouring his emotions into the dark-green paper and igniting it with his transcendent force. Death. Dying. What he'd materialized was the Dying Talisman. One by one, each fiendish life ended in a contagious cataclysm. Tens of thousands died in just a few seconds. Hundreds of thousands more joined them. This was the essence of death—even the destroyers were not exempt from it.

He roared in despair and charged into their ranks, wanting nothing more than to kill the lot of them for what they'd done. They did not respect life, so why should he respect theirs? His Clear Sky Pillar reaped them like wheat on harvest day, the kind of wheat that was filled with weeds and pests, the kind of wheat that you burned lest it contaminate the rest of your harvest.

His combat sigils manifested five blinding suns that burned thousands as they climbed toward the helpless refugees. His angry outburst inspired others to join him, and they dove into the fiends, looking to kill as many as they could. They knew they couldn't hold them back, but that wouldn't stop them from dying while trying.

In the distance, Cha Ming could see the fiend whisperer. He tried to reach him but was intercepted by the endless swarms of fiends that were birthed from the corrupted mountain itself. They pulled themselves from the stones and crawled out from empty caverns. Even more passed him and rushed toward the humans and demon refugees that were left. Not a single person, human or demon, would be spared.

And in that moment, when all seemed lost, when all seemed bleak, Cha Ming felt a tremble unlike anything he'd ever felt. It came from deep beneath him, through rock, soil, silt, and metal. It came from deep within the earth, from all it touched, and finally, from the mountain itself.

He looked to the top of the mountain, and to his surprise, the fiends had paused. They were frozen, as though they couldn't move, and the cone, which was still in its place where the broken mountain shrine lay, glowed an illusory purple. It vanished, and as it did, a gigantic violet projection appeared, crushing down on the fiends while holding up their victims. He recognized that illusory presence—it was Mr. Mountain. His presence enveloped all of Mount

Tai, the largest mountain on the continent.

What is real, and what is false? Mr. Mountain bellowed in a tremble that emanated from deep within the ground. *What is victory and what is defeat? You have claimed the core, the heart that pushes veins of metallic ore throughout the earth, the thing that breathes life into all living things. But you neglected what was most important. You neglected the body. Well, I have claimed the body, the immovable mountain. I AM the mountain, and you cannot claim me.*

Fiends tried to flee, but they were crushed to a paste under the pressure. The miasma dispersed, only to be replaced by a violet mist. It swirled into a giant character above the peak—the character for mountain—and when that character formed, the suppression increased. For a mountain wasn't quick, but it wasn't slow either. It simply was, and it was *mighty*. It blocked wind and rain for some, but it crushed others in rocky landslides. It could not be moved, and people could only helplessly travel around it. It was strength and suppression incarnate.

Cha Ming growled and charged at a nearby fiend, easily bisecting it with Splitting Heaven and Earth. Silverwing flew above, slashing his foes with wind and destroying those strong enough to escape. Ivan grinned and continued pounding the mountain with his fists, urging spikes to pierce fiends. The mountain seemed to aid and support him.

The battle was over in a few seconds. That was all it took to finish off the remaining fiends. And when they were dead, Cha Ming looked turned his attention to the fiend whisperer but found no one. Only a few residual wisps of gray spatial qi remained, just like last time.

He shook his head and looked around. There was death and destruction as far as the eye could see. Most of the fiends, demons corrupted by the miasma, had been destroyed. Only a small number of corrupted demons had survived, those that were strong enough to force out the black blood that had consumed them.

Beneath the clouds, which had now cleared, was a scene of ruin and rubble. The village on Mount Tai was nothing more than a distant memory. It was a graveyard for the daring, a resting place for those who'd dared to dream of peace.

Hours later, Cha Ming stood inside a freshly erected building. He and a few demons had built it using formations and their mastery of earth. Mr. Mountain had also helped. Mountains, apparently, supported those who lived on them. Under his direction, perfect rocks for building had worked their way to the surface, where cultivators and demons dragged them away to rebuild a substantially smaller village. And to everyone's relief, his surface shifted, burying those that had been slain in battle and giving them their proper rest.

"And that's how Mr. Mountain solved the problem," Cha Ming said to a hologram of Feng Ming that the core-transmission jade projected. "He just suddenly had an epiphany and crushed them. We no longer have to worry about the mountain, but I worry about all the other places where demons live. It's very likely that the fiend whisperer will go after them.

"We'll have to have Mr. Mountain and Silverwing go to other ranges and warn them," Feng Ming said. "I need you on the front lines. Are you sure this Yiwan fellow can't join us?"

"I was here only for my ore," said Ivan, who was sitting in a corner of the room. "Now that I have obtained it, I will leave." He held a fist-sized chunk in his hand. It wasn't a heavy metal, unlike most high-grade ores Cha Ming had seen, but a light silver-colored one that sparkled like a dozen crystals.

"I need you to head over to Golf Leaf City," Feng Ming said. "There are problems there, and we need to get to the bottom of things."

"Problems?" Cha Ming asked. What could be happening there? Hadn't Wang Jun taken care of things?

"Yes, problems," Feng Ming said. "The kingdom has been acting strangely, and they're sowing commercial chaos across the North. Though some might consider it commercial opportunism, I sense it's something more. It reeks of sabotage rather than coincidence."

"Strange," Cha Ming said. Feng Ming's image flickered, and a startled expression appeared on his face. At the same time, Ivan's expression grew grim.

"Change of plans," both Feng Ming and Ivan said at once. They looked at each other strangely, then Feng Ming continued. "I need you to hurry to the Evergreen Battlefield. The push has intensified, and…" He hesitated.

"What is it?" Cha Ming asked.

"Do you remember our dear friend from Bastion?" Feng Ming asked. "The large one that likes to devour all things in existence?"

"The Taotie?" Cha Ming asked, frowning. "I thought the South had sealed it away."

"I thought so too," Feng Ming said. "So did everyone else. Unfortunately, it seems it's been sighted at the Evergreen Battlefield. It's fighting *with* the Southern Alliance, devouring anyone, human or demon, who approaches it."

"I can't stop that thing," Cha Ming said, paling. "Dozens of transcendents had to join together to do it last time."

"I just need you to help evacuate the people there and diminish how much sustenance the beast can obtain," Feng Ming said. "Besides, didn't you say Gua was there?"

He was right. Gua was in the Evergreen Battlefield's swamps, condensing his mark. If the Taotie got to him, he'd be nothing more than an appetizer to the gigantic creature.

"I'll leave right away," Cha Ming said, though he really wished he had time to recover from his wounds from Bastion. "Though I think it's prudent if Silverwing and Mr. Mountain go protect the other demons."

"Agreed," Feng Ming said. "Please ask them to help us with this. As for you, Godspeed."

The image winked out, leaving Cha Ming alone with Ivan and Silverwing.

"This beast," Ivan said. "You cannot fight it."

"I know," Cha Ming said. "I'm only going there to save what I can."

"No, you don't understand," Ivan said, his voice urgent. "You cannot possibly know. Planes get destroyed by these things, Cha Ming. Planes die. You, someone who was born of this plane, do not stand a chance against it." He placed his hand on Cha Ming's shoulder. "You should leave now, but if you can't bring yourself to do it, remember, you always have another option."

"Which is?" Cha Ming asked.

"To leave everything behind," Ivan said. "Transcend. Leave this place like I must do now. Normally you can only leave via stable spatial passageways, but transcending is the exception. Let that be your hope when all other hope is lost."

"And you?" Cha Ming asked. "What will you do?"

"I had hoped to gather more things," Ivan said. "But I dare not wait any longer. Spatial channels will become unstable if I linger."

"You're not from around here, are you?" Cha Ming asked the Slavic body cultivator, wondering about the story behind his origins.

Ivan smiled. "Yes. I, Ivan Vladimirovich, am not from around here. Perhaps the name gave it away." He shrugged, then placed his finger against the nearby wall. The gray stone surface warped and crackled as he ran his finger down it, drawing a thin gray line that expanded, revealing a large gray portal into nothingness. "Remember my advice. You do not have to stay here. If you somehow survive this, and should those devils playing with fire not destroy everything you love and hold dear, perhaps we will meet again."

With that, he walked through the portal. It winked out, leaving Cha Ming and Silverwing with a situation that was much graver than it was five minutes ago.

Chapter 9: Discord

O rder, order!" a middle-aged man called out, smacking a gavel on a thick wooden plate in the center of a large room containing a ridiculously large table. An older man, his mentor, and the previous chair of these meetings, nodded in approval at the strength of his strikes and the severity of his tone as he scolded the others. The role of meeting chair was a ceremonial one, but it was also an important one. It took a strong and inflexible personality to keep this mismatched bunch in order.

Feng Ming stood from his seat in the position closest to the door. The square room had a relatively plain interior, its silver-white walls decorated with a half dozen Jun Xiezi paintings and white embossments pushing out from behind them. The wooden table where they sat was inlaid with silver patterns. It also had a seating order despite its circular nature. Where one sat depended on many things, like rank, size, and clout. In his case, Feng Ming had called the meeting, which meant he got to speak first and sit nearest the door, so that anyone looking to leave had to cross him. He looked over the few dozen representatives, which wore grimmer expressions than they had one year ago. Many of them were pale, while others were less ornately clothed than they had once been.

"I've called this meeting for two reasons," Feng Ming said as they quieted down. He looked to no one in particular, constantly shifting his eyes as he'd been taught by his public speaking teacher. "First, to brief you on the war situation—for everyone but the daftest fool would agree that we are at war—and second, to obtain commitments."

Unlike other times, he wore his black battle armor and black-and-gold marshal's cape to the meeting. His Lucky Spear, too cumbersome to sit down with, was safely tucked away in his storage ring where he could retrieve it at a moment's notice. The uniform, like the man at the gavel, was symbolic as well; everyone who could be armed, should be armed, no matter the time or place.

"The situation is dire," he continued. "The Eastern Desert, headed by the Desert Wind Kingdom, has just rebuffed an invasion that almost took over the Windswept Canyon to use it against the North. The Phoenix Cry Empire and the Long Kingdom have seen intensification of siege activities, with our Southern enemies bringing strange weapons that have managed to tear deep gouges in their fortifications but fortunately haven't actually pierced through yet.

"Near my own hometown, fighting has not broken out for quite some time. But that doesn't mean we can sit idly. There is an army amassing at the Southern Battlefield, and it is only a matter of days, if not hours, before they try breaking through again like they did a few years ago.

"The Evergreen Battlefield, as you know, is being overrun with enemy forces. They harness the powers of an ancient, world-ending being that even transcendents fear. No one knows how they struck a deal with it or even communicated with the thing in the first place. I've sent as many men as I can to help in the evacuation of their civilians, but the situation looks grim.

"All around us, devil worship is becoming commonplace. Devil cults incite rebellions too numerous to quell. Bandits roam our lands, causing chaos wherever they go. Senior officials disobey, and princes are resorting to petty internal power struggles, completely ignoring the situation at our communal border. I don't know how long they can keep their heads in the sand, but they are fools. Do they really think they'll get to keep what little power they claim after Southern forces arrive?

"Meanwhile, it's not only humans that are affected, but demons. Some of you might say: Who cares? I say that everyone should care. Even if the welfare of demons is of no consequence to most humans, there's been not one but two occurrences where fiends have tried conquering dense sources of demonic energy. The first was near the eastern edge of the continent, the Windswept Canyon, and the second at the center near Mount Tai. Both occurrences were *north of the wall.*

"My friend and fellow fighter, Du Cha Ming, has organized a resistance against the fiends in both of these cases, but he's just one man. In the latest case, the peaceful mountain village of Taishan was overrun. Tens of millions of people and demons are dead, and only a few hundred thousand remain. For make no mistake—these fiends are not like demons. They know no honor and they care not for value. They rush over demonic land like locusts, devouring everything they touch, proceeding to human lands after they've consumed everything.

"That is why, ladies and gentlemen, I beg for your support. Everyone here is contributing to some extent, but it was only enough during times of peace. Now, our forces near the border are dying by the thousands. Their weapons break and their medicines run low. Recruiting more able-bodied men is stretching the finances of those kingdoms to the breaking point. It's only a matter of time before one or more of them falls, and Southern forces rush into the North, gaining a beachhead into our fertile lands."

Feng Ming paused, then placed his hands on the table and stared at them intently. "I do not ask for charity. I do not ask for gifts. I ask for your self-interested support. If these border countries fall, you will be next—the South will spare no one."

Speech delivered, Feng Ming sat down amidst the gentle mutterings of various representatives.

"Nice speech," whispered Li Fei, who was seated beside him. Today, she wore her black hair in loose braids fastened with a dozen swordlike silver pins. The martial touch fitted the situation. Her silver cultivator's robes brought strength to her disposition that her lower cultivation did not. As Quicksilver's representative, her interests and Feng Ming's interests were closely tied together. If the Song Kingdom fell, Quicksilver would be next in line. Moreover, they wouldn't have the luxury of a transcendent-grade wall to aid in their defense. Only a wide mountain pass and its two flanking mountain chains would stand in their way.

"We'll see if it was good enough," Feng Ming whispered back, eyeing the representatives as they conversed. "We need their help. Not just in the Evergreen Empire, but everywhere."

"My intelligence says it will be difficult this time," Li Fei cautioned. "The political situation has become complex."

Feng Ming grunted. He wasn't any good at politics, and the mere concept of it interfering in the defense of their nations was ludicrous to him. What good was bickering about specifics and internal power struggles when you stood to lose everything, kingdom included?

"We of the Phoenix Cry Empire also echo your sentiment," a woman in red robes stood and said. As one of their lesser princesses, Feng Xia had inherited their rare phoenix bloodline and the beauty that came with it. Her fiery disposition complemented her magical origins, making her stand out amongst the mostly career politicians in the assembly. "We have defended our border with the South for thousands of years, and rarely do we ask for aid. Over the past few days, however, we have lost over five percent of our country's fighting force. In addition, Marshal Feng's warning of fiendish tides has us especially worried. Though not as well known as Huoshan's Fire Mountains, Phoenix Cry Peak is home to demonic descendants of the phoenix that aid us in our cultivation."

"It has us worried as well," the Long Kingdom's representative said. A muscular man, Long Wu specialized in body cultivation. He was also a marshal like Feng Ming. Their kingdom was extremely militaristic, which was exacerbated by the fact that their dragon bloodline liked to manifest in men. Dragons were overbearing creatures, with the power to back it up.

"I, Zhang Bo, cannot stress Marshal Feng's plea enough," the short old alchemist from the Evergreen Kingdom said. "We're dying out there. Our army is falling back. True North Country is doing what they can to help hold back the tide, but—" His teary words were interrupted by a message from his core-transmission jade. He looked at it and shut his eyes. "I'm sorry, I need to take this."

"I think True North Country's position is quite obvious," True North Country's representative, Mei Ling, said. "We also thank the rest of this council for their timely support in Beihai."

"Your words are all moving," Jin Yixing, the representative of the Golden Kingdom, said. "Unfortunately, I can do nothing for you. I am quite helpless in this matter. Both in terms of troops and finances, we are truly in a difficult position. And this isn't just my position, but the Church of Justice's position. We would love to do more, truly, but our hands are tied."

Feng Ming frowned. Though he'd heard about the turmoil in their kingdom, he'd at least hoped that they could receive token support from the Jin royal family, and by extension, the Church of Justice's chaplains. Perhaps the trouble there was worse than he'd feared, if righteous men couldn't even send a single cultivator.

"We of the Xia Empire are also in a difficult position," said Zhen Wei, a man in a tang-style suit.

"You're not fighting anyone, and there are no uprisings in your country," Feng Ming said, cutting him off. "How can you have the gall to call your position difficult?"

"It is difficult if I say it is difficult," Zhen Wei said stiffly, not skipping a beat. "You Southerners only know how to bleed and complain. You know nothing of trade and politics."

"I agree with Zhen Wei," another representative from a much smaller kingdom said. "Our situation is difficult, and you're disrespecting us by discounting what we're going through."

It only got worse from there. A half dozen kingdoms chimed in, and the room devolved into chaos, making Feng Ming wish he could bury his head in the sand and suffocate himself.

"I have something to say," a voice said suddenly. It was the representative of Huoshan, Ding Lei. Despite his long gray beard, no one would ever call him weak. He had been a prominent blacksmith before he eventually retired and went into politics.

Finally, Feng Ming thought. *Someone who can put an end to this chaos.* Huoshan was also an economic kingdom that didn't wage war often. The kingdom also produced a massive amount of weapons, and they usually supported motions that Feng Ming suggested. If anyone could calm them down, it was their representative.

"I regret to inform you that Huoshan can do nothing to help you," Ding Lei said. "Furthermore, due to financial turmoil radiating from the west, our production capacity for weapons has been reduced by a third. We apologize for this, and will do our best to prioritize military shipments to battlefields."

At that moment, Zhang Bo, who'd just walked into the room, held up a finger. "You... how could you? You pick *now* of all times to capitulate?" Judging by the pale and gaunt appearance of the man, the conversation he'd just had over the core-transmission jade had not been a pleasant one. It was likely yet another battle report, a mounting list of their kingdom's casualties.

"You of all people should know exactly what I'm going through," Ding Lei said. "The Evergreen Kingdom would be in the same position with alchemical goods if you didn't have more pressing matters to worry about, like keeping your kingdom intact. I dare you to say otherwise."

"I..." Zhang Bo could only utter a single syllable before slumping back down into his seat, defeated. Then, one kingdom after another echoed Huoshan's words, putting the final nail in the meeting's coffin.

It's all over, Feng Ming thought. There was nothing he could do to salvage this. There was still another session scheduled for after lunch, but what did they have to build off of? It was then that Jiao Ming, his wingman, chose to stand. He looked over the arguing representatives, who hushed to give him a chance to voice his position. Normally, they would be in for a good show. The man never supported Feng Ming.

"You bunch of cowards," Jiao Ming spat, disappointing them.

Instead of blue robes, he currently wore black armor, his golden sword fastened to his waist. His blue fan, a symbol of ostentation and riches, was nowhere to be seen. "Normally, I'd be the one causing a stink for the marshal, but this? This is disgusting." Many lowered their eyes in shame. "Let me tell you, I think Marshal Feng is a jackass. An arrogant brat who thinks too highly of himself, and I hate the way he talks, the way he looks, and the way he behaves. Most of all, I hate everything he says."

He pointed his finger to Feng Ming. "But that man is right. What he says is the truth. And as much as I hate him, as much as I resent him for my brother's death near Beihai, he puts his spear where his mouth is.

"When we were overrun at the Windswept Canyon and on our last legs, Feng Ming, who hates me just as much as I hate him, was the one to step up and fight for me. He saved my life at least three times, and saved many of my men as well. If not for him, our battlefield would already be lost. If not for him, you'd have Southern troops breathing down your necks. If a man can put aside personal grudges and save those he hates, can you not put aside petty things like economics and politics and bleed a little for those who've been protecting you, those you owe your lives to?"

He shook his head as he looked over them pityingly. "If this is all you can do or say, I don't know why I wasted my time coming here. Instead, I should have gone to Evergreen, where they could use a few extra hands to evacuate civilians. Or the Phoenix Burial Battlefield, where the South's army of corpse puppets is destroying their wall one stone after another. Or the Dragonglass Battlefield, or any other place than this godforsaken city—begging your pardon, Ambassador Li—where the only thing I can do is yell at the lot of you, then drink away my sorrows and regret the time I wasted.

"If this is all you can offer, then this 'alliance' of ours is meaningless. We may as well dissolve it now and tear apart whatever agreements we have and cast them to the wind. We might as well start fighting amongst ourselves while we're at it, killing each other while the South breaks through, if only because it's a tender mercy compared to what they'll do to us." He huffed, red faced, looking around and daring anyone to contradict him. No one did, so he swished his cape and turned around. "I'm done with this meeting. I've had it with you people." Then, Jiao Ming walked out the door.

Silence reigned in the meeting room. No one spoke, not even in whispers. Then, Huoshan's representative spoke. "We'll see what we can do, lad," the old smith said. "It won't be much, but we'll do what we can."

With that, the meeting was adjourned, and the representatives stood up and began discussing privately.

Bless that man, Feng Ming thought, making his way toward the exit where they'd find refreshments. Never in his life had he ever misjudged a man as much as he'd misjudged Jiao Ming.

"The situation's worse than I thought," Feng Ming said to Li Fei. He and Jiao Ming were seated in her office a short distance away from the meeting room, where many people were still discussing. They'd already done all they could to convince them and had chosen to remove themselves from the assembly lest they do more harm than good.

"From what I gathered in my discussion with Ding Lei," Li Fei said, "the situation in the Golden Kingdom is much worse than I had anticipated. It's gone on a downward spiral over the last few days. And it's not just trade. Apparently, a third of their royal family was assassinated overnight. They covered it up until now, for fear that the uprisings in their kingdom would get worse. Their kingdom is slowly but surely collapsing."

"A *third*?" Jiao Ming exclaimed. "In a single night? Don't tell me it was the Temple?"

"Who else could it be?" Li Fei said. "Apparently, they'd been sending in secret reinforcements and lying low. Then one night, they suddenly attacked, crippling the kingdom's government. To make matters worse, the Golden Kingdom's troops are committed to fighting rebels. They have no spare manpower to consolidate their hold on Gold Leaf City. The Wang family's move is just twisting the knife that's already in their back."

"The Wang family?" Feng Ming said. "I thought they were fighting amongst themselves in a battle for succession?"

"It seems that Wang Ling won and Wang Jun lost," Li Fei said. "Wang Jun is now his loyal lapdog, and he is currently throwing the North into economic upheaval."

"Impossible!" Feng Ming said. He didn't know Wang Jun all that well, but the information he'd gathered on him indicated that his relationship with his brother was irreconcilable. Wang Jun wasn't one to forgive and forget when his friends or family were involved. Of that he was certain.

Li Fei raised an eyebrow. "I'm only saying what I heard firsthand from the representative of the Golden Kingdom. In fact, it's the Jade Bamboo Conglomerate's actions that have thrown a wrench into our plans. They've paralyzed the economies of over half our member kingdoms in the name of standardization. Everyone knows it's a bullshit reason, but they can only bite back their words. One does not simply alienate their biggest commercial backer."

Feng Ming put his hand to his brow and massaged between his eyes. He looked over to Li Fei, then to Jiao Ming. "What can we do?" he asked. Trade wasn't exactly his area of expertise.

"We could send delegates," Li Fei suggested. "Quicksilver's economic clout is significant. We could also look to forge emergency trade agreements and expedite government approvals. Aside from that, I don't see much else we could do."

"We could kill the little bastards leading the Wang family," Jiao Ming interrupted. "That would go a long way in solving our problems."

"You're a marvelous man," Feng Ming said. "I'm not half as brave as you are."

"Brave?" Jiao Ming asked. "They're just a bunch of merchants."

In the Eastern Desert, it wasn't soft power that got you rich. You only got to keep what your sword could claim.

"Well, these merchants are as slippery as loaches," Feng Ming explained. "They've also hired the best bodyguards as mercenaries, supplied them with the best equipment, and if push comes to shove, they have the backing of many governments. Not to mention that it's common knowledge they have trusts in place as a deterrent. Should anyone assassinate one of their senior members, an enormous bounty would immediately be placed on the killer's head. The bounty would also extend to their friends and their entire family."

Jiao Ming went silent.

"But you're right, we need to do something about this. Once Cha Ming is done in the Evergreen Kingdom, I'll have to ask him to pay Wang Jun a visit. If anyone can convince him to change his mind, it's him." He'd have to shelve any notion of helping out Gong Lan. Though he trusted her, her warnings of the monastery being in danger just didn't make the cut. Regardless of whatever important tree it protected.

"I'll do what I can on my end," Li Fei said. "Now, are you gentlemen going to get the hell out of my office and let me do my work, or are you staying for dinner?"

Right. They'd barged in here during the intermission, interrupting whatever she was doing.

"Dinner sounds great, actually," Feng Ming said.

"I didn't know you were the type," Li Fei said. "Maybe I should call your wife and have a heart-to-heart with her. Clear up any misunderstandings she might inevitably get." She glanced to Jiao Ming. "And yours as well, perhaps? Will it be dinner for three?"

Feng Ming coughed uncomfortably. "On second thought, I was on my way to the bar for a drink," he said, standing up and grabbing his cloak off a door hook.

"I'll come along," Jiao Ming said, coughing lightly. They both exchanged a look on their way out. As good as they were at fighting and battle, they'd be fools to think they could win a war of words with a career politician.

Chapter 10:
Sunrise

Rabbits dodged out of the way, kicking off the stone platform as Huxian's massive form crashed down on them, breaking them apart into dozens of miniature replicas. Twin light and shadow domains constrained the creatures as his tails flailed about, projecting lightning, swamp, and a lesser wind domain, using them less as a concentrated attack and more like a blanket of diluted destruction. These domains, though powerful, weren't like transcendent domains. Rather, they were projections of his friends' powers, amassed in a crude way to constrict and attack his opponents. He swatted at the beleaguered rabbits with clawed hands and bit down on them with massive jaws. Despite the furious time-accelerated blitz, he only managed to destroy ten of the creatures, reducing them to piles of sand that rushed into his body.

The other 118 rabbits managed to dodge in time. They countered with lightning-fast kicks that hit the sorest spots on Huxian's body. Demonic rabbits were always good fighters, specializing in kicks with their powerful legs. Individually, they wouldn't matter much, but simultaneously? He coughed out blood as twenty kicks hit him, drenching the red stone floor in violet-red gore.

Plus, these weren't regular rabbits. They were just another lesson from the Candle Dragon, a manifestation of the monolith called time, and in this case, its passing. People died. People ended. But people were born and people grew. Demons were much the same. These rabbits broke apart and amalgamated just like he did. Moreover, if he didn't eliminate them fast enough, they multiplied, creating broods of children that grew without end. Only the setting sun would stop them, and by then, he would have failed this stage of the trial.

I need time, Huxian thought. *Time to mount a second offensive.* He shrank down to fox-pup size then blitzed away, leading the rabbits away in a furious chase. If they were distracted, they couldn't breed. Moreover, they couldn't think. Trails of distorted time slowed them down, granting Huxian a few breaths to recover from his injuries. They had the initiative, so he let them chase him for a while longer. And then, after gathering his energy, he countered their counterattack.

Huxian grew massive again as he landed on the platform, turning to face the oncoming horde. The rabbits had grown again, and they'd added dozens to their numbers. But despite being powerful and numerous, they weren't very smart; they didn't know how to lock down his movements like a proper demon swarm should, nor did they know how to accurately predict his movements.

The air around him shimmered, and the rabbits froze as his eyes shone red like the rising sun. Time stood still as he activated his newest technique, the first stage of Time-Torching Eyes: Sunrise. The rabbits squealed, begging for mercy as their furs ignited. The air around Huxian heated up from the flames as time accelerated within their bodies, filling them with too much energy for them to handle, which would eventually lead them to bursting. The first rule of time, Huxian had discovered, was that the sun rises. Time passes, no matter how one travels in the space-time continuum. The first stage of the Time-Torching Eyes simply accelerated that process. It took time out of his opponents' hands and used it to harm them.

As the rabbits squealed, Huxian took advantage of their misery. First, he locked time with a bagua symbol, buying himself precious seconds to slash with sharp claws. Each scratch destroyed dozens, and half of the rabbits were reduced to sand by the time his time-lock expired. Demoralized and broken, the rabbits fled. They tried to escape him and outlast the clock, but the sun was still at its apex.

Huxian chased them down, making short work of the ragtag bunch. He chased them out of holes and burrows in the platform, uprooting new "families" when they successfully multiplied. It took until the sun was almost setting. Exhausted, he yawned and stretched as the piles of sand, much larger than before, were absorbed through his body and migrated to his eyes. By the time he'd finished the process, a little less than a minute remained before the sun would set. Enough time for him to recover to full strength.

What a mysterious technique, Huxian thought. After much effort and twenty-seven piles of sand, the first cycle of the Time-Torching Eyes was finally complete. With it, the initial Devil-Sealing, Demon-Subduing, and Spirit-Banishing Intents had completely vanished. They had been replaced with raw power, control over time as it affected all things. His eyes were now reddish gold, and they were far more useful than the parlor tricks he'd learned thus far, like basic time acceleration and time-lagging techniques.

New weapons aside, this trial finally made a little more sense. There was a pattern, he'd discovered, and it was a funny one at that. The demons he faced were manifestations of time in the form of the twelve zodiac animals, with the rat—lousy cheater that it was—symbolizing decay, followed by the hardworking ox, symbolizing continuity. The tiger had come next, though fortunately, he'd faced a much tamer version than he'd expected. Still, in the story of the fox and the tiger, the fox won. It made sense that he, too, would prevail.

Animals aside, the number of them started with one and doubled every time. The ninth stage contained the highest number, 256 of them. This was a watershed, and also the most difficult of the nine stages. The next stage would only be a single animal, though it would be significantly stronger than any of his previous opponents.

The Candle Dragon's challenge was exhausting to say the least. That was especially the case, given that he didn't have time to rest at night and replenish his energy. The only time he could recover was the time he earned by finishing quickly. Unless, of course, he waited for night to come.

Huxian grew nervous as time trickled by, healing as much as possible before finally, the last sliver of sunlight faded off the edge of the platform. Like clockwork, the much slower-moving moon rose over the edge, and with it came the cold. He didn't move on like he usually did. Instead, he stood his ground. Tonight, he would face the killer pigeon assassin, ending it once and for all.

The snows came with the moon, their crystals dancing in the black sky, glittering in the silver moon's pale light. This time, he noticed that even these icy snowflakes were sharp as daggers, though these daggers were too small to do anything to him. He waited for the telltale growl of the pigeon, whom he'd faced several times before gaining his Time-Torching Eyes. He'd waited to familiarize himself with the technique before doing so again, as all his previous attempts had nearly resulted in his death.

This time was different, however. He sensed none of the usual trepidation at not knowing where his opponent would strike. Huxian looked around, frowning. The pigeon was nowhere to be seen. He didn't hear its telltale growl, nor did he feel the distortions in space that usually came with it. Instead, he only saw the blackness of night. The occasional flapping of wings reminded him that the bird was there, though he heard not a growl, but a caw.

Did pigeons caw? He walked about, his paws leaving footsteps in the fresh snow. Leaving a trail would normally be taboo to someone stalking prey, but how could he stalk what he couldn't see? At least this way, he could be found on his own terms.

Huxian looked around for some time before finally noticing something he hadn't seen before during these dark nights. It was a ripple in time, a distortion in space. There were eight such openings, each the same distance from the center of the platform. Could those be where the pigeon was hiding? He walked over to one of them and sniffed. He pawed the ripple, but his paw ran though it like it didn't exist.

Strange, he thought. He moved from the distortion and toward the center of the platform, in the middle of many such openings. When he reached the center, he finally heard flapping. Fluttering ensued, and a black figure rushed out of one of the eight distortions in space, stabbing straight toward him with sharp crystalline feathers. It wasn't a pigeon like last time, a smaller bird throwing crystal daggers as it pecked. Instead, it was a crow. Its feathers were mostly black, but a few sharp crystals poked out from them, gleaming with a lethal edge.

Huxian barely had time to dodge as the crow flew past him. It disappeared into a door, and before he could react, it leaped out of another, attacking his vulnerable flanks. He panicked, activating his Time-Torching Eyes. The crow burned as his eyes damaged it, but it seemed to ignore the pain and go in for the kill. Crystal feathers bit into one of Huxian's haunches, cutting deep and almost severing his leg. He felt a different sort of fear.

This wasn't the fear of unpredictability, the type where you didn't know where your killer came from. After only a few attacks, he could tell exactly where the crow was coming from. But still, he couldn't avoid it. It was lethal and unavoidable, a knife plunging to his back that he couldn't dodge. He felt the fear so vividly he could almost taste it. *Run!* It was all Huxian could think of to do.

He struggled to fly toward the exit as the crow unleashed one swift attack after another. This time, he was prepared for it. He activated all his suppression domains, including light, shadow, lightning, swamp, and wind. He left time distortions behind him, and blessedly, they were able to stall it. As a result, he only suffered relatively shallow wounds and chipped bones and severed tendons. These would heal with time. His poor life would not.

In that instant, Huxian realized he'd never feared death so much in his life. He'd never thought much about dying, but here was Death's sickle, fully sharpened for his waiting neck. He dodged and evaded the crystalline feathers that aimed not just for his vital points, but his eyes and legs. His fur became mangled and bloody, and it only got worse as time progressed. He looked up at the moon and discovered that it had only budged a smidgen; night here was extremely long relative to daytime. He couldn't stall like he might during the day. He needed to escape right away.

He ran with everything he had. He used his splitting technique but discovered that his injuries were too great to split into too many versions of himself. So he split into eight, and six of them were instantly cut down, puffing into smoke. He split again into another eight, much smaller versions. Every time one of his selves was cut down, his demonic energy was severely depleted. If not for the abundant ambient supply restoring him, such losses would have been too much for him to bear. He ran, and time slowed to a crawl as he did.

Six more of Huxian's clones fell, and by the time he left the platform and moved on to the next, crossing the invisible boundary at the bridge, there was only one small Huxian left. Demonic energy rushed into him, healing his wounds as quickly as they could. The wound on his haunch hurt, but the crow's feathers had cut to the core of his being, suppressing his regeneration. He waited a moment before stepping onto the platform, where the sun was already rising. Time would not pause while he was on the bridge. There, 256 rabbits appeared. As he limped, their ears perked up. He didn't move to agitate them, but rather circled around them for the exit. There was no way he could defeat them, wounded as he was.

Seeing what he was up to, the rabbits did something uncharacteristic. Usually, they were a lazy bunch and wouldn't attack unless provoked. This time, however, they all leaped toward him at the same time. Huxian could only grit his teeth and use time acceleration to dodge as many as possible. He didn't focus on destroying them, but rather on buying time and distance as his leg reknitted. He only healed it halfway before he finally gave up and left the platform. For the first time since the trials had started, he'd failed due to his injuries.

Was defeating the assassin impossible? And why was the assassin different? If his wounds were any indication, if he tried that again anytime soon, he would die a meaningless death. He needed an edge to defeat it, something that opposed the power of space it so easily wielded.

I'll have to wait for enlightenment on the next stage of the Time-Torching Eyes, he decided. In the meantime, he'd need to stall and recover, lest he lose these easy matches. Still, the prospect of facing the assassin filled him with dread. Would it be a crow next time, or something different? It seemed that the pigeon presided over the first three zodiac animals, and the crow was his newest opponent. If this trend kept up, he'd likely need to face a different bird upon reaching the second half of the trials.

Sighing, Huxian stepped toward his opponent. He didn't want to fight right way, but there was no avoiding it. Plus, there would only be *one* animal.

Now what comes next? Huxian thought. *First is rat, then comes ox. Mighty tiger comes next, and swift rabbit after that. Then… wait,* he wouldn't make me fight a dragon on the fifth round, would he? He eyed the creature in the middle and was relieved to see that it was a simple house cat. *I wonder why there's no dragon?*

"A dragon would not abase himself to run a race," the Candle Dragon's voice boomed overhead, scaring even the cat on the platform. "Men invented this result, for they wished to praise my kind's power and benevolence, and I allowed it. But in truth, it was a house cat that placed fifth."

I dunno, Huxian said. *My inherited memories—*

"Are mistaken," the Candle Dragon said with an air of finality. Huxian shrugged. The dragon's insecurities weren't *his* problem. The house cat didn't seem to care as it lay there, licking and cleaning itself as Huxian healed. What did it represent? The lazy inevitability of time? He recovered as much as he could in the time allotted, then attacked it. It only took a few breaths to defeat the creature, which dropped gold and red sand this time. He breathed it in, consolidating his eye technique.

Then, he rested. He rested and pondered his eventual bout with the murderous birds—pigeon, crow, or anything else the darkness would throw at him. In that moment, he realized something. That darkness frightened him. But he wasn't a coward. He refused to be one.

The next assassin I face, I'll beat it, Huxian thought as he licked his bloody thigh. He would beat it or die trying. Fear was a terrible dish, and after tasting it, it contaminated all other dishes that touched it.

Chapter 11: Sunset

Thirty-two horses ran around the red stone platform, galloping pleasantly as though it was the finest of meadows. The morning sun was rising swiftly over the platform's horizon, illuminating it but not eliminating the blackness in the sky above. It was only now that Huxian realized he couldn't breathe. While on the Ling Nan Plane, he would definitely have noticed it, but mundane things like that didn't even register, since here, there was both strangeness and demonic energy to spare.

I've finally achieved them, Huxian thought as he approached the horses, who looked at him like sheep eyeing a lone wolf roaming near their feeding grounds. *The second stage of the Time-Torching Eyes: Sunset.* It had taken him a bit longer to complete than he'd originally anticipated. Combined with the loss against the ninth stage of the rabbit trials, he'd also lost in the ninth stage of the cat trials and the last two stages of the snake trials. Overall, he was four stages behind. Fortunately, his reward two stages prior had been substantial. He'd cleared the next one with little trouble at all by taking advantage of his new ability.

Sensing the threat Huxian posed to them, the horses neighed, and their rich black manes suddenly erupting in shadowy fire. Their bodies turned slightly incorporeal as they took on their true forms: They were nightmares, elites among horses and a rather decent bloodline among demons. Over the past few horse stages, Huxian had realized they represented an aspect of time called memory. But these memories were twisted remnants that haunted the nights, the thoughts that you wished would go away but tormented you as you trembled in your sleep.

They ran at him in formation, their ghostly hooves beating at his soul like percussion instruments. He remembered the time when he was young and afraid, sucking at his mother's teat moments before she suddenly vanished. He remembered the time he'd lost Lei Jiang, and those first days he'd been separated from Cha Ming, afraid but not willing to admit it.

Then, he didn't have time to waste with horses. Cha Ming needed him, and the plane did as well. His eyes glowed red gold as he unleashed Time-Torching Eyes: Sunrise, which had gotten a substantial boost after he'd completed the second stage. The flames on the nightmares erupted, turning to red and gold and searing them, the concentrated sunlight forcing them out of the nightmare and into the physical realm where they were weakest.

Their greatest advantage negated, the horses still couldn't be underestimated. They hit Huxian with deadly hooves, drawing blood and cracking bones with every hit they landed. Huxian responded in kind, biting and scratching, his domains wearing away at them. Not long passed before one fell to the ground, then another, then in pairs. Piles of sand larger than his body accumulated faster than it could rush into his body, his light and shadow aura destroying and devouring their wounded bodies, returning to his ravenous eyes with sustenance.

Huxian let out a sigh of satisfaction as the last of them disappeared. He waited at the center of the platform, healing his broken bones and damaged flesh. He didn't go to the edge, as would be prudent—the time for games was over. If he didn't defeat the assassin, he would have trouble completing the third stage of the Candle Dragon's inheritance. Likely, he wouldn't be able to defeat sixty-four of the horses, as their power increased exponentially in groups. If that trend continued, how many of the remaining forty-nine stages could he complete? Twenty-three more failures and he was done for.

It's not even the mounting strength and teamwork that gets to me, but the lack of rest, Huxian thought as another bone reknitted. A quarter of his bones were still broken, and many of his muscles were bruised as the sun started to set. He would be too badly injured to compete in the next stage, and his troubles would carry on throughout the rest of the horse trials. If he didn't have time to rest, he might very well die. If he wanted more time, he would need to earn it. And that meant he needed to defeat the deadly bird that would inevitably appear.

The sun finally set, giving way for a solitary moon to rise in a starless sky. A familiar eerie blue glow covered the platform as snow fell all around him. The snow, he noticed, was much more beautiful than before. Entrancing even. He blinked and noticed that a bird had appeared between him and the exit. It wasn't an annoying bird like the pigeon, nor was it a bloodthirsty bird like the crow. Instead, it was a beautiful peacock with four crystalline feathers for a tail. They reflected the moonlight, illuminating the peacock to expose the wondrous details on its multicolored feathers. And it gave him not an ounce of trepidation, which was odd considering how he'd felt in his latest encounters.

It's a female, Huxian realized. Without knowing what he was doing, he walked toward the peacock. Typically, males had the most flamboyant tails in their species, but he could tell at a glance that this was no normal peacock. Her entrancing blue eyes and ornate patterns screamed of femininity. He wanted nothing more than to take a bite out of her tender neck. He was a fox, after all.

I just need to get close, he thought, stepping forward with glazed eyes that contained no guile, malice, or aeons of enmity with peacock-kind. The void peacock—his new nickname for it—opened its crystalline beak and sang a wonderful song that caused the lonely void in his soul to grow. He wanted the peacock. Needed it. His need was reflected in the four feathers of its tail. Come to me, and all your worries will be gone, it seemed to say. Come to me, and you can rest in blissful and eternal silence. Your wounds, I will heal them. Your bones, I will mend them. Enter my warm embrace.

He opened his muzzle and panted, letting his tongue roll out like a perfect fool. The peacock's feathers fanned out, void shards materializing around it. Huxian realized that not only was it trying to entrance him, but it had lured him into a formation trap; void shards were ready and waiting to attack him once he entered her reach. This *was* fearsome. It was the fear that accompanied you when asked out a beautiful foxy lady. It was the type of fear that you didn't see coming, that you felt but couldn't help but walk into. It was the fear of the lonely void that pushed you to seek out companionship.

A smarter fox would have kept his distance. A smarter fox would have known he was outmatched. But Huxian was desperate. There was a Taotie on their home plane, and he needed to defeat it. While he might be able to abandon the Ling Nan Plane, Cha Ming never could. Besides, there were people he liked there, including his friends. It would be poor form to leave them to a creature of nightmares.

Just a little more, Huxian thought as their safe zones intersected. Outside that range, both of them could escape without any problems. But within it, everything was up in the air. They were now both in reach of each other, an ideal distance to strike. Still, Huxian waited. These creatures, he'd discovered, were good at escaping into the void. Their control over spatial laws was beyond anything he'd thought possible for their realm, the peak of core formation.

He waited just a while longer until he could feel the peacock's breath. *Now!* he thought. The trap sprung, and hundreds of crystalline void shards dove toward Huxian. His figure blurred as he used time acceleration to zip past them, and a bagua symbol appearing around the peacock, whose eyes grew murderous. The charm faded, and Huxian finally noticed a terrible truth: He'd been deceived. The peacock was, in fact, male. Not that there was anything wrong with that, but he just didn't swing that way.

Huxian's eyes grew crimson as he activated the second stage of the Time-Torching Eyes: Sunset. Their surroundings turned red, and the blue glow around the peacock dimmed. The power surging from the peacock diminished as time took its toll on its body. Sunset contained a fundamental truth of time: that all things come to an end. All things eventually wear down, and even heavenly emperors fade. Yama was the only exception, but perhaps that was more because his fate was tied to the destiny of the universe itself. Or perhaps because he represented the end point and was the executor of the plane's ultimate will.

He roared as he pounced, crystal shards piercing his fur, cutting through muscle and bone. But he ignored the breaks, because the crystal shards could cut through anything no matter how hard. He bit into the void peacock's chest, and it screeched, whipping its fanlike tail. Four larger tail shards, the ones that had mesmerized him in the first place, began cutting toward him in tandem.

Now that you're weak, you're mine, Huxian thought. He held firm, sending out his light and shadow clones to deal with the shards. As incorporeal manifestations of his power, they re-formed instantly once cut. His domains activated, striking both the blades and the peacock with wind and lightning and suffocating swamp, and soon, the damage on the bird increased, to the point that not much of a bird remained.

Then it screeched a second time. It disappeared, entering a gray tunnel Huxian could finally perceive after much practice. It was risky, but he chose to give chase. His body blurred as his light and shadow clones joined him to chase the fleeing bird. It moved ridiculously fast through what Huxian could now see was a spatial maze. Carefully interlinked glasslike panes connected and separated the platform in strange ways. By using these, the peacock could go to several different exits, sidestepping the rules of time to instantly appear in another location.

Time doesn't affect this place, Huxian realized. *But what if it did?* His eyes changed color to red and gold as he activated Sunrise. Time accelerated all around him, and the void maze, which had previously been exempt from time's rules, suddenly began experiencing it. The formerly stable panes of spatial glass cracked and shattered, spraying him in a deadly shower of broken reality, the fragments turning into dust, as space could no longer clearly separate itself, and began to merge with its surroundings. Pane by pane, the maze began to crumble. If he didn't escape, he'd be caught in the void and shredded. So he jumped through a hole as everything collapsed, and the void peacock appeared not far from him as the void maze winked out of existence.

It was then that the void peacock screeched a third time, and this time, it sounded like death itself. Its feathers glowed blue, and they formed a massive storm around the bird, cutting like razorblades in a hurricane. Deprived of its feathers, the peacock resembled a nightmarish turkey that had come back to life just as it was being stuffed for a Thanksgiving feast. It was a sight that once seen, could never be forgotten.

Huxian's Time-Torching Eyes glowed red and gold, and red clashed with blue. The time-accelerating effects clashed with the peacock's spatial bewitchment effects, breaking the feathers apart but not harming the peacock otherwise.

With the void peacock's greatest weapons eliminated, the fight was hardly fair. Huxian pounced on it, light and shadow clones in tow. He bit its head off, crunching down on where its void core should be, only to realize there was none to be found.

Instead, he found a large pile of black crystal dust, its color blacker than the deepest night. He looked at it, then realized it reminded him of something. He stared upward and realized it was the night sky. He sniffed at the pile, and before he could react, it swirled around him before finally diving into his back instead of his eyes.

What the blazing hell? he thought. Information streamed into his mind, information on a new technique he was now condensing: Void Phoenix's Moon-Eclipsing Wings.

It all made sense to Huxian now, who finally lay down to rest as the moon slowly made its way across the sky. He'd won the fight, and as a result, he had earned time to rest, as well as the corresponding reward for another trial. The Candle Dragon, it turned out, had not been completely honest with him. He'd been having such a difficult time because he was taking on not just one Godbeast inheritance trial but two. *At the same time.*

Perhaps it's a blessing in disguise, he thought, licking his wounded leg. If he worked hard enough, it might be possible to obtain not one but two new tools. He regretted learning about this so late in the game, but with any luck, he'd be able to master the first stage of the technique, Void-Piercing Feather.

Regardless of the result, he now had hope. He'd gained the opportunity for rest. A new technique had always been there, but obtaining it had required him to be willing to risk his life. The Void Phoenix's inheritance was not for the timid or the faint hearted. Space was a dangerous thing, and failure in manipulating it could easily lead to death and dismemberment.

Time passed slowly beneath the moonlight. The snow was cool and refreshing, and the atmosphere a calm contrast to the heated trial up ahead.

"It sure took him long enough," the Candle Dragon said, his coiling body surrounding the entire line of trial platforms. They floated through the void, which came not from him but from his long time frenemy, the Void Phoenix. "I thought you said he was exceptional?"

"He can be a bit disappointing at times," Bagua Hushao, who was floating beside them, admitted with a yawn. "But he's got his strong points." Huxian's ancestor was resting on his own platform in the shape of a bagua. His black-and-white body rested on the central yin-yang portion of the diagram, and his eight tails were splayed out on each of their respective trigrams. "I happen to like him. I think he's worth the favors I'm trading in."

"Not that I'm complaining about getting off cheap on those favors, but why not give him your own path?" another voice said. A sleek bird with black-and-blue plumage flew down beside the two

Godbeasts and transformed into a human woman. She still wore feathers to protect her more tantalizing features, like her cheekbones, and that region between the navel and the hip bones. The power she possessed was no joke. She was every bit Bagua Hushao's and the Candle Dragon's equal.

Bagua Hushao grinned. His body faded in a mist of black and white, revealing a thin man with long black and white hair draping down over purple robes. Only younger, less-powerful demons were restricted to demon form, after all. The more powerful one grew, the more it grew necessary to restrain and contain the massive natural energies within. "And why let such a promising junior follow a path well trodden when he can experience a new way, unbound by his ancestors?"

"Why indeed?" the Void Phoenix said, winking with her piercing blue eyes. "Why lead him down the path where he's most likely to succeed?"

"You two always bicker so much," said the Candle Dragon, who took the form of an old man before floating up beside them. He had white hair and red eyes. His robes were made of the finest gold thread and covered in clawlike patterns, and on his head, he wore a golden crown inlaid with the brightest rubies.

"Shut up!" both Bagua Hushao and the Void Phoenix said simultaneously. They looked away from each other like squabbling siblings.

"I do not disagree with his approach," the Candle Dragon said. "I was intrigued when you said you had a high-potential candidate for me to test. Even more so when you suggested I should collaborate with this witch."

"You're one to talk, decrepit warlock," the Void Phoenix huffed. "For all your talk of honesty and truth, you were pretty obscure with the poor pup when you explained the rules down there."

"Why do *you two* always bicker so much?" Bagua Hushao said lazily, prompting glares from his two companions. He coughed lightly. "I think you'll be pleased by his performance. He'll do right by the both of you."

"Pleased?" the Void Phoenix said, looking toward the small fox resting on the red platform. "I honestly don't see how he'll survive. He was barely able to defeat one of my tamest minions."

"He's young," Bagua Hushao said. "And he's learning. You're forgetting that he has the most promising feature one can find in a young demon."

"Which is?" the Candle Dragon asked with a raised eyebrow.

"Daring," Bagua Hushao said. "The willingness to risk it all for his friends. I see your doubts. You think I tossed him out to die. You think I disowned him just to see how he turns out, and to satisfy my curiosity. Well, I assure you, my dear lady and dashing gentleman, that things won't end badly. This test is only beginning. Don't call the game before it's over."

"It's halfway done," the Void Phoenix pointed out. "And he's only got one portion of spatial dust. He'll never get enough to condense a space mark. Even condensing a time mark will be tricky if we help him."

"I stand by my words," Bagua Hushao said. He crossed his arms and looked down at the baby fox, one of his stray children. He loved every one of them, but demons were not caring and merciful creatures.

Though he put on a strong front, there was worry deep within his heart. His bravado hid a cruel truth: If things continued this way, if Huxian didn't shake things up, he would definitely fail, gaining a pittance instead of the fortune the Candle Dragon had initially offered. But there was always a chance, and he knew a way. He only hoped the young fox was clever enough to find it.

Chapter 12: Next Step

Small bells chimed as the door to the meeting room opened, revealing a half dozen waiters who busily served small dishes and poured tea. They were dressed in golden colors, matching the room's white-and-gold décor, and the dishes they served were of the colorful variety, as ornate as they were tasty or strange, if that was what you preferred.

As the number one restaurant in the city, the Gold Foliage House was an ostentatious venue, worthy of serving princes and princesses that occasionally visited the city. That was only fitting, since some of the people in the room were exactly that. Wang Jun seemed to be the only one at the table lacking any kind of noble title.

Though the food was wonderful, no one looked pleased to be there. That was especially the case for the delegates from Huoshan. The unorganized lot had six different representatives heading their many blacksmith trade associations. And naturally, instead of doing the smart thing and appointing someone to represent them, they'd all insisted on coming to personally bicker. Just as planned.

"Like I said, I'm not planning on making exceptions for every group," Wang Jun said, taking a sip of his tea—fresh mountain spring leaves nurtured with demon bone ash. He took his time enjoying the flavor, letting it wash over his tongue as he mulled over his next words. "We'll need to harmonize things across the entire North, and while there are many smithing associations, it makes sense to use Huoshan's standards as a template. Like Dong Guo's suggested standards, for example."

Dong Guo, a dense man with arms nearly twice as thick as his companions, looked confused for a moment. That confusion soon turned to self-satisfaction as he realized he was winning the argument he'd been having for the past twenty-four hours with his peers. The others ignored his exultation and glared daggers at Wang Jun, trying their best to cut him to pieces as nonviolently as possible. After all, Dong Guo's proposal was the most disorganized and different of the lot. It was clear that he'd picked it to sow dissension and chaos.

"Surely there must be some leeway," said Hua Lan, a slender but surprisingly strong woman with red hair. "We've spent decades trading with each other, and we've always been able to figure something out."

"Alas, I would love to," Wang Jun said. "Truly, I would. But this is beyond me. This is a directive from the Patriarch himself, and I am helpless to do anything but obey. If you would like, however, I could deliver your words to him. He's a busy man, but I'm sure he could get you a response in a few days' time while we hash things out otherwise."

Hua Lan was the most dependent on him of the lot. By giving her hope, he sowed seeds of doubt in their internal negotiation process. How wonderful it was to argue with this group of six, as opposed to the three others in the room.

"You shouldn't hold your hopes up, Hua Lan," said Feng Ye, one of the three princesses who were dining with them. "He's clearly stringing you along with empty promises, like a young man with no promise would do to a maiden before eventually running off without her." She drank tea in a dignified manner that befitted her royal status. The two other princesses beside her were refined and followed her lead. Unlike those from Huoshan, they were there to support their main negotiator if there were gaps in her knowledge or expertise. Regardless of their input, all decisions on their end would be made at her sole discretion.

Wang Jun didn't personally hate the fact that she was ruining his plans, but it did go contrary to what Wang Ling and the Patriarch wanted. He'd have to do something about that. "Their situation is a little different from yours," Wang Jun said.

"How so?" Feng Ye asked, reaching over with her chopsticks to grab a small steamed bun filled with a sweet bean paste. "Please explain. I'm curious."

"Last I checked, smithing was different than nurturing and gathering herbs," Wang Jun pointed out.

"And last I checked, they received the same treatment in your document," Feng Ye said with a smile. She looked to the side. "Correct me if I'm wrong, my dear sister."

Feng Li, who'd remained silent until now, shook her head. "Not wrong at all, sister. Since learning of this joint meeting with those from Huoshan, I looked into the matter specifically. In both cases, there is a requirement for harmonized standards. In fact, the wording is shockingly similar. It was as though the author had no idea about the goods he was trying to regulate, and simply copied over all the wording with minimal substitution."

"Imagine that," Feng Ye said. "Though I'm sure it wasn't intentional. Prime Director Wang?"

Point one for the Phoenix Cry Empire, Wang Jun thought. He looked to Wang Bing, who'd recently reviewed Wang Jun's draft.

"Things were moving very quickly," Wang Bing said. "And requests for refunds and settlements mounted, giving us no choice but to act before giving proper distinction to each sector. The reason the wording is so general is to give us all a chance to discuss specifics with each organization."

"And in doing so, drive a wedge between them," Feng Ye said. "How clever. I originally wondered what the logic was behind bringing us and the smiths from Huoshan together, instead of the herbologists from the Evergreen Empire or even the Song Kingdom. This conversation has made it clear that the prime director's intention is to send us all mixed messages. The way you've approached us is already different from those in True North Country. I should know. We just had a meeting."

"My dear lady, that is because each individual organization is different," Wang Jun said in a reassuring tone. "Tell me, do you pander to equality and representation in your kingdom, or do you respect strength, bloodline, and authority? Do those in Huoshan appreciate scalability and suitability for the masses like Quicksilver, or do they respect individual artistry and high quality? If I had them in the same room, how could I speak in terms each party would understand? Surely you can't fault me for wanting to speed things up by adding a personal touch to group negotiations?"

Feng Ye pursed her lips. In that exchange, Wang Jun had been the victor.

"I think that we should focus on things that aren't very different between standards and organizations and work from there," said Luo Xing, one of the older smiths from Huoshan. He had a kindly demeanor, and everyone in the group seemed to respect him to some extent. Wang Jun suspected it had a lot to do with his higher-level achievements in smithing; he'd only joined their trade association after forging one of the few half-step-transcendent weapons on the continent.

"And what might those things be?" Wang Jun asked, cursing Feng Ye for having bought the smiths time to regroup.

"Material quality and forging imperfection count," Luo Xing said. "We have the best refiners on the continent, and every smith prides himself on flawless work. There's nothing more damaging to a smith's reputation than creating a weapon that breaks when fighting an enemy."

"And which standard do you propose?" Wang Jun asked. "There two dozen for mortal-grade works alone."

"We'll leave that up to you," Luo Xing answered. "Pick one you like, and we'll get it done. Though bear in mind that it will impact cost. We'll negotiate with the other parties separately and come to our own agreements on how to handle quality control and implementation."

"But who will pay the price for not adhering to the standards?" Wang Jun asked.

"We'll worry about that," Luo Xing said.

"Unacceptable," Wang Jun said. "Individual responsibility is an integral part of this undertaking. Only by holding individuals and organizations responsible for their actions can we stamp out inconsistency at its root."

"If that is the case, we'll be sure to hold cross-border training to implement the standards as soon as possible," Luo Xing said. "I'll personally teach them if I have to, and I could teach a donkey to smith. As for individual risk, I'm sure that we could work out an insurance scheme with your very profitable insurance company. Surely you wouldn't be opposed to making extra money on risk mitigation when it's you yourself that asked for said mitigation in the first place?"

Wang Jun winced internally. He counted that one as two points. It was a good thing these meetings weren't so much about winning as they were about stalling for time. "I think you've made a wonderful suggestion," Wang Jun said. "It's unfortunate that all the standardization in the world can't solve inconsistencies in the soil. I'm really not sure how we'll solve this herb-quality problem."

"We'll divide herbs into generalized tiers based on properties," Feng Ye said. "Isn't that the most optimal solution?"

"I'm not convinced it is," Wang Jun said. "I'll need to talk with your counterparts from Evergreen about it first." She glared at him, as this was clearly a delaying tactic. Evergreen was especially unresponsive given their war situation. "Then if that's all, I think we'll adjourn for the day. You've given me much to think about, and it will take some time to collate today's discussions and present them to our council of elders for consideration."

He didn't wait for their response, and stood up. Wang Bing and Elder Bai, who'd been there but had been busy pouring tea for everyone who needed more, accompanied him outside the room. They'd been there for support, but thankfully, he'd only needed to tap Wang Bing once.

"That seems to have gone poorly," Wang Bing said as the door shut behind them.

"It was destined to go poorly," Wang Jun said. "When one is so unilateral as we've been, it drives the others to organize against us all the more quickly. If we'd been softer, we could have dragged this out for months on end."

"Then why not do that?" Wang Bing asked.

"Because we don't need months," Wang Jun said. "Tell me, how long do you think we can keep this up while still maintaining legitimacy?"

"Days," Wang Bing said. "Maybe weeks?"

"Then you have your answer," Wang Jun said grimly. "We're not dragging this out, because the goods interruptions wouldn't be as severe. We're not buying time for an extended siege, Wang Bing. We're trying to win a few quick battles. Even if they manage to bypass us and set up their own trade accords, the damage will already be done. When the South's forces are in Gold Leaf City, hijacking Northern trade will be so much easier than it is now."

"How did it go?" Patriarch Wuling asked Wang Jun, who stood in the center of the elder council chambers like a convict for interrogation. The man himself sat several rows back in his customary throne-like seat.

"Poorly," Wang Jun said. "As we discussed before, we can only stall for so long by being this blunt. Already, Quicksilver has jumped in to fill a void in the trade network. In two weeks, they'll have completely displaced us."

"What happens in two weeks doesn't concern us," Wang Wuling said.

"Agreed," Wang Jun replied, then waited for the Patriarch to continue.

Unfortunately, it wasn't the Patriarch who spoke next, but Wang Ling, who was seated just beside him. Heavens, he hated his poisonous voice. "How are our finances doing?" he asked. "Surely we're making a killing off the black market?"

"We're making a tidy profit, of course," Wang Jun said. "Though we're still losing massive amounts on the whole. Our property values have taken a steep dive, yet we still need to pay staff to maintain our future profitability. We need to continue renting prime locations, or we'll lose them to other bidders."

Wang Ling shrugged. "Lay some people off, then. Close some locations. We need to be flush with cash when war comes to this country."

Wang Jun clenched his jaw. "The laws of the Golden Kingdom mandate a certain severance be paid to employees let go, even in uncertain times like these. The expense will be astronomical. The same applies to canceling contracts where we rent our locations. In the short term, it will save us cash, but in the long term, we'll definitely lose out."

"Then don't pay them," Wang Ling said, grabbing a bunch of grapes off a plate beside him and eating one.

"Don't pay them," Wang Jun said blankly. He felt his rage bubble up again, as it often did when he spoke to him. "Do you know how much financial distress that will cause? To our own employees, who have worked for us for decades? The Wang family has always stood by the fact that employees are more extended family than disposable assets. That's how we're able to operate so efficiently with minimal corruption."

"At this point, I don't think we have the luxury of caring," Patriarch Wuling cut in. "Ling is right. We need the money now. We also can't sit on our cash reserves—we'll need to spend them."

Wang Jun took in a deep breath, then let it out. He cursed them for having seen the obvious move, a move he'd been hoping to delay by at least another week. "I'll see it done."

What they asked of him went against decades of learning and personal business experience. By betraying their staff in this way, they wouldn't just lose external reputation, it would also come back to bite them financially. That wasn't even counting the loss in morale in their company, or morality of the situation. Well, he shouldn't count on that last one, he supposed, with them siding with devils and all.

"You'll do it after you take care of some other matters," Wang Wuling said. "Stopping cash from leaking out means nothing if we aren't ready for the struggle. We need to hire mercenaries and guards, and we need to arm them."

"So, it's come to open rebellion now," Wang Jun said softly. Everything was happening too quickly for him to even react.

"Yes," Wang Wuling said. "If it were a year ago, aiding and interfering would have been enough. Since your meddling in the Ji Kingdom, however, they've asked us to take a very concrete role in the invasion. We will be spending eighty percent of our treasury toward the war effort. Though we're being punished, make no mistake—this is our chance to distinguish ourselves. Our goal at the end of all this is to own the kingdom."

Wang Jun bowed stiffly. "It will be as you say." He turned around and walked out of the room, ignoring the confused Wang Bing, who'd been waiting for him outside. He couldn't face her now, not with everything that was happening, so he jumped into a shadow behind a statue and traveled to an empty room in the mansion.

There, he clutched his knees and rocked back and forth. He let the pain wash through him and accustomed himself to it. He let go of his ego and let his senses seep into the shadows and become one with the darkness that was still getting to know him.

He'd been naïve in thinking he'd just need to run interference and sow chaos, he realized. One doesn't just commit treason halfway. His family was rotten to the core, and he could not judge them by the standards of reasonable men.

Then what can I judge them by? Reading people required insight on their character. *I suppose I can only judge them by the standards of devils. Only they could be so callous.*

"When will it all end?" Wang Jun asked Hong Xin. Once again, she sat on the couch, and he lay down on his back with his head on her lap. "Why must they ask me to do such things?" She looked at him in concern. She hadn't been privy to the contents of his meeting with the Patriarch, but the orders he'd sent shortly after filled her with worry.

War. Suffering. And at the same time, things that seemed petty like downsizing and "labor optimization." Unfortunately, she knew all too well what financial distress could drive men to do, and how desperation could transform them, destroying their families and their communities. The war would kill many, yes, but the change and poverty that would accompany it would kill ten times more. It wasn't just warriors she wanted to protect, but the little people. The people she'd forgotten existed until she'd lost her cultivation and became one of them.

"You seem surprised," Hong Xin said after some time. She petted his golden hair, running her fingers through the soft tangle like a large-toothed comb. "The Wang Jun I know would have seen it coming." She felt his cheeks and noticed no change in temperature, no flush of embarrassment. Though she'd lost kindling and dousing, there were certain tells she remembered. And with Wang Jun, she'd had to learn another skillset to read him, as her previous arts were worthless on him to begin with.

"I'd suspected, but I never dared think they would stoop so low," Wang Jun said. He sat up and put his head in his hands, letting his long hair droop over his face.

"Then expect the worst," Hong Xin said. "Not just for others, but for you and me." She placed her hand on his chin and lifted his eyes to hers. "Do you really think they'll let you off after all this is over?"

"I don't care much about myself anymore," Wang Jun said with a laugh. "It's only…"

She saw pain and worry in his expression, but Hong Xin said nothing, as the implication was obvious. When they had no use for him, everyone else who depended on him was fair game. Wang Bing would be punished, and so would Elder Bai. All of his loyal minions would get what was coming to them. And finally, they'd have no use for her. And given how much they hated Wang Jun, they probably had something special in store for her, if only to cause him even more agony before they finally twisted the dagger and put him out of his misery.

It begged a question: If she was going to die anyway, what was the point of playing along? Why shouldn't he make plans, assuming everything would happen exactly as he dreaded? That was the second stage of her plan, watering the seed she'd planted days ago. The seed would germinate and take root in his mind, growing until he could no longer ignore it. For him to act, he couldn't see her as living. It was vital for him to assume that, as far as his family was concerned, she was already dead.

Chapter 13: Preparations

It was a quiet night in Gold Leaf City as Wang Jun led his trio through silent streets. Wang Bing and Elder Bai were accompanying him, their figures wreathed in shadows to hide them from unwanted eyes. Undesirables could be found on every corner and every side alley. Though these were the dregs of society and went unnoticed by most, he knew perfectly well that it was exactly these eyes they were hiding from.

After walking awhile, they arrived at a building that could be mistaken for a tavern. It stank of ale and wine, had a steady stream of music, and was filled with drunken laughter that threatened to tear down its surprisingly firm walls. Wang Jun knocked three times on the even sturdier front door—it had to be, given how many times they had to throw people out through it—and it was opened by a large man with scarred knuckles. His face was greasy and dirty, his shirt torn in a few places, and his mouth was missing more than a few of its rotten yellow teeth. He looked them up and down before grunting and letting them inside. They were greeted by music and the mixed smells of sweat and alcohol, along with partially clothed bodies covered in scars or a variety of substances.

They didn't mingle with the other patrons, and the crowd only eyed them for a moment before returning to their drinks. These folks were not the type to ask questions; the fewer there were, the easier they slept.

"Right this way, esteemed patrons," said a woman in green silks instead of the leathers all around them. She led them to the back of the room, through a door, and down a hallway, which opened into a private dining room where three men sat. The largest man, Chen Yangjing, was a half-step-rune-carving cultivator, with some body cultivation to spare. He was also the head of the Gold Swords mercenary group, a loose alliance of men for hire in the Golden Kingdom.

"Prime Director Jun," Chen Yangjing said, wiping his mouth as he set down a large mug of ale. The alcoholic beverage wasn't the type that mortals drank, but rather a brew from Haijing, specifically tailored to intoxicate even the strongest body cultivators. "Please take a seat."

Wang Jun did so, and Wang Bing and Elder Bai followed suit. He accepted a cup of wine the lady in silks poured for him and took a sip. He held back a grimace as the strong concoction burned its way down his throat, and he held back the coughing fit that his hosts likely expected. Like in all negotiations, the drink was a test. A test of his sincerity for accepting the beverage, and a test of strength depending on whether or not he could tolerate it. Though the drink burned, Wang Jun refused to admit it. He choked it down without expression, then turned his attention to the group of cold-blooded killers.

"Thank you for taking the time to invite me to your game," Wang Jun said, placing his cup back down. "I realize this is a terribly busy time for you."

"Terribly busy indeed," Chen Yangjing said. "Terrible times are profitable times in our business. With the Golden Army overwhelmed across the country and the palace guard understaffed, even cripples and beggars can find fighting work if they're willing to sharpen their swords and grease their armor."

"How righteous of you, protecting the kingdom in its time of need," Wang Jun said.

"Righteousness has nothing to do with it," Chen Yangjing replied, grabbing a piece of apple from a plate an attendant brought over to him. It let out a large crunch as he bit into it, and a dense natural energy leaked out from the spirit fruit and filled the room. "Now, enough with the small talk. We're here for serious business. We're here to play a game."

The man on his left nodded and pressed a rune on the circular table. There was a bit of shuffling noise before four rows of neatly arranged face-down tiles rose up before each of them. This game, *Majiang*, had been around for ages and was usually played by aging couples and family members. There were 136 tiles, each one-inch thick, a simpler set than most, which often had regional rules specific to the city.

They moved simultaneously, pushing the four tile rows together at an angle. The man who'd pressed the rune rolled the dice and counted off several tiles to the right of Wang Jun and took four tiles. Wang Jun followed—most things went counterclockwise in this game, and they continued until everyone had thirteen tiles. The man who'd gone first drew fourteen and placed a single tile faceup in the center, starting the game. Wang Jun played next, and soon the game was in full swing.

"Truth be told, I'd do the opposite if the other side could afford it," Chen Yangjing said, placing a tile with three dots in the center. "Thing is, it's just too expensive to work against the kingdom you're based in. That kind of thing can get you killed even after you're done with the mission." The pile of face-up tiles was quickly growing as they played.

"How expensive are we talking?" Wang Jun asked. It was his turn, so he drew a tile. It was a northern wind, which he already had two of, so he kept it. In this game, one had to form four melds—runs or sets of three or four—and a single pair to win. There were complicated requirements, making the game very strategic, but Wang Jun didn't think too much about that; he wasn't here to win. He threw away the seven of numbers, which the one on his right conveniently needed, revealing the eight and nine required to complete the meld. You could only "eat" tiles to complete a run if it was the player before you that played it.

"Three times the price," the man he'd just fed the tile to said. His name was Hawkeye, and he was the leader of the Hawkeye Mercenary Group, men and women who preferred ambushes and covert work instead of brute force like the Gold Swords mercenaries. "And depending on the nature of the contract, there would be a set minimum purchase. You can't take those kinds of risks without enough of a payoff to justify it."

"Such as?" Wang Jun asked. "I ask only out of curiosity, of course."

Chen Yangjing, who was up next, answered his question. "Fighting alongside bandits can get a few people in hot water." He took a tile, shook his head in disgust, and slapped it face up on the table. Three tiles like it had already been thrown away by the others, making the tile almost useless. "I'd say that unless we were paid for ten initial-core-formation cultivator equivalents, it wouldn't be worth the hassle. Not for any of us."

The other two nodded in agreement. There was a price for the convenience of having all three of them in a single room. "And if it was something like protecting those damned cultists..." He shook his head. "I wouldn't do it for less than ten peak-core-formation cultivator equivalents, and even then, I'd need to think about it, and a year would have to be paid for up front."

"I suppose the consequences of being discovered, and the potential fallout, are important," Wang Jun said, confiscating a piece the man to his right had just thrown. Since he was stealing to complete a set of three, he got to skip the other two players. Turn order began anew as soon as he placed another tile faceup. "Now, as a man who likes to consider things on their extreme, I have a hypothetical question. How expensive would it be to back a rebellion? Surely such a thing would be the most dangerous thing you could do, wouldn't it?"

Chen Yangjing grinned. He ate the last piece of apple and chased it with a long pull of ale. "This is very hypothetical, of course, having never been asked to do such a thing. It's tricky because we'd need to commit every mercenary we have and get rid of those who refuse to participate. We'd only do it if all three of our mercenary companies were participating. We're a friendly bunch, and we really hate killing each other."

"Just wouldn't feel right to play *Majiang* with a man who killed your underlings," Hawkeye agreed.

"None of us would do that unless we had ten years' worth of wages," said Silver, the man to Wang Jun's left. He was a wiry man with a thin silver ring on each finger. Each ring had runic patterns connecting them, and their likely use was to reinforce his knuckles. "We'd also have to pay for things like deathsworn contracts and all that ugly stuff. And since we couldn't go through the Church..." He shook his head. "Such a thing would bankrupt almost anyone—save maybe you, of course."

"I suppose it would," Wang Jun said. "And it would be even more expensive if whoever wanted to hire you all were in a hurry."

"Exactly!" Chen Yangjing said, slapping his hand on the table, causing a few tiles to fall down. His two partners glared at him for the poor form. He ignored the looks and turned to the man on his right. "This is exactly the kind of understanding customer we're looking for, Hawkeye. They don't look for deals, and they understand the troubles you're going through."

Hawkeye nodded as he played, twirling a wicked-looking throwing knife around his fingers, tossing it up and catching it by the tip of the blade as he picked up and laid down another a tile. "Makes sense," he said. "There ain't many people like him with so much money to burn."

"Really, though, how much could it possibly cost?," Wang Jun said. "I only sense four peak-core-formation cultivators in this building, Silver and Hawkeye included. And then there's you, of course, the only half-step transcendent."

"Here, yes," Chen Yangjing said, nodding. He claimed a tile Silver had just thrown down, revealing his second meld in southern winds. His other meld was a set of three sticks that he'd picked up earlier, significantly narrowing the types of winning hands he could make.

To win, he'd need to complete something in dots and numbers now. He'd also need a one or a nine, which the others would hoard and not throw away unless they absolutely had to. "But you're not counting all the troops we have posted in the palace, within the kingdom, and even abroad. We're looking at nearly twenty peak-core-formation equivalents. That's awfully pricey, given how rare they are. What do you think, Silver?"

"Fifty million," Silver said after a short while. "It would scale up depending how many men we could find, non-negotiable."

Wang Jun winced. "That would definitely eat into a family's fortune. Though, I don't suppose anyone would bargain."

"Not a chance," Hawkeye said. "They'd have nothing to fall back on, and what's worse, we could report it to the kingdom. Those pricks wouldn't pay us nearly as much for our services, but at least it'd be less troublesome. You have no idea how many people we'd have to kill to keep the secret. Blood money isn't cheap."

"Fair enough, fair enough," Wang Jun said, chuckling. "Thank you for satisfying my curiosity. I came here for a completely different matter, of course."

"Of course," Chen Yangjing said. "I'd wager that like every damn rich fool out there, you need protection in turbulent times. Either for yourself or for your family. Just be warned, we might be on friendly terms since you were kind enough to join our table, but I'm going to gouge you just like I'm gouging everyone else in this city." He claimed another tile, meaning that he only had a meld and a pair he could keep hidden. "I heard you're hot stuff in merchant circles, but here, you dance to our tune."

"I completely understand," Wang Jun said, avoiding the tile he knew the man wanted and playing another. "I just need a lot of hired muscle to stay at the Jade Bamboo Pavilion as honored guests. Just in case someone wants to cause trouble."

"A few birds told me you upset a lot of people recently," Chen Yangjing said. "Quite a few of them tried to hire me to off you, but we're mercenaries, not assassins. Let the Temple deal with that dirty business."

"More than a few, actually," Wang Jun said, shaking his head self deprecatingly. "A few trade associations and some kingdoms are after my head. I should know—I put counter-bounties on each person who tried. It was ridiculously expensive."

"How interesting," Chen Yangjing said, his eyes narrowing. "The Spirit Temple doesn't usually renege on contracts and inform their targets. Goes against their principles, I'm told."

This time, it was Wang Jun who grinned. "It pays to have connections who can kill and silence just about anyone you want. All the money in the world won't help you if you're a dead man, business and political connections be damned."

The man gulped. "How many men do you need? I might not gouge you quite as much as the others if you hire a couple of my best men for a few months. It'll be like a bulk discount or something. We could each pitch some people in."

"Why settle for your best men?" Wang Jun asked innocently. "I want you, the strongest of them all."

"Not a chance," Chen Yangjing said, chuckling. He picked up a face-down tile, and after thinking for a moment, traded one for an existing tile. Was the tile related to what he was holding, or was it a bluff? Likely the former, given how the man had been playing. Luck had played a fairly significant role in getting him what he needed. "I need to stay here and mind the business. I'm not involved in all that guarding and traveling and killing. Somebody has to talk to the clients."

"But what clients would you need to speak to?" Wang Jun asked innocently. "I don't just need you, but every last man you have."

Chen Yangjing froze. Hawkeye looked up, and Silver's finger stopped tapping.

"You'll have to call them back from the palace, from outside the city, and any missions they're on. And they might need to stay in our pavilion for at least a year, if not ten. It would be best if you came along to command them."

They sat in silence for a moment until Chen Yangjing began to laugh uncontrollably. The entire establishment went silent as his laugh echoed throughout the building's thin inner walls. As the man kept going, his attendant, who'd seen them in originally, walked out the door to silence those outside. "I told you! I told you he was my kind of customer! I've never met a man with the brass balls to ask me what he just did!"

"Then I take it you're free to take the contract?" Wang Jun asked.

Chen Yangjing wiped tears of laughter from his eyes and nodded. "It might take me a while to get everyone together, but I can do it. Be warned, though, we take cash up front. And like I said, the price will scale depending on who else we can find."

"Find as many men as you like," Wang Jun said. "But they need to be at the Jade Bamboo Pavilion in three days."

"*Three days?*" Hawkeye said, frowning. "Are you crazy? Forget finding people, the paperwork alone will take weeks. We'd need to bypass the Church of Justice, and for that we'd need—" He cut himself off as a stack of black papers appeared on the table. Beside it was a promissory note. The man picked up the note and sucked in a breath. "That's a hundred million, not fifty," he said.

"You only get that much if you find enough men," Wang Jun said. "Everyone who signs the contract will get an employment mark for verification, similar to how things work in the South." Wang Jun looked to Chen Yangjing's forearm, which was adorned with a conspicuous black tattoo. "I take it you won't have a problem dissolving your own mark?"

Chen Yangjing shook his head. "You don't need to worry about it. It won't conflict. Though I wouldn't mind if you could connect me with that friend of yours in high places to get rid of it."

"Consider it done," Wang Jun said, standing up. "But remember, three days. You have until dusk." He left the three men at the table and walked out of the room with Elder Bai and Wang Bing in tow. The two of them had gone pale near the end of the conversation. They finally realized just how ugly things had gotten.

As guilty as he felt, he'd given them ample chances to leave. Now, they knew too much. They were stuck with him, whether they liked it or not. Still, Wang Jun led them down a few streets at a slow pace before stopping. They sat in a small park, a green space designated by the city for leisure. Though there were many people in the park, their group was wreathed in shadows. Everyone avoided them unconsciously, as the shadows eased them away.

"Tell me that didn't just happen," Wang Bing finally said. Her eyes were pleading for denial on Wang Jun's part.

"I'm afraid this is the path we're on," Wang Jun said. "If you're not willing to follow me, if you won't have faith in the direction I'm going in, you can still resign. It's not too late, but I'll have to put you on surveillance so that news doesn't leak out, and you'll be under house arrest. I should be able to ensure that you're safe as long as I'm still alive. I owe you that much at least."

Wang Bing gulped and shook her head. "I won't back out now. Given what you're doing, I doubt anyone in the extended family will be able to come out unscathed regardless of the end result."

"You're right," Wang Jun said. "We're going all in."

Wang Bing firmed her resolve. "What do you need me to do?"

"The same as I did today," Wang Jun said. "I need you to go to ten noble houses in the city. They're independent enough of the crown that they'll likely accept my proposed protection contract. You'll need to start from the top of the list, though, and make sure you leak out news when each of them accepts. Once they see their allies capitulate, they'll have no choice but to take sides."

"I'll get it done," Wang Bing said.

Wang Jun gave her a storage ring containing another thick stack of contracts and ten promissory notes. He also gave her another item—a Wang signature jade. By using it, she could sign any document as though she was Wang Jun himself. "Be sure to use that signet to stamp these documents. No other one will do."

"Is there something special about it?" Wang Bing asked. "I still have the other one you gave me."

"It has to be that one," Wang Jun affirmed. "In fact, give me the other." Wang Bing did so, and he crushed the expensive item and tossed away the jade dust. "Now there can be no mistakes. When can you leave?"

"Immediately," Wang Bing said. "I don't dare sit on anything this important."

"Do it as soon as possible, and please get your husband to lie low, or better yet, get him to stay at the Jade Bamboo Pavilion for the next three days. I doubt my family will allow him to leave the city."

"Won't that be dangerous?" Wang Bing asked.

"It will be safer there than anywhere else," Wang Jun said. "And it will stop our opponents from taking hostages."

She paled but nodded. "I'm on it," Wang Bing said. She ran off down the street, taking her wreath of shadows along with her. It obscured her movements and sounds as she made her way to one of the rich areas of the city.

"And what would you have me do, young master?" Elder Bai asked stiffly. "I hope it's nothing so hard as you've tasked the little lady with." What he'd seen at the mercenary association had clearly gotten to him. Wang Jun had expected as much.

"Alas, I'll be asking you to do something much harder," Wang Jun said. He shook his head and took out two envelopes. "The first letter, unfortunately, is your letter of dismissal. Due to our current family policies, I'm unable to give you severance. You'll have to sue us through appropriate channels if you want any type of official compensation."

Elder Bai's eyes reddened as tears came to his eyes. He did his best to stop them, but they broke through like tiny rivers from an overflowing lake. Elder Bai didn't look anything like the capable assistant he was. Instead, he resembled a frail old man with nothing left in the world.

"There now," Wang Jun said, walking up to him and hugging him tightly. The older man didn't reject the gesture. "What's going on now is far more than you can handle. I know what happened to your family. I know how they died. You'd rather kill yourself than go through with this."

"There's no need," Elder Bai said, choking up. "If there's something you need me to do, I'll do it."

"That won't be necessary, old friend," Wang Jun said. "You're like an uncle to me. No, a father that my father never was. I can't do that to you. That's why, in this second envelope, there's a gift. Please open it."

Elder Bai did so, his aged fingers fumbling as he took out a letter opener and pried it open. He wiped his eyes before looking at what was inside, and when he did, his eyes widened. "You must have made a mistake. There's no way this is accurate."

"It's very accurate," Wang Jun said, smiling. "These are illicit funds—they have nothing to do with the family. I'm giving them to you because I have no need of them any longer."

"B-but…" Elder bai stuttered. "I wouldn't know what to do with so much money. *Kingdoms* wouldn't know what to with it."

"I don't know what to tell you," Wang Jun said. "But since you mention it, it's dangerous for you to have so much money, and the family leadership probably won't like you leaving anyway. That's why I'll give you a third gift."

He grabbed Elder Bai's wrist and clamped a black metallic object on it. It resembled a soul-sealing collar, but instead of suppressing his soul, the shadows around Elder Bai deepened. "No one will find you if you don't wish to be found, my dear Elder Bai. As for what you should do, I'm really not sure. You're a righteous man, so perhaps you could put that money to good use."

He looked up at the sky, thinking. "If I recall correctly, the family has tasked me with buying weapons for our troops. Fortunately, these are all elite troops, so I've been able to do so by buying out stockpiles everywhere. Alas, there are so many lesser providers of weapons out there. I recall us starting an entire industry when we rolled out the cultivation-endowment pills. They're too small to be bound by large contracts like these. I'm afraid a buyer with enough money would have considerable sway over them.

"That aside, I've heard that there are a lot of disgruntled craftsmen in the city. They'd want nothing more than massive offers to get their workshops rolling and buy them the time they need to live out the Wang family's madness." He shook his head. "That's all speculation, of course. You're free to do whatever you like, Elder Bai."

Hearing these words from Wang Jun, Elder Bai's resolve strengthened. "I won't let you down," he said. The stooped man stood a little straighter.

"You're not working for me, Uncle Bai," Wang Jun said. "You're working for the people you want to protect. Remember that."

The older man nodded, and after a moment of hesitation, he flew down the street. No one else noticed him as he flitted by.

Wang Jun was finally alone, and the concept both pained him and reassured him. "You've never disappointed me, Uncle Bai. Don't start now." He then turned his heels and headed back toward Gold Leaf Square. Not toward the Jade Bamboo Pavilion, but toward a different destination.

"I can't say I'm surprised at your visit," a man said to Wang Jun. "But I can't say I expected it either. You're an enigma, you know. I think there's maybe a handful of people with your constitution in the entire universe."

The man was none other than Elder Zhong, the mysterious manager of the Greenwind Pavilion. Wang Jun sat at a small table on the top floor, enjoying tea the man in green-and-silver robes poured for him.

"My teacher speaks highly of you," Wang Jun said. "He says you have a finger in every plane, and a wider web of information than anyone has a right to."

"Worthless things," Elder Zhong said, brushing him off. "They're nothing compared to the darker secrets Daoist Obscurus keeps."

The fact that the man knew his master's name and remembered it spoke volumes on its own. Aside from the few disciples the man had, Elder Zhong was the first to ever mention him to Wang Jun directly.

"Now tell me," Wang Jun said, "can you get these things for me? Can you get them to me now?"

"I can," Elder Zhong said with a smile. "Though whether you can afford them is an entirely different matter. I had a kid in here who asked me for a priceless treasure the other day. Similar age, high potential like you. He thought you could just buy peak-transcendent treasures using local goods. All to refine his body, of all things. What a waste, I thought, until I noticed some deeper secrets on him."

"I sure hope it wasn't Zhou Li," Wang Jun said, frowning.

"That old geezer?" Elder Zhong said. "Naw, I only see him personally because he pays me a lot of money for the service. Otherwise, he's not worth my time."

"I see," Wang Jun said. He could only think of one other person who fit the bill, assuming they were talking about people on the Ling Nan Plane specifically. "Then tell me, will this suffice?" He passed over a black card to the man.

Elder Zhong whisked it over and whistled. "Wow. Just… Wow. How many people did you have to kill and steal from to get this much? This is more than you could loot from years on a battlefield."

"You'd be surprised by how much wealth rich men carry on their persons," Wang Jun said. "For someone good at preserving themselves like I am, that makes sense, but mere initial-core-formation cultivators? I just don't know what gives them the courage."

Elder Zhong nodded understandingly. "Money gives all sorts of courage to inferior men." He snapped his fingers, and the gray formation at the back of the room flashed. A ring appeared on it, which Elder Zhong threw over to Wang Jun. "I don't know what you're going to do with these things, though. Only darkness-aligned demons and void creatures would ever want anything like that. Smiths won't touch them, even on immortal planes."

"Then it's a good thing I'm one of the handful of people in the universe that has a use for them," Wang Jun said. "It's only the low demand that balances out the short supply and makes it possible for me to afford them."

Elder Zhong grunted. "I've had the stuff shoved in a warehouse for millennia. Though, to be honest, I thought you'd haggle more."

"I only haggle when I have something to fall back on," Wang Jun said. "What will I do if you get upset and raise the price on me?"

"Speaking of falling back," Elder Zhong said, avoiding the question. "I already spoke to another three high-potential individuals on the plane. I told them to get the hell out of here. Not a single one of them will listen to me, though, and I'm hoping you'll at least have the sense to listen. You see, there's this creature—"

"The Taotie?" Wang Jun asked. "Coming to destroy the plane? It's probably too late, and spatial portals are becoming unstable. I doubt even you have much time left."

"How did you…?" Elder Zhong shook his head. "I should expect no less from the disciple of old DO. Chaos and destruction always follow that man, so it's no wonder he was the first to know about it."

"Master?" Wang Jun said. "I doubt he'd mess with something like this."

"I didn't say he was involved, but I won't deny the possibility," Elder Zhong said. "Correlation isn't causation, but there's only so much coincidence I'm willing to tolerate. Regardless, do you want a way out?"

Wang Jun shook his head.

"Kids these days. They don't know what's good for them." He waved his hand to the door. "Be gone with you, then. I'm not staying much longer. Three or four days, tops."

"Worse comes to worst, I can always transcend," Wang Jun said, getting up from his seat and draining his cup of tea. "Transcending doesn't rely on artificial spatial passageways like you immortals do."

"I suppose it doesn't," Elder Zhong grumbled as he walked back to the spatial portal. The formation flashed, leaving Wang Jun alone in the empty room.

Chapter 14: Evergreen

The bright sun and marshy jungle weren't as beautiful as Cha Ming remembered. The green landscape, once peppered with small green-and-blue lakes, was now a grayscale caricature of the beauty he knew existed. There were still demons inhabiting those trees, and there were still humans prowling the wilderness. But now they were running, both man and beast, scrambling like frightened kittens. And he looked at them from the top of city walls that could do little to protect its inhabitants.

At the edge of his senses, Cha Ming could feel an army fighting. Dozens of soldiers fought and bled, their blood seeping into the marshy carpet beneath the treetops. Lives winked out one after another as they fought to stall the inevitable. They were glad to fight the army, for that meant not having to fight the other more frightening thing, that spot of darkness not far from them, feeding. At the very edge of his perception, Cha Ming could sense a spiritual emptiness. It was a spot of darkness that writhed and grew, expanding with every life that vanished.

"I can't believe they had the nerve to try and tame the damn thing," Cha Ming muttered. He remembered how much devastation it had brought to Bastion before they restrained it. Shaking his head, he flew down from his vantage point just above the city gates. Down below, all was chaos. Street urchins barely avoided busy shopkeepers as they piled goods into wooden crates. They were low-quality goods—things like plates and decorations that took up little space but weren't worth using spatial treasures to carry.

Everywhere he looked, people hurried, guards harassing them. The lush greenery Evergreen City prided itself on was lost in the crush of panicking people, and what hadn't been smashed had already been packed away into pots and jade boxes by fast-working herbologists.

Every second, someone finished packing and joined the long, snaking caravan making its way northeast to the northern gate of the city. They didn't just use the main gate, but side gates as well.

Fortunately, Cha Ming didn't have to walk through the busy streets. Far fewer people traveled aboveground, as most of the powerful cultivators had either run away or joined the army in the Evergreen Battlefield. From his vantage point above the buildings, the city was a fifty-mile-wide hive of activity. Even the wealthy, those with access to the best moving resources and storage treasures, were scrambling to leave. The alchemists, who resided in their tall glass tower shaped like a medicinal flask, were no exception. The tall chimney, which usually spat smoke and deadly chemicals into the skies, did no such thing today; an ordinance had been issued, and all activities not related to the evacuation were forbidden.

The only order Cha Ming saw in the nearest fifty miles was near the palace, where messengers rushed in to receive orders and bring them out to waiting soldiers. These men, weary as they were, were the only thing preventing the city from collapsing. Without them, the city would descend into total anarchy.

The guards looked up warily as Cha Ming landed between their assembled platoons and made his way to the palace. A short man in green robes greeted him at the entrance and opened the door for him. "Are you Grand Elder Cha Ming?" asked the man, who was obviously an alchemist. He was a younger man, quite possibly in his twenties, but his strength had impressively reached the peak of foundation establishment.

"I am," Cha Ming said. "What's the situation?"

"Marshal Feng asked us to receive you," the man said. "Please call this one Junior Yao. I will lead you to the central conference room where the government officials are deliberating."

Cha Ming took the deference in stride and followed the man through the corridors. It was a wonder they were able to spare even him, given how things were faring south of the city.

"Right this way," he said, taking him through the jade-pillared entrance hall of Evergreen Palace. Golden vines snaked up the pillars and formed an intricate latticework across the walls and ceiling. The floor, made of a strange brown marble with black swirls, perfectly complemented the elaborate décor. They walked through several tall hallways before arriving at a door in the east wing of the palace. The man gulped, then opened it, allowing Cha Ming into the den of lions.

"We won't make it far if things keep going on like this," one man was saying. He had a long gray beard, and like Junior Yao, he also wore green robes. "The people in the city barely have time to pack. At the rate we're retreating, we don't have more than three hours to evacuate millions of people, leaving many behind."

A middle-aged man wearing royal green robes and a golden crown answered him. Though seated at the head of the table, he lacked the authority a king usually had, but he did his best to project confidence. "I don't see how we have any other options," he said, massaging his forehead. "We're going to need to start forcing people out, whether they're ready or not. We have alchemists aplenty—I refuse to believe they'll starve if we set out now."

"We would have more time," another man in green armor said. "If only you would authorize us to attack the creature." The man was half a hand taller than Cha Ming and wore a golden sword at his waist. Like Cha Ming, he was a half-step-rune-carving cultivator. He also wore a black-and-gold cape like Feng Ming's, the traditional mark of a marshal across the continent.

"Marshal Dong, you of all people should know to heed Marshal Feng's advice," the weary king said. "He said we shouldn't fight it under any circumstance, and I don't doubt the authenticity of his words."

"But the man fought the beast for months," Marshal Dong objected. "All I want to do is stall it for one more day. If we don't buy time, at least three quarters of the people in Evergreen City will perish. That's not even counting the many villagers and farmers we'll have to leave behind."

"This..." the king said, hesitating. Another round of loud arguments broke out.

Unsure of how to insert himself into the conversation, Cha Ming looked around the room. To his surprise, he saw a familiar figure waving him over. He smiled and walked over to Jin Huang, who was seated with the king's councillors. Specifically, he was seated with the alchemists and other trade representatives, though instead of the golden badge with a cauldron they wore, he wore a black badge with a skull and crossbones.

"Jin Huang, it's nice to see you well and alive," Cha Ming said while evaluating his disciple. To his surprise, the young man's cultivation had shot to the peak of core formation. He also had a heavy aura around him that reminded Cha Ming of the poison master, Zhou Bei.

"It's good to see you, Master," Jin Huang said. "I normally skip these meetings, but I made sure to attend when I heard you were coming."

Cha Ming nodded. "It's pretty chaotic out there. What's the situation?"

"There seems to be a deadlock between the king and his advisors," Jin Huang explained. "The alchemists want to evacuate but want more time. The army thinks we should win more time, but more for the civilians rather than the alchemists and merchants. The king, on the other hand, wants to call an immediate evacuation with no packing allowed."

"That will cause a lot of panic and confusion," Cha Ming said, frowning. "Even just a few more hours to pack would calm everyone down."

Jin Huang shook his head. "The problem is that we don't have hours. The South is routing us on the battlefield. We need to be out of the city soon and moving fast."

Cha Ming nodded. He could sense the entire city with his transcendent force, and the exits from the city were all bottlenecked, and the guards had even destroyed portions of their own wall to facilitate the exodus. Despite this, it was clear that it would take at least a day for everyone to leave. Packing didn't actually matter if physically leaving would be a problem.

"I'd like to speak, but I'm not exactly sure how to interject here," Cha Ming said, looking toward the king. He and five other men were arguing, and others argued less loudly in the background. "I might have been sent here by Marshal Feng, but I don't have a shred of authority or credibility with these men." It wasn't like Mount Tai, where his Demon-Subduing Eyes would give him instant recognition. Even in the Eastern Desert, it had been Feng Ming who'd given him legitimacy.

"Oh, that's not a problem," Jin Huang said. He lifted his hand and shouted, "Everyone, I have something to say."

To Cha Ming's surprise, the man's boyish voice almost instantly silenced everyone around him. The silence spread across the room until the king himself finally nodded to Jin Huang. Everyone seemed straight-up terrified of the man, which was funny considering he was the kindest and gentlest of all his disciples.

"That is, my teacher has something to say."

Everyone looked to Cha Ming even more fearfully. Embarrassed, Cha Ming coughed lightly. "Hello, my name is Cha Ming, and I've come at the request of Marshal Feng from the Song Kingdom. I have some suggestions if you don't mind."

No one objected, and everyone paid perfect attention to him. It was like everyone here had suddenly become a group of high-performing students at their first university class.

"The first thing you need to consider," Cha Ming continued, "is that even if I destroyed the entire northern portion of your wall—which I will—it would still take a full day for everyone to evacuate.

And even if I set formation traps to delay the enemy—which I can—you'll still need a day's head start to make it to the Golden Kingdom's borders. The second thing to consider is that we need to evacuate more than people. The demons of the Evergreen Battlefield must also be evacuated to other demonic territories."

Several people frowned at that, but most kept their mouths shut. It was only Marshal Dong, who matched Cha Ming in cultivation, who dared speak up. "Respected Grand Elder, it's not that I question your judgment, but... why must the demons be evacuated, exactly? Is it not enough to evacuate our own citizens?" There were nods of agreement.

"Normally, you would be right," Cha Ming explained. "Demons like to mind their own affairs, and they don't often interfere in human matters. But you must consider the nature of the enemy you are facing. The Taotie, which you are so keen on fighting for a few hours, is growing stronger by the minute. It is far stronger than when Marshal Feng and Gong Xuandi fought it months ago. I have heard from Marshal Feng that it wreaked havoc in Bastion, and over twenty transcendents and hundreds of peak-core-formation cultivators were needed to restrain it. Tell me, is that something you are capable of? Because I'm not."

Marshal Dong shook his head. "I suppose we aren't."

"Unfortunately, the creature grows stronger with every life it takes," Cha Ming said. "The South is playing with fire, and we must prevent the creature from growing. If we do not evacuate the demons, and in turn get them to mobilize others, it won't just be this country that is lost, but the entire continent. We must accomplish both of these objectives if we are to have a chance at surviving."

"But how?" asked the king, who'd been silent until now.

"Jin Huang and I will journey to the Evergreen Battlefield and meet with a strong demon there," Cha Ming explained. "We will get him to mobilize his forces and harass the Southern army and somehow distract the Taotie. Meanwhile, you will use all your remaining troops, destroy your city walls, and get everyone moving as quickly as possible. We'll buy you the time you need, but you must be swift and decisive. Save who you can and save what you can. Burn the rest. Don't dare leave anything to the enemy, because anything we leave behind can and will be used against us on the battlefield."

A grim silence ensued. Then, one after another, the officials began speaking. "We can move key equipment in the top-grade laboratories and twenty percent of lower-level equipment," one of the alchemists said. "What ingredients don't fit in movable storage, we can blend in an incendiary mixture that will detonate when enemy troops enter the city."

"There's no need for you to destroy the wall, Grand Elder," another man said. He was clearly a geomancer. "We'll collapse the northeast wall by shifting the earth, and we'll rig the rest of it to collapse easily when the South arrives to buy us time."

"There's no need for Grand Elder Cha Ming to set up formation traps, either," a woman added. She wore a formation-master medallion from Haijing. "We'll take care of these low-level things using excess formation flags."

"We can start forcibly removing people from the city," Marshal Dong agreed. "But we'll need the geomancers to break some unneeded structures. Meanwhile, I'll take my elites that aren't needed for the evacuation and reinforce our army."

One after another, people chipped in where they could. Seeing that everything was in motion, Cha Ming and Jin Huang left the meeting room.

"Who knew you had so much clout in this city?" Cha Ming said to Jin Huang.

Jin Huang shrugged. "I may have bullied my way back into the city after they tried extorting me. Something about being a walking poison calamity makes people treat you with a lot of respect."

"I could totally destroy a city within a few minutes," Cha Ming muttered.

"Yes, you could, but how painful would it be?" Jin Huang asked.

Cha Ming considered that, then was forced to agree with Jin Huang. Agony was definitely an important factor to consider when deciding who to antagonize.

"So, what's the plan?" Jin Huang asked.

"I haven't figured out that part yet," Cha Ming said. "I guess it depends on how strong and how fast your living poisons are."

"Oh, I wouldn't worry about that," Jin Huang said cheerfully. "We're going to the Evergreen Battlefield, with swamps and poisons aplenty. You couldn't find a better place for me to fight."

"Tell me more," Cha Ming said, and together, they flew out of the palace toward their destination.

Chapter 15:
Five Poisonous Monarchs

"Here is good," Jin Huang said, flying down to where a large number of enemy troops had assembled. He proceeded not to the troops themselves but to a nearby stream. There, the young man extended his arm, releasing thousands of tiny green, blue, and brown dots into the pool, which immediately changed to match their colors. The leaves of the plant life around the pool also began to change; their surfaces developed a slick coating of blues and browns that made even Cha Ming, a half-step-blood-awakening cultivator feel danger.

"You're confident this will buy us time?" Cha Ming asked, following him as he proceeded to another group of advancing troops. He'd originally been planning on going directly to the demons, but Jin Huang had insisted on coming here first.

Jin Huang nodded. "If we get the demons to help, whatever we do will be loud and draw attention. It's best to give my friends some time to spread first before we give them an opening to strike."

Cha Ming sweated a little inside as he realized the "friends" Jin Huang was talking about were, in fact, poisons. Since he couldn't help the younger man with his task, he kept a lookout with his transcendent force. Even blind, he could see the subtle changes affecting the nearby land, enhancing its lethality without alerting nearby troops. He maintained the camouflage formation he'd erected, though he noticed that it was growing weaker the deeper into the jungle they went. Something was obstructing it, diminishing its usefulness.

Perhaps ten miles to the south, Southern forces clashed with the army. Marshal Dong had joined them, significantly easing their burden and casualties. He was a swift blur that fought against a growing mass of black tentacles and horns and mouths that tried to eat everything they touched. With every blow they exchanged, the creature paused for a half second, buying time for his forces to execute their strategic retreat.

Like this, Cha Ming and Jin Huang continued advancing toward their enemies. They stopped three miles away from the battle, carefully sowing poisons in many different places. Though doing so was risky, the trap would strike at the enemy's back lines when instructed. These living poisons, as Jin Huang called them, were intelligent. The tiny spots were deadly and would follow instructions to the letter. They were even potent enough to damage Cha Ming, though they were far from strong enough to be able to kill him.

After skimming the edge of the enemy encampment, he and Jin Huang doubled back and proceeded deeper into demon territory, which they'd sidestepped thus far. All sorts of creatures began appearing—snakes, frogs, crocodiles, and other swamp-dwelling demons. Each one lay in wait for unsuspecting prey; they were perfectly suited to their environment, which, as far as Cha Ming understood, was filled with terrible poisons and diseases, and bogs that could suffocate the life out of even the strongest men on the continent. It was a place no sane man would enter, yet here he was, taking his youngest apprentice with him.

The farther they traveled, the stronger the swamp creatures grew. Though they glared angrily at the duo and seemed to want nothing more than to tear them apart, they shrank back fearfully when they came too close for comfort. At first, Cha Ming thought they were frightened off by his powerful aura. But soon, he realized he was mistaken. They weren't shrinking back from him, a half-step transcendent, but Jin Huang, a much weaker cultivator. They were frightened by his poisons, which seemed to grow stronger the deeper they went.

They flew another two miles unimpeded before the trees parted, revealing a small lake nestled in the bosom of the forest. The water wasn't blue like most lakes, nor was it green. Instead, it was sickly iridescent brown, and a poisonous cloud clung to the surface of the water where lesser demons didn't dare travel. Larger carcasses of powerful demons lay decomposing there, a terrible warning for any who dared think of trespassing.

Submerged in that lake was Gua. The giant toad sat cross-legged in a swamp so poisonous Cha Ming didn't dare touch its waters. Surrounding him were five other massive demons—a scorpion, a spider, a snake, a centipede, and a toad like Gua. Each one was a powerful peak-core-formation demon. A natural formation glowed around them as they each drew from the power of the lake.

"I don't think they're helping him," Cha Ming said, hesitating. "I think they're fighting him."

Jin Huang nodded gravely. "The poisons in the area are confused and uncertain. They're unwilling to favor either one of the monarchs." He cocked his ear and nodded. "They say it was this way when there were five. With six, their choice is even more difficult."

"Hmm..." Cha Ming thought for a moment before flying above the lake. Jin Huang followed him and caused the poisons to part. They flew until they were only a few feet from Gua's face. "Gua, it's me."

Hearing his words, Gua opened one eye. He glared at Cha Ming, then scowled. *Come here to gloat, have you?*

Cha Ming shrugged. "Silverwing and Mr. Mountain succeeded. I expected you to be done here, but I guess I overestimated you." He shook his head. "Just wait until they find out. They'll laugh their heads off."

What do you want? Gua asked grumpily.

Cha Ming smiled. "There's an army coming. Can you feel them?"

Gua nodded lightly. *It's what I told these five geezers. I told them a big threat was coming, but noooo, they wouldn't listen. Do you have any idea how long they've been fighting here?*

Cha Ming shook his head.

Nine hundred years! Nine hundred bloody years fighting over this swamp. Isn't that crazy?

"And you decided to be the sixth?" Cha Ming asked. "Anyway, you should know about the creature, the Taotie." Gua's expression darkened. "You know you can't stay here much longer. You have to evacuate."

We all need to move, Gua agreed. *Which is exactly what I told these five geezers.*

"To complicate things, the creature is backed up by an army, speeding it up," Cha Ming said. "What's worse, there are humans to the northeast. They need time to evacuate. We'll help you win this swamp, but I need your help fighting the army to buy the humans time."

Gua licked his lips. *I can buy you three hours.*

"Two days," Cha Ming said. "And you won't be alone. I'll help you fight them."

One, Gua shot back, glancing at the other demons, who'd slowly begun opening their eyes. *No more than one.*

"This isn't a negotiation," Cha Ming said. "Everyone is doing their part. In the east, Silverwing is rallying demon monarchs against a fiend whisperer. In the center of the continent, Mr. Mountain is reinforcing the North–South wall. This is something everyone needs to contribute to. You can't just fight on the sidelines."

Gua hesitated. He looked to the snake beside him, who slithered menacingly. *Fine. I'll do it. If only to teach this old thing a lesson.*

Cha Ming nodded and summoned the Clear Sky Staff. His figure flashed behind the snake and crashed against its skull. To his surprise, however, the staff didn't even touch the snake's skin. Instead, he struck a thick poisonous liquid. The water in the lake below had come to the creature's aid, forming a barrier that even the Clear Sky Staff couldn't part.

If it was as easy as beating them up, I'd have done it ages ago, Gua said with a snort. *The swamp protects them. You're going to need to convince them to give up somehow. Otherwise, it's impossible to win against them.*

Cha Ming frowned. The situation here was very different than Silverwing's. Near the Eastern Desert, he only had one competitor and had gotten him to submit. Mr. Mountain, on the other hand, had no competition, and only he was perfectly suited to the mountainous energy. Here, unfortunately, there were no less than five opponents. Further, they were all fully harmonized with the land around them, likely due to the hundreds of years they'd spent soaking inside the lake.

Should I cook the frog? Cha Ming thought. *I could heat the water until he's nothing more than frog soup.* Or would that even work? His cloaking formation was basically useless near the lake, which meant that he likely couldn't draw on combat formations to move him. Curious about what would happen, Cha Ming extended his flame pseudo-domain to his hand, which he extended toward the uncaring snake. The moment his hand was about to touch the snake, the poisonous water shot up. It formed a thin film around it, protecting it from his intrusion.

Frustrated, Cha Ming opened his eyes. They burned painfully as his Demon-Subduing, Devil-Sealing, and Spirit-Banishing Intents washed over the crowd of demons, weakening them. Unfortunately, he couldn't focus his power on any one of them. It washed over all of them, communally weakening all six, Gua included.

"Master, may I try something?" Jin Huang asked.

"We've got nothing to lose," Cha Ming muttered, pulling his hand back and letting the lake waters recede. "What did you have in mind?"

"I was thinking about your formation earlier," Jin Huang said. "I think the reason it failed was because it didn't fit the environment. The qi it harnessed was too balanced, while this place is imbalanced. The qi is allocated, unlike the heaven and earth energies formations often manipulate."

"I suspect you're right," Cha Ming said. "Unfortunately, it seems even pseudo-domains can't help us. No formation I create will be able to move them."

"Then my suggestion isn't to fight with the swamp, but to work with it," Jin Huang said. "Let me give it a try."

Cha Ming stepped back and looked on in interest. Jin Huang stepped toward the snake, but instead of unleashing an attack like Cha Ming had, he held out his sleeve. Tens of thousands of small poisonous dots traveled out and floated toward the snake. As they approached it, the poisonous lake water responded to shield it, but to Cha Ming's surprise, it pulled back and let the poison through. The snake shivered as the dots entered its body.

Jin Huang nodded in satisfaction. "I thought so. The water is poisonous, so it's fine with any poisonous creatures. That includes living poisons."

"So, you can kill this snake?" Cha Ming asked. "Or at least knock it out?"

"Heavens, no," Jin Huang said. "What I did was just a shove. If there's a little brawling in the schoolyard, teachers won't bother interfering. If I really tried to kill or incapacitate him, the swamp would shut me down."

"Then how are you planning to make him submit?" Cha Ming asked.

"You remember what I said about painful deaths?" Jin Huang asked. Cha Ming nodded. "Well, it's a similar concept. Let's just say I can make this snake's life extremely painful. As a demon, he'll survive mostly anything I throw at him, but will he want to?"

As they were speaking, the snake was looking left to right wildly. It shivered again as Jin Huang's poisons began attacking it and let out a soft moan soon after.

It's working! Gua said, opening his eyes excitedly. *You're breaking its concentration!*

"I'll need time," Jin Huang said, sitting cross-legged in midair next to the snake. "By the time I'm done, we'll be the best of friends." He patted the snake's head for good measure. The lake waters didn't block him but welcomed him like its dearest friend. Cha Ming could swear he saw the snake sweating.

To the south, the Southern army was swiftly approaching. The Taotie was giving Evergreen's army a hard time, with losses growing with each passing second. "I'll buy you as much time as I can," Cha Ming said, flying up.

"Wait!" Jin Huang yelled.

Cha Ming turned back to Jin Huang and saw a soft green-and-blue mist floating in the wind. It was much thicker than the batches he'd previously released. "These are my friends. Why don't you spread them around while you're there?"

Friends? Cha Ming thought, curiously observing the small creatures as they flew around his body and plunged beneath his robes. He reached out to them, and to his surprise, he heard voices.

Is it time? a voice asked.

Are the others ready? another asked.

Soon, Cha Ming said, uncertain if they could hear him. That answer seemed to satisfy the group of living poisons, and the chattering stopped. Shrugging, he flew two miles before stopping near a group of scouts. They traveled through trees, scaring away demons and revealing poisonous obstacles for their main forces.

One of the unlucky scouts met an untimely demise. He walked behind a tree and was destroyed by a vicious black palm. An identical-looking man walked back the way he'd come and made his way back toward his superior. He'd discovered a threat, and it was imperative that they stopped to investigate it.

"You lot are, without a doubt, the saddest group of scouts I have ever had to manage," a sergeant named Lin Ba barked to a group of four soldiers. Three of them stood at attention, eyes straight, but one of them held his eyes downcast. He looked guilty through and through, a perfect specimen in need of some punishment. The sergeant paused in front of him and shook his head in disgust. "Who the hell gave you the gall to stop us?"

The three straight-backed soldiers didn't answer. They waited for the trembling third to lift his head up and speak. "It was my fault, sir," the soldier said. "I thought I'd spotted a king-level beast."

"A king-level beast," the sergeant said flatly. "Are you sure it wasn't just your own shadow?" Many nearby soldiers snickered, drawing a glare from the sergeant. Now wasn't the time for levity. Their work here was more important than any of them realized.

"I'm not sure, sir," the soldier said, eyes still down. "It was my mistake, and I accept responsibility." The fact that his sergeant was the one who'd ordered the search was irrelevant. If he didn't take a dive for the team, his fate would be far, far worse.

"You'd better think twice before you do something so foolish again," the scout sergeant said. "Report to the latrines."

"Yes, sir," the scout said. He bowed rapidly and made his way to the back, where a temporary camp had been set up. He wasted no time and approached an old one-eyed man, who scowled when he saw him.

"What did you do this time, Li?" the man said, shaking his head as he picked his teeth. "Mustn't have been too bad. People don't often get latrine duty every day of the week."

He was right, Li knew. Punishments were usually a lot heavier. That was the main reason he volunteered to be the fall man so often. He wasn't strong or smart, but no man took punishment better than Yijing Li.

"Shoveling or mucking?" the old man asked.

"Shoveling," Li answered. Too quickly, he realized.

"Mucking it is," the old man said, spitting out his toothpick.

Li groaned as he dragged his feet to a large wheelbarrow. He took it over to a nearby pile of excrement. There weren't just soldiers in the army, after all, but enslaved demons aplenty.

Li gagged as he made his way to a stinking pile. An equally miserable man ran over when he got there, shovel in hand. He scooped the poop into the wheelbarrow Li would eventually take to the incinerator. No one, friend or foe, wanted feces on their territory.

Is here good? Li asked. Some answered affirmatively and moved into the pile of excrement. Others remained. Excrement wasn't well suited to them.

Once the barrow was full, Li rolled it to a large fire. He dumped the load into the fire, and to his surprise, he heard voices again.

Here, they said.

In the fire? Li asked. A few wisps of poison surged into the incinerator flames, changing their color in the process. This poison, it seemed, liked heat and combustion. The many poisons Jin Huang had given him each drew on different aspects of the five elements. They were similar to his poetic talismans and their dual nature. Poisons weren't just made of wood and water—they stemmed from all of creation.

Seeing he could do nothing else around here, Li—or Cha Ming—turned into a mouse. He crawled through camp, eventually finding the quartermaster's stores. There, he crawled through a formation trap that had been specially designed for vermin like him and released another round of poison.

"Gotcha," a voice said, slapping down a box. Cha Ming squeaked in fear as a mouse should, and the one who'd caught him lifted him to eye level. The middle-aged man wore robes instead of armor, and only a few stray teeth still hung in his mouth. "You thought you could steal from me, did ya?"

Startled, Cha Ming burst out of the box. He avoided a demonic crow watching overhead and ducked into a tent where a captain was dressing down sergeants. To his surprise, Sergeant Lin Ba was one of them. Having his soldier take a fall apparently wasn't enough to avoid all punishment. He moved to leave the tent, but as he did, a chill washed over him. He reached out with his soul force, and to his surprise, someone reached back.

That's not supposed to be able to happen, Cha Ming sent mentally to Sun Wukong, who was resting in the Clear Sky Brush.

Looks like you're unlucky, Sun Wukong replied. *A strong medium's latched on to you.*

Just what he needed. Cha Ming turned into a house cat and trotted between legs. He turned into a captain when other heads were turned and walked in a different direction. A few tents later, he was an alchemist, a hunched-over man carrying a large cauldron to his laboratory. Unfortunately, his actions seemed to have little effect on the presence locking on to him. In fact, they seemed to encourage its attention and draw it closer.

Run, Sun Wukong sent. He didn't have to say it twice. Cha Ming jumped up from the ground, and a giant ghostly palm struck down where he'd been just been. The palm killed half a dozen men and drew the attention of hundreds more.

"Looks like my cover's blown," he muttered. Then, he erupted in violence.

Combat sigils surged out, burning everyone within a hundred feet, and he swung the Clear Sky Pillar, clearing swaths of troops that managed to avoid the flames in the process. Sure as rain, the enemy's elite forces all darted out of their tents. They threw swords at Cha Ming that he deflected with ease and pulled out spears, sabers, and staves not much different from the staff he wielded.

If you have a plan, now's the time to act on it, Cha Ming said. The poisons on him pulsed in response, and to his surprise, they dove into the ground. Black tendrils shot out in every direction as Cha Ming fled from the center to avoid being encircled.

A scythe on a chain flew past Cha Ming, threatening to cut and inject him with a lethal poison. To answer, he covered his hand in a golden pseudo-domain and grabbed the core treasure, throwing it back at the attacker, then ducked as a swordsman struck through the air above him three times in succession. Cha Ming kicked off from another man, sending himself hurtling toward a fat one who threw a meaty fist at him. In response, a staff appeared in his hand and pierced forward with Origin Strike, destroying the hand and the arm attached to it, reducing it to formless gray mist.

Below him, troops of all kinds were amassing together. They

looked up at the spectacle but were powerless to stop a powerful cultivator like Cha Ming. They weren't here to fight decisive battles but to act as cannon fodder, threats, or distractions. Ultimately, they were here to hold ground and subjugate the population in any territories they claimed.

Four more men joined the brawl, forcing Cha Ming to retract his combat sigils. They formed a prison of ice around two of the new arrivals, strong blood masters bearing wicked curved blades. He struck out with Splitting Heaven and Earth, destroying weapons that tried to block and cutting two core-formation cultivators apart. The ice prison broke, releasing his two opponents. Six more flew up and completed their encirclement.

"You're outmatched, Grand Elder," said a man in black armor, clearly the leader of the enemy forces, as he appeared just outside the six. "Leave now or die."

The offer surprised Cha Ming, but he soon realized the reason for it. If they fought here, his forces would be devastated unless a transcendent interfered.

"What if don't want to?" Cha Ming asked innocently. "I was just walking around peacefully before a spirit medium attacked me."

"I'm sure it was all a misunderstanding," the enemy marshal said.

"I'm sure," Cha Ming agreed. Endless moments passed as enemy reinforcements closed in on their encirclement. He wasn't waiting to bargain, but rather to achieve a specific goal.

Found him, Sun Wukong said, appearing outside the Clear Sky Brush and pointing. Cha Ming followed his ghostly finger's direction and saw his target—a spindly, ghostly man hidden behind a protective formation.

Cha Ming wasted no time. His combat formations formed a spear that pierced through his encirclement and widened, forcing enemies out of his way. He used the power of wind and lightning, the weight manipulation in his bones, and his pseudo-domain to cut through the air as quickly as possible. Then, just a moment before reaching his target, he opened his eyes. Devil-Subduing, Demon-Sealing, and Spirit-Banishing Intents oozed out around him, surrounding the spirit medium with a sea of devastating energy. A single Origin Strike took him out, and the Spirit-Banishing Intent finished off his corrupted soul. Then talismans exploded all around Cha Ming, reducing the area around him to rubble.

Guess where I am, Cha Ming called out mentally to those floating above. They looked around and didn't see Cha Ming. Surprised soldiers helped their injured companions recover from the blast.

Clap. Clap. Clap.

The black-armored leader chuckled as he gazed down at his soldiers. "I see you can disguise yourself," the marshal said. "Very resourceful, and very difficult. I confess, without our medium, we won't be able to find you easily."

Then, to Cha Ming's surprise, he slashed out with his spear. A wave of gold flew out and struck a tenth of the wounded soldiers, killing them before their companions could reach them.

"Unfortunately for you, you *overestimated* the value of soldiers and underestimated how much I want you dead. Further..."

A gray light appeared beside him and materialized into an old hunchbacked man with a redwood cane. Space around the man shattered and distorted with his appearance, and the heavens brewed up a storm in response. "It's not just me who wants to kill you. Let's see if you can survive a transcendent head-on."

He swung his spear again, and more men died. All but a single man, Cha Ming, glaring up defiantly with a staff in hand.

"Listen, things will be a lot easier if you just cooperate," Jin Huang said to the half-submerged scorpion convulsing in the lake. "Think about it. Snake and toad have already given up. It's only a matter of time until the pain gets to you."

The scorpion, confident in his strength, stubbornly clung for dear life as the poisons rampaged through his body. As the waters of the lake came up to support him, Jin Huang eased up. Torture was an art, not a science.

I'll never give in to you, human, the scorpion hissed. It struck out with a bright-red stinger, forcing Jin Huang to dodge.

Jin Huang responded by summoning a living poison cloud and catching it. He appeared beside the instrument of poisonous death and used his finger to wipe a glob of glowing poison off it, then put said glob of poison in his mouth. Then, just like a gourmet, he licked his lips and dove in for more.

"It's not like it's me you're giving in to," Jin Huang insisted, chasing after the stinger. "It's more like you'd be giving up to the insufferably ugly toad. Just like the others did." The serpent and the toad, who were sitting obediently to the side, nodded profusely. The frustrated scorpion moved to sting Jin Huang again but abruptly pulled back when it remembered that the young man regarded his deadliest weapon as candy.

"I'll tell you what," Jin Huang said. "I offered a carrot to the others, and I can do the same for you." The scorpion paused as it considered. "To them, I offered some poison companions. They were lonely, that's understandable. Within you, on the other hand, I sense great strength. So I'll tell you what, I'll awaken your strength, and if I can make your bloodline increase by a tier, you'll promise to throw your support behind good ole Gua, and we'll be done here. What do you say?" The scorpion paused. Then, shivering as it remembered the pain from before, nodded. "All right, hold still."

Jin Huang activated the poisons again. The scorpion roared in pain. *You promised!* it yelled. *You promised us!*

"I promised," Jin Huang said, nodding. "Just bear with it for a while."

The scorpion fought with everything it had, and the snake and the toad did nothing to stop Jin Huang. The ignored the writhing frenemy they'd spent a full nine hundred years with. Minutes passed as the scorpion writhed, but unlike before, the lake didn't interfere.

As the twitching slowed, the scorpion was close to dying, and Jin Huang flicked his sleeve. Another poison flew out. It was a much darker green than the scorpion's exoskeleton, and it shimmered with an oily sheen that matched the lake the scorpion was bathing in. The poison dove into the scorpion monarch, and as it did, the deep-brown poison he'd injected it with in the first place returned to Jin Huang. The young man, who'd gone pale from sending out the dark-green poison, regained a bit of a color as he consumed it.

Finally, the scorpion twitched one last time. Then it fell still. The snake slithered over to where his body lay and nudged it with its head. *You promisssed him,* the snake said. *Why did you break your promisssssse?*

"Break it?" Jin Huang asked. "When did I break it?"

The scorpion shivered, and suddenly its exoskeleton to began to crack. A thin layer peeled off as the scorpion, who had technically been dead for three seconds, came back to life. It glowed deep green, the same green color as Jin Huang had sent into him. No poison left to return to the younger man this time. The poison belonged to the scorpion now, who was significantly more powerful for it.

As agreed, I yield my portion to the obscenely ugly toad, the scorpion said. It floated up from the lake, and the demonic energy flowed toward Gua. At long last, the balance was fully tilted. Seeing no reason to resist any longer, the horrendous hairy spider and the blue centipede floated up and prostrated themselves.

It's Gua time, baby! Gua shouted as the poisonous lake's power poured into him. Above him, a single character representing "swamp" appeared. As his strength soared, Gua flicked out his fan and struck a daring pose. *How do I look?*

"Wonderful, Uncle Gua, wonderful," Jin Huang said. "But what about the evacuation? I can feel my poisons wreaking havoc on the enemy forces."

At that moment, Cha Ming appeared, bloody and bruised. "I'm sorry, I can't hold them off any longer. A transcendent is after my skin, and I was only able to escape because Jin Huang's poisons started destroying their army, and…" Then, confused, he looked toward Gua. "Well, that was fast."

I'm stylishly early. What can I say? Gua said. He swung his fan again, and this time, the swamp, which the five poisonous monarchs had been fighting over for ages, swirled around Gua. It surged toward his mark, which began to glow brightly. Then it transformed into a mist that hung in the air. Millions of creatures in the swamp and the surrounding jungle floated to Gua and dove into the swamp.

Everyone, there's an ugly monster knocking on our door. We're moving. The monarchs floated up beside him and nodded. In the distance, they could see that the South had finally coaxed the Taotie into abandoning its pursuit of lesser prey and turned it back toward the retreating Northern forces. The Evergreen Kingdom's soldiers were dying, and so were True North Country's soldiers. All in a bid to buy them as much time as possible.

"We need two days' worth of time," Cha Ming said. "But I have no idea how we'll do that against this creature. The Taotie has grown stronger since the last time I saw it. Now it barely gets fazed when the Evergreen Kingdom's marshal strikes it."

Amateur, Gua said, snorting as he flicked his sleeve. *To stop a dog, you don't need to hurt it. You just need to hurt its owner and it'll stay at home for days with him.* Gua's eyes narrowed and focused on where Cha Ming had been causing havoc. The troops were just beginning to form ranks again. It seemed they'd recovered from Jin Huang's Poison Nova, the self-destruction of living poisons to inflict maximum short-term damage.

Let's hurt them badly this time, what do you say? Hold my fan. He tossed his fan to Jin Huang, who caught the core treasure. Then, to their amazement, Gua charged straight at the enemy transcendent. The five poison monarchs charged alongside him.

"To bait a bear, carry food, I guess," Cha Ming said. He flew after Gua and shot toward the transcendent. They didn't have long before the Taotie arrived, but by then, their advance forces would be a skeleton crew. They'd have no choice but to stop for reinforcements.

Chapter 16: Understanding

Daytime in Gold Leaf City was a time for family. It was a time for peace and business, for rest and relaxation. Despite the undercurrents in the city, the inhabitants still went about with increased fervor. They played in Central Square with their families, enjoying the warm weather granted by the clear skies and hot sun and drank cold drinks they could purchase just outside the square proper.

Daytime was a time for business, though some business was best done at night. As such, it was a curious sight when Wang Jun, prime director of the Wang family, entered the Red Dust Pavilion at high noon. Mistresses who had either been cleaning, resting, or preparing for the upcoming evening, scrambled to greet the man at the entrance.

"Kindly wait here, esteemed guest," one of them said politely. He smiled and obliged them, sitting down in their well-decorated lobby, enjoying leftover snacks from the night before as he waited for tea to brew.

It took a few minutes for a small group to finally come down and greet him. Bai Ling, their chief tactician and wonderfully competent *Angels and Devils* player was in her full Red Dust Mistress regalia, phoenix coronet included. As expected, she'd taken on Hong Xin's mantle after her resignation. By her sides were Ling Fei, an ex-vice-head of the Icy Heart Pavilion, and Ji Bingxue, one of Hong Xin's old companions.

"I'm happy you could take the time during this busy day," Wang Jun said, clasping his hands and bowing lightly.

"The days are hardly busy for us," Bai Ling said, leading the way to their best VIP room. "I'm sure you and everyone in the city knows that."

"I wasn't talking about *your* business in particular," Wang Jun said.

"I wasn't either," Bai Ling replied. It was a soft jab at the city's deadlocked trade and paralyzed economy. Likely, this had affected the Red Dust Pavilion's income, as they'd maintained a neutral position in the entire debacle thus far. The Red Dust Mistress pushed a door open for Wang Jun, revealing an assortment of snacks and dishes that had somehow been prepared during his short wait.

"I suppose we haven't been silent about our intentions," Wang Jun said, taking a sip of tea after it was poured for him. He nodded in satisfaction. Hong Xin, despite all her good intentions, had never been good at brewing tea. Bai Ling, on the other hand, took it up as a serious hobby, as businessmen and businesswomen often did.

"If I'm to use a metaphor to describe the Wang family's actions, I'd say you've been as silent as a burglar ransacking a house of glass in a busy neighborhood in broad daylight," Bai Ling said, drawing her lips into a line. "You know that even if you manage to find something in that house, the guards will catch you, and the entire town will know who you are."

"A fisherman must use a worm on his hook when fishing, just as a man must make a ruckus when pretending to be a burglar," Wang Jun replied. "Otherwise, how will people see him for what they think he is?"

"I know why you're here," Bai Ling said, sighing as she topped up his tea. "No need to beat around the bush. You want us to join you in your efforts, despite us knowing full well that you're cooperating with the Spirit Temple, those we fought so hard to extricate ourselves from. What exactly made you think we'd be amenable to this?"

Wang Jun shrugged. "Survival, I suppose. Though that's only half the reason I'm here."

"Without sugar to make the medicine go down, you can be sure that the answer is no," Bai Ling said. "And even with sugar, we still know it's not medicine, but poison. We're not soft persimmons, ripe fruit just waiting to be squeezed."

"Then it's a good thing I wasn't shopping for fruit, but strong independent women," Wang Jun said. He looked to her two attendants. "Could we have some time alone? I promise to behave and not do anything unseemly to your headmistress."

"I strongly advise against this," said Ling Fei, who'd been silent until now. "The man is dangerous, and his reputation of late is less than stellar."

"Peace, Ling Fei," Bai Ling said. "Prime Director Wang and I have an understanding. Ji Bingxue, could you fetch the board before you leave?"

The woman nodded and retrieved a thick box with four short legs that had been tucked into the lower part of a shelf. She also placed two bowls of stones beside it before leading the suspicious Ling Fei out of the room.

"She's a keeper, that one," Wang Jun said, playing first. "It's good to have aides willing to contradict you. I've only ever had two such people in my life, and I have no idea what I'd do without them."

"I used to be that person," Bai Ling said. "For all the good that did her." As always, she assumed Wang Jun knew a great deal more than he let on. Usually, that was a good tactic to confirm your opponent's knowledge. In this case, however, it was just convenient.

Their game was a fast one, with neither of them giving each other time to think. They progressed through the early game, claiming territory, and the middle game, waging fierce battles but never deciding them. This continued until the endgame, where Wang Jun started a ko fight for life in his corner. Neither of them had spoken during the entire game.

"Your suspicions were right all along," Wang Jun finally said as he placed a stone. "I was the one who did it." He responded to one of her threats and passed the turn.

"If you're willing to admit it, there must be more to the story," Bai Ling said, returning ko. "What was it—did you misjudge the situation? You did not grasp the full intricacies of the city's politics, and the strength of the Spirit Temple?"

"It was lack of over oversight, actually," Wang Jun said. "A minion of mine, for which I'm fully responsible, carried tasks out without my authorization. Unfortunately, he reports only to me; I can't escape blame for what happened."

"It provided a good opportunity," Bai Ling said, continuing her attack on his precarious groups. "Unfortunately, it came at a great cost. If I could turn back time to avoid paying it, I would."

"Hindsight is the most accurate vision humans are gifted with," Wang Jun said wistfully. "Both of us didn't anticipate this consequence, and if we didn't, who would have? You did your best to protect her. You didn't put up a shred of resistance when Mistress Huang accompanied her into retirement."

Bai Ling nodded. "It seems we're both responsible for her death, then, in a way. And we both lost something dear to us. I, a friend, and you, a lover."

"No," Wang Jun said. "You lost a friend, but I gained a vulnerable family member." Bai Ling looked up sharply. "Or did you think I'd change so quickly for something other than family?"

Bai Ling hesitated a moment, composing herself before asking. "Is she safe?"

Wang Jun shook his head. "I'm afraid I can't speak much about this. My negligence could make things very difficult. So here I am, asking for your support, all to protect the woman I love. Ironic, isn't it? Given how much trouble she went through to fight these people."

"Ironic indeed," Bai Ling said, continuing the game. They fought for some time, but ultimately, Wang Jun had more threats. He saved his group, prompting Bai Ling to start another fight elsewhere.

They continued playing for some time until the situation reversed. Now, Bai Ling started a fight of her own, forcing Wang Jun to find weaknesses in her position. The woman, who usually played to lose, was fighting tooth and nail to destroy him. To date, it was the first game in which they'd actually played seriously. There was a subconscious battle raging between both expert players, a war of wits between two schemers whose decade-long plans had been tossed to the wayside.

"You know she wouldn't like what you're doing," Bai Ling said, ignoring one of his threats and continuing to defend her beleaguered group. "You know she'd tell you it wasn't worth it."

"I know that because I hear those words every day," Wang Jun said. "But unfortunately, without different circumstances, I have no choice in the matter. I'm trapped, Bai Ling. I'm sinking in an ocean with chains wrapped around my hands and feet and weights at my ankles, and there are very few people in this city— No, on this continent, who will help me."

"And you want me to be one of those people," Bai Ling said, raising an eyebrow. "Despite what we went through all those years ago."

"Heavens, no," Wang Jun said. "I want you to join me in an ultimate betrayal: overthrowing the currents of power in this kingdom and tilting the scales in my family's favor." He made another threat, which Bai Ling decided to ignore, defending her group again. In compensation for the loss, he captured a group of stones for ten or so points. Now, neither of them had many threats remaining on the board, and they'd need them for the final struggle for the center they'd been putting off until the very end. There, he would be on the defensive. There was a group there he needed to protect at all costs, and if he didn't, he would lose the match.

"Assuming I decide to entertain you," Bai Ling said. "I would throw my support behind you and not anyone else."

"I'm afraid that isn't in my power," Wang Jun said, retrieving a stack of black papers as he continued his defense. He also took out a green jade stamp, though unlike most stamps, this one was surrounded in a subtle cloud of black shadows. "I've been instructed to stamp any contracts with this specific stamp. It's a special stamp, and I'm afraid I can't deviate from this order."

Bai Ling frowned. "I can't say I've ever seen a stamp like this."

"You haven't," Wang Jun said. "It's one of a kind, and it contains the blood of the leaders of my family. Not my blood, of course. They wouldn't trust me with that. Regardless, it's this seal I've been using for all my recruitment activities."

"I see," Bai Ling said, realizing something. "Then if it's this seal, I think I can agree to your proposal."

"Then I'm glad," Wang Jun said. He began stamping contract after contract with the shadowy seal, leaving the Wang family's imprint on each one. Signing on to these employment contracts would bind the Red Dust Pavilion to the Wang family's leadership, and it ran seven levels down, making it very difficult to escape the contract even if Wang Ling and Patriarch Wuling died.

The seal left a shadowy mark, though the shadows disappeared as the green ink dried. And with each paper he stamped, they played a move, poking at each other's weaknesses, tightening the noose around Wang Jun's center group.

"You sure like to gamble," Bai Ling said, eyeing the group. "If you secure this position, you'll win a landslide victory, and if you don't, you'll lose by a landslide as well. Is it worth the risk, playing such a dangerous game, when you can win by half a point?"

"Maybe it isn't," Wang Jun said softly. "In my experience, however, winning by a half point is hardly satisfying. Only big victories can be savored for an entire lifetime." He tapped his hand on the side of the table, indicating it was her turn to play. "I pass. I'm afraid I can't bear to continue this battle."

"Then let's call it a draw this time," Bai Ling said. "A draw after the many wins I've given you."

"I earned those wins fair and square," Wang Jun said with a grin. "Just like you earned your losses."

"I suppose we've all gotten what we've deserved," Bai Ling said. "Ladies, please come back in."

At her command, Ji Bingxue and Li Fei reentered the room. They glanced at the black contracts warily.

"After much discussion with Wang Jun, I've decided that it's in our best interest to throw our support behind the Wang family."

"What?" Ji Bingxue exclaimed. "How could you possibly think that? After what the Spirit Temple did to us? To her?"

"There are reasons behind this, reasons which, unfortunately, I can't tell you," Bai Ling said. "Regardless of whether you agree or not, I'm following through with it." She bit her thumb and pressed it against one of the black contracts. A shadowy employment mark appeared on her arm. "I trust Wang Jun. If you desire for me to relinquish my leadership, I will do so. Otherwise, I expect you to follow me."

Ji Bingxue eyed Bai Ling. "Are you sure. One hundred percent sure?"

"I've already staked my life on it, Vice-Mistress Ji," Bai Ling said. "Are you with me?"

The woman hesitated, then pressed her thumb against the sheet. Then, after much grumbling, Ling Fei followed.

"I won't disappoint you, ladies," Wang Jun said. "Or rather, if I do, I'll be the first one taking a trip to the Yellow River."

"I'm not afraid you'll disappoint me," Bai Ling said. "I'm just afraid you'll disappoint those closest to you."

Understanding reached, the three women summoned their members for a mass signing. Though hesitant, they followed through with Bai Ling's decision one after another. Work complete, Wang Jun gathered the contracts and returned to the Wang family mansion.

It was time for the most painful part of the entire plan.

Hong Xin's mood sank when she heard news of Bai Ling's capitulation. All hope she'd held for the future of the Red Dust Pavilion shattered in an instant. Her scattered thoughts wandered aimlessly as Wang Jun entered her cell just in time for their daily visit.

A guard opened the door to her cell, then shut it after Wang Jun entered. Noting her mood, he sat down on a chair beside the sofa she lay on.

"You could have tried," she said, breathing in and out to calm herself. "You could have tried less hard for that wretched family of yours."

"And endanger you?" Wang Jun said. "No. No, I could never bring myself to do that. And if you think about it, although I'm dragging your friends into this mess, they'll be safest this way. They'll survive. That's the most important thing, Hong Xin. When there's life, there are options."

By now, she'd made it abundantly clear she could receive news from the outside world. First it was the mercenaries, then the royal family. Elder Bai's termination had been particularly hard on her. Had the older man, Wang Jun's closest confidant and pillar of moral support, finally had enough of him? Was he beyond redemption now?

"You knew what you needed to do," Hong Xin said. "I had hope for you. But now, my only regret is not ending my life sooner." She reached for the red pin stuck in her hair. Though it seemed dull, it was, in fact, extremely sharp. A glamour hid its deadliness, and only a transcendent could pierce its clever veil.

"I'm afraid I can't let you do that," Wang Jun said. His arm flashed, and his hand grabbed her wrist pin. Guards scrambled inside the room and retrieved the deadly object. They exchanged looks of disbelief as they confiscated it, then all her jewelry for good measure. That included the pin, her only source of information from the outside world.

"So you choose to preserve me," Hong Xin said bitterly. "The only thing that doesn't matter, while throwing the rest away. You've kept the box but thrown away the ring, Wang Jun. You're a fool. I'm disappointed."

"I won't have you die on my watch," Wang Jun said. "I won't be able to live with myself if I don't try my best to free you from this situation."

Hong Xin laughed a hopeless laugh. "Get out of here. I don't want to see your stupid face." All her efforts had gone to waste, and all that was left was a useless shadow of her former self. She'd tried her best, but there was no turning him back. His heart was corrupted, through and through.

She waited for him to protest, to say something to contradict her, or to insist on staying. But to her surprise, he left her in her cell. Those precious minutes he'd bargained for were cast to the wayside to make time for his darker deeds. She waited for him to clear the stairs before finally breaking down. She sobbed for hours before her tears finally dried up.

"Are you ready?" Wang Ling said as Wang Jun entered the elder council chamber. Like before, only Wang Ling and Patriarch Wuling were there.

"As ready as I'll ever be," Wang Jun said. "I've shattered trade in the North, and I've deprived the Golden Kingdom of its protectors. I've recruited all the best families, forging an alliance the Spirit Temple can use to destroy the Church of Justice once and for all. From here, we'll soften the North's western flank. It will only be a matter of time before the rest of them fall in line. It's a decisive victory, an achievement we can proudly show off to our dark leaders." He said this without emotion or sympathy. His voice was that that of a man who had lost everything.

"Good, good," Patriarch Wuling said. "Then I finally have your third assignment in this great war for our survival. As you know, Junior Patriarch Ling is suited for battle but not commanding. We'll need someone like you to marshal our forces and lead us to victory on the battlefield."

"I've been told you're the best *Angels and Devils* player in the North," Wang Ling said. "I've heard many grandmasters admit to it."

"You want me to be your commander?" Wang Jun asked bitterly. "You want an unmotivated man like me to head your rebellion and destroy this kingdom? Why not just assign a donkey, or better yet, the junior patriarch?"

"You're hardly unmotivated," Patriarch Wuling said, ignoring the insult. "In fact, I would argue that you have the strongest motivation of all: protecting someone you love. Not many conquerors can claim the same advantage."

Wang Jun took in a deep breath, then sighed. "What are your orders?"

"We are holding a meeting tomorrow, a discussion with all the major powers in the city," Wang Wuling said. "Although we're not against using bloodshed to force the Church of Justice out, we're hoping they'll surrender for the good of the common people."

"A show of force," Wang Jun said. "To intimidate them into submitting without a fight. For why fight when you can win without shedding a single drop of blood?"

"Victory and defeat are decided before the battle," Wang Ling said. "And why fight when you don't have to? I've reviewed your business history. You often use this tactic for business negotiations."

"There are similarities between business and warfare," Wang Jun said. "What time will the meeting take place?"

"Dusk," Wang Ling answered, in that annoying, hateful voice. "A fitting time for the end of a dynasty, I think."

"A fitting time indeed," Wang Jun replied. "If that will be all, there are some things that require my attention. These new duties leave me pressed for time." Wang Jun bowed and excused himself from their presence. He returned directly to his chambers, feeling more alone than he ever had. Though he'd known this was coming, it was still a lot to take in.

He took a minute to calm himself before looking up at the mirror. His shadow was there, returned from whatever duty it had been accomplishing. "Come," he said, beckoning. The shadow oozed out of the mirror like liquid broken glass, its form twisted and sharp, the space around it crumbling. A malevolent and bloody aura filled the room as it did.

"Take it," Wang Jun said, offering his arm. He slit his wrist, and blood dribbled on the floor. "Take it all."

The shadow complied, first lapping up the puddle and clamping onto his arm, draining away freely. Wang Jun would gain many white hairs this evening, but if he could complete the item on time, it would all be worth it.

Chapter 17: Samsara

Winds buffeted Cha Ming's body as he flew through the clouds, revealing his next destination: Gold Leaf City. The sun was setting, its body a red half circle providing dim illumination to the few wild places so far from the spirit woods. Demons and wild beasts of the day sought shelter, and even the day's predators warily made their way to their lairs. Humans also followed this natural cycle. Farmers returned from tending their fields. People in villages made their way back lest they get caught out in the dark. Everything was connected, a great circle that bound all of creation.

As creatures of the day retreated, creatures of the night emerged. They mercilessly displaced their counterparts, claiming the lands as their own. The bloodred tint to the clouds as they did so would normally seem beautiful to Cha Ming, but blind as he was, he saw nothing. And although he couldn't see the red colors in the clouds, he could remember them and the omen they represented.

As Golf Leaf City grew on the horizon, he examined his condition. The past two days fighting against the South's forces and baiting the Taotie, though dangerous and taxing, had been surprisingly easy, all things considered. Strangely enough, the South hadn't sent many transcendents to supervise their troops. The one transcendent there hadn't dared interfere too much, preferring to keep right next to the creature to give it instructions.

They had run it around in circles, and as they did so, Cha Ming had taken medicine to recover from his injuries. His soul was nine-tenths recovered, and his vitality reserves were fully replenished. His qi was finally full again for the first time since the battle in Bastion.

The evacuation of the Evergreen Kingdom was completed without a hitch, with half its population taken into neighboring countries. Not many had been sent to the Golden Kingdom, however, which was likely related to his most recent assignment. Wang Jun, it appeared, had switched sides. Within minutes, they would be staging a coup to overthrow the Golden Kingdom's rulers and eliminate the Church of Justice. Wang Jun had sown chaos in the North's economy and rallied troops to cripple the kingdom and prevent it from resisting the South's invasion. The man was a traitor, they said, but Cha Ming refused to believe it.

He isn't a simple lad, Sun Wukong said, appearing beside Cha Ming. *And his master isn't simple either. Do you really know him? Can you truly know a man as obscure as him?*

"I'll find out soon enough," Cha Ming said, dreading the confrontation. It didn't help that immediately after Feng Ming had sent his message, Wang Jun had sent him one as well. It wasn't an assurance that everything was well as he'd expected it to be—it was a plea for help.

I need you, it said. *Come to Gold Leaf Square. Come at dusk. Make a lot of noise.* There were no other specific instructions and no other explanations. Whatever it was that Wang Jun wanted, he might not be able to explain. That, or it was trap.

Keep your guard up and you'll be fine, Sun Wukong reassured him. *There aren't many people who can kill you if you have a mind to escape.*

"That's the thing, isn't it?" Cha Ming said. "Wang Jun knows me too well. If he wants to trap me, he'll make it so I won't want to escape. He'll make it so I have to risk it all to accomplish an objective."

Sun Wukong grunted. He returned to the Clear Sky World, leaving Cha Ming alone to plan his entrance. Wang Jun wanted noise, did he? Then why not do a public service and destroy something garish? That was one way to test his friend's motives. Only then would he decide whether he should help him or put him down.

"It's time," Patriarch Wuling said, looking at the crowd of assembled elders in the room. He nodded to Wang Jun, who stood up to make his announcement.

"My dear council of elders," Wang Jun said, leaving a dramatic pause before continuing. "The time has come. Many of you might be confused by our actions until now, but you need wonder no longer. Tonight, we will witness the end of a dynasty. Our actions will usher in a fresh start for our family, which has always been denied the power it deserved. As of right now, it's official. The Wang family declares its allegiance to the Southern Alliance." Murmurs ensued, but nothing too drastic. "Most of you don't seem surprised," Wang Jun continued. "All of you are the brightest minds in our family. The truth is that this plan is hundreds of years in the making. The South's victory is inevitable, and only by toppling down the wall ourselves can we gain amnesty and prosperity."

"That's insane," one of the elders, Elder Bei, said. Though his voice was calm and loud, his face was flushed as he stood and pointed. "You can't make such decisions on your own. This is madness."

"It wasn't his decision," Wang Ling said from the side.

"Both of you are mad," Elder Bei said. He looked up to Patriarch Wuling with a pained expression. "You too? What gives you the right to make such a big decision?"

The elders began arguing, and many drew their weapons. After days of the family's unseemly behavior, around a third of their elders had finally had enough. "You've taken the good name of the Wang family and dragged it through the mud," Elder Bei continued. "Our ancestor founded this family on principles, and you've thrown them all away. There were three simple rules: Prioritize family wealth, empower the competent, and don't involve yourself in politics. In recent days, you've broken all three of them."

"Are you done?" Wang Jun asked calmly. "Will you put your sword away, or do I have to take it?"

"I'm to let you disarm us?" Wang Bei said, incredulous. "You're crazier than I thought. No, we're leaving. We're taking a third of us, a third of the wealth of the family, and we're leaving."

"No one is leaving," a deep voice said. It penetrated everyone's mind and soul, rendering them as helpless as kittens. Then, to Wang Jun's surprise, a figure appeared beside him. He was tall and thin, and whatever was left of his long blond hair was lost in a sea of white. And while his skin seemed young and healthy, his eyes were ancient. Centuries had passed under his watch.

At long last, the king finally appears, Wang Jun thought. It was the transcendent presiding over the family, Ancestor Wang. It was undoubtedly him who had taken an active hand in mixing up Hong Xin's karma.

"The elder council, of all people, should understand a simple fact," Ancestor Wang said. "Nothing happens in the family without my knowledge or my will. I instructed you juniors so you wouldn't go astray, and I protected you so our bloodline would be preserved. I gave you freedom so you could grow, but at no point did anything happen unless I wished it to happen. Is that understood?"

Elder Bei, who'd gone pale after the appearance of Ancestor Wang, prostrated himself. "Is there really no other way, Great Ancestor?"

"No," Ancestor Wang said. "I value my family, and I care much for virtue. When both are weighed, however, I value family most. To preserve you, we must join the South. You are not like me, a man who can flee the plane whenever he wishes."

Elder Bei rose, then bowed again. "We will do as instructed," he said. The elders who'd taken up arms put away their weapons. With grim determination, they bowed first to the ancestor, then to Patriarch Wuling, Wang Ling, and Wang Jun in that order. Seeing that everything was taken care of, Ancestor Wang disappeared.

Wang Jun cleared his throat and continued.

"We've recruited noble families and mercenaries, and even the Red Dust Pavilion," Wang Jun said. "The Spirit Temple has our back, and the Church of Justice and the royal family has been crippled by them. Since we don't want an all-out war, we have invited them to Gold Leaf Square to discuss the future of the Golden Kingdom. Their response will determine our actions. Blood need not be spilled this day.

"Still, it is wise to take precautions. I want every one of you who has reached core formation to join me downstairs in five minutes, ready for battle. Though I expect a peaceful surrender, the righteous often like to go out in a blaze of glory. We've invited the Jin royal family, and we want them to know what to do to protect their people when we show them our might and our resolve. They *will* capitulate."

At that moment, a frantic knock sounded at the door. "Enter," Wang Jung said.

A nervous messenger boy ran through the door, then bowed to the Patriarch. "The Jin royal family is making its way through the city streets to Central Square," he said.

"As expected," Wang Jun said. "Are they alone?"

"No, sir," the messenger said, shaking his head. "Many nobles have taken their elites to escort them. The Church of Justice has sent their paladins, their inquisitors, and their chaplains. They've emptied their churches, it seems, and have come with everything they have. I don't know what they're up to."

Wang Jun nodded. "You are dismissed." He turned to the elders as the boy left the room. "Change of plans. Meet me downstairs in *three* minutes, armed to the teeth and carrying potential burning pills if you have them. I understand you're all weak, but this might be a difficult battle. Furthermore," he said, staring at a specter that had appeared in the room unbeknownst to any but him, "the Spirit Temple might need a show of sincerity. Nothing shows sincerity like bleeding for a cause." The elders gulped, and the shadow vanished. It had gotten the confirmation it needed.

As the elders ran out of the room, Wang Jun walked over to

Wang Ling and Patriarch Wuling. "I've done what you asked, and now you'll need to do what I ask," he said softly. "I'm worried for Hong Xin's safety. We'll be taking her with us to Gold Leaf Square."

"We'll do no such thing," Patriarch Wuling said.

Wang Jun raised his hand to silence him. "You will, or you will lose your marshal and commander at the most inconvenient time. If she's protected, I can rest assured. But I will *not* leave her in the Wang family manor when we've emptied out all our able-bodied fighters."

Patriarch Wuling pondered for a moment, then pulled his lips into a thin line. "See it done," he said to Wang Ling. "We'll deal with this insubordination later."

Wang Ling grimaced but nodded, and in that moment, something struck Wang Jun about both of their expressions.

"No wonder, no wonder," Wang Jun said, chuckling. "Everything makes sense now."

"What's so funny?" Patriarch Wuling said, glaring at Wang Jun.

"Nothing, nothing," Wang Jun said. "I've just always wondered why you preferred Ling so much over Hua and I. Perhaps it's because he reminds you of your long-lost son, or maybe it's just a coincidence. But you *have* to admit, he looks a lot like you, doesn't he? Even his name, which I heard my mother and father had an argument over, resembles yours."

"Whatever you might think, it changes nothing," Patriarch Wuling said coldly.

"You're right," Wang Jun said. "Which is why I was laughing instead of crying. This changes nothing. The dead are dead, and there's nothing I can do to bring them back. I can only worry about the living." He nodded to Patriarch Wuling and excused himself. He had something to fetch in his chambers. Something he hadn't wanted on his person when the Ancestor appeared to quell the rebellious elders.

"That's a lot of troops," Sun Wukong said with a whistle, eyeing the city along with Cha Ming. In Gold Leaf Square, small armies of elites were assembling. The Golden Kingdom's forces marched in step, their expressions grim as they walked toward their destination. They were flanked by gold-armored forces from the Church of Justice, whose eyes burned with zeal and self-sacrifice. He'd seen men with similar expressions over the past few days. They weren't fighting to win. They knew full well that they would die, and they sought only to take down enemies with them.

Behind them, nobles sent forces to support the brave knights. But Cha Ming could see that those who did sent the bare minimum required to be considered as participating. This did not bode well for the Golden Kingdom, as twice as many mercenaries were pouring out of the Wang family complex, and hidden in the shadows, Cha Ming could sense the souls of the dead. The Spirit Temple had sent Spectral Assassins, and there were far more than he'd fought in Bastion.

"I'm not worried about the pawns," Cha Ming said, looking up to where a few figures were floating. He saw an angel and a devil, transcendent cultivators from the Alabaster Group and the Obsidian Syndicate. An old man with long white hair floated nonchalantly beside them, supervising the Wang family household as it organized its rebellion.

There were two others facing off a short distance away. A smiling man in golden robes holding a religious book and a ghostly figure in black robes. Cha Ming had seen a man like him before; he was a shepherd, one of the leaders of the Spirit Temple. And though he wasn't technically a transcendent, a half-transcendent soul cultivator like him was a force to be feared. If he went all out, he could easily destroy a transcendent.

"They're too heavily outnumbered," Sun Wukong said. "It's best for them to run away and shore up their defenses."

"Perhaps," Cha Ming said. "We've yet to see what Ancestor Wang will do." He'd been given a description of the man by Feng Ming.

Though he wasn't very powerful for a transcendent, he was not to be trifled with.

"You're telling me he has nothing to do with what's happening down there?" Sun Wukong asked. It wasn't only mercenaries and nobles that assembled down below, but elders of the Wang family as well. They lined up with leaders of devilish cults that had finally come out of the woodwork after so long in hiding. To Cha Ming's surprise, the Red Dust Pavilion had also joined them. That made sense, now that he thought about it; any organization that preyed on the hearts of men was bound to be opportunistic.

"I just see a man who cares for his family," Cha Ming replied, spotting Ancestor Wang. "He'll do whatever it takes to protect them, and that might change depending on the situation."

Likely, that was what Wang Jun was doing. The young master of the Wang family hadn't yet left the Jade Bamboo Pavilion, and the leadership of the Red Dust Pavilion had not left theirs. The Spirit Temple's forces were an exception, leaving only token defenses to guard their spirit pool. Only the Greenwind Pavilion was unaccounted for. They never took sides, and he knew firsthand they had the power to back that up.

"Knocking on the front door isn't very useful when the city gates are so far away from the party venue," Cha Ming said. "I was thinking of a more dramatic way to make an entrance."

"A giant illusory display showing how awesome you are?" Sun Wukong asked, his eyes bright with excitement.

"No," Cha Ming said. "I was thinking a show of power would work better."

The Golden Kingdom's forces had entered Gold Leaf Square. They were forming ranks and preparing to parley. Any minute now, Wang Jun and the other ringleaders would come out. Only then would he make his appearance.

"Let go of me," Hong Xin said, biting at her guard as she struggled against the robes binding her arms. Her eyes were red from crying all day, and her wrists were red and bleeding from all the struggling she'd been doing.

"Please gag her if she continues," Wang Jun said, leading the way out, ignoring Hong Xin's glare as he walked down the steps. Wang Ling smirked, as did Patriarch Wuling. Anything that caused Wang Jun misery was music to their ears. Their group walked at a relaxed pace toward the enemy forces assembled in Gold Leaf Square.

They were joined by a few powerful Spectral Assassins, priests from the Spirit Temple, and the headmistress and vice heads of the Red Dust Pavilion. Though the animosity between the two groups hadn't faded, they could put such grudges aside for now. Moreover, Hong Xin's presence wasn't lost on the uncomfortable members of the Red Dust Pavilion. Bai Ling's lips were drawn to a thin line, and Ji Bingxue and Ling Fei gasped. The reason they were there finally dawned on them, firming their resolve.

A few heads of noble houses also joined their group, if only to add legitimacy to their claim that this was all for the good of the people. Their mercenaries stood off to the side facing the opposing army; they weren't here to talk, but to fight and bleed for money.

"Prime Director Wang," King Tai, the ruler of the Golden Kingdom, said as he arrived, "the customs of Golf Leaf City appear to be lost on you. Typically, when meeting with someone important, you arrive on time or slightly early."

"That is only if both parties are equal," Wang Jun said, eyeing the final trace of red disappearing behind a curtain of darkness. "In this case, I'd say we showed up precisely when we should." He turned to the local chaplain of the Church of Justice. "How nice that you could make it, though I don't remember inviting you."

"I showed up because I was needed, not because I was wanted," Chaplain Wu said. He and his guards struck an imposing figure, and even Wang Jun's shadow trembled under the influence of their light-based cultivation.

"I will assume, then, that you've decided not to go quietly," Wang

Jun said to King Tai. "Which is regrettable. The loss of human life will be astronomical if we are forced to stabilize the kingdom after deposing you."

"Better to die an honest man than live at the whims of evil tyrants," King Tai said. His voice was tired, and his face was tired. He'd lost much family over the past few days, which added to the toll of putting down constant rebellions.

"Brave words, but they are accurate ones," Wang Jun said, looking at the army assembled. Perhaps a third of the forces on the square were allied with the Golden Kingdom, an impressive showing given the lackluster support he had from each of the remaining nobles. "I just don't see how you'll make a difference in the end. You can't win here, King Tai."

"The difference will be in the hearts of men and the eyes of the goddess," Chaplain Wu said. "Our reward will not be in this life but the next one."

"Truer words could never be spoken," Wang Jun said. "Should we—" He cut off as a powerful force erupted in a corner of Gold Leaf Square. Everyone turned their heads to the source: a blazing beacon of light above the Spirit Temple. It was a man, a powerful one. An oppressive aura filled the air, sickening the nearby devils and causing the evil spirits to shiver. Beside the man, an object appeared. It was a large pillar, black and white, with gray on its bottom edge. Everything around that edge disappeared and turned to gray mist. The man took the pillar and shoved it down, straight into the center of the Spirit Temple. Spirits screamed as they blew out like candles in the wind, and in the starry sky, a yellow river appeared, snatching away souls as they were banished.

"It's *him*," one of the priests of the Spirit Temple said.

"He must have been the one behind Bastion," another spat.

The entire temple caught fire, and a cloud of dust appeared. As it cleared, a figure with brown hair and closed eyes walked up to them with a light smile. "Did I miss the party?" he asked.

"So now it's clear," Patriarch Wuling said. "That man is called Du Cha Ming. He's much stronger than the last time I saw him. He was the man who destroyed Bastion's Spirit Temple."

"There's no use hiding it now," Wang Jun said, chuckling. "He owed me a favor, and I cashed it in."

"Well, ask him for another one," Wang Ling said. "This isn't the time to get someone like him involved."

Power fluctuations had appeared, and occasional waves of transcendent power washed over them. The transcendents had started fighting in the skies.

"I'll see what I can do," Wang Jun replied. He walked over to the man he still considered his dearest friend. All he could hope for was that the man cooperated. He was Hong Xin's—no, his entire family's—only hope.

She was with him all this time? Ji Bingxue sent to Bai Ling. *They captured her and used her against him?*

That's the gist of it, Bai Ling said. *They used her as a hostage to get him to do their dirty work.*

That still doesn't explain why you capitulated, Ling Fei said. As the leader of the Icy Heart Pavilion's people, she understood Bai Ling best of all. *Hong Xin has a bleeding heart. You of all people know what she'd want you to do.*

I capitulated because I had to, Bai Ling said. *And because of a hunch. I hate the Spirit Temple as much as anyone else here, but often, deception is needed to win when playing a complicated game. Hidden pieces your enemies don't know exist until the very last minute.*

Is that what we are, then? Hidden pieces? Ji Bingxue said. *We're pretty useless, considering that mark on our arm.*

And that's where the hunch comes in, Bai Ling said. *It was that or run. Did you want us to run?*

Ji Bingxue shook her head, and Ling Fei did so as well.

We're fighters, but we're not very strong. However, our command over minds and souls is excellent. You want revenge on the Spirit Temple? You want to get back at them for what they did to those innocents and what they did to our sisters? Then wait. If I'm right, our time will come. And if I'm wrong... well, at least I'll have saved as many sisters as I could.

With that, they turned their attention to the two men at the center of the square. Wang Jun and Cha Ming, two of the most powerful men on the continent, were talking. Everything hinged on this crucial discussion.

"Cha Ming, it's nice to see you again," Wang Jun said. "I really wish it could have been under different circumstances."

"As do I," Cha Ming said, noticing Wang Jun's weary expression and the excess of white hairs on his head. "You should know as well as anyone that I can't let you destroy the Golden Kingdom. I can't let you serve the North to the South on a silver platter."

"It's regrettable, but alas, it's what I must do," Wang Jun said. "If you'll just look behind me, you'll see the reason for my change in temperament."

Cha Ming did so and saw a person he hadn't noticed. She was weak, barely recognizable, with not a shred of cultivation. Though her soul was sealed behind a peak-core soul-sealing collar, he recognized her. She was the very first friend he'd made in the cultivation world, Hong Xin.

"You lied to me," Cha Ming said, his calm expression not betraying his rising emotions. "We spoke when I was in the city. You said you hadn't found her."

"I lied because she wanted me to," Wang Jun said. "This, unfortunately, is a rather recent development. She was the headmistress of the Red Dust Pavilion, you know. They're very upset about her situation, but ultimately, for her safety, they accepted my invitation."

"This changes nothing," Cha Ming said, remembering the millions of lives lost in Bastion and the millions of lives lost in the North. "She isn't worth a whole kingdom of people. Her life isn't worth what I know will happen here once the South takes over."

It was a cruel choice to make, friendship over the fate of many, but one he had to make regardless, if he wanted any chance of ever sleeping again.

"Alas, it's the hand we've been dealt," Wang Jun said. "You know what you need to do, and I know what I need to do. Patriarch Wuling and Wang Ling are her keepers, and I believe you now know who watches in the shadows."

Cha Ming had sensed him earlier. As the shepherd of the Spirit Temple and the vice chancellor of the Church of Justice clashed up above, the angel of the Alabaster Group and the devil of the Obsidian Syndicate fought as well. Only Ancestor Wang wasn't fighting. He'd appeared among the Wang family's elders, hiding himself. Not many people could see him. As a transcendent, he could hide from prying eyes with ease.

I have a favor to ask you, Wang Jun sent mentally. *I'll give you my life if that is what you wish. I wish to save her, but I also wish to save this kingdom. But for that, I need your help. I need you to fight a transcendent. Are you up for it? Can you do that for me?*

Now was the moment of truth. Things had gone full circle, and every interaction with the man flashed before Cha Ming's eyes. He remembered meeting Wang Jun in Green Leaf Academy, and he remembered their time in the Spirit Woods. He remembered getting rescued, and he remembered him pouring out his heart and soul as they drank in the Red Dust Pavilion. Was it a trap? Was it a ruse? Was it all to bait him into a fight he couldn't extricate himself from, or was there more to the situation than met the eye? He looked to the uncertain elders of the Wang family, who had drawn weapons as they looked warily at their supposed foes in the square. He looked to the mercenaries who stood at grim attention as they waited to slaughter the king's men, the protectors of their country. He looked to those from the Spirit Temple, smug men who could almost taste victory. The odds were stacked against them, and if he chose poorly, he would be buried with the dead.

Finally, he looked to Hong Xin, who was looking down, ashamed. Tears fell from her eyes as she wept for what was about to happen. She cried not for herself, but for others and their fate. They weren't tears of desperation, nor tears of remorse. They were tears of a woman who wanted to die.

Breathing in, he made his choice. His body flashed, and he swung the Clear Sky Staff.

Cha Ming blurred past Wang Jun, appearing suddenly beside the elder council. Wang Ling, who guarded Hong Xin, pulled her back by the wrist. An explosion of raw power erupted as the staff, laced with destructive black lightning, clashed against a golden sword. Lightning came down from the heavens and struck Ancestor Wang, who'd just defended.

Cha Ming's actions hadn't been expected by anyone else, who could barely see the man. He was fast, swift, and powerful, giving Ancestor Wang no time to flee. And the distraction that ensued was exactly what Wang Jun was waiting for. It was time to strike.

He blended with the shadows and flitted through the shadow plane, emerging beside a stunned Patriarch Wuling. Unfortunately, the man wasn't a rookie when it came to battle; he raised a transcendent saber to block Wang Jun's black sword and flew toward Wang Ling.

Do it, Wang Jun commanded.

His shadow complied. It congealed into a massive scythe that Wang Jun grabbed and swung with all his might. The scythe extended, rushing past the Patriarch then pulling back, bisecting the surprised man, cutting through his body and soul, and life left his eyes. The first part of his plan had succeeded splendidly: Get Cha Ming to distract the Ancestor while he used his new weapon, Void Shadow Scythe, to rid himself of one of three problems. Though Patriarch Wuling had poisoned her, needing an antidote in a few minutes was the least of his worries.

The man didn't even whimper as his life left him. The scythe disappeared in the shadows, and Wang Jun rushed to Wang Ling. He swung out with the scythe again. This time, it met a golden sword, one of the many transcendent treasures in Wang Ling's possession.

"You're crazy!" he shouted. "If you kill me, she'll die!"

"And if you don't fight me, you will as well," Wang Jun said. He disappeared and reappeared behind Wang Ling, who'd anticipated his movements. Reacting fast, he sent his sword out for a quick stab. Wang Jun evaded it, and just as Wang Ling was about to follow up and finish him, the man's expression jolted, and he disappeared, avoiding a scythe of shadows to his neck as he reappeared ten feet away, wiping blood trailing from where the scythe had nicked him.

"You're stronger than I am," Wang Jun said. "I'll admit that. Without making a transcendent treasure of my own, there was no way I could face you. In fact, I'm still no match for you. One on one, there's no way I can win. But you miscalculated, you see. I'm not one person. I'm two people." His shadow appeared beside his body, and a scythe appeared in his hands again. Another scythe, a projection of his own, appeared in his doppelganger's hands. "Any last words?"

"Attack!" Wang Ling said. The cultivators in the square, who had been waiting for orders, moved in on the king's men.

"Attack the Spirit Temple's forces and rebel nobles!" Wang Jun shouted out loud so everyone could hear it. Men cried out as the mercenaries Wang Jun had recruited turned on their own people. The nobles Wang Bing had recruited joined them as well. She wasn't there personally, as she was too weak to fight in this struggle, so she'd stayed behind in the Jade Bamboo Pavilion with her husband in a safe house. The Red Dust Pavilion, those he'd recruited, turned on the stronger members of the Spirit Temple, who were conveniently right beside them and blissfully unaware of their impending demise. Fire and ice crashed down on them, destroying many souls with the powers of kindling and dousing. King Tai's troops took this in stride and began a slaughter, cutting down traitors with blades of light.

Under normal circumstances, such a thing would never have happened. These men and women had signed an employment contract, and such things could never be violated. Those who'd signed the contracts would follow their master's orders to the letter. Unfortunately for Wang Ling, those contracts hadn't been stamped by a normal seal. Shadows had corrupted it, forging a new, hidden name to be imprinted on each document. It wasn't the Wang family they had signed on with, nor was it Patriarch Wuling or Wang Ling they'd agreed to serve. Those were only fallbacks, necessary for his subterfuge. They hadn't signed with the family, but Wang Jun himself.

Light filled the skies as the Church of Justice attacked evil spirits alongside the Red Dust Mistresses. Knights and women of ill repute fought side by side to slay a common enemy. Mercenaries turned against allied forces and began to slaughter them. On this battlefield, these soldiers of fortune were angels of mercy granted by the goddess of light herself to preserve men of good faith.

Devils fell by the dozens, returning to their base elements as their souls left their corpses. Everything happened in an instant, and by the time Cha Ming and Ancestor Wang had exchanged fifty blows, a tenth of the men below were dead.

"*You* did this," Ancestor Wang said, cutting through the void and stabbing into Cha Ming's chest. "You made him do this." He pulled out his sword to deflect a counterstrike from Cha Ming's staff as the wound healed.

"On the contrary, you did this," Cha Ming said. "You made your family take sides. Their blood is on your hands, Ancestor Wang. You never should have betrayed the North." As he spoke, more men died, many of them elders of the Wang family that were suddenly caught up in the chaos.

"The North will fall, regardless of what we do here," Ancestor Wang said, preparing for another strike. Though the man was a gold cultivator, the air around him distorted strangely when he struck, hinting at the man's superficial knowledge over a rare element—space.

"You won't be there to see it," Cha Ming said, smashing down with Crushing Chaos. The man grunted as he blocked his blow, and as he did, tribulation lightning finally snuck past the man's spatial defenses and struck true, singeing his weak transcendent flesh.

"I should have killed you when I saw you meeting with that brat," Ancestor Wang growled, summoning a dozen needles that tore through space toward Cha Ming. Cha Ming replied by summoning a half-step-transcendent ice shield, stalling the needles just long enough to strike in a wide arc, destroying six of them before six others pierced through his bones at different points, destroying large reserves of vital energy in the process.

"And why didn't you?" Cha Ming asked, repurposing his ice sigils to a five-colored runic-sealing array. He threw five talismans on key nodes, activating the formation. Ancestor Wang, who could normally fly through points in space with ease, became slow and sluggish, unable to fully avoid him. The storms overhead intensified as they spotted that weakness, and some of the lightning that bathed the battling transcendents above them diverted to the older man, who could no longer evade its detection.

"A transcendent bitch from the Red Dust Pavilion didn't let me," Ancestor Wang said. "But that's irrelevant. The situation is now out of control, and either Wang Jun or Wang Ling will win. Either way, my family line is preserved. In fact, you could call this situation ideal."

"Then why fight?" Cha Ming asked. "Why not let juniors decide what happens?"

"Why indeed?" Ancestor Wang said. He ceased resisting Cha Ming's formation, and the lightning stopped. The formation was meant to seal and stabilize space, something he'd figured out while observing Elder Zhong's formation. "Let's just say I don't like our kids making bad friends."

"You have a lot of time on your hands, then," Cha Ming said. "What are you, nine hundred years old?"

"Nine hundred sixty-eight," Ancestor Wang said. "I have very little time left. Why care if I live or die?"

Cha Ming gripped the Clear Sky Staff uncomfortably. The air around him began to shimmer and break as Ancestor Wang's aura exploded.

"Now let's see if Wang Jun has made friends worth keeping," said Ancestor Wang. "Let's see if you're worthy of your soul-bound treasure, a rarity among rarities that perhaps only me and my silly descendant could detect. Let's see if the many transcendents who have been protecting you from the shadows all this time knew what they were doing."

Runes appeared in the air all around him, runes Cha Ming could barely understand. They were runes of gold that filled the air with an inviolable pressure.

"I know you fought a blood-awakening blood master. Consider this either a death penalty or an education. Each rune-carving cultivator, by carving his core, forms a domain. Mine is a golden domain of stability. Everything inside it is under my control."

Blades appeared out of thin air, and golden chains wrapped around Cha Ming without any warning. Fortunately, they'd taken to the skies, sparing many others an untimely death. Cha Ming reached out for ambient qi but realized there was none to be had. It was all under Ancestor Wang's control, manifesting as transcendent golden power.

"Demigods are tough to kill," Ancestor Wang continued. "Your body is halfway there, so the energies of heaven and earth resist harming you, but every cut I land depletes your vitality, while I wouldn't last a few strikes myself.

"Transcendents, on the other hand, are hard to touch. We control natural energies around us, wresting it away from our opponents.

Everything around us is our domain, and within that small circle of influence, the heavens obey. There, we are immortals among mere men."

The golden power squeezed and cut at Cha Ming, draining him as surely as the lightning that struck Ancestor Wang's domain drained him. Blood leaked out of the older man's mouth as he used his power to put Cha Ming in his place. If not for a thin film of water pseudo-domain on his skin, Cha Ming would have already succumbed to the man's influence. It was only through this half-transcendent qi that he could control energies of heaven and earth. "Any last words?" the man asked.

"Go to hell," Cha Ming spat, and blood leaked from his lips.

"A pity," Ancestor Wang said, piercing Cha Ming through the heart, depleting his vitality that much further.

Hong Xin blinked tears out of her eyes as she watched Wang Jun fight her captor, Wang Ling. This time, they weren't tears of sadness but tears of joy. She'd mistakenly thought her efforts had meant nothing. Yet here he was, fighting for the sake of the Golden Kingdom, fighting for the sake of the North despite the inevitability of her death. It worked. At long last, she'd succeeded. His heartbreaking actions and selfish words had all been an act to set the stage for something greater.

Despite her joy, she was mostly helpless. Without her cultivation, she could do nothing but watch the battle. Gold Leaf Square was no longer a place for family fun and reunion. It was a place of death and carnage, where blood filled the streets and watered the gold-leafed trees like a fresh spring drizzle. Nobles fought with their lives on the line, and mercenaries cut down men for paltry spirit stones. Inquisitors summoned light and heat to burn apart their adversaries—devils, evil spirits, and men who had simply chosen the wrong side. The Wang family was taking especially large casualties. Now that their leadership was fighting amongst themselves, they, too, had taken out weapons and were fighting with their own blood relatives.

There was one scene, however, that warmed her heart. Bai Ling and the Red Dust Mistresses, whom she'd thought had betrayed the North to side with the Spirit Temple, were now fighting their adversaries with everything they had. They used their arts to inspire the men of the North and calm their fears. Music filled the air and left their enemies awestruck. They cowered as the music attacked their minds and lashed their souls. Never in their wildest dreams would they have thought that mere musical performances could inflict such damage. Their betrayal had been a show, a smokescreen to set up an ambush. They weren't here for survival; they were here for vengeance.

All is well that ends well, she thought, for the end was swiftly approaching. The poison in her body grew stronger with every passing minute, and without the antidote, she would die without anyone having to do anything. This assumed, of course, that Wang Jun didn't outright kill Wang Ling, something she fully expected to happen by the time this was over.

Soon, she would find peace. Soon, she would sleep.

Bai Ling threw an *Angels and Devils* stone on the floor, creating an area of black flames that was impassible to foes. It connected with several other such stones she'd laid, closing a circle and surrounding a group of Spectral Assassins with soul-searing fire. They cried out in agony as inquisitors from the Church of Justice charged through the wall of flames unimpeded, punishing the trapped souls that could do nothing as the light consumed them.

On her right, she laid down a white stone, completing another chain. It cut off a group of devils and encased them in soul-sealing ice. This time, sisters of the Icy Heart Pavilion rushed in, swords and sabers slashing at frozen devils, leaving behind cold puddles of water, wood chips, or ashes in their wake. They joined with her group as she walked toward her destination: the Wang family elders, the most important part of their mission. Fighting had broken out between the merchants, so it was difficult to tell who to kill and who to save.

"Will we be killing the entire elder council?" Ling Fei asked from beside her. She was cold-hearted and practical, exactly what someone wanted in a subordinate.

Ji Bingxue, who hadn't left her side, paled. "We wouldn't, would we?"

Bai Ling massaged her temple with her left hand as she placed a few other stones with her right. Hers was a delicate art, requiring much planning as she laid out treasures infused with her qi to mark out territory. It required a great deal of mental energy, and she didn't appreciate others not connecting the obvious dots.

"Do you both remember the contracts we signed?" Bai Ling asked. "The ones which, predictably, had been doctored by Wang Jun to have us swear fealty to him instead of his family members?"

"Predictably?" Ji Bingxue asked. "That was a madwoman's gamble!"

"It was predictable," Bai Ling said. "His insistence on the stamp, along with other tells, gave it away. Likely, he'd done it this way so he wouldn't be spotted giving away any information by specters or the like. Now tell me, do you remember the contract?"

"Yes?" Ji Bingxue said hesitantly.

"Then tell me, what was the order of succession on the contract?" Bai Ling said.

"Well, Patriarch Wuling is dead, so that leaves Wang Ling, Wang Xing, Wang Song..." Ji Bingxue answered, uncertain. "Wait, why do you want to know that? Isn't it moot?"

"It's a double attack," Ling Fei exclaimed. Bless that woman, she was a bright one. "If Wang Jun dies, we actually revert back to Wang family authority, as per the chain of command. As do the others.

That aside, Wang Jun was never on the other contracts the Wang family had others sign. But if we kill all the successors, the ones they contracted will no longer have to obey."

"Remember, it's important to pursue several objectives with each move," Bai Ling said, nodding. "Think strategically. Though the list means nothing to us unless Wang Jun dies, it means everything to the turncoats right now who are forced to fight. If given the option, they might surrender, lessening the burden and casualties on our side."

She pointed her head in one direction. "Ling Fei, take care of the one I mark with a black stone." The stone didn't fly out like it usually did but appeared above a man's head and slammed down with full force. He coughed up blood as he fought it off, but with his attention diverted, Ling Fei was able to execute him by summoning a few blades of ice.

"Ji Bingxue, sing for me," Bai Ling said, slamming down a white stone on another man. As he defended himself from the unexpected strike, a gentle song invaded his soul. He said not a word as fire reduced his body to ashes.

Three down, six more to go.

Fortunately, Ancestor Wang had thought it beneath him to place his name on the contract. Therefore, the only difficult part would be finishing off Wang Ling, whom Wang Jun was clearly having a difficult time with. Moreover, Wang Jun had hinted that his life was tied to Hong Xin's. How would they solve that problem?

She wanted nothing more than for her sister to pull through this, but if it meant thousands more dying, she knew what Hong Xin would want her to do in the end. That woman, bless her heart, would gladly sacrifice herself for the sake of the many. She only hoped the heavens remembered her intentions when assigning her next life.

Calm, focused, Bai Ling placed another stone. A few seconds later, another name vanished from the list. Only five remained.

A blade of gold slashed into Cha Ming's gut, where it expanded and cut into his body, reducing his tough flesh to a few droplets of blood. The droplets fled and evaded the golden energy before coming together and growing. Almost in an instant, they grew a new body, with no injuries remaining despite his greatly diminished vitality.

Being a body cultivator was paying off, as he'd narrowly avoided death many times now. Fighting a rune-carving cultivator, it seemed, was far more dangerous that fighting a blood-awakening one. At least blood-awakening cultivators were predictable. Rune-carving ones were unreasonably powerful if they managed to stay out of your reach.

As though reading his thoughts, Ancestor Wang spoke nonchalantly, his arms behind his back. He still viewed it as a mini lesson, a lecture to a promising junior. "We rune-carving cultivators are actually not stronger than blood-awakening cultivators. Rather, we have different strengths. Body cultivators rely on resistance and resilience. They're able to take a lot of punishment and can basically fight indefinitely, unless they use some sort of divine ability.

"Rune-carving cultivators, on the other hand, are glass cannons. If you get past our domain's constriction, if you escape our control, you win. We won't last a single hit."

As he spoke, Cha Ming tried to cut through the man's entrapment once again. He lashed out with Crushing Chaos, but unfortunately, the golden chains hampering his movements didn't break. They were impervious to the fiery pseudo-domain Cha Ming had infused into the staff beforehand. Their level was much higher than the weak mastery he had over his own elements.

I need some way to close in quickly, Cha Ming sent to Sun Wukong. *Can you help me?*

In this case, no, I can't, Sun Wukong sent back. *This is a matter of supremacy in domains. He's taking a lot of damage from the plane with every second he keeps you trapped, but who knows if you'll outlast him in the end.*

Cha Ming cursed as another blade struck true, destroying his shoulder and upper torso. It regrew in the blink of an eye, just in time for him to avoid another blade strike and dodge another chain. The air smelled like blood and lightning, a symphony of charred flesh and sharpened steel.

I just had a crazy idea, Cha Ming said. He shared it with Sun Wukong, who appeared beside him and cursed.

Are you crazy? the Monkey King yelled, blocking a strike of his own with the power of his very strong soul. The heavens rumbled when he did so, forcing him back into the brush. *In principle, you can do it. But I wouldn't dream of it until you've familiarized yourself with actual domains. Doing this could kill you.*

Doing nothing will kill me, Cha Ming pointed out.

Touché, Sun Wukong said. *Fine, in this case, I'll be useful. If I combine my power with yours, you'll gain some extra vitality and regeneration. It'll only buy you a few seconds, though, so make every moment count.*

"Interesting," Ancestor Wang said, stroking his beard in bemusement. "You've even been blessed with a spirit companion, but you still only amount to so much. It will be my great pleasure and final service to my family to eliminate you. The Wang family doesn't need bad apples like you spoiling the entire basket."

The man took a step forward, and the golden chains, which had mostly been slow and stable, began whipping around chaotically without any semblance of order. He took another step, and the few swords that he'd summoned before became thousands, all piercing toward Cha Ming's vitals in unison. Lightning roared above them.

Now! Cha Ming thought. He summoned a pseudo-domain, this one for wood. He then summoned a second, one for gold. It destroyed the wood domain, but before it could fully do so, he summoned a third, fire. Then a fourth, then a fifth, until a full destructive cycle was summoned. A dark film coated his skin, and the pseudo-domain, which he didn't fully understand, began eroding away at his vitality, his qi, and his soul.

Fortunately, he wasn't alone. As he summoned the black film, Sun Wukong's soul merged with his, just like it had on the Heaven Ascension Platform. A crown appeared atop his head, and a tail sprouted from his rear. His teeth sharpened, and he found himself brimming with strength and vitality. And for a moment, he felt invincible. That is, until he felt this newfound strength quickly slipping away.

Hurry up, you foolish boy! Sun Wukong yelled.

Cha Ming nodded. He flashed toward the chains, which sought to entrap him. They wrapped around his body for a split second before shattering into nothingness. Swords came out to cut him, but they disintegrated to dust before they could cut more than an inch into his flesh. Meanwhile, his entire body was burning. This pseudo-domain of destruction was something he'd thought of on a whim. It was a last-ditch effort, a Hail Mary pass for his own survival.

Ancestor Wang's eyes widened as Cha Ming executed Origin Strike, piercing into his chest with the Clear Sky Staff just before letting go of the black domain. His teeth returned to normal, and his tail disappeared as Sun Wukong returned to the Clear Sky World, completely drained from the encounter.

"Ha. Haha." Ancestor Wang laughed wetly as his life began to leave him, the staff still sticking through his chest. "So you're not trash after all. Good for you. Good for him." He laughed one last time before his body slumped. Ancestor Wang was dead, and Cha Ming had almost died with him.

He looked up and saw the angel and the devil, who were still fighting over the chaotic battlefield. He looked to the Spirit Temple's shepherd and was surprised to see that not only was the vice chancellor fighting him, but a second person. It was a woman surrounded in red dust he could see despite his blind eyes.

The battlefield was winding down, and the Golden Kingdom was winning. Everything would soon be over.

Wang Jun's shadow stretched out, forming a bridge in space that he used to dodge a slash from Wang Ling's sword. He threw out three daggers, which the man blocked effortlessly before raising his sword, deflecting a blow from Wang Jun's scythe. Despite having a doppelganger and a new weapon, they were evenly matched. If only his abilities had more to do with offense than flight and subterfuge.

"It might seem like you're winning, but you're not looking at the big picture," Wang Ling said mockingly. "Even now, the North is losing. Tell me I'm wrong. Deny me that truth."

"Maybe you're right," Wang Jun said, continuing his assault. They were evenly matched, yes, but Wang Jun had momentum, something he was using to his advantage. "The South has broken through the Evergreen Battlefield and is taking up a foothold near the Golden Kingdom and True North Country. It won't be long before they make it to the Great Redwood Forest. Meanwhile, I've heard they're mobilizing troops on another portion of wall. Likely, that means they have the ability to break down another section of the mighty partition."

"And you still think you're fighting for the winning side?" Wang Ling mocked. He thrust his sword at Wang Jun's chest, coming far too close to ending his life. Wang Jun's shadow scythe appeared and blocked the blow just in time, then disappeared along with Wang Jun, reappearing above Wang Ling and slashing downward. Wang Ling brought up his sword to block, but this time, something different happened. This time, there was a soft crack.

"I fight for what is right," Wang Jun said, cutting down again faster than Wang Ling could react. More cracks appeared on the transcendent weapon, something that should be indestructible in a mortal realm. "The cost might be high, and the situation might seem hopeless, but I still need to fight, or I'll live the rest of my life regretting it."

"She *will* die," Wang Ling said, struggling to maintain his grip on his sword.

"We will see," Wang Jun said. Wang Ling's sword broke, shattering into a hundred pieces, and as it did, shadowy chains enveloped him, completely restraining his movements. "There's no way you can't dissolve your bond. A father would never put his son in such a terrible position."

Wang Ling laughed. "Maybe you're right. But do you remember why you did all this in the first place? It was all for Wang Hua, your sister."

"And how is that relevant?" Wang Jun said, summoning his black scythe and bringing it to Wang Ling's neck. It drew a thin line of blood that leaked onto the man's green robes.

"By all means, kill me," Wang Ling said. "I've lost everything. All I want now is to see you suffer."

Clenching his teeth, Wang Jun muzzled him with shadows and looked around. The fighting was winding down, though many were still at it. The trickiest and riskiest part of his plan wasn't to double-cross the Wang family but to keep Hong Xin alive while that happened.

At that moment, Cha Ming arrived. He landed beside Hong Xin, who was barely breathing, and felt for her pulse. "She's been poisoned," he said, frowning.

"Yes, she was poisoned by Patriarch Wuling," Wang Jun said. "Can you keep her alive until we find a way to karmically detach these two?"

Cha Ming nodded. "I'll do what I can. Worse comes to worst. I'll call Jin Huang over. There's no poison he can't solve."

One problem gone, Wang Jun thought. He scanned the crowd and found Bai Ling making her way toward him. "We have a problem," Wang Jun said. "Hong Xin is karmically attached to Wang Ling, and we need a way to resolve that. If he dies, she goes with him."

Bai Ling frowned but nodded.

"I take it you want to us to convince the Church of Justice to help out?" she said.

"They won't do it for my sake, but they might do it for yours," Wang Jun said.

"We will naturally do our best for the Red Dust Mistress's disciple," a man said as he floated down from the sky. It was the vice chancellor of the Church of Justice, Vice Chancellor Lin. A woman in red appeared behind him. He'd seen her likeness in historical records. She was the Red Dust Mistress who'd transcended a few hundred years back, Hong Yinyue.

Wang Jun sighed in relief but frowned as he realized something. Was his shadow prison weakening? He turned back to Wang Ling and noticed a trickle of black blood from the man's mouth. Poison.

"Wang Jun, come quickly!" Cha Ming shouted.

Wang Jun ran up to Hong Xin and fell to his knees beside her. To spite him one last time, Wang Ling had apparently ended his own life. Hong Xin's life-force was fading fast.

"I don't know what do," Cha Ming said. "I fed her one of my most powerful spirit pills, but it's not working."

"This isn't something medicine can fix, Cha Ming," Wang Jun said softly. He shivered, and his tears, which he'd thought had dried up long ago, began flowing again. Hong Xin's hand, which Cha Ming had been holding, fell limp inside his. Life left her, and the shadow of the Yellow River appeared once again.

No, no, no, Cha Ming thought. He reached out desperately as her life slipped away, using his wood and water qi to feed the small well of life-force within her. It drained away like water between his fingers and leaked out of her body like it was a perforated container.

Everything was happening far too quickly.

He'd been too naïve, and his opponents too sinister. Hong Xin, the first friend he'd ever made in the cultivation world, was dying, and he was powerless to save her. Though his eyes were open, he could barely make anything out. His soul could faintly feel hers leaving, and the gentle river coming to take it. He heard Wang Jun shout something, and a black tether appeared, anchoring the soul. The river insisted, and the soul was moving away, little by little.

How can a soul live without a living body? Cha Ming thought. And how can it return when its destiny has changed? Her soul was moving to the river of the dead. It was moving toward samsara, toward reincarnation.

Cha Ming thought about her embarrassed smile on the day they'd met. Her family had helped him, a dirty boy who couldn't even feed himself, out of the kindness of their hearts. He owed them, but because of her disappearance, he could no longer face them, and now that his chance had finally come, he couldn't even keep her alive. It was like karma was a vengeful spirit, punishing him for his prior failures. He laughed and cried at the same time, not knowing what to make of himself.

Life and death. Images of people dying superimposed with laughing voices in sorry situations. A grandfather smiled as he ended his lonely life, the last one in his immediate family. A little boy knowing nothing of the world was crying, but an angel was bending down, holding the boy's ghost closely and whisking it away before the Yellow River could take it.

Life and death. Images of people fighting superimposed with warriors dying with smiles on their faces. A man roared in defiance as a city burned around him. A wolf pup whined as it drank the last few drops from his dead mother's breast. A cold wind burned the skin of a freezing man, while flames felt like cool ice to a man who was burning.

Images of his own life flashed before his eyes. Not just this life, but his past life. More than ever, he felt a strong connection between past and present, anchored by that yellow river. If he could simply open his eyes, if he could glimpse into that river and find her soul, he could latch on to it and drag her back. She hadn't yet reincarnated, had she? She hadn't even left.

He blinked, but in his eyes, there was only pain and hatred. He

PATRICK G. LAPLANTE

knew in that moment the truth of Ivan's words. He'd painted the world in black and white, removing the gray, and in the process, blinding himself. These eyes were his heart demon, a consequence of his way of thinking. But how could he make that hatred go away? How could he see things as they truly were when his vision had become so clouded? Good and evil stood in stark contrast, but the distinction was blurred on the battlefield, which ran slick with the blood of good and evil men alike.

Cha Ming took in a deep breath. He let go of Hong Xin's palm and sat cross-legged, ignoring all movement around him. As transcendents tried to keep her soul anchored, he let go of everything around him and sent out two important treasures, the medallions Ling Dong had once crafted and the painting Jun Xiezi had made, *Samsara*. Every truth had a dual nature. Perhaps by discovering this one, he could save her.

Cha Ming saw the beasts of Taishan village falling to a swarm of fiendish demons. He saw their decimated population taking root again, a fraction of what they once were, but trying to make the best of the situation.

Cha Ming saw Bastion and its soldiers dying. But in their death, they bought life for their countrymen, and they stole life from the Taotie that threaten to kill them. The South hated the North because they envied them. As a result, they did the best they could to steal what they thought should rightfully be theirs. The irony of the situation was that while the North decayed in abundance, the South thrived in scarcity. Who was truly lucky? And what would happen if the South won? Would history not simply repeat itself? Perhaps it already had, and life and death were just a vicious cycle. Time was an illusion, a wheel that turned around and around, spitting out the same spiteful reality to the same people again and again.

The medallions representing life swirled, and the two portions of *Samsara* blended together. Cha Ming blinked, and in that moment, he realized something. Tears fell from of his eyes, tears he didn't know he had in him. The first tears were jade tears. They glowed brightly with their loathing for evil things. The second pair of tears were

- 213 -

violet, and though they didn't hate, they commanded the respect of nature, bending it to its will. The third pair of tears was golden, and it hated karma above all other things. Cha Ming blinked again, and the world came to life. His eyes were gray, he realized, and for the first time in his life, he could see the world in all its colors.

The Devil-Sealing, Demon-Subduing, and Spirit-Banishing Intents, he realized, were all within these six tears. He stowed them in the Clear Sky World and stood up, looking all around him. His new eyes weren't derived from three scriptures. Rather, he'd broken the scriptures with understanding, letting him see the world as it truly was.

People were dying, and spirits were drifting. He saw karmic attachments he'd never dreamed of before. Every man and woman, their physical tells, their cultivations. He saw truths he never would have imagined before, and they were many, and overwhelming.

And above Hong Xin's body, he saw the Yellow River—the rush of souls and the reaper that stood there shaking his head.

"Her time is over," Yama said. "Let her go."

His timeless eyes were filled with pity. Wang Jun, at a high cost to his own life, had anchored the soul just inches away from the yellow stream, and though it had ceased moving forward, it saw no inclination to return. He saw the truth in the soul's motions. Its time was up. It wanted this farce to end.

"Her body is dead," Yama said. "She has nowhere else to go. Let her go to where she's meant to."

Cha Ming ignored him and summoned a Living Talisman and threw it on her body. The body's heart began beating, and technically, it lived.

"Her body lives. Surely she can return," Cha Ming said, turning to Yama.

Yama shook his head again. "She needs a medium, a powerful one that bridges life and death." Hearing these words, Cha Ming held up a hand. A green talisman materialized out of creation qi.

"Dying leaves carpet the forest floor," Cha Ming said. *"Man is*

left pondering his demise. Living life to its fullest potential; Never questioning his struggle."

The Samsara Talisman that had just appeared burned like a phoenix undergoing nirvana, and from it shot a powerful aura of life and death. It linked Hong Xin's soul and body, pulling her a short distance from the river.

"I know that accepting death is difficult, young one," Yama said like a wise grandfather, "but the bond isn't powerful enough. You know nothing about her, and that weakens your ability to help her." He waved his hand, and the shadowy tether Wang Jun had made quivered and broke. "He had the knowledge, but not the power."

"Please?" Cha Ming asked. Then he looked to Hong Xin's body and saw something. He looked to her soul and saw another. At that moment, he thought of his time in the Spirit Woods, when Wang Jun had explained Huxian's situation.

"Everyone has a true name," Cha Ming said as he realized the truth. He looked up to Yama, whose hand paused. "Elder Ling once said that devil sealers used the true names of devils to seal them. A name is enough, isn't it?"

Yama said nothing. Cha Ming looked to Hong Xin's soul and focused. Strange characters he'd never seen before appeared. He took the Clear Sky Brush and painted on the bond of samsara he'd drawn between her body and soul. He copied the meaningless characters a bit at a time until they were fully written, and the moment he finished the last one, something changed.

The tether shivered. Its nature harmonized with Hong Xin's body and soul. They began to drift closer, and Yama shook his head. "Your attachment means little, young man. She lives, but she will eventually die. You've only saved her for a few dozen years, if that is what she's destined for."

"Living is a struggle," Cha Ming said. "Trying your best doesn't contradict the laws of life and death."

"You're right," Yama said. "It doesn't. Life is a struggle, even for the dead." With those words, the Yellow River vanished, taking Yama away with it.

Hong Xin breathed, and her eyes opened. Though Cha Ming wanted nothing more than to hug and speak to her, he collapsed to the ground in exhaustion. He'd spent too much of his strength, and now it was time to rest.

Chapter 18: Moving Forward

"Come in," Cha Ming said, not waiting for the knock to land on the door of his room in the Wang family mansion. The door opened, revealing Wang Jun. He looked haggard and gaunt, like he hadn't slept in weeks. Exhaustion aside, only a few blond hairs remained on his head of white, making it obvious at a glance the steep price he'd paid over the last few months. Though the battle was far from over, his friend didn't have much time left. Not unless he transcended.

"It's time," Wang Jun said, still standing in the door frame. "The Jin royal family and the Church of Justice are done rooting out the rebels who escaped. The city is clean as a whistle, which is more than can be said for half the North. Ironically, betrayal has led to stability. We have the luxury of thinking ahead and supporting the other kingdoms."

"Let's go," Cha Ming said with a wistful smile. They walked in silence for a while, wandering about the mansion to pick up a few of the surviving elders to escort them. The great irony of the entire affair was that Wang Jun, as prime director of the Wang family, was technically supposed to be next in line for the family leadership. Patriarch Wuling had overwritten this rule, putting nine others between Wang Jun and him for succession. None of them had made it out of the battle alive, leaving only the second young master to fill the vacant role.

"You could have told me," Cha Ming finally said as they left the mansion. "You could have told me she was safe."

"And if I asked you not to share a secret, would you?" Wang Jun asked. Cha Ming thought about it and supposed he wouldn't. "Things were relatively peaceful then. I never anticipated these consequences. By the time I wanted to tell you, it was already too late."

Cha Ming sighed. "Where is she?" He hadn't seen Hong Xin since the battle, as he'd been asleep for a while, too busy recovering to search for her.

"Sleeping," Wang Jun said. "In the Red Dust Pavilion, where very capable people are taking care of her. You may have noticed her condition when you brought her back from the Yellow River. She's not as strong as she used to be. Not anymore."

Gold Leaf Square was far less frightening than it had been a few hours ago. The blood in the streets had been washed away, leaving only red stains on the concrete, to be cleaned off at a later date. Burnt-down trees had been cut at the stump, as these trees were apparently quite resilient, able to regrow a replacement if the roots were intact. The fountain, however, was gone. The battle had been too much for the structure, and its bath and foundation were so full of cracks that all water had leaked out, making it better to do away with it rather than repair the damage. The Spirit Temple was in ashes, and inquisitors had followed up on Cha Ming's quick destruction of it, hunting down stray ghosts that had managed to hide away from his Spirit-Banishing Intent.

Spirit-Banishing Intent. Cha Ming no longer had such a thing. And though he'd lost his ability to see and interact with evil spirits, he now saw the world as he never had. Several other dimensions now complemented the original three, giving life to the many colors that lit up the world. Many things that had been hidden from his eyes before could be read like an open book. Exact cultivation levels, cultivation types, the names of techniques, and the true names of people and things. He could see merit and sin and demonic energies, and thick and thin lines of karma that connected people and things. The best analogy he could think of was that he'd been a near-sighted man with no concept of three-dimensional vision that suddenly gained fully functioning eyesight along with full stereoscopy. It was... overwhelming.

Fortunately, this change in vision had been the result of a change in mindset. His memories had become clearer, and he was able to analyze things with great clarity. He even wagered that his *Angels and Devils* skills had improved from the transformation. Formations that might have seemed challenging before were no longer an issue, as his fine control over runic energy had gone up by leaps and bounds.

"I wish I could do more for her," Cha Ming said, spotting a group of three women up ahead. Bai Ling, the new headmistress of the Red Dust Pavilion, wore the same ceremonial outfit she'd worn in battle. Her two vice heads, Ling Fei and Ji Bingxue, followed slightly behind her. *One is a dancer and the other a... painter?* The ice-cold woman, Ling Fei, apparently had a few hidden talents she never shared with anyone, including her sisters. Small secrets like these brought a smile to Cha Ming's face. They were the unnecessary frosting that brought sweetness to the cake called life.

"How is she?" Wang Jun asked as they drew nearer.

"Well enough, given that she'd had her heart broken twice and died once in the past six hours," Bai Ling said. "She asked about you before we forced her back to sleep. She wanted to see you."

"I'm afraid I can't face her quite yet," Wang Jun said. "I still have much to make amends for, and the war doesn't seem to wait for the whims of mortals. But I'm working on it."

"Very well," Bai Ling said. "Let's get on with it."

They joined Wang Jun and Cha Ming's group as they made their way to the north of the city where the royal palace was located.

Neither Wang Jun nor Cha Ming had ever set foot in this supposedly holy place. Every building within the palace walls was said to be hallowed. At first, he'd discounted such a thing, but then he noticed a light golden glow clinging to every building, protecting them from external forces. He recognized this glow as something similar to the glow he kept inside his own body: divinity. They were indeed blessed buildings, he realized. The revelation gave credence to what he'd originally assumed was a strange but unfounded religion.

At the center of the royal palace wasn't the royal audience hall but a grand cathedral to the sun goddess, a wondrous structure with alabaster walls that sported intricate golden patterns and tinted glass windows. The audience hall off to its side was much smaller. Though similar in décor, it had clearly been built to show the crown's subservience to the Church.

They walked into the palace complex unimpeded. Cha Ming wondered whether this had to do with their newfound trust for them or their lack of manpower after the battle in Gold Leaf Square. Everyone showed telltale signs of exhaustion and overdrafting their strength. They made their way to the audience hall where guards opened the door for them, allowing them entry. Several dozen nobles had already entered. These were the king's closest allies, the ones who had remained loyal through thick and thin. There were also several high-ranking figures from the Church of Justice, including the vice chancellor who'd fought alongside them.

"I have come as instructed," Wang Jun said as they entered.

"As have we," Bai Ling said.

"Forgive our tardiness, but I had to recover after my battle with the late Ancestor Wang," Cha Ming said.

"It is impressive that you managed to last so long against him, let alone defeat him," said Vice Chancellor Lin, the only transcendent in the room. He bowed to the king. "Forgive my interruption. I'll be standing to the side unless you request my input."

"Thank you, all of you, for coming," King Tai said as the man retreated. "Time is short, and we've all suffered devastating losses. Many friends and family members have died, and much was lost in battle today. And the battle was just the beginning. Afterward, I sent out my elites. We put down the weaker forces our opponents had left behind, and we imprisoned the families of those who rebelled to ensure their future cooperation. Now, we must rebuild our great nation to weather the upcoming storm. I ask all of you: What have you lost? And what are you prepared to contribute given those losses?"

There was silence for a moment before a member of the Church of Justice stepped up.

"The Church of Justice has lost fifty percent of its fighting prowess," announced Chaplain Wu, who'd lost an arm in the battle. Only a bandaged stump remained of his left arm, as he'd had time to heal it but not enough time to regrow it using expensive spirit medicines. "Though our losses were great, we will commit our entire force to fighting back the darkness."

"The Chen family has lost eighty percent of its fighting force," a tall man with broad shoulders said. "But we will commit all we have left to fighting back the darkness."

On and on they went, with everyone present mentioning their casualties. Eventually, Bai Ling spoke, revealing that the Red Dust Pavilion had lost forty percent of their members.

"The Wang family has lost eighty percent of its fighting force," Wang Jun said. "But we will commit our entire force to fighting back the darkness."

"You?" Chaplain Wu asked, raising an eyebrow. His comment drew stares. "You, the master of darkness, would fight it? Even when fighting, you plot and scheme, and stab your family in the back."

King Tai raised his hand. "It was only his clever ploy that allowed us to uproot our foes and the Spirit Temple," he said. "And never forget that warfare employs deception, and that light can create illusions that trick minds and blinds foes."

"Yes, my king," Chaplain Wu said. Though the Church of Justice technically oversaw the Golden Kingdom's monarchy, the king was considered the head of the Church, and chaplains only his spiritual advisors. Only the chancellor and his vice chancellors, transcendents in the Church, had any sway over him.

"Patriarch Jun, please forgive my chaplain, but he did express legitimate concerns," King Tai said, turning his attention back to Wang Jun. "In this time of great darkness, we are looking for some assurances."

"I understand," Wang Jun said, stepping forward, unarmed. "A creature like me is reviled by all. It is reviled by the Church for being born different and reviled by its family for much the same reason. I have never been treated like anyone else, nor do I ever expect to be. Though I wonder, what is the reason for the difference in treatment? Is it because no matter how hard you run, you'll never catch me? Or is it because if I decide to finish someone, they'll never see the dagger coming?"

"Are you threatening us?" Chaplain Wu said, stepping between him and the king.

"I'm simply stating facts," Wang Jun said. "And don't forget that the Wang family still controls vast wealth, and the eighty percent losses did not include the thirty percent losses to our impressive mercenary force, which, might I add, is still in our employment for a full ten years."

The king's expression turned cold. "Are you really going to use this delicate time to negotiate? Are you sure you wish to do this?"

Wang Jun smiled. "I'm not here to negotiate, I'm simply here to state facts."

Heavens, Cha Might thought, rolling his eyes. Why did his friend have to be such a drama queen? In some ways, he was worse than Gua, who made a mountain out of a molehill whenever the opportunity presented itself. Already, men were drawing swords and cultivators releasing their qi. The audience hall was like a powder keg waiting to blow. The only thing stopping them from attacking was the king's raised hand. The man was a powerful cultivator, and if he couldn't take care of a threat to his life, likely no one else in this room could, save the lone transcendent.

"Henceforth," Wang Jun said, his voice carrying across the entire room, "the Wang family turns full control of its mercenary forces to Marshal Feng Ming of the Northern Alliance, to do as he deems fit without need of our consultation. Did you hear that, mercenary leader?"

"Loud and clear," said Chen Yangjing, who'd been lurking about in a corner of the room. "Such a generous man, giving away such a pricey contract."

"I don't understand," King Tai said, frowning in confusion.

"As I said, I'm not here to negotiate; I'm here to state facts," Wang Jun replied. Then, he looked to the back of the room, where Cha Ming noticed a shadow walking through the half-open door unimpeded. The shadow walked up to Wang Jun and took the form of a white-haired old man.

"Young master, I did as you requested," the old man said. It was Elder Bai, whom Cha Ming had been told Wang Jun had let go a few days earlier.

"How did this man get inside?" King Tai exclaimed once Elder Bai appeared. "Guards, throw him out!" A pair of inquisitors lunged for Elder Bai, who seemed to blink out of existence and blink back into existence a short while later.

"I dare you to touch a hair on this man's body," Wang Jun said crisply. "His arrival is timely, and he comes at my request. Three days ago, I entrusted a secret task to him. Tell me Elder Bai, how much did you manage to spend?"

"Alas, out of the fifty million you entrusted me with, I spent only forty," Elder Bai said. "I'm a terrible spender, and very frugal. The goods have been delivered to various major cities and battlefields, where the common people have joined forces against the South. In fact, there's a stockpile that's been delivered here just now."

"My king!" a voice yelled from outside the door. "A massive pile of armaments has been abandoned before the palace gates!"

"That was also the largest shipment," Elder Bai whispered not too quietly with a hand beside his mouth. "I figured you needed a larger one here as an apology."

"What is going on here?" King Tai said. "Why am I constantly being interrupted in my own court?"

"Relax, King Tai," Wang Jun said. "You will soon be getting a flood of reports. The people of the North have been coddled, you see. They haven't had to suffer through hardship like the Southerners have. The weather here is temperate, and the lands arable. They've been safe, not knowing war all along. This makes them weak.

"But the comfort that led to this weakness has its advantages. These same people, through no small effort on my own part, have been given cultivation bases they weren't lucky enough to be born with. They've been given wealth beyond their wildest dreams and are members of the first wave of a cultural revolution.

"These men and women are the future of the North, King Tai. They see the South coming to take their newfound wealth, and they're not about to give it up. These people might be weak individually, but together, they're strong. The South isn't just fighting our armies, my king, but billions of qi-condensation cultivators. These men and women, once the rabble of society, have gotten a leg up in life and aren't willing to give up their newfound wealth.

"Elder Bai has, at my request, purchased forty million top-grade spirit stones' worth of weapons. Most of them will be spirit weapons and low-grade magic weapons, crafted and delivered. In addition to this down payment, the remaining funds of the Wang family are now officially available for the war effort. We will be placing orders with every weapons manufacturer, big or small, to arm the many Northern armies. The embargoes and negotiations are over. The North is back in business. As for myself, I will personally spend every penny I have fighting the encroaching menace.

"You asked for assurances? My assurance is that I have nothing left. You will never be able to kill me, and my fortunes have fallen into other good men's hands, so you can't take that either. My staff will work tirelessly to help procure much-needed supplies, and we will continue coordinating logistics for the battle. In addition, our elders will fight when required, though my advice is that they are best used for organization and management, which is their strength. That is our assurance, and our apology, King Tai. What say you?"

King Tai looked at him gravely. He looked to Chaplain Wu, who was speechless. He looked to the vice chancellor, who nodded and smiled. "Very well. Since this small matter is settled, let us switch to discussing tactics."

A light glowed, and a giant map of the continent appeared at the center of the room. King Tai walked through the illusory map and stuck his finger on Gold Leaf City. "We are here." He pointed southwest, where a dark spot was moving. "The Southern forces and the Taotie are here. They are moving at a strange angle toward True North Country, likely so they can have the entire west coast to themselves."

He tapped one of the partitioned territories, the Evergreen Kingdom, and it turned red, joining the rest of the Southern Alliance territory. The Northern Alliance territory was blue, and everywhere they looked, tiny red spots peppered them. There were much larger red spots near battlefields, including the Eastern Desert, the Long Kingdom, and the Phoenix Cry Empire. Even the Southern Battlefield had started fighting, its forces bolstered by the Quicksilver Empire.

"Wang Jun, Bai Ling, I hear you have excellent tactical minds," King Tai said. "Come join us in planning the North's defense."

"As you command," Wang Jun said.

The king then turned to Cha Ming. "I have no authority over you, and speaking to Marshal Feng, it seems he has some ideas where your efforts would best be utilized. Since the situation here has stabilized, I think it is best if you contact him personally."

"I will do as instructed," Cha Ming said. He bowed and left along with several other people who weren't needed for the planning meeting. The gloom in the room had lifted, and everyone was speaking in excited whispers. These men and women had expected a confrontation. They'd expected a condemnation. Instead, they'd gotten funding. They'd gotten men. They'd gotten closure. Most importantly, however, they'd gotten hope. A bright ray of sunshine was finally peeking through the clouds.

"So you're leaving?" Sun Wukong asked, appearing beside him. "Just like that?"

"Just like that," Cha Ming replied. He walked out of the audience hall and flew into the air despite the indignation of the guards in the palace complex. No one dared stop him, though a patrolling angelic transcendent nodded to him as he left the city. "Hong Xin is safe;

Wang Jun's problem is resolved. There's nothing left for me to do here."

"Always so low key," Sun Wukong said. "You need to learn to show off a bit. Bask in the glory. You fought a transcendent, boy! And you won! Think about how great an achievement that is!" They continued flying, and Cha Ming said nothing. "Is something on your mind, boy?"

"I remembered something," Cha Ming said. "Something I saw long ago. I had doubts about the place before, but now I have many more questions that need answering."

"Which place?" Sun Wukong said. "What could have possibly escaped my wonderful senses?"

"You were sleeping," Cha Ming said. "And I was in a hurry. Besides, I'm not sure you'll be able to see what I see. Not anymore." Through these gray eyes, Cha Ming could see much farther than ever. He could see wind currents, energy patterns, and karmic attachments. He was currently following a very specific karmic thread: his attachment to a place he'd thought he'd never revisit.

They were headed toward the Silverwing Mountain Range, where the Pure Jade Defensive Formation was still happily waiting for him. And in the center, something else. Something powerful Something ancient.

Chapter 19: Pushing Ahead

Feng Ming flicked a playing card up in the air, catching it effortlessly as its chaotic tumble brought it back down in perfect alignment with his ready fingers. He repeated the motion over and over, using the repetitive task to preoccupy his overwhelmed mind. The Northern Alliance was in danger. And of all things, it was crumbling from the inside, a fatal flaw in its foundation that crushed it beneath the weight of its own disagreements.

"Who would have thought luck would be so useless in some situations?" he muttered, continuing the flicking. Luck could make this card fall as it should. It could make battles unfold as he wished. Hell, it could even find him the perfect wife, Song Guo, who was currently pouring him a cup of tea and confiscating the half-finished bottle of baiju before he could get back to it. Yet for all the good it did, it couldn't even unite them to fight a common enemy. Petty squabbles now ruled over life and death, completely overturning what their alliance was created for in the first place.

"Come now, it can't be that bad, dear," Song Guo said, sitting beside him. He straightened up and accepted his tea, grimacing as he took the first sip. It wasn't normal tea, he realized, but a medicinal one. His intoxication reduced substantially with only a single mouthful. She was doing what she thought was best for him—he knew that—but with the intoxication gone, the massive load of self-doubt and despair filled the gap.

"The South has breached the Evergreen Battlefield," Feng Ming said with a sigh. "Gold Leaf City is fighting an all-out rebellion, and many kingdoms will soon follow. There's fighting everywhere, whether with swords or with money, and everyone is being selfish. To make matters worse, a world-ending creature has somehow been tamed by the South. They've recklessly turned it against us, but it's only a matter of time before it turns on the plane itself. We can't win, Song Guo. We've lost."

"Look at me," Song Guo said, but Feng Ming averted his gaze. "Look at me!" she repeated. Reluctantly, Feng Ming obeyed. He was greeted by a smarting slap to the face. "How dare you give up!"

"Coming to grips with the facts is not giving up," Feng Ming said, doing his best to ignore the sting on his right cheek. "It's only by facing reality that we preserve what we can." Another slap came, but this time, he intercepted it and grabbed her wrist. She yanked it away with tearful eyes.

"This isn't the man I married," Song Guo said in a hurt voice. "The man I married would never give up. He would see great difficulties and overcome them like a true hero. You aren't my husband. You're a coward."

"The difficulties are too great," Feng Ming repeated.

"And how will you know unless you try?" she said, her tears continuing. "You tried for as long as you felt comfortable, and you failed. You know what I think? I think your luck has made you soft. It makes everything easy without as much work as normal people need to put in. If you don't succeed on your first try, you think it's impossible.

"But what about the second try? And the third? What about the ninety-ninth try? Don't you care about me? Don't you care about your children?" The cries of their youngest interrupted them. She looked back, then, red-eyed, walked out the room to care for her.

"I just don't know what I can do," Feng Ming muttered, retrieving a jade tablet from a side table. On it, he saw briefings of major events all across the continent. A casualty report from the Phoenix Burial Battlefield. Another refusal to a trade agreement from Quicksilver. Another rebellion, this time in the Xia Empire.

The sheer amount of news was overwhelming. Song Guo blamed him for not trying. She thought he'd given up after a few refusals. But she didn't know that he'd tried and failed many more times than ninety-nine. Hundreds of situations had cropped up over a matter of days, and he'd failed in alleviating all but a handful. There simply weren't enough men to take care of these problems, and where there were, there wasn't enough money or supplies. And with the economic lifeline of the North in shambles, more than half of their kingdoms were turtling on themselves, hoping to strike as best a deal as they could once their enemies finally came to their borders. A deal he could never make, given how many times he'd personally offended the South. His kingdom and family were doomed.

Feng Ming frowned as he scrolled through the many entries. He saw red where he shouldn't—he usually checked every one of these red-tagged entries, as they were important news that couldn't be missed. But then again, he'd been drinking, and he'd stopped checking the jade a few hours back. He scrolled to a spot that caught his eyes, an entry from a few hours ago. The battle that had finally erupted in Gold Leaf Square and had concluded. Through some trickery and double-crossing, the Golden Kingdom had won. *That* was a pleasant surprise. Most of the Wang family leadership had been killed in the conflict. Cha Ming had been involved as well.

Time to see if I've lost yet another friend, he thought, typing out a quick message to King Tai. Though they hadn't been close, he and Wang Jun had gone to school together and cooperated many times. Just as he was about to send the message, however, another entry appeared on the tablet. It was red.

Wang Jun pledges twenty peak-core-formation equivalents to Marshal Feng Ming of the North.

"What in the..." Feng Ming muttered. Where did that come from? Hadn't Wang Jun died? If most of the elders in the Wang family were dead, that meant the rebellion had failed, and their ringleader would either be put to death or imprisoned. More entries began to roll in.

The Wang family has opened up its coffers for the war effort.

The Golden Kingdom has mobilized to help True North Country in repelling the Southern Alliance.

A stockpile of weapons has been delivered to the Golden Kingdom.

A stockpile of weapons has been delivered to the Quicksilver Empire.

A stockpile of weapons has been delivered to the Xia Empire.

On and on it went, listing every country, and every major city in the North.

Gold Leaf City's Trade Association has announced expedited production of war goods.

Huoshan's Spiritual Blacksmiths have begun wartime production.

The Xia Empire has announced its full support to the war effort.

Feng Ming could barely believe his eyes.

Just what had happened over the past three hours? They were a drunken blur, a haze he'd willingly pushed himself into to numb himself to the upcoming bad news. Moreover, this was too much, too fast. He'd tried his best for days to solve the North's problems, but to no avail, and then out of nowhere, problems were solving themselves?

"Li Fei, are you seeing this?" Feng Ming sent through his core-transmission jade. A small jade figure appeared on the other side.

"It seems that though the Wang family was severely damaged," Li Fei said, "Wang Jun seems to have gone along with the betrayal to set up an ambush and completely obliterate Northern influence in the Golden Kingdom. Now he's actively throwing money around to solve all our problems. Judging by the recent deliveries, it seems he'd already been working on it but hadn't wanted to reveal his ploy early in order to lure the snake from its hole. Currently, production lines are running smoothly. Troops are being deployed and armed, and if this keeps up, we might even be able to organize a resistance."

Feng Ming summoned a map and sifted through the red dots indicating rebels and cultists. It also included the relative military strength of each country. He frowned, however, as red dots began disappearing, and small cities that had been lost began reverting back to friendly status.

"What's going on in those kingdoms?" he said. "I haven't seen any battle announcements on my news feed."

"It's been going on for a while now, but we're finally seeing the results," Li Fei said. "I tried to contact you earlier, but you responded in so drunk a fashion I doubt you can even remember."

"Just tell me," Feng Ming said with mild irritation. The North didn't have enough troops to force out such widespread incursions so quickly.

"It's the civilians," Li Fei said. "Apparently, someone went ahead and armed them, and we forgot to consider that we have billions of cultivators in the North now, all unregistered, that very much like their homes and would hate to lose them. They've organized themselves into militias that fall outside our chain of command, and through sheer force of numbers, they are forcing back the cultists and bandits and retaking their occupied cities."

"Wang Jun, you bloody genius," Feng Ming muttered. He summoned a large map from his tablet to survey the situation in more detail. "We're making progress, but we're not out of the woods yet. Let's get in touch with the Xia Empire first. They joined so quickly because they were desperate, and their local Spirit Temple is actively making things difficult for them."

"Is that something we can even help with?" Li Fei asked.

"It wasn't a few days ago," Feng Ming said. "Fortunately, the Golden Kingdom is stabilized, and the Church of Justice has inquisitors to spare. I'll contact King Tai to get his support." He didn't wait for her reply and immediately hung up and placed a call.

"King Tai?" Feng Ming asked. "I'm going to need to ask you for a favor."

In the western woods of the Quicksilver Empire, a storm raged. Tribulation lightning filled the skies, and the monarch and three sovereigns of the nearby mountain range cowered beneath the clouds. Though they feared what would happen when their foe emerged, they also knew running was senseless. After all, he was facing tribulation lightning with his bare body, and all it was doing was strengthening him.

I doubt we'll survive this, the Clay Dragon Sovereign said to his companion, a rather large butterfly. *I insulted his mother, which is definitely a low blow in the demon code of conduct.* His draconic body, though large and covered in stone, seemed especially fragile under the lightning's illumination. Many of his tile-like scales were broken from his initial clash with their opponent, despite being the most physically tough of their group when adjusting for cultivation.

I didn't do anything, the Nightmare Butterfly said. *But Master Sun once said that good friends can be your prop, and bad friends can be your downfall. Be careful when choosing friends, and even more careful when choosing allies.*

Master Sun did not *say that*, the Razorback Sovereign said. It wasn't a butterfly or a dragon, but a crow. While the butterfly monarch had illusory and ethereal features, the Razorback Sovereign's were hard and sharp. Every one of her feathers was a lethal blade that could easily rend the skin of demons equal in power.

I think you will all be fine, said the Storm Tiger Monarch, the leader of the bunch. *You are beneath him in cultivation. I, on the other hand, am in deep trouble. My kind and his have an irreconcilable enmity. As Master Sun said, a mouse will never miss out an on opportunity to slay a tiger.* He gulped as the lightning in the skies began to subside.

I don't think Master Sun said that either, the Nightmare Butterfly muttered.

Quiet, the Razorback Sovereign said, cutting her off. The clouds, which had hung over their valley for hundreds of years, began to part. Thunder roared as a small figure emerged—perhaps six feet tall and half as wide. It was the creature's small stature that had led them to insult it in the first place. Who would have known that the small creature asking to take over their territory so politely would be such a fearsome beast? In hindsight, they should have given the mouse the benefit of the doubt. Calamity-Swallowing Mice were far too rare, and they could be forgiven for making the mistake.

The mouse flickered and appeared beside the Clay Dragon Sovereign. *Who was it that insulted this general's mother again? Was it you?*

I—the Clay Dragon Sovereign started, but the mouse zipped over to the Nightmare Butterfly Sovereign.

Were you the one who got him say it? Lei Jiang asked, glaring at the oversized butterfly.

I apologize for my negligence in controlling my acquaintance, the Nightmare Butterfly said, bowing her head. But by the time she was done bowing, he'd already zipped over to the Storm Tiger Monarch.

Look at you, big tiger and all, the mouse said. *If I, Lei Jiang, wasn't so high and mighty, I might bring myself down to your level to teach you a lesson.*

This one accepts his inferiority, the Storm Tiger Monarch said. As he spoke, however, a small claw tore a deep gouge on his cheek.

What was that? the mouse said. *I couldn't quite hear it.*

This one accepts— the Storm Tiger Monarch said just before being struck by another claw. Then another, then another.

You tigers always think you're hot stuff, bullying mice wherever you go, the small gray mouse said. *I think it's high time I corrected that.* A black lightning initiation mark appeared above it, crackling with the power of half-step initiation. The clouds rumbled with power, and the sovereigns trembled in fear. They prostrated themselves before the mouse alongside the tiger, their master.

It was over. They were done for. Or that's what they thought before an actual physical voice chimed in, one they hadn't heard in years. "Uncle Lei Jiang, don't you think you're going a little overboard?" it said.

They looked to the source and noticed it wasn't a demon but a human, and a human they recognized. It was Ling Dong, and the power he emanated gave them hope.

Wait, did he say Uncle *Lei Jiang?* the Razorback Sovereign whispered to her companions. If it was an uncle-nephew relationship, they might truly be doomed.

Junior Ling Dong, butt out, Lei Jiang said. *I'm exacting vengeance for all mouse kind!* He continued beating the tiger.

"That's terribly unfortunate," Ling Dong said. "I'm sure what you're doing is fair and just, but unfortunately, I owe this tiger a favor. Could you give me this face and spare him? Spare all of them?"

Lei Jiang glared at the tiger, then to their surprise, withdrew his claws. *I suppose I can give you this face, Junior. Have you heard from my friends yet? Was I the fastest as predicted?*

Ling Dong shifted uncomfortably. "Unfortunately, you were the slowest," Ling Dong said. "Silverwing finished first. Then came Mr. Mountain, then Gua. I came here to check up on you, but I guess that wasn't necessary."

Unacceptable, Lei Jiang said. Lightning began to fall around him, destroying rocks and striking trees. *Unacceptable!* he yelled, and the lightning storm expanded, threatening to destroy the entire mountain.

"Silverwing wanted me to mention something, however," Ling Dong said. "You might technically be last, and as per the agreement, that makes you the fifth brother. However, Huxian hasn't finished gaining his initiation mark. He says it's a gray area, and everyone has agreed to start calling Huxian 'Little Boss' from now on."

Little Boss? Lei Jiang said, the lightning still raging. Then, it stopped. The skies became quiet, and the clouds disappeared. *I like it. Let's go.*

He flew up into the empty sky, leaving behind the four weaker demons. Ling Dong joined him.

"There's an issue I need your help with," Ling Dong said once they were a short distance away. "There's a man called the fiend whisperer. He's been corrupting demons all over the continent. Silverwing and the others have been rounding them up. We're gathering in Quicksilver, but we need a staging area."

"Leave it to Uncle Lei Jiang," Lei Jiang said. "I'll set one up for you in a jiffy."

"Um, please don't raze a forest to the ground with heavenly judgment," Ling Dong said. "That's a request from all of us. We feel quite strongly about it."

Lei Jiang rolled his eyes. "Fine," he said. "I'll threaten heavenly judgment and mete it out if warranted. Happy?"

"Delighted," Ling Dong said. "I'd love to stay and chat, but time is short. I need to make a trip to Huoshan before all hell breaks loose. And remember, act quickly. Those fiends aren't just popping up everywhere; they're moving."

"Where are they going?" Lei Jiang asked, then his eyes widened in realization.

"You've got it," Ling Dong said. "They're grouping up in a forest just to the south of the Quicksilver Empire. We're not just staging demons; we're hosting a welcome party."

"It's time," Luo Xuehua said, waking Yue Bing from her meditation. "Are you sure about this?"

"Desperate times call for desperate measures," Yue Bing answered, straightening out her bloodred robes as Luo Xuehua led her down the stairs. "I thought all night about it, and I see no reason to back down."

A few attendants nodded as they journeyed to the bottom of the building. They wished her luck, and she would need it.

They were now in the basement of the Alabaster Group's

headquarters, under the personal protection of Lu Tianhao himself. No one would dare interrupt them here, save another transcendent, and even then, they'd have to think twice about it. As higher-ranking members, they were privy to some information. Transcendents weren't all equal in power, and Lu Tianhao was one of the strongest among them.

They opened a door that led into a large stone room, which had been painted with bloodred runes. Though they were red, they were aligned with many elements, for blood flowed, was metallic, had weight, and had energy. But what many people didn't know was that blood *lived*. Before cultivating Hua Tuo's legacy, she'd never realized it herself. Soon, others would also know. She hadn't come here to cultivate; she had come to teach.

Though Yue Bing had taught others before, they had been weak, and they had only been taught the basics. Actual blood cultivation was dangerous for many reasons beyond the obvious ones. But what they needed now was strength, so strength she would give them.

Five men and five women sat in the room cross-legged. Each one was a late-marrow-refining cultivator, glowing bright with a jade aura. Though she could endow anyone she wished with the power of blood, it helped if the subject already had deep vitality reserves, as this would reduce the strain on her own body.

"You have one last chance to turn back," Yue Bing said as she entered, placing a red vial on one of four points in a runic circle inside the room. She walked clockwise, not looking at them. "What I'm placing here is the blood of our enemies, forcibly harvested to enhance your cultivation."

"We aren't scared of dying," one of the men said. "Nor are we scared of harming devils and evil men."

"I wasn't talking about that," Yue Bing said, placing a second vial. "Blood is a strange element, and it can arouse hidden passions in men and women alike. The first blood masters are prime examples. They were students of my master, led astray by sinful thoughts and the allure of power." She walked over to another corner and placed a third vial. "In peaceful times, blood cultivation is useless. It is best practiced during war, when one can cultivate blood with righteous purpose. When there is peace, your cultivation will stall, forever unable to advance further. Then you'll be tempted to kill others, if only to pursue the peak like all the others around you are doing."

"I am ready to make that sacrifice," one of the women said as Yue Bing placed a fourth vial. "We need strength now, not later. I never hoped to achieve godhood, and I only joined the Alabaster Group to protect."

"And do you all feel the same way?" Yue Bing asked. Firm nods followed. "We'll need privacy," she said to Luo Xuehua. "Will the next batch be ready in a day?"

"How many can you transform?" Luo Xuehua asked.

"Each inheritance carries great risk, but desperate times call for desperate measures," Yue Bing said. "I'll endow as many as I can, and if I don't make it, it will be up to the Alabaster Group to police them."

"We'll make sure they don't get out of control," Luo Xuehua said. "We're not toothless spirit doctors, so picky when enforcing justice."

"If all goes well, I'll keep them in line myself," Yue Bing said. "What can be given can also be taken away."

Luo Xuehua nodded and left the room. She didn't see the red glow that filled it, but she heard the screams.

Yue Bing would hear them for the next full day. Converting one's cultivation was very different than starting from scratch—to transform them, she needed to destroy them and heal them, over and over, replacing their bodies from the inside out.

"No means no," Gong Shuren, the Sea God Emissary, said to Gong Xuandi, who was kneeling in the emperor's audience chamber. Several royals were there enjoying the spectacle, the prostration of a former emperor.

"I understand your reluctance, but things are really getting out of control," Gong Xuandi said. "It's different than last time. Things have changed."

"Have they?" Gong Shuren asked, leaning forward in her throne. "We remain neutral for a reason, Xuandi. Right and wrong, good and evil, they change their minds like a woman changes clothes. Luck favors one then the other on a whim. No one knows when this will change. We sow karma at our own risk."

"I'm not talking about good and evil," Gong Xuandi said, stubborn but eyes still looking down. "I'm only talking about the creature. If the Taotie isn't handled properly, it could spell the doom of our lineage and would mean a great loss to the Sea God Plane."

"Perhaps," Gong Shuren said. "But it has not come to that yet. Return with your few men and fight as Feng Ming orders. That is your punishment."

"Forgive me for correcting you, but my orders are to follow Marshal Feng's orders, and he did not ask me to fight, he asked me to beg," Gong Xuandi said. "And though we argue and bicker a lot, I'm afraid I agree with him. If we don't defeat the creature, our empire is in danger. I came here because there's no greater power on this plane than the power of the Sea God, which is manifested in his emissary and his personal treasure, the clock tower."

"Perhaps I will act. In time," Gong Shuren said. "But that time hasn't come yet. Go, before I throw you out."

Gong Xuandi shook his head and looked her in the eye. A sign of great disrespect, but desperate times called for desperate measures. "I will remain kneeling here until you agree to help."

Gong Shuren shrugged. "Then stay kneeling. You watch and learn how a real emperor should rule. Next!"

A Haijing royal stepped up to answer her call. "I've come with a plea for aid in fighting a territorial group of demonic dolphins," the man said.

Gong Xuandi recognized him. He'd dealt with the annoying man many times in the past.

Gong Shuren, sensing his irritation, prodded the man along. "Please, tell me more." And he did so. Gong Xuandi rolled his eyes but didn't rise. He was here on a mission, and he wouldn't leave until he accomplished it.

Chapter 29: Last Chance

An eagle screeched loudly, and the screech ripped through Huxian's mind like a claw through tender flesh. It was difficult to move, difficult to think, but think he did, barely avoiding a spatial blockade. He maneuvered around them as he dodged the slashing wings of the terrifying bird. Not a normal bird but fear incarnate, complete with eight wings.

Huxian wasn't sure if there was a point to this battle, nor was he sure if he would gain anything. But it was the last portion of the trial, and he'd be damned if he didn't try to squeeze every last bit of space dust he could out of this place. His eyes burned bright with the third stage of Time-Torching Eyes: High Noon. He used the first stage of Moon-Eclipsing Wings, Void-Piercing Feather to shuttle through space and appear on the eagle's left flank.

They collided and tumbled to the ground in unison. As Huxian bit into its tender underside, the void eagle used its sharp beak and talons to rip into Huxian's large body. A common tactic when fighting such a creature would be to hop on its back where it was defenseless. But this eagle represented a simple truth of space—it was fearfully all-encompassing. It didn't use its eight wings to fly, but rather as extra limbs. Each appendage seemed to have a mind of its own, stabbing into his body in whichever way they could without wounding their master. They cut through his skin like it was tofu, causing severe damage to his demonic energy reserves. Battles with assassins were always like this. They were a life-and-death struggle he sometimes won, but he often had to escape with quite a lot less fur than he'd entered with, limping with a wounded body to fight off the next wave of daylight denizens.

This time, Huxian didn't need to worry about facing another opponent. This was the last platform in the trial, and he would give it his all. He flashed once more with Void-Piercing Feather, a movement skill that ignored distance and cut straight through the fabric of space. He bit down with his teeth, and the damage was amplified by his Time-Torching Eyes. High Noon was unlike the other skills in that it didn't do anything on its own. Instead, it magnified whatever abilities he used, doubling their effect by compressing time. Though he wasn't sure he understood the physics behind it, or if this physics made any sense it all, it was the best ability out of the bunch. Killing twice as fast meant living twice as quickly. Every second mattered when fighting with your life on the line.

Black dust sprinkled on the cold white snow. Before long, it became a slushy mess of violet and red. He didn't use his largest form, preferring to maintain a middling size lest he provide the bird with an unmissable target. He dodged one of the spatial wings, narrowly avoiding it by switching his Time-Torching Eyes to Setting Sun, dulling the energy in his surroundings, then piercing through space once again, dodging another wing and landing on the creature's back.

The void eagle screamed as he activated High Noon again, scratching into its blue and black feathers, ripping out its spatial wings. It blinked out of existence, but Huxian latched on, traveling through channels in space before appearing in another spot on the platform. Seeing that it couldn't shake him off, its wings detached, forming eight massive glass shards that attacked him in unison. The odd wingless bird fell to the ground as Huxian was forced to evade the furious onslaught.

Fortunately, he'd done this before many times. He rushed away from the eagle, projecting Setting Sun to weaken the spatial fragments and slow them down. *Not quite yet... Not quite yet... now!*

He'd discovered through trial and error that the eagle would recall its wings when they went too far. Having lured the wings away, he pierced through space yet again. This time, he grew to his largest size and bit down on the eagle, using his swamp and lightning domains to bog it down and using High Noon to double the damage he inflicted. The eagle, without enough time to summon its wings back, could only stand there and take the punishment. As the creature crumbled to dust, eight massive glass shards flew through space toward Huxian's chest. But Huxian was expecting this.

The large fox split into two, then four, then eight. He split a final time just before the shards were about to strike, narrowly avoiding them before recombining into his giant form once more. His eyes flared red as High Noon activated, and Huxian bit down once again. The rest of the void eagle's body disappeared, leaving nothing but black dust on the bloody snow. He breathed, and the dust poured into his back, growing the single feather that sat there. With enough dust, the feather would become a pair of wings. Not that any dust remained to be claimed.

Depressed by the fact that the fight hadn't gained him anything, he limped over to the edge of the platform. As always, the contents were shrouded until he physically crossed the threshold to the next. Once past it, a force kept him from going backward, and the next platform appeared in all its glory.

It was his final destination in the trials—he could tell by the lack of bridge or neighboring island. It was much different than the initial platform he'd appeared on at the start. He hadn't noticed it at first, but every platform had become progressively darker. This one was black as midnight, blending in with the blackness of space. Only the bright sun and moon that shone above him enabled him to differentiate between up and down.

There was one more odd thing about the place. Just like the first platform, a large object floated in the air. It wasn't an hourglass like before, but a giant needle. He'd sensed it back when he started condensing the Moon-Eclipsing Wings. Now that he could finally see it, and he recognized it as the Void Phoenix's Space-Piercing Needle.

"I made this artifact for my descendants long ago," a voice said. A beautiful woman appeared beside the needle, touching it. She had long black hair and silky white skin, and every step she took was entrancing. And her eyes—they were fearful eyes—bored into him like the spatial shards those evil void beings had used against him. "Only my inheritors can use the thing. And even then, only if they're strong enough."

Madam Void Phoenix, Huxian said, *I've completed the trial. Will I be able to condense a space-time mark?* Might as well cut to the chase.

The woman shook her head. "You haven't condensed enough of my power. At least the third stage is required, and it would need to balance out the stronger power of time you've accumulated within your eyes. I'm sorry, but the first stage of the Moon-Eclipsing Wings is all I can give you."

Then I thank you for your blessing, Huxian said. A strong ability like Void-Piercing Feather would be useful regardless. He didn't regret his decision to fight for it. In fact, he felt he was a better fox for it.

Beside the woman, the Candle Dragon appeared. This time, he took the form of an old man with glowing red eyes. "Don't be sad, young one. You've inherited enough of my power to condense a time mark. That's far better than what you could have gotten otherwise. I confess myself impressed. I never knew you had it in you."

Is there truly no other way? asked Huxian. It was a pity to have come so far and settle for the lesser prize—even if that prize was the one he'd come for in the first place.

"Perhaps there is," the Candle Dragon said. "Heaven never seals off all exits. But you know how the rules work—I can't tell you anything concrete. And even if I could, nothing comes to mind."

So it's useless, Huxian said. The Candle Dragon would never lie about such a thing.

"Will you be condensing your mark now or later?" the Candle Dragon asked. "If you do it now, I can help you shape your mark. In any case, this needle is the key to your return home. By activating it, you can pierce through tremendous barriers, including the barrier in and out of this independent space."

Thank you, Huxian said, bowing his head. *I just need time to think and rest.*

"As you wish," the Candle Dragon said. He and the Void Phoenix disappeared, leaving Huxian to collapse in a pool of his own blood. His wounds had not yet healed from the previous trial.

Was it truly the end of the line? Or was it just another trick? Although he'd tried very hard, he'd started on the Void Phoenix's inheritance too late. If only he'd risked his life earlier, then he would have gotten enough time to rest. More time to rest would have gotten him more dust, and he could have aced this entire exam.

Alas, life never gives second chances, Huxian thought. Second attempts, yes, but you could never erase your first. It was through these failures that you improved yourself, and through each experience that you grew. *Or does it?*

He looked at the floating black needle that seemed to connect all of reality. An idea sprouted in his mind. It was daring, life risking, and completely based on conjecture. He was sure the Void Phoenix would like it.

"It's really too bad," the Void Phoenix said as she and the Candle Dragon appeared a short distance away. "He has a lot of potential. If you hadn't said what you did in the beginning, he might have even succeeded in condensing both inheritances."

"Nothing I could do about it," the Candle Dragon said. "The Demon Conventions dictate that inheritances must contain riddles that test the candidate's intelligence. A full inheritance must never be given if the riddle isn't solved."

"But he's really good," the Void Phoenix said. "Maybe I'll find him after this and teach him a bit."

"That goes against the fourth rule, and you know it," the Candle Dragon said. "No second chances." He turned to look at Hushao. "Unless you're going to butt in and side with her?"

"No, I'm all right," Bagua Hushao said. He was lying on a haystack of all things, chewing on a stalk with his sharp foxy teeth. "And I think Huxian is all right too. Look at him. Does he look like someone's who's given up? At worst, this will make him a better fox. At best… Anyway, who cares about condensing some ultimate mark."

Above him floated a picture of Huxian. The small fox was currently sniffing the needle, inspecting it. He was looking around suspiciously, probably because he knew full well that workarounds could theoretically exist for such a complicated trial.

"I'm afraid I don't see a way out of it," the Candle Dragon said. "I didn't lie to him when I said that. He only had a single day and a single night for each phase of the trial. Further, the platforms only let him go one way."

"We made the rules pretty ironclad," the Void Phoenix said in agreement. "You approved them yourself."

Bagua Hushao grinned. "You're right, I did. I left a pretty big loophole, though. Let's see if he's smart enough to find it."

His two companions frowned and looked to Huxian. The black needle was glowing brightly, generating enough power to send him back home.

"See? He's given up," the Candle Dragon said. "He's already going home, even without condensing his mark. In my opinion, he's too embarrassed to do it here. I mean— What *is* he doing?"

The needle suddenly began to glow with a sharp dark light.

"He's feeding it with the void dust he condensed his feather with…" the Void Phoenix said, raising an eyebrow. "… sacrificing his technique to increase the piercing power. Does he think we tricked him? Does he think he won't make it back unless he gives something up?"

It was unusual but not unheard of. Some demon emperors were known to force their descendants to give something up. They were not of the same mindset, however, and the fox should know it.

"Maybe he thinks he needs a bit more piercing power where he's going," Bagua Hushao said with a grin. "Watch and learn, my friends. There's a reason that out of all the demons, foxes are still considered the most cunning."

Stupid trial, stupid games, Huxian thought as he poured the hard-earned space dust into the absurdly pointy needle. Void crackled around it as it generated far more power than necessary to pierce out of this demi-plane. Sure, it should be enough to get where he was going, but why take any chances? For all he knew, space was firmer inside the plane than at the borders between. And he was *not* going to get tricked again.

As the last of the black dust disappeared along with the single feathers on his back, the needle pulsed. He'd reached a milestone, it seemed, but for what, he didn't know. All he knew was that if what he had in mind didn't work, he might get trapped here for all eternity, never able to return. He could beg all he wanted, but the rules of inheritance were clear: You don't get second chances. They'd leave him to rot in this place between realms.

The Void Phoenix Trials rewarded bravery and daring, Huxian thought as he prepared himself mentally for the next step. He placed his paw on the glowing needle with hesitation before making his final decision. *Go big or go home.*

The needle let out a surge of power, forming a gray slit in reality. As he'd predicted, going where he wanted to go was much harder than simply leaving. The slit began closing immediately, so he zipped through, using his rudimentary knowledge of space and time to rush through the portal, but even as quick as he went, he clipped his tails in the process.

He appeared on a familiar platform. He'd been here before, at the start of the trials. One could only go forward here, but the Candle Dragon never said anything about going back to where you started. Piercing space wasn't normal movement. He'd simply gone forward in another direction. It wasn't *technically* cheating.

One problem solved, one more to go, he thought, walking up to the hourglass. The sand in his eyes began drifting out, filling the bottom of the container. He was back to where he started, yes, but that didn't change the fact that he only had one day to claim each trial's reward. The dust had disappeared, and he wouldn't get a chance to fight those demons again.

The glow in his eyes faded and as they reverted to their original three colors. Though the hourglass was only three quarters full, he had a feeling it would be enough. At his signal, he flipped it, and it began flowing. Time went backward everywhere else in the realm, and only he was immune to it.

He saw no changes at first, but that was likely due to distance. A few minutes later, he saw a strange sight on each platform in his line of sight. One after another, dust returned to them from their surroundings. Some of it came in the form of animals returning to their homes, while a larger portion came from the bottom of the hourglass itself, drifting out to where it had once belonged. The rate at which it left the hourglass increased as time passed, which made sense, as his success rate was higher in the beginning. And though he couldn't see the black dust appearing on the platforms, he had a hunch that it would be there as well. The murderous birds, defeated or not, were back. He'd have to face them all over again, without the help of all the tools he'd acquired.

You think you're so smart, making these trials, Huxian grumbled as he walked to the first platform. It was obvious, wasn't it? Why the hourglass? Why the needle? Why not just tear him a hole in space to send him back home and be done with him? There must be a final trick to this test, and it finally clicked. He might not be able to travel backward, but spatial piercing could avoid that. And he might not get a second chance, but he could always get another first chance. Though he hadn't yet completed a single trial, he had an advantage. He knew how the rules worked, and he knew how to fight for what he wanted.

He pounced on the first platform, smashing the first rabbit to a pulp. It transformed to gold dust that rushed into his eyes, alleviating their itchiness and irritation. Then, having used barely any of his energy, he waited. He waited until the sun set and the moon rose, and the blue snow covered the platform under the pale moonlight.

The pigeon growled but didn't reveal itself. Its mission was to strike fear in him, to instill a lesson on the fearful unpredictability of space. But he'd already learned that lesson. He didn't wait. Instead, he dove into a barely discernable slit in space and appeared right beside the creature, who growled again in confusion.

He struck before the bird could react. The pigeon wanted to be unpredictable? Fine. He would do the same thing. He bit into its neck, but before it could pierce him with a feather, he disappeared into the material world. The pigeon looked around in confusion, but before it could come out, he reappeared at another point in space and bit it again.

It wanted to play hide-and-seek? Fine. Two could play at that game. They played and played, until finally, the pigeon lost. Huxian walked over to the next platform a pocket of space dust richer, completely healed and well rested.

Everything was as it should be.

Chapter 21: Destiny

It didn't take long for Cha Ming to reach the Silverwing Mountain Range, but in that time, the winds of change swept across the entire continent. A constant stream of information from the Northern Alliance appeared on the jade tablet Feng Ming had conveniently given him. It told of him of battles won, secured supplies, and militias rising to defend their kingdoms. It was an awe-inspiring display of solidarity, a puzzle that finally clicked together. The North was no longer crumbling. It was fighting for its survival.

The Evergreen Kingdom was lost, but militias were giving the Southern army pause. There were skirmishes at their new borders, but fortunately, the Taotie had been reined in as they solidified their defensive lines. In every battlefield, the fighting intensified, but with new men and weapons, the battles were no longer as one-sided as they once were.

There was another change, Cha Ming finally noticed, though he wondered if that had been happening all along. Light clouds filled the skies above the entire continent, sending strikes of lightning down as transcendents clashed in probing battles. It would soon be time for them to join the fight in earnest. Though it might kill them to do so, when and where they died was of utmost importance.

With everyone doing their all, Cha Ming couldn't sit still either. He had an important task to complete here in the Silverwing

Mountain Range. *Who daresss trespasss?* a voice said. Cha Ming didn't bother answering the Geomantic Sovereign. He broke through the Pure Jade Defensive Formation and proceeded straight to the center of the mountain range. There, he saw a familiar owl staring at him with wide-open eyes.

You've finally come, the True Seer Great Owl said, twisting his head sideways so far Cha Ming thought it might break its neck. *You finally see. It is late, but better than never.*

"You knew it was here all along, didn't you?" Cha Ming asked, looking over the flat, infertile land between the mountains. "You could have told me, you know. Saved me time."

The owl hooted. *There was no use in telling you back then,* the True Seer Great Owl said. *Is there any use in telling a blind man the color of a rose? Or a deaf man the sound of a wonderful tune?*

"No, I suppose there isn't," Cha Ming said. "It might even cause more confusion than its worth. But there's something else you want to tell me. An unrelated matter."

Very observant, the True Seer Great Owl said. *I just thought you might like to know where your brother the fox is.*

"Is he well?" Cha Ming asked, looking around the central jade plate. As he thought, many energy lines extended from it, some of them demonic and others, surprisingly angelic. They were lines he couldn't see when he'd first been here.

He entered an ancient portal to claim an initiation mark, the True Seer Great Owl said. *His destiny is uncertain, as is yours. But I'm sure you know he still lives. Otherwise, you wouldn't be here talking to me now, would you?*

"I suppose I wouldn't," Cha Ming said. "Do you see it now?"

Sun Wukong jumped out of the Clear Sky World and nodded as he looked at the formation. "I'll be damned," the Monkey King said. "A formation that should take a fortune to make and years to mature, set up ahead of time. After this, I don't know how much luck you'll have left."

"It was all planned," Cha Ming said, taking note of various karmic threads, powerful ones he could see but not interfere with.

They were not just connected to the jade plates, but to his body, and his soul as well. "These jade plates. The protective formation. The True Seer Great Owl here to guard it all. All as a last line of defense."

The True Seer Great Owl hooted. *Though the plan was to seal up the creature indefinitely, the heavenly emperors could not directly destroy it. Not without destroying the plane. They were concerned that at some point, devilish forces would give into desperation and cooperate with it.*

"Therefore, they set up a failsafe," Cha Ming said. "A karmic mechanism, tied to the Devil-Sealing, Demon-Subduing, and Spirit-Banishing Scriptures." He held up his hand, and the scriptures appeared. Along with them appeared diagrams that had appeared in his mind after he'd completed the third stage in each one. "The Devil-Sealing Plates, the Demon-Subduing Pillars, and the Spirit-Banishing Wards, they're all complex creations that require much time and many resources. They draw on different inspirations, and their shapes are not the same. They do, however, share the same root."

"Five elements, one instrument," Sun Wukong said, pointing to one of the diagrams. "But when combined..."

"It has to be done perfectly and elegantly," Cha Ming said. "An immortal artisan likely had a hand in this, judging by the aura. All that's missing is five extremely rare energy sources, even in transcendent realms." He flicked his sleeve, and five round objects appeared. They were the elemental source cores, the greater components that housed the elemental source marrow he'd used to refine his body to half-step blood awakening. They floated out to five other jade plates and landed on perfectly shaped depressions within them, and the jade plates glowed.

"You're not mad that this was all orchestrated?" Sun Wukong asked. "A story you're just playing out a role in? I'd be mad. I'd be fuming."

"Isn't it the same for everyone?" Cha Ming answered. "Doesn't everyone start off as a character in someone else's story? Every story happens in three parts, teacher. First, you go with the flow and let fate take care of you. Then you break free of those shackles and change your own fate."

"And the third part?" Sun Wukong asked.

"Then you go back to the beginning," Cha Ming said. "You write a story for others, and you get lost in the river of time." He shook his head. "There's no sense worrying about it. It's a problem for another day. For now, we're playing out the first part as best we can, simultaneously struggling to break free. That will come when I transcend, when I open my wings and soar." Behind him, a thin outline of jade wings were forming. There were five elemental seals on the wings, though a final step was lacking for them to finally congeal.

"We're still missing a few components," Sun Wukong muttered. "Maybe we can bother your disciples for their Devil-Sealing Intent or something."

"No need," Cha Ming replied. He summoned six drops from the Clear Sky World, the tears he'd shed to gain his Eyes of Truth. He threw two jade tears at a pool of naturally occurring liquified elemental essence, which had filled up when he'd placed the five elemental source cores moments prior. "There are five elements and three instruments. The first instrument is aligned with creation. To seal devils, one must create an everlasting seal that will never dissipate." The elemental essence, normally light blue, turned white as the tears landed, and they began to glow with devil-sealing jade light, so powerful that it was blinding.

"Next comes destruction," Cha Ming continued. He threw out the golden tears into their own liquified elemental essence pool, which began to crackle with destructive black lightning. "To banish spirits, one must sever their karma, breaking their attachments to the mortal realm, and send them back to the Yellow River."

He then threw out the two violet tears. The pool they landed in turned just as violet as the original. They didn't represent a basic element but another thing entirely—heart. It was the same power illusions used, and it was also the power of demons and nature. It embellished things that were already there and brought order and discipline alongside anarchy and chaos.

"And the key?" Sun Wukong asked. "Where are you going to find Grandmist Essence in a short amount of time?"

"I thought of something better," Cha Ming said. He summoned the Clear Sky Staff and walked over to the final, central pool. It was much smaller than the others, and according to the original instructions, would fill with Grandmist Essence within weeks of inserting the source cores. This Grandmist Essence would harmonize all three instruments, acting as the final key to the formation. "I don't have weeks for this pool to fill. But I know this brush has Grandmist Essence within it, if it's willing to cough it up."

He willed the staff to change, and it did. It transformed until it was three feet in diameter and twelve feet long, the exact dimensions of the pool in question. It settled into the empty hole, and a multitude of lights flashed as the entire formation came to life, lighting up the entire mountain range in the process.

Through his Eyes of Truth, he could see that these changes didn't just apply to this mountain range. It reached out to the five leylines of the Ling Nan Plane, drawing from them as well. The Leyline of Gold in Bastion, the Leyline of Fire in Huoshan, the Leyline of Water near Haijing, and the Leyline of Wood in the Redwood Forest. Even the Leyline of Earth located deep beneath Mount Tai was connected. Power poured into the Clear Sky Staff, the five elemental pools, and the black, white, and violet ones. Nine was the perfect number, and the weapon he created here would be unsurpassed, something that transcended the rules themselves.

Time rushed by in the outside world as everything within the valley slowed to a crawl. The presence of Grandmist distorted everything, and the sheer power involved was overwhelming. Clouds appeared overhead to destroy the transcendent treasure as it was being formed, but several transcendent formations had been activated in the process, powered by the very leylines of the plane. It was a loophole that only gods could dream of, a loophole only immortals could enforce. He was creating a transcendent treasure on a mortal plane, and this time, there was no fear of repercussion.

"It makes me wonder," Cha Ming said as he reached out to the central pillar, where the glow was finally fading. Everything had happened in an instant, and weeks had been replaced by seconds. Yet his eyes saw that things weren't so simple. Days had passed outside the mountain range.

"Wonder?" Sun Wukong said. "About what?"

"About the plane," Cha Ming said. "Its rules, its judgment. It seems there are some cases where they can be bent. Maybe we can use that to fight the creature."

Sun Wukong frowned. "Maybe. But don't get addicted to trying. You saw what happened last time we did."

"Only as a last resort, my friend," Cha Ming said. "Only if things become desperate." He reached down, and the central pillar shrank and floated up. The eight other pillars did the same. He moved to store them in the Clear Sky Staff, but to his surprise, they merged together in a single gray object. "That's the glutton I know," Cha Ming said, chuckling as the staff vibrated in indignation. The soul-bound treasure had already absorbed them, incorporating them into its large arsenal of potential transformations.

"What will you call this one?" Sun Wukong asked. "You've already got Clear Sky Pillar. You wanna go with Clear Sky Sealer or Clear Sky Banisher?"

"Let's go with Tri-Sealing Pillars," Cha Ming said. "It's not perfect, but what is?" He stowed the staff and took out his core-transmission jade. "Speaking of imperfect, it looks like we missed a lot."

"What happened?" Sun Wukong asked, floating and scratching his hairy red chin.

"Evergreen is losing ground, same as always," Cha Ming answered. "The other battlefields suffered ferocious attacks and immense casualties. After drawing enough men away from Southhaven Wall, they dispatched ten transcendents, who sacrificed their lives to destroy it. Seventy-five percent of the Song Kingdom's fighting force was annihilated in an instant."

"But why?" Sun Wukong said. "Is Songjing fine?"

"They were never going to Songjing," Cha Ming said softly. He saw the writing on the wall, the many words of warning. "Nor were they going to the Evergreen Kingdom. It was all a ploy, a diversion. A false trail to let us underestimate them. The same day they broke the wall, they walked straight past Songjing, ignoring it. They broke through the Northern defensive lines and entered the mountains."

"The North wasn't their goal," Sun Wukong muttered.

"Karma was their goal," Cha Ming said. "To change the fate of devils, occupying Northern lands means nothing. They're after the World Tree, and if we don't do something about it, they're going to destroy it."

Chapter 22: World Tree

It took no more than a few minutes to fly from the Silverwing Mountain Range, crossing the northern pass and entering the mountains to the west that divided the Song Kingdom and the Quicksilver Empire. These western mountains were far taller than those he'd come from, and their jagged peaks were covered in snow all year round. Between them were green valleys filled with trails and wandering rivers. Normally, they'd be quiet, pristine things filled with demons, beasts, insects, and just about anything else that wasn't human.

The previously peaceful mountains were swarming with foundation-establishment cultivators. Those same cultivators fought to scale the precarious slopes and find a place hidden from the naked eye. Cha Ming skipped over these minor figures and flew straight to the peak of one of the smaller barren mountains. Its rocky slopes weren't exactly treacherous, but neither were they a walk in the park to scale. There were no steps or stairs, and there was not a soul in sight.

But karma didn't lie. With his new eyes, Cha Ming could see thousands upon thousands of tiny strings. They weren't tangled or corrupted like those binding evil spirits to the world, but neither were they jade or ochre, or red or black like others he'd seen. Instead, they were of the purest white, and the connection extra thin. He followed these strings, and soon the illusion vanished. The *real* mountain appeared.

Cha Ming had never been to a Buddhist temple in this life, but he admired their views on nonviolence and nonattachment. The monastery he saw was simple. Orange-robed monks lived there and maintained the buildings on its flat surface. There was no snow, and plants grew in abundance. There was also a path he'd missed before. It ran from the bottom of the mountain all the way to the top. In fact, there were many paths, all of which crisscrossed and eventually led to a massive bewitching staircase, which in turn led to the plateau.

At the back of the plateau, past the temple and simple dwellings, was a bridge that led to the enemy's objective: the World Tree. It was a massive thing that towered over the rest of the plateau, yet at the same time felt small and insignificant. Its drooping branches cast long shadows, but these shadows didn't block out the sun; rather they illuminated everything, bringing clarity to the confused and overwhelmed.

It was only as he flew toward the World Tree that he noticed the *real* strangeness. The air, he realized, was still. Completely and utterly still. The leaves on the World Tree shook, and the robes on those assembled to discuss the upcoming battle flickered a bit, but he felt none of it. The wind seemed disconnected, in another place entirely. And he heard very few of their sounds as they spoke. It was as though he'd entered a separate dimension that didn't quite connect with the one those people stood in.

He focused on one group of people: Gong Lan and a few head monks were speaking to Feng Ming, who'd assembled a few ragtag soldiers. They were standing at the edge of the mountain plateau just before the stairs, surveying the literal flood of invaders forcing their way up the mountain passes. And on the back of the mountain, he felt many strong presences: There were demons, and beyond them was a nightmarish flood that, at any moment, would begin their ascent. They were fiends, far more fiends than he'd ever faced.

The dialogue he heard from Feng Ming and Gong Lan was fleeting, but through it, he discovered the Song Kingdom's situation.

The elites of the Southern army had come here, but the laggards had already taken three cities. They'd have taken Songjing already if it weren't for the militia that had assembled to defend it. But it was only a matter of time unless more substantial troops went back to guard it.

"Where am I?" Cha Ming said, looking away from Feng Ming and the rest and flying closer to the tree, where he finally saw a man. The wind avoided the man just like it did Cha Ming. And he knew the man: He was none other than Zhou Li, his long-time nemesis. Despite the mountain's powerful defenders, he was somehow standing here right next to his objective. Zhou Li smiled when he saw him.

"At last, you've come," Zhou Li said. His hands were folded behind his back. He was unarmed and completely relaxed. Though Cha Ming knew he could crush the man with ease, something within him prevented him from acting on it.

"Is this real?" Cha Ming asked, landing on the ground near where Zhou Li was standing.

"Real as real can be," Zhou Li said. "Though I made some modifications."

Cha Ming looked where Zhou Li pointed and noticed the air was filled with thin lines that extended in three dimensions. They encompassed the World Tree, the demons and fiends, and the troops at the base of the mountain, and he could tell at a glance they would encompass anyone else who entered the area.

"You weren't injured before you went to Bastion," Cha Ming noted. "I know you didn't get hurt in Beihai." That was the excuse that had been given for why Zhou Li was late to face the Taotie. Now, he saw there was more to the story.

"Quite right," Zhou Li said. "I was working on this, my masterpiece. It's the board on which we'll play, though to be honest, I was hoping you wouldn't be my opponent. I thought perhaps the monk would be chosen, or perhaps Wang Jun—that would have been utterly disastrous. I suppose it's a happy medium."

Cha Ming frowned but did nothing. The situation had exceeded his understanding. "What now?" he asked cautiously. The wind, he observed, was still absent.

"Now?" Zhou Li said. "Now we wait."

So they did. And as they did, a flight of white figures flew in. These cultivators were of the Alabaster Group and flew under the leadership of jade-winged angels. There were hundreds of core-formation cultivators there, many more than Cha Ming thought possible. Two dozen transcendent angels, Lu Tianhao included, were at their head. Then, as though their presence required opposition, an equally large group of devils appeared. The ochre-winged devils flew in from the south, and they were members of the Obsidian Syndicate.

Angels aside, there were others standing guard on the mountain. Not only were there monks, but Cha Ming finally noticed soldiers stationed at various key points on the passes, ready to hold off invading troops should they venture too closely. Though Cha Ming wasn't sure if the weak cultivators that climbed could even hurt the World Tree, he supposed a single spark could light a fire that burned down an entire forest. As such, it was reassuring to see the mismatched lot defending them. They were men and women from all over the continent, standing together against a common enemy.

"If this tree falls, we'll be in for dark days," Cha Ming said, looking back at the World Tree and the peace it emanated. He could see that this peace wasn't only concentrated on the plateau; it expanded all across the continent—no, the plane—like a gentle mist that blessed every creature.

"That's rather the point, isn't it?" Zhou Li said. "We don't want the North—that's trivial territory, which we can fight for south of the border. The true prize is this tree, or rather, its removal. Only by uprooting it can we truly level the playing field. Devils will come in waves like they should, performing their duties as the proper checks and balances against the angels, and when the scales tip, the angels will do the same to the devils that rule the land after so long in silence. It's all about balance, Cha Ming. That is all it was ever about."

"You're crazy," Cha Ming said. He'd seen what this "balance" entailed.

"I'm evil," Zhou Li countered. "Don't call every evil man crazy. It's insulting to their intelligence."

There was an unusual ripple in the air on the plateau then. The ripple turned into a black slit, and soon, a man emerged from it. A gentle breeze blew past him. The man was none other than Brother Wang Jun, black robe and black scythe included. Following his appearance, the black slit widened into a large portal, and troops filed out in orderly lines. There were inquisitors of the Church of Justice, mistresses of the Red Dust Pavilion, and some of the more powerful mercenaries he'd seen in Gold Leaf City.

It didn't stop there. Wang Jun walked over to an empty spot and cut the air with his scythe. Another portal appeared, and a blue-armored man with a golden sword walked out leading men from the Eastern Desert. They were soon joined by green-robed cultivators from the Evergreen Kingdom and a dozen beautiful princesses from what Cha Ming could only assume was the Phoenix Cry Empire. Portals opened one after another, filling the plateau with a flood of most of the powerful men and women north of the wall.

"God, I hate that man," Zhou Li said, looking toward Wang Jun. "I really thought I had him there, when we found out the Red Dust Mistress was his little lady."

"I'm sure the feeling is mutual," Cha Ming said. "Though it seems you're a little outnumbered."

"Just wait a little while longer," Zhou Li said. "It's not time to start yet. The tree and I have an agreement, and it's vital we respect the terms we discussed."

It was then that Cha Ming felt a chill, though the chill didn't come from a wind or breeze but from a shivering stillness. He looked and suddenly knew to expect them. The South's forces had finally arrived. Feng Ming, Gong Lan, Wang Jun, and Lu Tianhao assembled and flew to the front of the Alabaster Group, forming their vanguard. The cultivators who'd just arrived flew up as well, though they stayed a good distance away.

It was slow at first. A few dozen cultivators at a time. Enemy troops began to trickle in from the south. There were powerful soldiers from the enemy army, colonels and higher who had fought dozens of battles and hundreds of duels to achieve their ranks. There were hundreds of blood masters, each one reeking of ten thousand mortals, sacrifices that had been made for a final strengthening before their departure. There were only half as many Spectral Assassins, however, as many had been killed in Bastion and Gold Leaf City, but each of them was a deadly weapon.

There were devils too. Too many to count. They formed the vanguard much like their own angelic cultivators. They were black-robed devils with sinful auras so thick they could choke the life out of a normal person. Two of them were especially prominent at their head, though Zhou Li, who would have been the third of them, simply stood beside the tree, waiting. The black-armored general from the Eastern Desert stood on the right, and the fiend whisperer in black leathers flew on the left. They met with the Northern leadership and exchanged curt and taunting words, but he could barely hear them in this place, the realm between realms.

"That's all of them, I think," Zhou Li said. "A few more taunts, and we'll be ready."

"I don't suppose you'd consider letting go of your grudges and reincarnating like a proper person?" Cha Ming asked.

"After all I went through to get here?" Zhou Li said. "No, I think not. I'll play this game to the bitter end."

"And what game is that?" Cha Ming asked, looking at the massive grid that encompassed all reality in this pocket dimension. It reminded him of something.

"I assure you that you know how to play it," Zhou Li said. "That was a requirement. Though I'm not sure if you know the full rules this specific variant entails." As he spoke, Feng Ming and Wang Jun flew down to the plateau where their normal soldiers were fighting. They were chasing after the enemy general and his crackling blade of lightning as soldiers began a steady climb.

At the same time, the fiend whisperer flew to the back of the mountain and joined the sea of blackness facing off against demons, which he knew included Gua, Lei Jiang, Silverwing, and Mr.

Mountain. He also felt Ling Dong there, standing strong.

Gong Lan, on the other hand, flew toward where the monks and the red-and-blue-robed ladies were fighting against the black-cloaked preachers and assassins of the Temple. Her opponents were three of their shepherds. She sent golden light out to suppress them as best she could.

Finally, Lu Tianhao summoned a sword. It seemed to be made of the wind itself. He flew up, and the opposing devil went with him. It was none other than Yang Mubai, the senior partner of the Obsidian Syndicate who'd offered him a job in Quicksilver.

The air trembled, and space shattered as they soared up above the mortal cultivators. Lightning clouds gathered, and flashes alerted everyone that the battle had begun in earnest, and the remaining transcendents joined the battle. It was a spark that set off a powder keg, and fighting erupted everywhere. Alabaster and Obsidian mixed as angels and devils killed.

"Angels and devils," Cha Ming whispered, finally seeing the connection. "The black lines connecting this entire space. This dimension is just a giant *Angels and Devils board*, a three-dimensional one painted over this entire reality."

"Two dimensional, but projected over the landscape," Zhou Li said, shrugging. "But yes, I painted it myself. I prefer chess to the game, but I couldn't get the presentation where I liked it, so here we are. We'll play a game, just you and I, and the winner can leave this place."

There were five distinct battles that Cha Ming could see. First, there were the mistresses and the monks and their spectral adversaries. Second, the cultists, who were fighting against the inquisitors and chaplains of the Golden Kingdom. Third, the battle on the slopes, the gentle dance between Feng Ming, Wang Jun, and the enemy commander. Yue Bing and her newly minted blood doctors had joined this fight to counter the enemy blood masters that had joined their opponents. Thus far, it was fairly even, though it seemed that eventually the Southern forces would find their way up here.

Fourth, the demons and the fiends. The fiend whisperer had taken out a flute and was playing a fiendish melody, and the fiends, which resembled waves slapping against a rocky shore, suddenly began to boil over with strength and ferocity. Ling Dong fought back by projecting his Demon-Subduing and Devil-Sealing Intents in ways that Cha Ming could never have dreamed of, and Gua, Silvering, Mr. Mountain, and Lei Jiang clashed with their leaders overhead. But still, the odds seemed against them.

Or that would have been the case, if not for timely help. The lesser fiends had the advantage and were felling their opponents mercilessly when suddenly, a change occurred. Poison novas erupted everywhere in their ranks, and poisonous creatures emerged. Jin Huang, who'd been conspicuously absent until now, appeared within the demonic ranks. He was cheering on his faithful pets, encouraging them, and somehow, it was working, tilting the odds back in their favor until it became an even battlefield. The energized poisons cooperated with the demons, a large portion of which were poisonous in nature and drew from the even larger swamp Gua had summoned, the same swamp he'd taken from the Evergreen Battlefield and brought out to assist them.

Fifth, the angels and the devils and their accompanying transcendents. Only beings like them who felt so strongly about their convictions would stay on this plane, forgoing advancement for the sake of the cause they supported.

"I'm required to ask you if you're ready," Zhou Li said. "Well?"

"I don't suppose you'll explain the rules of this game to me?" Cha Ming said.

"No, your sponsor thought it would be counterproductive, actually," Zhou Li replied.

"No time like the present," Cha Ming said.

Zhou Li smiled, raised two fingers, and summoned a black stone, throwing it out to where the demons were fighting.

"Devils play first," Zhou Li said, then he attacked Cha Ming. Cha Ming defended with his staff, deflecting Zhou Li's surprisingly sturdy sword strikes. White stones appeared around the initial black one Zhou Li had played, defending against it while even more black stones piled on to reinforce the first. As the stones appeared, Cha Ming noticed tiny ripples. A warping in reality. And threads of karma.

And still, a windless stillness.

Chapter 23: Opening

Like it or not, Cha Ming was playing a game. He defended against Zhou Li's attacks, clashing against his black sword, which spewed endless black sin flames. As they exchanged these probing strikes, stones continued to land on the board. Black and white pieces alternated in familiar positions, Zhou Li on the offense, and Cha Ming on the defense. The demons and fiends danced back and forth as they played, and the stones seemed to influence not only the players, but the battlefield itself.

The first rule of the game is that what happens in the game affects the outside world, Cha Ming decided. The placement of the stones respective to the changes in the battlefield couldn't be chalked up to mere coincidence. Further, he could see slender threads of karma connecting the stones, the combatants, and the land. And the more they fought, the more stones and strings appeared. Zhou Li had the initiative, and if this game was like any other, that was a big problem.

Cha Ming knew that he needed to take back the initiative. Even if he didn't know what he was doing. If he failed to do that, he would lose, plain and simple. Not exactly sure if it was the right decision to make, he focused on one particular endangered flank in the demon army and attacked Zhou Li with simple staff techniques, using little more than his pseudo-domain to coat his attacks. They exchanged a few blows, and this time, it was Zhou Li on the defensive. Stones appeared near the endangered flank, securing it, relieving the pressure. The demons fought back the fiends and secured their battle lines.

The exchange was short but very telling. There was a second rule to the game: Whoever was on the offensive got to decide *where* to play stones and force the defender to do the same. Moreover, now that a few stones had been placed, Cha Ming felt a difference in his own energy levels of all things, something he hadn't worried about since taking a half step into transcendence. With every stone he placed, he felt his power mounting.

No, that wasn't right. He focused his eyes on the black lines that covered the battlefield in a strange combination of two and three dimensions. The battlefield actually *suppressed* him, and the stones released that suppression. To his surprise, however, it didn't just supress Cha Ming. It also suppressed Zhou Li, the one who'd instigated the game. Which, he supposed, made sense, as the constraints of the game were far too powerful and the stakes too great. Try as he might, he could find no way to even attempt breaking it.

Seeing there was little more they could do on this flank of the demonic battle, both Zhou Li and Cha Ming switched in tandem. Their focus changed to another area in the demonic battlefield, setting down stones and claiming a sort of subtle "territory." Doing so used fewer stones and fewer moves than before, and with each of these territory-marking stones, Cha Ming saw a much greater easing of the invisible shackles on his power. Zhou Li's strikes became increasingly elegant, forcing Cha Ming to summon his combat formations to supplement. Or try to.

I can't use my techniques, Cha Ming realized as he was forced to dodge backward, narrowly avoiding a deadly slash to his chest. He tried to conceptualize a frozen shield formation, but his sigils didn't fly out. He tried to summon talismans, but they stubbornly remained in his storage space. Blow after blow, he lost territory as Zhou Li gained, and with each gain, his meager skills increased by leaps and bounds. The logical conclusion, then, was a difficult-todefine third rule: claiming territory was the quickest way to gain an edge in this battle.

"I think the demons and fiends have had enough of our interference," Cha Ming said after a few preliminary areas were anchored to their stones. "You can stay here and play if you like."

He flew away from Zhou Li and soared above a group of monks that were fighting Spectral Assassins. Naturally, they didn't see him. His world was windless, and their interference only extended to the game. The movement caused a stone to appear, but another appeared in response alongside Zhou Li's cloaked figure.

"Smart move, not letting yourself get tied up in the battlefield of my choosing," Zhou Li said. "It's too bad you're losing."

Cha Ming attacked him with the Clear Sky Staff. Despite lacking techniques, the staff's transcendent nature and his superior body strength were something he could rely on. Zhou Li slashed out with his sword and summoned a blade of black flames that Cha Ming could only partially block. It bit into his chest, taking a small chunk of his vitality reserves as the flames extinguished themselves and his body regenerated.

"Not that I want to be generous, but it seems you've figured out the first three rules of our game," Zhou Li said. "I'm afraid that, as per my contract, that means I need to inform you of the fourth."

"Please, don't hold back," Cha Ming said.

"This is more than a game, Cha Ming," Zhou Li said. His words were chilling. "You and I are bound to the board. As we play, our actions affect reality. But in the end, that's only a side benefit. The game's true purpose, you see, is to tie you up. You have to stay here and keep playing or face a terrible consequence."

"You don't have to tell me. I see it," Cha Ming said, gazing at the edges of the board, the black lines that made it, and the stones around them. By building up territory, they were building up karma. That karma all led to one place. It was a standoff between the two of them, a final showdown. Whether he liked it or not, whoever lost this game was fated to die.

"Mantra of peace," Gong Lan said, humming as she mouthed short syllables that formed golden words around her. They reinforced a golden temple that was under assault from three black-cloaked figures with tremendous power. They reeked of death and were surrounded by vengeful thoughts. They were evil spirits, or as close to one as a mortal could get without transcending.

"All you monks know how to do is defend," one of the three said. His voice was hoarse and grated like sandpaper. He summoned a crook that was black as midnight, then waved it, bringing forth a sea of souls to bombard the golden temple. The man was a shepherd of the Spirit Temple, a herder of souls. The ultimate adversary of anyone in her lineage.

"One need only walk a thousand steps to see the way," Gong Lan said. Her words resounded with the temple, the tree, and the world. "Why not put down your arms and embrace the solitude of the road?"

Golden bricks appeared beneath her feat. Her resplendent golden energy poured into them and radiated outward, searing the souls attacking the crumbling temple. She took a step, and more bricks appeared. They expanded into a road that accelerated before crashing into the shepherd, knocking him back as he coughed up black blood, one of the few remaining vestiges of his mortality.

"I was mistaken, it seems," the shepherd said. "You Buddhists are just hypocrites."

"Salvation is for the many and not the few," Gong Lan said, forming hand seals and summoning blades of light. They plunged toward the other two shepherds who'd thought they were flanking her, exploding as they struck against their crooks and forming pages of scripture that wrapped around them, binding them. She used the short respite to look at the Spectral Assassins fighting with monks and Red Dust mistresses, strange battlefield companions in this time of great struggle. Bai Ling, their leader, used Soul-Searing Flames and Soul-Sealing Ice, very effective against the Spirit Temple's denizens.

They were outnumbered, unfortunately, and Gong Lan's monks were young and not well trained. If only the Violet Wind Monastery hadn't been destroyed. If only she'd arrived in time like she had for the Blue Lagoon Monastery, saving half their monks before they were destroyed by the encroaching corruption. She turned her attention back to the shepherds, who had regrouped and were executing a group technique. A giant herd of ghosts was circling around them, mutating as they poured their corrupted powers into the shepherds.

The monks and mistresses would be fine, Gong Lan decided. Spectral Assassins were tricky to deal with, but ultimately, they only used brute force and swiftness. Monks and mistresses alike were experts in dealing with this sort of opponent, redirecting attacks to deal with aggression. Speaking of which, she lunged forward and drew the twin blades at her back. They were rulers, technically, bladeless swords that could maybe bruise a living person or break bones if she hit hard enough. But against this churning sea of souls, they were brutally effective. Two quick strikes to the stewing spirit formation forced the three shepherds to abort and salvage what souls they could.

Though Gong Lan knew nothing about formations, she had much outside help. She drew strength from the World Tree and guidance from the Bodhi Seed. With it, she was able to handle three of the shepherds, who could rival initial transcendents in power. That left six other shepherds to senior monks who had to handle them in pairs.

But shepherds and Spectral Assassins aren't the only ones in the Spirit Temple, are they? a voice muttered inside her mind. *Where are the others?* She scanned the crowd and noticed an anomaly. One of the assassins was fighting very poorly, considering the type of creature he was. *Bai Ling,* she rapidly sent. *You're fighting more than just assassins.*

A lotus of flames went off at this moment, threatening to

consume two of their black-robed opponents. They backed away but were chased by three Red Dust mistresses who sensed blood and went in for the kill. Gong Lan's golden eyes saw threads of crimson karma tightening around them, around the assassins, and connecting to reinforcements.

"Watch out!" she yelled.

The mistresses, unaware of their current situation, continued forward. The karmic threads tightened, and black characters appeared, causing them to stop unexpectedly. They were bound in place, and the assassins pounced. They killed the three mistresses without missing a beat.

What the hell just happened? Bai Ling sent urgently.

It appears there are Soul Priests among the ranks of the assassins, disguising themselves, Gong Lan said gravely. *Your sisters thought they'd outmaneuvered the relatively simple assassins, but in doing so, they stepped into a karmic trap. They were dead the moment they chased those assassins and caused the noose to tighten.*

What do we do? Bai Ling asked. *How to we fight that?* She wasn't panicking, but instead making a calm threat assessment.

Strategically, Gong Lan said. *You're good at that, right?* She shook her head and sheathed her two rulers. The shepherds, who had taken advantage of her distraction, slammed their crooks in the air, sending ghostly wails that echoed in her ears. She countered with a quick mantra, raising her right hand with two index fingers pointed upward. A large golden bell appeared and tolled loudly. The shepherds were pushed back, giving her time to trace karmic threads she'd just noticed. They were small filaments that pierced through from another dimension, influencing their battle.

She traced these filaments back to her source and frowned when she realized where they were coming from. They weren't from the Soul Priests as she'd expected. Instead, they came from above, where two figures fought, unnoticed by the rest. She could barely make out their figures. They were Zhou Li and Cha Ming, who'd been conspicuously absent from the battle. And though their exchanges weren't mighty, each exchange had a lasting impression. The echoes of their battle could be felt by the entire battlefield.

The northern side of the mountain was a chaotic mess of blood and gore, fur and feathers. Claws and teeth savaged and bit as demons and fiends alike struggled to kill as many as they could before breathing their last.

The battle had just begun, but already, the battlefield was beginning to resemble a sea of corpses more than the side of a mountain.

Fortunately, we have Lei Jiang and the others, Ling Dong thought as he jumped over a demonic badger and cleaved into a scaly creature of nightmares with the eyes of a toad but the feathers of a swan. Black blood spewed onto the ground, bathing lesser fiends in corrupting power. Fortunately, they had nothing to fear. Four half-step initiation demons were apparently enough to stop the fiendish blood from claiming them.

"Look out!" a voice said, one of the three humans on the mountain. Ling Dong dodged in time to avoid a strangely placed claw on the tail of a fiendish lizard. He threw out his greatsword and impaled the crazed fiend, then summoned it back to his hand as he saluted Jin Huang, his apprentice brother. The little imp was usually never up to anything good, but now he was busy planting poisons that determined their life and death. The third human on the mountain, however, was actively trying to kill him. The man in black war leathers, who was commanding from the back of the battlefield, supporting fiendish forces wherever he went.

Two could play at that game.

Ling Dong flew through the skies, projecting a violet light that reinforced allied demons and subdued opposing ones. They glowed with a jade light that suppressed the fiend's devilish heritage, weakening them even further. It only somewhat made up for the sheer deadliness of their opponents. Fiends weren't creatures of balance; they were creatures of destruction.

Fly. Kill. Fly. Kill. He repeated the process over and over. But the demonic and fiendish tides were massive, and he couldn't see this battle coming to a conclusion anytime soon. Moreover, it was getting weirder by the second. An eagle he slew had fur instead of feathers and snakes instead of talons. A badger had worms for teeth and talons for claws.

In the madness of the moment, it was difficult to think, but it allowed him to tap into something darker, stranger. He felt it then. A dark presence appeared on the fiendish portion of the battlefield. He racked his brains and found nothing that could describe it. Lei Jiang would know, but unfortunately, that demon was tied up with a large catlike fiend with tails of black fire. He looked around and found the next-best choice, a falcon fighting in the air with a featherless peacock.

"Uncle Silverwing, do you have a minute?" Ling Dong asked as he blocked a blow for the bird.

I'm kind of busy, Silverwing said, flying over to a swarm of bats with claws instead of teeth. He slashed out with his wings, destroying hundreds. Black blood rained from the sky, covering a dozen antelopes in fiendish refuse. *What's up?*

There's something over there you should see, Ling Dong said, looking to where the fiend whisperer was now gathering a large crowd. Silverwing looked, then ruffled his feathers.

Bad, bad, bad, Silverwing said. *Hop onto my back.*

"What's happening?" Ling Dong asked as he obeyed and clung tightly to the bird's sharp feathers. They flew over to Lei Jiang first, finishing off his opponent as the small rodent obediently climbed on.

Is that a fiendbone totem? Lei Jiang asked as he looked to where they were headed. Gua and Mr. Mountain flew up beside them as they spearheaded their troops, pushing deep into fiendish territory. The smoky purple mountain was a curious sight, usually incorporeal, but sometimes becoming solid out of nowhere to slam into a flying opponent.

I'm afraid it is, Silverwing said gravely.

"What's a fiendbone totem?" Ling Dong asked.

As implied by the name, it's a shamanic artifact using the bones of transcendent fiends as a medium, Silverwing said, giving the impression of an instructor at an academy. *There are no records of such fiends on the plane, which means they probably imported it from a transcendent one at great expense.*

"How bad as it?" Ling Dong asked.

Very bad, Silverwing said. *These fiends are already very powerful, but with a fiendbone totem, their energy reserves will be limitless. We'll be overrun in no time.*

"Can we counter it?" Ling Dong asked.

Yes, the good old-fashioned way, Silverwing said. *Boys, are you ready?* They nodded and crashed into a new group of fiends that had appeared just above them. Ling Dong looked around and saw a human floating beside the totem. The man had black hair, black eyes, and a thick beard with bones tied into its many black braids. And in his hands, he had a giant truncheon covered in black metal spikes. It wasn't a demonic weapon, but a fiendish one.

"The good old-fashioned way," Ling Dong muttered, drawing his heavy sword. If someone had something nice and you didn't want him to have it, you stole it. And then you broke it. The good old-fashioned way.

"You know, we couldn't get better terrain to defend if we wanted it," Feng Ming said as they overlooked the mountain passes and the enchanted stairway leading up to the monastery. Enemy troops snaked through treacherously narrow pathways and cliffs, careful not to fall to their deaths as they pushed toward the monastery.

"I don't see how much help it will be, my friend," Wang Jun said, shaking his head. "We're sorely outnumbered, with nothing but a ragtag bunch of soldiers, poorly trained monks, and mediocre defenses. Though, I guess the blood doctors help."

"Well, you know what they say," Feng Ming said. "Terrain is the most important part of a winning a battle." He summoned four jade slips and touched each of them, sending a message to their sister pair held by a group of men waiting by a small bridge. They waited for several dozen cultivators to pass, as instructed, before cutting the bridge's supports. Though no one was killed by the act, it did separate a good portion of enemy troops long enough to eliminate them and retreat to higher ground as the enemy arranged for an alternate method of crossing.

"I disagree," Wang Jun said, summoning a replica of the mountain. The hologram, made completely of shadow, was somehow able to show the finest details. He touched a spot, triggering a trap that had been laid by one of their formation artists. A cliff collapsed and crushed a dozen foundation-establishment cultivators before they knew what hit them.

"Then what's most important, in your opinion?" Feng Ming asked.

"Planning," Wang Jun said. "And knowing your enemy." In response to his triggered trap, the enemy had somehow used it as a smokescreen for their movements, surprising an unprepared group of defenders and ambushing them. Wang Jun traced a pathway with his fingers, opening a portal of shadows for the troops to escape, but not before three of them were killed. As he was busy doing that, however, the enemy used an artifice, jumping across a chasm and attacking one of their other groups. It was too late to evacuate them, so Wang Jun was forced to summon another portal, reinforcing them with a couple of blood doctors while weakening one of their other positions.

"He's good," Feng Ming agreed. "Very good. Half my plans don't work half as well as his, even with my luck."

"And that is exactly why planning trumps everything," Wang Jun muttered, using his fingers to control the battlefield much like a puppet. "One doesn't need to get lucky. One plans for contingency after contingency, trying plan after plan until one eventually wins."

"Can we beat him?" Feng Ming asked.

"We don't have to," Wang Jun said. "We just have to stall him long enough to win the other battles."

"You didn't answer the question," Feng Ming said.

"I'm afraid you already know the answer," Wang Jun replied.

As he'd expected. They were severely outmatched.

Blood splashed on Zi Long's purple robes as he stabbed a devil through the chest with a spearing thrust. The blood wasn't his own or his opponent's, but from a man flying above him. The battle had started so fast and so furiously, with the angelic cultivators not giving the devilish ones a chance to think about organizing themselves.

Above them, transcendent angels exchanged fierce blows, their domains erupting and going all out in venting their anger. After centuries of stewing on old grudges, it was finally time to end them. Lu Tianhao led the charge. His jade wings stood opposite his opponent's ochre ones, his windy sword against his opponent's fiery blade. And above him, lightning raged. It struck both him and the devil, chastising them for causing a ruckus on the mortal plane; spatial fragments fell to the ground with each blow exchanged.

The devil impaled on Zi Long's staff finally breathed his last. He scattered to ashes as wrath devils usually did. At the same time, the man above him, the one who'd bled, tumbled to the ground, his white robes unblemished save a single spot of red on his chest.

He didn't have time to care for the man, however. He was looking for a certain woman. He couldn't just fight his way to her—he didn't have a powerful body like his brother Ling Dong, nor did he have strong qi like Jin Huang. He relied on tricks and illusions to defeat his opponents, or tricks of the mind that completely bypassed their usual defenses. *There. I found her.*

Luo Xuehua was fighting alongside Xi Lang, one of their senior members and someone they'd gone on missions with together. Like him and Xuehua, the man had scars and a painful past. And like all of them, he fought his devilish opponents with subdued fury. Jade and ochre clashed as Xi Lang formed hand seals, summoning a forest of thorny vines to encapsulate his enemy, a bark-skinned giant with arms as thick as tree trunks. He squeezed the life out of the creature as Luo Xuehua pierced him from afar with shards of ice.

Zi Long flew through the air—not to her side but in front of the man who was sneaking up behind her. As an illusionist, he was especially sensitive to the ways of water devils who beguiled their prey. The blue-skinned, black-haired man moved like a snake as he closed in on her bare back. Zi Long did likewise, but as he approached, he sent his holy spirit ahead and into the man's spiritual sea.

The air shattered, and clouds that burned the lungs encased the man in a tiny box. The box grew larger but was cut in half by a machete. The pieces were sucked into a vortex and compressed, the life squeezed out of them by a pair of giant hands. Bizarre illusions mesmerized the man as Zi Long appeared behind him and slapped out with his palms three times consecutively, once for wood, once for earth, and once for water. The man splattered into a puddle just behind the shocked Luo Xuehua. She smiled when she realized Zi Long, her silent protector, had saved her. She and Xi Lang got back to work, and before long, the resilient gluttony devil was gone, his body no more than a pile of wood shavings scattering onto the bloodstained plateau.

"It's not looking good," Xi Lang said, breathing heavily. "There are too many of them, and they're too strong."

"When did we ever let that stop us?" Zi Long asked.

"True," Xi Lang replied. "Where to next?"

"Let's find someone else who needs help," Zi Long said. "There's strength in numbers, and this battlefield is too chaotic."

They were about to leave, but Zi Long felt a chill running down his spine. Xi Lang must have felt it too, as he drew a large saber and swung upward, deflecting a black sword that threatened to cleave him in half. It missed his head and struck his arm, lopping it off halfway between the shoulder and the elbow. He yelled out in pain and clutched the bloody stump that remained.

The bearer of the sword was a black-armored devil, one of the most dangerous kinds. Pride devils were few by necessity. Lightning crackled around his blade as he ignored his wounded opponent and cleaved at the seemingly defenseless Luo Xuehua. Fortunately, Luo Xuehua had been in many battles. The blind fighter flowed like water, her twin blades drawing black blood as they found kinks in the man's armor. She retreated as the devil's gauntlet swept toward her, clipping her jaw as she jumped back.

"You're no match for him," Zi Long said, flying and catching her. Not only was the man a peak-core-formation cultivator, but he was a pride devil, one of the two types of indestructible devils. He'd found that devils like these were extremely self-confident and resistant to illusions. Only a half-step-marrow-refining cultivator would be its match in a normal situation.

"It doesn't matter," Luo Xuehua said, wiping blood from her lip where she'd been struck by the man's gauntlet. "I know that man; I'd recognize him anywhere." Her gaze went cold and her normally blank expression twisted with anger. "He's the man who killed my family and my village. He's the man who took my eyes." She didn't wait for his support. She didn't wait for a plan. She just rushed in headlong, leaving Zi Long little choice but to charge in with her.

All around them, there was more of the same. Hatred filed the air. Most of them had joined the Alabaster Group for a reason: they were there for revenge.

Cha Ming and Zhou Li jumped across the mountain, laying down initial stones and making probing attacks where foundation-establishment cultivators battled. Cha Ming won some but lost some. The soldiers fought and lost in much the same way, causing him to wonder exactly how much influence he had over the fates of these lesser cultivators.

"You fight very conservatively. Did you know that?" Zhou Li said, throwing his hand out and summoning a thick chain. He tied it to his sword and threw it out at him, using the chain's flexible body to make the attacks unpredictable and awkward to block.

"I'm sorry, I didn't spend much time studying parlor tricks," Cha Ming said. That was only partly true. Though he knew many lower-level techniques, the fact of the matter was that they just didn't match up to simple staff strikes using his strength as a half-step-blood-awakening cultivator. And until he unlocked his more powerful abilities, he could only keep losing ground to his opponent, who'd clearly been aware of these rules from the outset. "You know this is kind of pointless, don't you?" Cha Ming said, trying once again to execute Splitting Heaven and Earth. It came out as a simple horizontal staff strike that was easily parried by Zhou Li's sword.

"How so?" Zhou Li asked, stepping back and dodging his follow-up thrust.

"I'm much stronger than you in the end," Cha Ming said. "You might be able to use a few tricks early on, but once I unlock a few abilities, you're going to start losing. "

"We'll see," Zhou Li said, stepping back and throwing out a pouch that belched out black dust. It filled the air and entered Cha Ming's lungs through his mouth and nose, burning him from the inside. It was a small trick but one that hurt immensely. Zhou Li took advantage of the distraction to lay a few more stones.

Cha Ming smothered the pain and flew to another end of the battlefield. He laid down five stones along the way, each one in relatively empty areas. Finally, something clicked. He threw up an Ice Shield Combat Formation just in time to block a dragon of black ink, freshly summoned from a painting in Zhou Li's hands. The dragon froze for only a fraction of a second before breaking the sigils apart. It crashed into Cha Ming, destroying half his body before ultimately running out of energy. Cha Ming regenerated just in time to block a few quick sword strikes, though one of them managed to barely nick his shoulder, deviating the white stones protecting the mountain's valiant defenders.

"I've prepared for this moment for dozens of lifetimes," Zhou Li said. "I've evaluated your strengths and weaknesses. There is no way I'll let you reach your full potential. You might think there's hope at the end of the tunnel, but I have seen the end: you'll die weakened and alone."

Zhou Li took out another scroll with another painting. This time, it was a humanoid pig holding a giant rake. Cha Ming charged at him as he summoned a storm of blades to attack Zhou Li, placing two stones simultaneously. The pig soon melted, but not before tearing a deep gouge across Cha Ming's back with a skillful sweep. He cried out in pain as the flesh re-formed, using a smidgen of vitality in the process.

The part of the board corresponding to the Alabaster Group and the Obsidian Syndicate quickly filled up with aggressive black stones shifting the tides in the devils' favor. Mortals played to their tune, providing a brutal backdrop for the transcendents warring above them. These lofty angels and devils ignored Cha Ming's and Zhou Li's game, however. Not only did it have very little influence over their actions, but it was like the plane's lightning. They would ignore it and only rest once their opponents were dead.

Tentacles, horns, claws, and feathers swirled together, combining various fiends into four opponents that crashed into Ling Dong's four apprentice uncles. These creatures resembled nothing Ling Dong could have ever imagined. No twisted prank of nature would ever generate such abominations.

Up above, Silverwing now fought a winged velociraptor with sword-wielding human hands. Gua and Lei Jiang were busy fighting an octopus conjoined with a rattlesnake, both of which spewed poisonous black blood that not even Gua could tolerate. Mr. Mountain was fighting as a humanoid mist with blades on his forearms. His opponent was a projection of a horrid moth that was covered in rotting skin and tiny scales.

"What the hell are you doing to them?" Ling Dong said, gripping his blade.

"Perfecting them," the fiend whisperer said. "I am an artist. I give life to creatures in my imagination." He held up his hand and summoned his spiked club again. He held it over his shoulder while standing guard over the demon totem.

"I know art, and that isn't it," Ling Dong said, charging at the man and clashing. Vibrations ran through his arms and torso and legs as both were knocked back equal distances. If he'd only been using his body cultivation and qi, Ling Dong would have died for certain in that exchange. Fortunately, he'd been borrowing power from the demons. He was growing increasingly certain that the fiend whisperer was doing the same with his fiendish friends.

Ling Dong wasn't a normal craftsman. He was a demonic smith. The process wasn't like smithing, where humans beat metal into submission, forcing it into forms they didn't understand. Instead, he coaxed and convinced, bringing out the truest, most beautiful form for every creation. These creatures of the fiend whisperer were the exact opposite. Their unholiness and incongruity would never be allowed in the natural world without devilish interference. It was a perversion of all that was right and honorable, a twisted escape from the balance demons were known for. Fiends were monsters through and through.

"I could do this all day," the fiend whisperer said as they circled each other. They clashed again, and this time both of them felt it. They coughed up blood and went down on one knee. Though Ling Dong had tons of fighting experience, he wasn't sure how to approach a fight with this fiendish man. Normally, he caged in lesser opponents alongside him, forcing them to fight him them like a wild animal. But not this time. This man was fearless, and entering a cage with him was out of the question. He needed new tactics, new ways of doing things.

What if I use demonic qi like normal qi? Ling Dong thought. He felt for the earth and gathered its potential, then in a moment of inspiration, unleashed it. The earth shot up as spikes of rocky clay. The fiend whisperer dodged, but when Ling Dong moved to charge at the totem, some of the fiend whisper's twisted creations transformed into ashen snakes that spewed poison toward him.

How the hell am I going to get past him? Ling Dong thought, looking at the totem that was now glowing vivid black. The fiends nearest it were mutating incessantly, their twisted forms growing in power as energy poured out from the bone relic and into their flesh and blood. Demons were dying by the thousands as monarchs plundered their powers to do battle. Fiends fell likewise, though slowly but surely, their ranks were replenished by the totem's malevolent energy.

Ling Dong knew he needed to help to succeed. He knew there was no getting past the fiend whisperer on his own. Unfortunately, help seemed increasingly unlikely. Still, he kept trying. He was never truly alone. His heavy sword, almost too heavy for him to swing, sang as it whizzed through the air. His blade would keep him company.

"He's too good," Wang Jun said with a frown as his fingers moved across the mountain projection. Feng Ming was there as well, occasionally sending out orders whenever he noticed a situation. "It's like he's ten people. And my normal strategies aren't paying off."

On one ridge, his troops suffered an ambush, which he had them defend via carefully concealed traps. They were forced out almost immediately by support troops that made clever use of flight treasures. Arrows rained down on their position, though thankfully, Wang Jun had sent a squad of geomancers to them. They constructed a swift earthen shield that blocked the projectiles, buying them enough time to retreat through a shadow pathway.

"Should we go down there?" Feng Ming asked. "Should we fight?"

Wang Jun shook his head. "We're way more useful here, and besides, neither of us can multitask like he can."

On another path, they won a quick victory, forcing their opponents back. It was a consolation prize for their loss, as troops there had been mobilized from a place where the opposing general subsequently launched an ambush. War was a give and take, and there was seldom a clear winner or loser. More often than not, the result was little better than a draw.

"How lucky are you feeling?" Wang Jun said, holding his hand to his chin. As he thought, their troops began getting clobbered, and Feng Ming was forced to relay emergency instructions to minimize the fallout.

"I can feel as lucky as you'd like, but whatever you're thinking, do it quick," Feng Ming said.

A full minute trickled by, and at the end of it, Wang Jun got to work. His fingers blurred, and black strings linked up various game pieces on the mountain projection, setting up a chain reaction of events. On every front, they either attacked or retreated. There seemed to be little method to their madness as some forces joined, some split, and some defended. Their opponents reacted quickly. One after another, the situation in each skirmish stabilized. This continued for a good three minutes, after which one group of fifty men finally won a landslide victory. Literally. What would normally have been a terrible place for an ambush due to their troops position lower down suddenly became favorable due to a series of shifts in positioning.

"I have good news and bad news," Wang Jun said gravely.

"Start with the good news," Feng Ming said.

"The good news is that he's not invincible," Wang Jun said. "He's just very good, and he can think farther ahead than any man I've ever met."

"And the bad news?" Feng Ming asked.

Wang Jun grimaced. "A master chess player can think roughly twenty-five to thirty moves ahead in simple situations. That's not to say that they can predict a game's outcome, but whenever they make a move, they consider the consequences that deeply.

"In more complex situations, they can think maybe ten to fifteen moves ahead. And if the game changes to a more complex one like *Angels and Devils*, they might only think roughly five to ten moves ahead. This is because there are many possible lateral moves. Through quick judgment, it's easy to think of favorable positions after so few moves, so there's no need to calculate further. It's better to consider more options across the entire board than to think through every move in such detail."

"That's a game," Feng Ming said, sending out another set of orders. "Battles are infinitely more complicated. I only think maybe three to five moves ahead in any given situation. How much better could he possibly be?"

"To find out, I just tested him," Wang Jun answered. "I used precious time to lay out a complex strategy, forcing him to play my game. I considered five moves in most cases to funnel him down a specific path, where my calculations ran twenty deep. Near the end, and only on three separate pathways, I ran my simulation fifty moves ahead. He managed to keep up until the forty-second. Even then, the result was a bit of a gamble. I bet on your luck to eventually pull us through, and in the end, I succeeded."

Feng Ming whistled. "That's tough to compete against. It's a good thing you're on our side. At least with you here, we can win."

"That's the bad news," Wang Jun said grimly. "If it takes forty-two moves deep and a gamble to beat him, it will take hours to win. But we don't have hours, Feng Ming. Their objective is very clear." He looked back to the World Tree, which sat there peacefully. Throughout the entire conflict, despite the occasional attempt on the large Bodhi Tree, they'd always managed to defend it. It also seemed that the tree had some defenses of its own. "A single extra straw can break a camel's back. Considering how many incendiary treasures they are carrying, if we let too many through, we can kiss that tree goodbye. The only thing that confuses me is that thus far, the invaders don't seem to want to attack it. Or more accurately, they can't."

"Is the tree preventing it?" Feng Ming asked.

"I don't know," Wang Jun said, shaking his head. "The tree is very mysterious, and even beasts or devils would find calm between its leaves. Those around it are naturally nonviolent, but I think there's more to it than that. There's a battle being played on another level. It's not that someone *isn't* trying to destroy the tree; it's that someone else is stopping others dead in their tracks before they can even approach it." He looked above them, where he saw two shadows dancing in a place beyond them. With every blow and every exchange, the tides of battle rose and fell. "By the way, I'm not sure if you noticed, but where the hell are Zhou Li and Cha Ming?"

Luo Xuehua let out a bloodcurdling scream as the black-armored man's greatsword cut a deep gash in her arm. The wound wasn't deep, but the lightning within it caused much more damage. It wounded both her body and her soul.

We need to retreat, Zi Long sent, summoning a projection of what could be. Unlimited riches, power beyond description, and respect were just within the devil's grasp. They caused him to pause for a few moments, giving Zi Long enough time to sneak up behind him.

First illusory staff, flame, he thought. A projection of himself, a clone, appeared behind the armored man and swung downward.

Second illusory staff, water. Like a raging upside down wave, a water projection swung upward.

Third staff, earth. This projection appeared in front of the man, unleashing a stunning, vibrating lunge straight into his chest.

Fourth illusion, wood. A fourth Zi Long appeared beneath the man, and his staff wrapped around his legs, entangling him.

The earth projection struck first, knocking back the armored man. He ran straight into the downward flame strike, then was knocked back up as he fell down from the water projection. His knockup was interrupted by the wood projection, which held him fast and lurched around. The man was completely open Luo Xuehua and Zi Long's fifth projection, gold. Zi Long's staff became a sword, and he swung it three consecutive times before unleashing a blade of metal. It cut deep into the man's armor, opening it up for Luo Xuehua, who landed on his chest and slashed at his throat. The man's head was lopped off, falling to the ground. The body crashed down as well, but as soon as it did, it dissolved to lightning and re-formed.

The disappearance didn't surprise Zi Long, but Luo Xuehua, who'd been standing on him, lost her footing. The man swept with his giant sword, threatening to cleave her in half. Zi Long's sixth projection, which also happened to be his true body, superimposed itself with the others via illusion and charged out. His holy spirit rushed into the devil once again, this time causing him to pause for only a half second as Zi Long pulled Luo Xuehua back, barely saving her.

"Let go of me!" she yelled, running toward the devil.

Zi Long sighed, appeared behind her, and struck the back of her neck. He picked her up and slung her over his body, then summoned the illusion of a devastating battlefield to cover their escape. They merged with retreating soldiers, confusing the pride devil long enough for him to find another target. They'd barely escaped with their lives.

Zi Long held up a pill and brought it to Luo Xuehua's lips. "Do you want revenge? Do you want this pill?" She tried to bite it, but he pulled it back. "You're not thinking clearly. Calm yourself." He summoned a different kind of illusion, this one a memory of the calm swordswoman he knew she was. He let it play in her mind as a dream accelerated ten times, and only once she calmed down did he let her go. "I know it's hard, but you need to face it. We're not his match, and we need help."

"How?" Luo Xuehua said, eating the pill. The wound on her

arm closed up, and she sheathed her swords, which were covered in electrical burns.

"We'll start small," Zi Long said. "Find a friend. These men and women hate each other so much they're basically ignoring tactics. This is like a barroom brawl, not a battlefield. It makes both sides easy to kill."

"Xi Lang is dead," Luo Xuehua mumbled. "He killed him so fast."

"Well, there're a lot more people out there," Zi Long said. He'd liked the man, but there was no time for grieving, and they were no strangers to loss when on missions against devils. "With the two of us helping them, we'll be able to round up enough members to take care of that monstrosity. Sound like a plan?"

The pride devil who they'd just lost to had joined another battle. The tide was quickly turning in the devils' favor. With a wildcard like that fighting, it wouldn't be long until their casualties became unbearable. They had to act now, and fast, to contain it.

"All right," Luo Xuehua said. "Let's do it." They looked around and found a courageous woman, a middle-core-formation cultivator who was close to getting her wings, holding her ground against three wrath devils. They charged in toward her.

Chapter 24: Middle Game

"You're very good at this game," Zhou Li said, moving about with Cha Ming as they claimed key points on the invisible game board. Though they traveled quickly, the wind was still quiet. The stillness around them persisted. "You don't make unnecessary moves. You always play for value and ignore traps."

"You're losing," Cha Ming pointed out as he started a new offensive to chase Zhou Li's stones into a corner. He wrapped around them, causing the man to flee until he'd secured life for the lone group, then moved on to begin again in another location.

"You're so competitive," Zhou Li scolded. "A very good trait in a rival. You play to win—that's good. But so easily distracted." With this, he summoned two scrolls. It seemed by that by securing life for the latest group, Zhou Li's abilities had increased once again. Twin dogs of black ink appeared, their bodies wreathed in black flames. They joined together as one before stomping down, causing Cha Ming to stagger. The newly formed Cerberus breathed deadly flames he was forced to dodge. In the process, a few scattered stones he'd set up for territory went on the defensive, losing ground to Zhou Li's increasingly secure territory.

"It's not always about the opening," Zhou Li said. "The middle game is extremely important. I'd say people make their most fatal mistakes in this stage of the game, before they can become nitpicky and compete for trivial points."

"I agree, the middle game means everything," Cha Ming said. He laid down a few more stones, and with them came a surge of power. His peak-core-formation combat sigils suddenly felt a lot lighter. He poured transcendent force into them, summoning a gigantic mountain that weighed down on the Cerberus. He picked another part of the board where they'd played a few stones, the part where angels and devils were fighting. The angels were losing, and many stones were appearing and disappearing of their own volition. It seemed the game was a two-way street, and allies could even play stones for him.

The Cerberus let out one last cry of agony as it exploded in a nova of flame. The flames became a massive tidal wave that spat out dozens of voracious fish, courtesy of yet another three paintings. These paintings were much like talismans, but instead of using characters to imbue truth and power, they used imagery to lock essence.

Well, two can play at that game, Cha Ming thought. He threw out three talismans that summoned a whirlpool, sucking the fish into one central location. Then, just like fish in a barrel, he slammed down with the Clear Sky Pillar, dissolving the fish into ink that blended with the water.

"So focused on one spot of the board," Zhou Li mocked. He appeared on the mountain where the Alabaster Group's blood doctors and Feng Ming's ragtag forces were defending alongside lesser monks. Cha Ming scolded himself and joined the man. Where he stepped and fought, stones appeared. They materialized as hidden Alabaster Group reserves and surprise breakthroughs in the battling monks.

"You forget quite quickly as well," Cha Ming said, stepping back. "Never play elsewhere if your group can't be defended." He returned to their original position, and as stones appeared, Yue Bing and a few dozen late-core-formation cultivators joined the battle. This group was late, but their appearance made a distinct difference. The doctors began gathering the blood of the fallen and healing injured troops, surrounding and removing some of Zhou Li's stones in the process.

"Touché," Zhou Li said, grinning. By now, all four corners of their virtual board were basically filled. It was only the center that was unclaimed.

Wait, the center? A chilling thought ran through his mind as Zhou Li placed a single stone. And where he placed it, another stillness, and it was superimposed with the absence of wind. He placed it at the center of the board, straight above the World Tree.

"I know you like to play this move, especially in the beginning. You really should have done it, especially this time. Don't you remember what we're playing for?"

Right. They were fighting to defend the World Tree. He'd forgotten all about it when he'd learned his life was at stake. He looked at their board position and realized that many moves he hadn't understood before were actually perfectly positioned to support Zhou Li's bid for the center.

"Well played," Cha Ming said. He moved to attack Zhou Li's stones and displace them but was met with an army of inky creatures summoned by ten other scrolls. Zhou Li summoned a black paintbrush, which he used to draw a quick formation that linked them all together. The man had been holding back until a critical moment.

Fortunately, Cha Ming had also been holding back. Cha Ming threw out five talismans as he retreated, one for each of the five elements. Though they were only peak-core-formation treasures, he used them in combination with his combat sigils to create a compound formation. Five-Element Destroyer was a good name, wasn't it? Thinking up names for new techniques on the fly was exhilarating.

The army of ink disintegrated, and though he was forced to cede the absolute center, he was able to build substantial influence on every side of it. It would be difficult for Zhou Li to expand now. Strictly speaking, that meant that Cha Ming was winning the game. But he couldn't shake the feeling that something fishy was going on.

Just what *was* Zhou Li doing? The man wasn't playing like he should, trying to reduce gains from Cha Ming's foray into his territory. Instead, he was expanding the center as much as possible, ceding hard-earned ground from a game well played.

Three Spectral Assassins dove in for the kill, their gleaming crimson blades guided by threads of karma weaved by a Soul Priest. Gong Lan, spotting these new threads, severed them. The Spectral Assassins became confused and disorganized, and they let the opportunity slip between their fingers.

They would normally attack, she thought, noting their retreat to the proximity of the Soul Priests. That wasn't like Spectral Assassins. When cornered, they always fell back on their failsafe strategy: Kill everything in sight. Leave no survivors.

Near her, Bai Ling was busy baiting their opponents. Soul fire and soul ice was very effective against evil spirits and their ilk, but only if it hit. Unfortunately, spirit mediums had joined the battle, using their expanded senses to navigate these carefully laid traps. Seeing that her attacks bore no fruit, she flew back up to Gong Lan.

"I have good news and bad news," Bai Ling said, cracking open a pill bottle and taking a qi-replenishing pill. "Which one do you want first?" Her two vice mistresses were still down there exchanging blows with two shepherds as she recovered.

"Good news or bad news, it matters not," Gong Lan said.

"Then I'll start with the bad news," Bai Ling said. "It's always good to air out dirty laundry when you can. Unfortunately, it seems that they've reined in their vengeful hatred and are actually behaving themselves. I've tried kindling arts to prod them along, but to no avail. They can't be baited."

"That shouldn't be happening," Gong Lan said, frowning. "Evil spirits are vengeance incarnate. Unless something much greater is at stake, another target to their hatred we haven't yet spotted."

"Well, I'm not sure what that is," Bai Ling said. "The good news is that their newfound attitude means they're playing conservatively. They can't make it to the World Tree with us defending it. And our casualties are much lower than they could be."

"That is a blessing," Gong Lan said, frowning as she looked at the calm back and forth of battle. "This isn't fighting," she said, realizing what bothered her. "This is peace. I sense no intent in them to get past us and harm the World Tree."

"What could they even do to harm it?" the Bodhi Seed asked, popping up on her shoulder.

"Pardon?" Gong Lan said. "You mean they can't harm it?"

"I mean, look at the thing," the Bodhi Seed said. "Its vitality source stretches down to the core of the plane itself. It was planted there for a reason, and nothing short of a devastating blow will stand a chance in harming it. Plus, you try hurting it, if you even manage to get close to it."

"Then why are they even fighting?" Bai Ling wondered out loud.

"Who knows?" the Bodhi Seed said. "They like killing monks, don't they? That should be reason enough, right?"

Gong Lan ignored him and stepped up into the grid she'd noticed floating in the air. It was faint, and she could see stones everywhere. They were tied to their forces and the Spirit Temple's forces by karma. At the same time, she noticed they were tied to the spectral forms of Cha Ming and Zhou Li, who fought up above, and others couldn't see. It was… a two-way relationship?

"We're game pieces," Gong Lan realized. "And Zhou Li and Cha Ming are players. They don't just influence our battle—the opposite is also true."

Bai Ling appeared beside her, and though she couldn't see the karmic strings binding them or the men fighting, she seemed to have a grudging respect for the powerful monk. "If what you're saying is true, then that would explain their behavior."

"The Spirit Temple is here to support Zhou Li," Gong Lan said softly. "Their job isn't to kill us but to hold ground for him and feed his power base."

"If that's the case, then that's everyone's goal," Bai Ling said. "Every man and woman on this mountain supporting one or the other. But there's a key difference between our two goals."

"They're here to destroy the World Tree," Gong Lan said. "We're trying to defend it."

"Two different games entirely," Bai Ling said gravely. "This is worse than I thought."

"How is this worse?" Gong Lan said.

"It means Zhou Li doesn't have to play optimally," Bai Ling said. "As long as he destroys the tree, he wins." They looked down at their troops in worry. The monks and mistresses danced with evil spirits, and neither side was winning. Balance, it seemed, was the enemy. If they wanted to win, defending wouldn't cut it.

Ling Dong channeled the power of the mountain, its violet strength surging through his veins as he hefted his greatsword, sweeping from the ground as he did so. It unleashed a veritable storm of gravel that crashed into the fiend whisperer, who'd spun his club in a whirl of black wind. The man didn't press the attack—he didn't have to. The fiendbone totem was all the advantage he needed, and the advantage grew with every passing second.

Below them, Silverwing and the others were caught up in their respective brawls. The large bird was currently at a disadvantage, a furry snake coiled around his body as blades of wind lacerated it from the outside. Gua, on the other hand, was winning. The massive swamp he'd brought from another demonic mountain was slowing, poisoning, and suffocating his wolflike opponent.

A little help here, Lei Jiang yelled, prompting Ling Dong to come to his rescue. He swung his greatsword like a bat, slapping away spiky projectiles that resembled sea urchins as the small rodent dug into his tentacled opponent.

Mr. Mountain had taken the appearance of a rocky golem. He exchanged punches with a mostly humanoid fiend. But Ling Dong had no time to linger; he rushed back to the fiend whisperer, who'd taken advantage of his absence to attack Silverwing. The helpless bird was on the verge of being crushed. Ling Dong placed his hand on the mountainside, and a fissure appeared before the bird, spewing hot gasses and forcing the fiend whisperer back. He swung his club, barely avoiding Ling Dong's greatsword strike, and before long, they were back to where they started, floating in the air above the fiendbone totem.

We can't win this, Ling Dong thought as he drew in demonic power, replenishing his reserves. "Not without help." With near-infinite fiendish energy coming in at a greater rate than the mountain's demonic defenders, it was only a matter of time before they lost.

Another victory, another rout. Their battle had entered a steady rhythm. Wang Jun and Feng Ming took turns commanding, giving precious time for the former to come up with well thought-out battle plans. And their efforts were paying off. Their casualties weren't nearly as bad as before. The enemy had ceased taking ground so quickly and was now cautiously approaching.

But why the shift? Why the change? Did the enemy know something he didn't? All these worries bogged Wang Jun down as he thought through his plans in silence.

"We've entered a groove," Wang Jun said finally. "A steady rhythm. What are some reasons for that to happen in real battles? I'm used to games, not life-and-death struggles."

"Stalling," Feng Ming said instantly. "You only ever hit a groove if someone's stalling."

"*We've* been trying to stall," Wang Jun said. "To prevent them from going up the mountain. That much makes sense, at least."

"It's not that simple," Feng Ming said, taking a seat as Wang Jun issued orders. "If you're the attacking general, the last thing you want is a steady rhythm. You want to disrupt it, put the defenders on edge. When you have an advantage in manpower, you want a battle of attrition to disrupt the enemy until you win."

"That's what they started with," Wang Jun said. "And what we prevented. Yet I can't help shake a strange feeling."

"You're right to have that feeling," Feng Ming said. "I feel the same way."

"It's like we're flies caught in a web," Wang Jun said. "Or snakes dancing to the piper's tune."

"There are many reasons to stall," Feng Ming said, tapping his chin. "One reason is to conserve manpower if you're not in a hurry to achieve your objective."

"Which they are, in this case," Wang Jun said. "More to the point, lives are meaningless to them. Their transcendents are killing each other as we speak." Five had fallen so far, destroyed by either other transcendents or the plane's will itself.

"Usually, though, you stall to hold important ground," Feng Ming said reluctantly "You don't want to leave favorable territory, because it's easier to rout you outside it. When attacking uphill, you need to be careful and only attack when you have a decisive advantage. Likewise, you don't want to storm a keep right away. Instead, you want to take up important positions around it, isolating it as you bring up your main army."

"Damn it, that's it," Wang Jun said, stopping his orders. He sent a generic defensive plan to their troops and dropped all his current plans. "He's not trying to climb up the mountain. The mere thought that these troops could actually damage the World Tree is laughable."

"Then what are they here for?" Feng Ming asked.

"To hold ground," Wang Jun said. He summoned an illusion of an *Angels and Devils* board, an imitation of the game between Cha Ming and Zhou Li that others couldn't see. "We're all pieces on the board. But it's the players who ultimately win or lose, Feng Ming."

"Are you saying there's nothing we can do?" Feng Ming said. "Because I don't really like the game-piece analogy."

"It's more than that," Wang Jun said. "There's a karmic relationship between us, our troops, Cha Ming, and Zhou Li. I didn't see it before because I was distracted, but the karma flows both ways."

"So *we're* the players, and he's the game piece?" Feng Ming asked, confused.

"We're still the pieces, but we're not entirely under his control," Wang Jun said. "Our actions strengthen him, and their actions strengthen Zhou Li. Holding ground is ideal for Zhou Li, as it's feeding his power base."

"In my experience, giving your opponents the initiative is a bad idea," Feng Ming said. "It's best to do the opposite, to shake things up and at least disrupt their plans."

"I'm afraid that to upset the balance, we're going to have to make sacrifices," Wang Jun said gravely. "None of the other sides are winning. They've all hit a groove. Zhou Li's influence is expanding in the center, but the center is all he needs, isn't it?"

"Your orders?" Feng Ming asked.

"Queen's gambit," Wang Jun said. "We're going to need to free our best pieces to make something happen. We're going to lose a lot of pawns in the process."

Sacrifice. It was a difficult concept to accept. But the Alabaster Group was used to sacrifice, and Zi Long knew they needed to sacrifice lives to achieve anything here. Even those fighting above them knew what needed to be done. Nearby, a transcendent angel plummeted to the ground, his wings clipped and a sword sheathed in his chest. He'd defeated his opponent, who was now nothing more than a smoldering pile of wood shavings, but was it worth it? He thought so. He died smiling. They were happy for him.

Zi Long pulled Luo Xuehua past an overwhelmed member of the Alabaster Group. She was fighting three against one, impossible odds for anyone at the same level, let alone when fighting devils. They knew her, and she knew them. They'd shared wine and fought together. But now was not the time for tender feelings. They traded knowing nods, and they left her to die alone.

"There!" he said, spotting an opening. Three men were fighting three, as even a battle as they could find. They leaped in, Luo Xuehua with her icy swords and combat formations and Zi Long with his illusory staff arts. As he landed among the four devils, he unleashed his Devil-Sealing Intent. His holy spirit let out a chime, paralyzing them just long enough for their allies to land a killing blow. Seeing that they were overwhelmed, the two remaining devils fled. One of them acted too late, however, and his last burning act of anger was to latch on to one of the Alabaster Group's junior members and self-detonate, leaving behind only ashes and a charred corpse.

"Now we're four," Zi Long said. "Move out!" They left their comrade behind. The living needed their help far more than the dead.

"No you don't," Cha Ming spat, swinging out his staff and repelling an inky lion. He summoned a combat formation of flaming blades that tore into the creature, opening a path toward Zhou Li. The man had apparently been waiting for him, for he thrust forward with his sword, unleashing a black dragon of sin flames that sought to engulf him.

That was new. Zhou Li smirked and followed up with a spiraling motion. Ten more dragons erupted and surged forward. As they closed the distance, Cha Ming realized he'd regained a few more abilities. He unleashed Splitting Heaven and Earth, infusing water into his creation qi and forming a barrier of ice with his staff. The dragons puffed away as the ice melted, giving Cha Ming the opening he needed to unleash Crushing Chaos on Zhou Li, who'd evidently anticipated this and summoned an inky black shell to absorb it. Unlike the last shell he'd used, however, it fully repelled Cha Ming's powerful blow.

I can't pass if he has a solid wall of stones, Cha Ming realized, noticing the black stones on the ground in front of Zhou Li. He flickered to another side and started another offensive, forcing Zhou Li to block. A burning phoenix of black flame with evil eyes let out a piercing cry. It paralyzed Cha Ming and caused him to cough up blood. Heat built up inside him, and before he could escape, the phoenix exploded.

Cha Ming's flesh burnt away. His bones burnt away. Most of him evaporated with the intense flame, leaving nothing more than a few bones in his torso. They grew back in less than a second, drawing on his large vitality reserves, but to his dismay, Zhou Li's territory had expanded significantly during his absence.

He returned to damage control, limiting the expansion, accepting that a solid wall would be built once again. But he dared not slack, as time seemed shorter than ever. Zhou Li's obsession with the center was unnerving.

"Have you ever wondered what I am?" Zhou Li asked suddenly, appearing beside him. His swords slashed out a few times, hitting Cha Ming on the chest, but not before he could throw out a creation-infused palm blast. The palm crashed against a qi shield, sending Zhou Li a few feet back.

"I know exactly what you are," Cha Ming said. "You're a monster." He swung out with Crushing Chaos, using his combat sigils to form entangling vines to constrict Zhou Li's movements. Just as the staff was about to hit, however, the air sizzled, and Zhou Li's skin turned black and red, matching his dark eyes and red pupils.

It became clear in an instant, as his Eyes of Truth finally saw through the intricate veil Zhou Li had intentionally lifted.

"You're not just a devil," Cha Ming whispered. "You're a hybrid." Black veins of corruption ran across all of Zhou Li's body. Now that his form was unsealed, Cha Ming could finally see the telltale signs of both lineages.

Devils were far more common than evil spirits, and the main requirement was a perversion in personality. Wrath devils, those with the greatest resentment, channeled their anger in intense flames that resulted in extreme strength. But that strength had never been present in Zhou Li. Instead, it was bound by corrupted karma to his qi, resulting in the black flames that had become his trademark. Cha Ming had never seen the sin flames anywhere else.

It was no wonder that Zhou Li was so bitter. It was no wonder he held grudges and wanted nothing more than the North's destruction. Two evil forces had twisted his personality beyond recognition, making it impossible for him to focus on anything *but* revenge.

"Now that I've gathered sufficient territory, I can finally unleash my true power," Zhou Li said. "It's time to end this." Black sin flames oozed out of him, filling the nearest thirty feet with an ocean of liquid fire. Cha Ming was forced back as even his half-step-marrow-refining body could handle it no longer. Zhou Li was far stronger than he'd ever imagined. Black stones began spreading out form the center at a frightening pace. They broke through Cha Ming's carefully crafted enclosures, spreading out in all directions.

"Are you sure you want to do this?" Bai Ling said. "It's no better than killing them."

"What is death to those who've done their best to rid themselves of karma?" Gong Lan said, sending out mental instructions to her monks. At Bai Ling's own instructions, several mistresses flew out and joined her.

"They won't last long out there with the balance upset," Bai Ling said.

"It is an acceptable sacrifice," Gong Lan said. "They've been preparing for this their entire lives."

Bai Ling nodded, and at her instructions, their group broke off. They flew into the skies, avoiding Spectral Assassins that sought to box them in.

"Besides," Gong Lan said, "your mistresses are better at supporting others."

They flew past Wang Jun and Feng Ming, who were busy fighting their own battle. They flew past the demons, who were also in a deadlock. They proceeded past the invisible forms of Cha Ming and Zhou Li, who seemed to have transcended to their own plane of existence. Interfering with their game would be difficult, if not impossible.

"Let's go for the low-hanging fruit," Bai Ling said.

Gong Lan nodded, and together, their group of mistresses and a few monks flew toward a smaller battle where inquisitors and devil cultists were fighting.

"You know, we're just wasting time here," the fiend whisperer said. His black club struck against Ling Dong's forearm, which grew a thick layer of bark that absorbed the shock. Ling Dong swung his greatsword in turn, and black scales appeared on the man's leg, stopping the blade from digging too deep into his bones. Both jumped back, and their wounds reknit. Ling Dong couldn't help but notice his healed just a little bit slower than the fiend whisperer's.

"Isn't that your goal?" Ling Dong asked. "Wasting time?"

"Perhaps," the fiend whisperer replied. "But I grow stronger as you grow weaker. How long do you think you can keep this up? I respect you. I *like* you. Why don't you just run away, and I'll pretend I wasn't able to catch you?"

Ling Dong knew the truth of those words. He felt them. During their battle, thousands of demons died and thousands of fiends were born. Meanwhile, the existing fiends grew increasingly powerful. Soon, the entire mountain would fall under the horde's vicious onslaught.

In that moment of helpless realization, however, a soft breeze blew across Ling Dong's sweaty chest. It was a refreshing wind, a wind containing something he hadn't felt since the start of the battle. The fiend whisper frowned when the wind hit him as well.

"You feel it, don't you?" Ling Dong said, grinning. "Not so cut off from nature as you thought, are you?"

"This means nothing," the fiend whisperer said. "Fight me or run."

"Oh, I'll fight you," Ling Dong said. "It's far too early to be running." He looked over his shoulder and saw a group of inquisitors, Red Dust mistresses, a few scattered monks making their way toward the Alabaster Group. He let out a laugh of relief as he brought up his sword to block the fiend whisperer's spiked club. The winds of change were blowing, and the fiend whisperer knew it.

"The tides of battle are shifting," Wang Jun said, his fingers manipulating various strings. Their troops fought and retreated, combining as they lost ground faster then ever on their way up the mountain.

"Yeah, they are," Feng Ming said with a frown. "You're making us lose."

"I'm freeing up manpower," Wang Jun said. "Have you ever run a business?"

"Can't say I have," Feng Ming said, shaking his head as small dots on the illusory mountain vanished. Though there weren't as many as there were demons, there were still far more men here than with the Alabaster Group's forces and the monks. Each one represented a human life, its price incalculable and its worth immeasurable.

"I learned this in Green Leaf City, of all places," Wang Jun said. "Where it all began. My uncle, upset at my insistence in competing with my late brother, sent me to that backwater place with barely any investment capital. He told me that if I wanted to leave, I'd need to grow the Song Kingdom's business tenfold in three years."

"A tall order," Feng Ming said, focusing on key parts of the mountain as instructed and distributing his luck as much as he could. They lost ground quickly, but their losses were tolerable.

"Too tall," Wang Jun said. "To generate capital, I had to renegotiate contracts. I had to increase my accounts payable, decrease my accounts receivable. I cut down our working capital to the bone so I could reinvest it. I lost out on every trade to do it, and only then was I able to grow the company."

"That's what you're doing here," Feng Ming said. "You're reorganizing our forces to free up manpower. But what will you do with them? A general must have reasons for every action."

Wang Jun ignored him. He continued guiding troops and creating portals of darkness until finally, they'd ceded two thirds of the mountain. "Not them," Wang Jun said. "Just you."

"Me?" Feng Ming said, aghast. "You're going to handle him all on your own?"

"I won't be playing commander anymore," Wang Jun said, summoning his Void Shadow Scythe. "I'll be playing frontline general. Our troops are set, and their orders steady. I'd love to see him outmaneuver me tactically when he has a scythe-wielding madman on his tail."

Feng Ming blinked, and the man was gone. He looked around him and saw tiny imperfections in the flow of battle, all leading to one destination. All that was left was making sure they got there.

"Charge!" Zi Long yelled.

"Charge!" Luo Xuehua echoed. The Alabaster Group's forces, their cloaks soaked in blood and devilish gore, cut into a group of twelve devils and saving five members of the Alabaster Group. Their group's total swelled to thirty-six, though it was a far cry from the army the pride devil was gathering.

Above them, another angel died. This one was a peak-core-formation cultivator. These men and women were the future leaders of the Alabaster Group, and the merit they wielded made it very likely for them to succeed in rune carving.

Angels and devils. Strictly speaking, his merit glow could be considered angelic, just like those lesser devils, which were abominations created via diabolical ritual. He had not yet surpassed his limitations and condensed his ideals into wings like Luo Xuehua had. And like many of the devils here had. Perhaps he was just too pragmatic for the process.

Angels were luckier than most, and they found advancing easy. Devils were stronger, and their advancement more difficult. It was a careful balance maintained by the universe, between parties that wanted to wipe each other out of existence. They were eternal enemies since the dawn of time, like oil and water that could never mix.

"Things aren't going very well," Luo Xuehua said, frowning. "The devils are organizing quickly, but we are not."

"We just need to buy some time," Zi Long said. "Can you see the inquisitors? They're fighting their way over as we speak. With their help, we might just save a few more members."

"And then what?" Luo Xuehua said. "Even if we save a few more, we can't win. This is already unsalvageable." She was right, unfortunately. At best, they were saving lives and buying time.

"You guys are very terrible at tactics," a voice suddenly said. It was a black-armored man wearing a black cape. He recognized that man.

"Uncle Feng?" Zi Long said. "Aren't you needed on the mountain?"

"Looks like you all need my help a lot more," Feng Ming said, looking over the squabbling devilish and angelic forces. "There. We strike there."

"That's not a weakness," Zi Long said. Luo Xuehua quickly agreed.

"See, that's the problem with you good guys," Feng Ming said. "Always so righteous and straightforward. You charge straight in and clock someone in the face, but you never worry about the big friend standing right behind him." He held his spear out and pointed toward two other groups nearby. "We'll strike there and force them back a bit. "We'll join up with those beside them and free up a few men. I like to call it freeing up investment capital."

"I could use my illusions to drag in a few more survivors," Zi Long added.

"Now you're thinking," Feng Ming said. "You guys are bad at strategic thinking, but fortunately, you have me. Let me show you how it's done."

Chapter 25:
End Game

The scorching heat of Zhou Li's black flames seared flesh off Cha Ming's bones as he formed hand seals, summoning a half-step-transcendent crystal of ice. It completely encapsulated him, giving time for his flesh to reknit before the fire melted it once again, forcing him to retract the sigils lest they be damaged. And his bones would be damaged too, if it were not for the protection of his pseudo-domain. A thin layer of inviolable water covered him, though it was barely enough to keep him in one piece.

Being a body cultivator was a wonderful thing. Strength, stamina, defense, and healing. All combined into one package that made him a nigh-invulnerable adversary. But these black sin flames, the combined might of Zhou Li's powers as a wrath devil and an evil spirit, pushed the limits of what a mortal should be allowed to accomplish in this realm before transcending.

"You're not looking so good," Zhou Li said in his usual annoying voice. He flapped his crimson-and-ochre wings, appearing behind Cha Ming and stabbing with his flaming black sword. Cha Ming could only twirl his Clear Sky Staff, using Splitting Heaven and Earth to create a circular shield. The strike forced him back, both cracking his bones and leaving behind a long row of black stones where he traveled.

Too strong, Cha Ming thought, reaching out to Sun Wukong. *Can you help me?*

Not directly, Sun Wukong said. *There's a karmic field blocking me. The board you're playing on, it's locked you both in and is keeping everyone else out.*

Figures, Cha Ming thought. Another attack came, this time taking the shape of a murder of flaming black crows. He summoned a mountain to block them off, and it lasted only a few seconds before dissociating into combat sigils like the ice crystal before it. *I need the Tri-Sealing Pillars,* he thought. *If I have those, I can restrain and fight him.*

But how was he supposed to do that when he was losing ground? His influence was receding with every blow they exchanged, and Zhou Li was far too powerful for him to hold back. He flickered and attacked, preferring to take the initiative rather than remain in passive defense. Using his Eyes of Truth, Cha Ming detected a flaw in Zhou Li's technique and jabbed out with Origin Strike, which until now had been sealed. The gray mist sucked in black flames, destroying them, converting them. Zhou Li was forced back, though by the looks of it, he'd barely suffered any damage.

Wait, how did Origin Strike suddenly become available? he thought just as Zhou Li whispered a few words and black chains appeared around his body. He tried slashing through them with the Clear Sky Staff, but they were unreasonably solid. They wrapped around his arms and legs, which were coated in a golden pseudo-domain. Zhou Li formed hand seals, standing in midair and directing the chains as they crushed the life out of him.

He was missing something. Something important. He'd been losing ground to Zhou Li, so how did Origin Strike become available? His Eyes of Truth looked around the board and soon noticed an anomaly. Some stones, some boundaries, had already been set. He remembered them clearly. Yet now, these borders had shifted. Some stones had moved, and even some white stones had appeared.

He looked to the mountain, where their forces were holding off the last few passes. He looked to the demons, who were fighting in deadlock. The monks weren't faring any better, even with the support of the few mistresses.

But where was Gong Lan? Where was Feng Ming? He finally spotted them, one backing up the Alabaster Group's forces and the other helping the chaplains. And in that moment, he felt a gentle wind blow past him. It cooled his skin, despite the scorching black chains, breaking the stillness that had once filled this dreadful dimension.

Cha Ming smiled.

"Just give up," Zhou Li said. "It's hopeless."

Cha Ming laughed. "Don't you feel it??

"Feel what?" Zhou Li said.

"The wind," Cha Ming answered.

"What wind?" Zhou Li said. "There is no wind."

"The winds of change," Cha Ming whispered. "There's hope. I can feel it." He felt a shiver down his spine, and on his back, where the five elemental dualities were inscribed, a glowing white wind blew in a clockwise motion. And in that moment, he realized that all was not lost. He might be losing, but his friends were fighting. Others were doing their part, and their results were showing themselves on the game board. He didn't have to fight alone. He just had to have faith. Faith in his friends and everything they could accomplish.

Faith was the eighth virtue, independent of the seven others. Though many of his insights hinted at certain ones, they all shared faith as a common feature. A broken stone could be mended, and a stagnant ocean could flow. A dull blade could be sharpened, and a doused fire could be kindled. New life could spring forth from death, and together, they made the great cycle of samsara. Change was possible, but it only happened for those who willed it.

That small wind blowing from the fierce fighting and the risks his friends took to gain precious ground inspired him. The jade wings that were transparent before suddenly appeared in full splendor, though they weren't jade like the other wings he'd seen, but the purest white. They represented something that transcended the other seven virtues. For faith wasn't just a virtue—it was the willingness to move on. It represented positive change. No matter the damage, no matter the odds, no matter the wear and tear one suffered, hope could always be found. And with these wings came inspiration on the five elements, followed by a wonderful surge of power.

His pseudo-domain, which could previously only extend a microscopic distance, grew. It grew until it was a full ten feet wide, forming a bubble and forcing apart the chains that bound him. Zhou Li coughed up black blood as they broke, and Cha Ming summoned the Clear Sky Staff. With his newfound strength, he could now see many flaws riddling Zhou Li's body as a result of his corruption. And just above him, he could see a blurry outline, words that would help him if he could finally pierce the veil.

"Let's try this again," Cha Ming said. He rushed forward, executing Splitting Heaven and Earth. Zhou Li dodged and sent plumes of black flame back at him. They homed in on him using karmic tethers and crashed into his fledgling domain, almost causing it to shatter.

Definitely not invincible, Cha Ming thought, making a note to dodge future attacks. Their exchanges went from being one-sided to being equal for both sides. Cha Ming continued pushing Zhou Li, forcing him to wall off his meager but worrying center. Though he was winning once again, Cha Ming couldn't shake a feeling. What happened when he completed the enclosure around the center? He didn't know the answer, but one thing was certain: he couldn't stop Zhou Li from claiming it.

That thought worried him, since Zhou Li definitely knew something he didn't. Like Cha Ming, the man played the game to win. In Cha Ming's experience, however, that could mean a lot of things. This was real life; victory and defeat were often subjective.

"I see you know how to fight, peace-loving heretic," Chaplain Wu said to Gong Lan, his rosaries turning to beads of light that obliterated the three nearest devils. He held out another hand, and an angelic beam descended on another group, reducing them to ashes in just a few seconds. Now that he had room to breathe, he could finally unleash his full potential. Chaplains weren't there to defend the Church, but rather to destroy evil.

"The sixth company is secured, Chaplain!" a golden-armored man said, saluting.

"Good, go help the fourth," Chaplain Wu responded. The man did as instructed and charged at a group of devils with shield and longsword.

"Though we seek to shed all karma, mercy for all living things is paramount," Gong Lan said. "Eradicating evil does great justice to all. Much karma can be resolved by meting out punishment."

They flew out together, clashing against one of the devil cult leaders. The devils were split into two main groups—the Obsidian Syndicate and the cultists. It was these devil-worshipping foes that they fought, the wicked men and women who sacrificed regularly to their dark gods to obtain their powers. They weren't timid like their business associates.

"Well, we can agree on that at least," Chaplain Wu said, grunting as he blasted away an assailant with two palms.

"Thank you for coming," Gong Lan said, throwing one of her rulers and plunging it into a wrath devil's foul chest, destroying the core of its sinful power.

"We've almost wrapped things up here," Chaplain Wu said. "What do you say we go help those angels?"

"Unnecessary," Gong Lan said. "Feng Ming is there, and the situation is stable."

"Then the mountain?" Chaplain Wu asked.

"The demons," Gong Lan said, causing the man to frown. "I know you value human lives over demons, but I'm sure you value the World Tree's influence. If it falls, much goodness will be lost; many fewer people will worship the sun goddess."

"Fine," Chaplain Wu said, holding his hand up and calling for his people to assemble. The last of the devils had been dispatched, and their men were now treating the wounded. "But why the demons?"

"Because the demons are the biggest wildcard," Gong Lan said. "They are the most numerous, so a win for either side will cause a landslide victory. If this drags on too long, many of them will die."

"Who cares if a few more die if we eventually win?" Chaplain Wu said.

"It's not about the life and death of demons," Gong Lan said. "We're all pieces in a great game. Losing ground brings us closer to the edge of oblivion. Are you ready?"

"Ready as I'll ever be," Chaplain Wu said. He looked to his commanders, who nodded.

"Let's go," Gong Lan said, holding out a golden ruler and pointing it toward the far side of the mountain.

"She's coming," Ling Dong said, grinning as he spat out a mouthful of blood.

The fiend whisperer was bleeding as well, this time from a wound to his abdomen. Both wounds healed quickly and were nothing more than a tickle. Demonic and fiendish powers poured in to replenish their soft human flesh.

"You would dare accept the help of others?" the fiend whisperer spat. "What of your honor?"

"Honor is between equals and demons," Ling Dong said coldly. "You are a fiend, not a demon, and that makes a world of difference."

Golden scriptural characters appeared as Gong Lan landed. She whispered a few words, and a thousand and eighty golden pearls formed an intricate restraining matrix around the enemy commander. Bai Ling also landed. Shards of soul ice and wisps of soul fire stood ready to strike at any moment.

"Are we doing this?" Bai Ling asked.

"We'll support and you fight," Gong Lan said.

Ling Dong bared his teeth and growled as he charged.

A dark portal appeared in the middle of a river, broaching the concealment on an island. Wang Jun entered with a vicious slash, his scythe hitting nothing but empty air. He dissolved into darkness, reappearing just in time to meet a silver greatsword. His bones creaked and his qi shields trembled under the impact. His opponent was *strong*.

A boot flew his way, and Wang Jun disappeared again. He appeared above the man, who predicted this and swung in an upward arc. Then, the man cursed before sliding backward, barely avoiding Wang Jun's shadow and its very large scythe.

"Clever," the man said. "But I wasn't born yesterday."

They clashed several times before the man escaped in a flash of gray, revealing one of the cards he'd been using to ensure such rapid reinforcements. Wang Jun followed the man through darker paths and appeared in front, striking him again.

"Spatial affinities," Wang Jun said. "Impressive. And rare."

"A great tool for any general," the enemy commander said, grinning as he deflected the scythe blow one-handed and took out a dagger with the other. He struck Wang Jun in the chest, but to his surprise, the dagger only pierced shadow. Wang Jun's face split in a wolf's grin as the tip of his scythe extended and slashed the man's back with a bladelike whip. Chunks of armor fell off but were quickly regenerated. The armor wasn't a treasure after all, but lightning incarnate.

"I've never understood how this works," Wang Jun confessed as he summoned a writhing pool of shadows, dark tentacles reaching up to trap the man.

"How what works?" the man said, plunging his sword into the pool. Black lightning crackled and disintegrated the bindings before they could fully form, and the man charged at Wang Jun with a bull rush.

"This whole reincarnation thing," Wang Jun said, grunting as he landed. "I'm not an expert, but as far as I know, it's very difficult to retain identity and memories."

"We have our ways," the man said, forming hand seals from the ground and summoning an array of lightning. It shone with a hundred characters that turned to tiny bolts and attacked Wang Jun.

In response, Wang Jun waved his hand. A dark barrier sucked in the lightning, devouring it as it would a delicious snack. "Those ways must be straining. What do you have, another one, two, or three lifetimes? This is your last chance, isn't it?"

The man grunted and fled once again, this time appearing beside a group of mountain defenders. His greatsword cut a gouge in the stone and slew dozens of foundation-establishment cultivators before they knew what hit them. Wang Jun hadn't been idle during this time. He'd gone to the attackers, skillfully executing a half dozen captains, crippling their leadership.

"I could do this all day," the enemy general said.

"As could I," Wang Jun said. "But you don't have all day, do you? This will end in hours, if not minutes." The man didn't answer. He teleported yet again, but this time, he was met by a shadowy Wang Jun and his wretched scythe. "Not these ones, they're too important."

"You're not winning by doing this," the man said, swinging his great sword again.

"I'm not losing either," Wang Jun countered. He was done with winning and losing. If he could tie up this man and prevent him from taking any more ground, that was good enough. Other people—better people—would do the rest.

"You think you're doing the world a favor?" a black-robed devil said, hurling a ball of black flame across the sky. It struck a windy shield that appeared in front of Lu Tianhao. The two transcendents moved unnaturally fast through their surroundings, so quickly in fact that the heavens thought to send them a punishing bolt in retaliation for the reality they'd carelessly shattered.

"The world will be a better place without you, Yang Mubai," Lu Tianhao said. "You've killed countless people in your lifetime and corrupted many others."

"All because of your weak ways, of course," Yang Mubai said. "Am I to blame for your failures or are you?" The devil spread out his wide ochre wings—he had two pairs that burned like a dark sun—and fire erupted all around him. It formed a heaven-encompassing net that sought to strangle his opponent.

Lu Tianhao, not to be undone, gathered the winds and clouds. He ignored the heaven-punishing lightning that coursed through his veins and formed millions of tiny blades that cut the net, causing it to disperse. Space broke apart as the two forces collided, and the heavens roared again, singeing skin and burning hair.

Strictly speaking, this was his domain. Everything here was under his control. But it was also Yang Mubai's domain. They were overlapped and vying for power, while the plane fought with all its might for them to surrender.

"My failures are inexcusable," Lu Tianhao said. "I've never argued that. But your actions even more so. I'll tell you what—let's let the heavens judge us. We'll see who lasts the longest." The winds around him whirled and buffeted them both, bringing them close enough for Lu Tianhao to grab Yang Mubai. He bound them in chains of wind that drew the ire of the heavens.

"You're mad!" Yang Mubai said. "You're all mad!"

All around them, transcendents were giving it their all. Unlike the mortals below, they knew the nature of the battle and what was at stake. Mortals had somehow locked them away from the World Tree's influence, so it was now a battle for territory. Every single transcendent they could eliminate lessened the karmic encumbrance on their participant.

A mile away, the chancellor of the Church of Justice and two vice chancellors fought two brothers from the south. Though not devils, the two were blood masters and insane to boot. In another direction, Hong Yinyue was fighting the ancestor of the Fierce Puppet Sect, a group of cultivators who used strings of soul-infused qi to control reanimated corpses.

Every one of them, without exception, was dying. They'd suffered irreparable damage to their bodies and transcendent souls from the plane's lightning. Most of them would perish soon. Such was what fate had in store for them the moment they decided to stay behind instead of ascending to other realms.

"You just don't get it, do you?" Lu Tianhao said, digging deep claws of wind into his opponent's back. Yang Mubai countered with his own set of burning claws, which tore into the man's domain, which had been fashioned into a runic armor. "We're out for blood, and we won't stop until every last one of you murdering psychopaths are dead. We didn't come here to win, Yang Mubai. We came here to die." He roared in agony as his opponent's claws hit his vitals but laughed in triumph as he found his opponent's lungs and heart.

He'd been waiting for a long time for this, waiting centuries for this final battle. They'd told him his revenge would need to wait. His daughter's killer, though reprehensible, would get his due when the time was right.

Transcendents walked a fine line, and doing something the plane didn't like had deep consequences. Well, the time had finally come. Revenge was within his literal grasp. Slowly but surely, he squeezed the life out from his mortal enemy. Lightning raked their bodies and souls, but he couldn't care less about it. He'd rather die than let the man live another day.

Three more extensions, Cha Ming thought. Only three extensions and the center would be locked in. He both anticipated and dreaded the result. On the one hand, he'd have basically cinched the game, as

Zhou Li would no longer have any anchor points. On the other hand, it was clearly Zhou Li's goal to take as much of the central area as possible.

He didn't know what would happen when their borders were finalized, but there was no way to stop it regardless. All he could do was contain the threat as best he could, minimizing the eventual consequences that this play resulted in.

Two more extensions, he thought, parrying blow after blow. His staff arts were back, as were his sigils. His wings had finally congealed, increasing not only his elemental affinities but also his physical strength. Though Zhou Li was both a devil and an evil spirit, Cha Ming could somehow match his power and even exceed it. It ran counter to what he'd been taught—that good-aligned cultivators were weaker than evil-aligned ones. It was as though he'd unearthed a hidden truth of the universe, a truth that applied only to him.

Black flames broke apart under the influence of his earthen pseudo-domain. Space shattered, and the plane grumbled in protest but didn't take actions against them. They hadn't technically broken any rules, and as damaging as they were, it was nothing compared to the heated battle up above them, where transcendents broke space with a single wave of their hand and shattered time whenever they unleashed one of their terrible techniques.

One more extension. This one was the smallest. Four more exchanges later, Zhou Li's stones finally formed an impenetrable black wall, and the center, which he'd carefully enclosed, was impossible to invade. Then, to Cha Ming's surprise, Zhou Li didn't turn to another portion of the board. Instead, he began to fill his part of the territory with black stones.

"This isn't like you, remaining quiet like this," Cha Ming said. He paused, awaiting the usual reply, but no witty banter came. As black stones filled the space, Zhou Li's energy grew. The devilish man had a solemn expression about him, something Cha Ming had never seen on the usually condescending man.

"Let me throw that back at you, Cha Ming," Zhou Li finally said. He looked up. "This isn't like you. Expecting me to talk and banter.

You usually ignore me when I ask you questions or prod at your weaknesses."

He lifted one hand, then another, and black flames denser than anything he'd ever seen formed at the tip of his fingers. Cha Ming flashed toward him, piercing with Origin Strike, but the Grandmist-infused strike simply hit a black barrier that appeared out of thin air. Unable to comprehend what had just happened, Cha Ming struck again. He tried flying through without a weapon and piercing with his mightiest gold formation. His pseudo-domain was also equally ineffective, as were his talismans.

"Game over, Cha Ming."

The power at Zhou Li's fingertips continued to grow, and it finally dawned on Cha Ming. Zhou Li only needed this small central space. At Cha Ming's power level, he couldn't enter. Given enough time with Zhou Li's black flames, even the mighty World Tree, with roots that ran miles deep, could be burned to ashes.

There was only one thing Cha Ming could think of to stop it. He looked around the board and all its unfilled spaces. There were many areas to capture, much unclaimed territory to gain. In the past, he'd gained back strength when claiming it. Was it possible that he could somehow increase his power past his normal limits?

He didn't know, but nothing else he thought of could help. He looked around and spotted a turning point on the board. It was the largest contested area, with black stones aplenty. Yet without a player, these stones were defenseless. He appeared there and began playing stone after stone, and little by little, the tide of demons expanded, and the fiends receded.

Ling Dong's greatsword hacked into the sturdy fiend whisperer, and the enemy commander let out a whimper as it cut a gash in his flesh. It didn't cut through bone, but the damage was obvious. It was quickly repaired by an infusion of fiendish miasma.

"This guy's bones are tougher than transcendent treasures," Bai Ling remarked, her soul flames searing into the man's flesh. His soul, it seemed, was inseparable from his body. They were fused together with the fiendish miasma as a medium.

"He's nigh immortal," Gong Lan said, sighing as a hundred and eight rulers appeared around the man and pierced into him. Though they couldn't break bones, they pierced through his ribs, damaging his vital organs and scriptures spread over his body.

The man took in a quick breath and blew out, throwing the swords out from his torso. Icy black air formed around him, forcing the heat out from his bloodstream and blowing it away.

"You can't defeat me," the fiend whisperer said, summoning his spiked club again. He swung at Gong Lan, who summoned a bell to defend against it. The club struck true, but the bell let out a loud toll. He was dazed for a brief moment, giving enough time for Ling Dong to hack at him again. This time, the man caught the blade. His fierce grip crushed the metal, breaking a piece off Ling Dong's precious demonic weapon.

Fools! a voice squawked inside their minds. Silverwing, who was finally able to escape his opponent due to help from a few inquisitors and templars, flew toward them. He rushed past the fiend whisperer and toward the fiendbone totem. His sharp claws raked the black bone, and a few small pieces crumbled off. The fiend whisperer roared in pain as it happened. *Just kill this thing and he'll fall over. Easy.*

The enemy commander flew backward and batted Silverwing away. He stood on the totem, and one of his mightiest fiends stood beside him.

As this happened, Gua also broke free. He flew up and hefted a large fan. *We doing this?* he asked.

Yeah, we're doing this, Silverwing said.

Wait for me! Lei Jiang yelled.

Mr. Mountain simply floated over. Fiends all around them congregated, and all the demons on the battlefield poured their power into Ling Dong and the four half-step-initiation demons.

They'd finally broken the deadlock, and they were already well on their way to victory.

"Charge!" the Alabaster Group yelled, weapons in hand as they barreled toward their ochre-winged foes.

"Charge!" the Obsidian Syndicate yelled, gathering under the leadership of a few pride demons. These black-armored devils seemed to be natural generals, with shape-shifting envy devils their commanders and others mere foot soldiers. They fought a bloody battle, and men and women died by the dozens. Luck was not on their side, however, as all sorts of misfortune befell them, tilting the odds in the favor of their angelic opponents.

They, the Alabaster Group, were winning this battle, though not by as much as Feng Ming would have liked. Luck could only go so far when outmatched and outnumbered. By the time all this was said and done, only a quarter of the original Alabaster Group would remain. That wasn't counting the transcendents, of course. Their battle seemed even harsher than it was for the mortals below. Over half of the transcendents were dead, and another one or two died every minute or so. They seemed to die in pairs, taking each other out by all means necessary. Most of these men and women were angels and devils; they'd remained either to destroy their opponents or protect their factions. They weren't like solitary transcendents such as the late Ancestor Wang and Hong Yinyue. Many of those still fought, and none of them seemed to want to fully commit to anything.

How many transcendents would be left when all this was done? A dozen? Half that? The plane would undergo a great upheaval after this, as their greatest protectors and adversaries would be nothing more than legends to remember.

"We'll be done soon enough," Zi Long said, floating up beside him. Luo Xuehua was with him.

"We should help Ling Dong and the others once we've cleared out the rest," Feng Ming said. "They're winning, but time is everything." The two nodded, but as they were about to relay orders, another burst of energy appeared in the sky. Inevitably, such a burst would be accompanied by a fallen transcendent. There had been many over the course of their difficult battle.

"Teacher!" Zi Long yelled.

"Master!" Luo Xuehua cried out.

They moved to interfere, but Feng Ming put his hands on their shoulders and restrained them. "That burst of power is them both burning their transcendent souls," Feng Ming said gravely. "It allows them to surpass their limits, but it leaves them vulnerable to the plane's wrath."

Clouds were building around them, and the frequency of lightning strikes was increasing. Their domain, normally a barrier against the lightning's potency, no longer blocked it. They were dedicating everything they had to mutual destruction.

"We have to save him," Luo Xuehua said.

"I'm afraid it's already too late," Feng Ming said. "Either he kills his opponent, or he dies. Even if he wins, he won't last very long afterward."

Luo Xuehua teared up but nodded. She looked to the sky as her master shone with his final brilliance. It wasn't until someone close to you died that you truly understood the cost of war. Feng Ming knew that firsthand. It had taken his father's death to make him realize it. And though it would devastate her in the short term, she would grow stronger for it. Or at least that's what he told himself so he could sleep easier.

There, Cha Ming thought as spark lit up inside his mind. A key turned, and a lock unravelled. The last mental shackle was gone, and as they left, his Tri-Sealing Pillars returned. Cha Ming didn't linger around the demonic battlefield, where inky black fiends were being repelled. He appeared beside Zhou Li, where a great ball of fire was forming. The man was sweating profusely, and vitality seemed to drain from his black hair. He was pouring everything he had into this strike, leaving nothing for defense.

First Pillar: Water, Cha Ming thought, and a blue pillar appeared and slammed into the earth beside the World Tree. The pillar was massive, several tens of feet in diameter, and several hundred feet tall. It pierced into the ground where beasts were somehow still meditating despite the fighting. Leaves rustled as the ground beside the tree tore open.

Second Pillar: Earth. The ground shook as a massive pillar crashed into a rock garden. The ornament was destroyed, forever marring the sanctuary. Cha Ming could only sigh with remorse and summon the next three pillars. Wood, Metal, and Fire followed, and a complex sealing matrix soon expanded from them.

That gentle sealing energy invaded the entire plateau, causing devils and evil spirits to shriek. They wailed as he summoned two more pillars, one black and one white, and had them slam down above Zhou Li and his fireball. The man coughed up blood as the pillars stopped in midair. The fireball still grew, and its power still increased. The sealing matrix couldn't quite pierce the array of black stones he'd carefully laid.

Why wasn't it enough? What was he missing? He pondered over the failure, wondering how he could possibly reinforce it. Did it work like the Devil-Sealing Scripture? Did he need his opponent's true name? Back in the day, devil sealers would slay devils using the names of their commanders. Very seldom would they know the name of a specific devil. Unfortunately, only scattered remnants of names had been shared in the scripture, but those were lost to time. If he wanted a name to increase the power, he'd need to discover it for himself.

Unfortunately, all he could see above the man was set of blurry characters. Even with his Eyes of Truth, he couldn't make them out.

They were covered by a thin veil he couldn't pull away. So, unsure of what he should do, Cha Ming sat cross-legged. He stared at the blurry mess of characters and attempted to decipher it.

Talons raked across the totem's surface, taking off large rocklike chunks that evaporated into black smoke. Lightning scorched it, blasting off thousands of miniscule pieces. Likewise, Gong Lan's twin rulers stabbed into it, creating two large fissures that expanded into hundreds, structurally weakening the piece of black fiend bone.

Only seconds had passed since Silverwing's revelation, but already, the battle was swiftly changing. The fiend whisperer let out one last desperate yell as Ling Dong appeared above the totem, channeling the power of ten thousand demons and cutting down with his greatsword, which weighed as much as a mountain.

The totem shattered, and black smoke filled the battlefield. It was quickly consumed by a violet tide of natural energy that reclaimed its plundered wealth. The fiends began evaporating one after another, most of them becoming desiccated husks of demons but some returning to their normal demonic selves.

"Finish him," Gong Lan said.

Ling Dong nodded. The man was weakened and kneeling, his lower body encased in ice and his upper body burned beyond recognition. A sickening slice filled the air as Ling Dong dispatched the man, making the world a much better place in the process.

Though Ling Dong had done the deed, Gong Lan wasn't washing her hands clean. Instead, she held her 10,080-bead rosary and chanted a mantra. The 10,080 pearls became 10,080 swords and cleaved at karmic attachments surrounding the man's soul. An edict of Yama, written long before, appeared from his storage treasure. Gong Lan summoned a massive golden pagoda that crashed down on it, destroying it.

If only it were so simple.

One did not simply destroy an official document of the Underworld without repercussions. She coughed up blood from the inevitable backlash from the document, and her soul suffered serious injuries. Eliminating one of the three lead reincarnators, however, was well worth the price. His soul would be unencumbered and enter the cycle of reincarnation just like it should. The Yellow River appeared, whisking the man's soul away.

"Go help the others," Gong Lan said weakly. "Help the Alabaster Group. Help Wang Jun."

"What about Master?" Ling Dong said, staring into the sky where a battle between giants was taking place. Others couldn't see, but Ling Dong was special. His saw more than the average person.

"You can't help him," Gong Lan said. "But worry not—I will." She took a deep breath as she sat her injured body down and closed her eyes. Her soul flew out toward where the battle was taking place.

It wouldn't be easy getting to Cha Ming through this maze of black and white stones and karma. Any one of them could entangle her in her weakened state, potentially trapping her for all eternity. Cha Ming had done all he could to help her and protect the World Tree. He'd risked his life for her twice before, saving her from a wretched fate.

She owed him. Now, it was her turn to save.

"Was it worth it?" Wang Jun asked, the haft of his scythe crashing down against the enemy general's greatsword. The man became lightning and charged at him, forcing Wang Jun to retreat into the shadows and avoid the crackling storm. The man was burning his pride, significantly boosting his fighting prowess. Though it cost the man greatly, it let him fight a few moments longer.

"Every battle has a price, and every life an intangible value," the general said. His right arm became six lightning serpents that shot out at Wang Jun.

Wang Jun read the attack, and instead of disappearing, he twirled his staff. A portal of void energy appeared, consuming the lightning and sending it back out miles away.

"You're losing," Wang Jun said. "Now that you can't command and you're locked away with me, your men are dying. You picked the wrong terrain to fight on, reincarnator."

Now that the rhythm was broken, his troops were building momentum. Their terrain, the World Tree itself, was finally beginning to show its advantages. Their men fought harder for longer periods of time, and wounds that shouldn't have healed did so in much less time than they should have. "You could have fought anywhere. Weakened us. But you had to choose this place of all places."

"You know nothing," the general said. He struck out with his fist, but shadows took it, and a scythe bit down on his neck, forcing him to dissociate into lightning again and re-form a few feet away. "Things aren't always as they appear to be."

"We're losing too many of them," Feng Ming mumbled as he stared in the sky in horror. Like dying embers, the lives of transcendents disappeared, one after another. "It's too late for your master, but we can save some of the others. Come with me. Let's help."

Zi Long and Luo Xuehua nodded and flew into the skies alongside him.

The skies were a treacherous place. Lightning flashed incessantly, scorching the many transcendents as they made their last stands.

"You get that one," Feng Ming said, pointing to a wounded angel missing an arm, pursued by an equally wounded devil wielding a giant greataxe. Luo Xuehua flew out to help her in silent agreement, and Zi Long went to aid an older man at his direction, leaving Feng

Ming a choice between two others. He hesitated, then flew to the hopeless case, Lu Tianhao.

"Sneaky bastards," he muttered, flashing across the skies. He dodged lightning and cut through wind with his spear, pulling the angel back just in time to prevent his opponent from beheading him.

"Let go of me!" Lu Tianhao bellowed, throwing the surprised Feng Ming backward, forcing him to use his transcendent spear to block. He was forced backward toward another wounded transcendent and exchanged a few blows with the surprised man. The transcendent wasn't a devil nor an evil spirit, but the sins he bore were nothing to scoff at.

"Get lost!" Feng Ming yelled, stabbing out with all his might at the transcendent, who smirked and summoned an icy shield. *Come on, time to get lucky.* The shield shuddered on impact and shattered, allowing the spear to pierce through and stab the transcendent through the chest.

The transcendent, wide eyed with disbelief, stared down at the gaping hole where his heart was. Feng Ming's blow had pierced clean through, and as a qi cultivator, such a blow was lethal. Life left the man as he crumpled to the ground, broken. Merit rushed into Feng Ming, bringing his glowing pool to the limit of what the mortal realms could tolerate and then some.

No, not now. You'd better not carve yourself now, he scolded his core. It seemed to listen, and the jade aura that was about to form a sharp knife and cut into it dissipated, disappearing to heavens knew where for the time being.

"Gah!" a voice yelled, bringing Feng Ming's attention back to the battlefield.

"Teacher!" a voice yelled.

"Master!" a woman's voice followed.

Zi Long and Luo Xuehua flew out with their transcendents in tow, but they were too late. A sword was stuck inside Yang Mubai's chest, while a saber had cut through Lu Tianhao's shoulder straight down to his abdomen. Feng Ming caught the man as he fell, bringing him to the ground along with the few remaining wounded transcendents.

"It is done," Lu Tianhao said. "He's paid the price at last." His devilish opponent's body burned to ashes, and Lu Tianhao's sword plunged to the ground.

"Master, don't go," Luo Xuehua said with tears in her eyes.

"I never expected to survive this battle, little one," Lu Tianhao said, reaching up weakly to her face. "Now that he's dead, one of my final wishes is accomplished. Do you remember what I said?"

Luo Xuehua nodded, choking back her tears. "I'll take care of them." She put her hands on his, which were growing colder by the second.

"And I'll protect her," Zi Long said, kneeling down and placing his hands on both of theirs.

Lu Tianhao smiled and coughed up blood. "Then I die a happy man," he said. He took in a ragged breath and let out a long sigh as his life left him. His jade wings, usually transparent, appeared beside his body. A gentle wind blew and carried them away, their feathers like petals on a spring breeze.

Sadness was inescapable in war. Feng Ming knew firsthand how the two of them must feel. Losing a father figure was devastating, and it would take them months to piece themselves back together. They would get over it in time, but for now, they had done enough. The Alabaster Group, or its remnants at least, weren't needed any longer. The demons had joined in, and the Obsidian Syndicate would soon perish.

It was all up to Cha Ming now, and whatever mysterious battle he was fighting. "Heavens above, if you can give him even a fraction of my luck for these final moments, please do it."

Cha Ming's gray eyes bled as he stared at the wispy, undecipherable words floating around Zhou Li. The orb of black fire above his opponent's head had grown to fifty feet in diameter and was showing no signs of slowing. Unfortunately, Cha Ming could do nothing to stop him. His Tri-Sealing Pillars, including both the Devil-Sealing Formation and the Spirit-Banishing Formation could only struggle helplessly against the array of defensive stones.

Just a little more, he thought, staring at the characters that were so close to firming up. He could feel them, the many stones shifting across the board as the angelic forces started winning. The fiends had been completely annihilated, and most of the devils were gone. Only stragglers remained on the mountain, but even those were being uprooted.

The fiend whisperer was dead. Feng Ming had joined Wang Jun in fighting the enemy general. Meanwhile, Silverwing and the remainder of Huxian's friends were saving whatever transcendents they could. Only a dozen or so remained from the original hundred that had been fighting.

"Relax," a voice said from behind Cha Ming. It was Gong Lan's voice, though it was much softer than before. He felt something like a hand on his back, though it was ghostly and transparent. It reached through his body and into his soul. "There's no need to read something new. You've always known his name. You've seen it before, many lifetimes ago, even though none of your incarnations remember."

Life and death blurred as he watched the characters slowly take shape. Time stood still as Zhou Li's fireball reached eighty feet in diameter. The tree below them grew blossoms as a tiny spirit that usually accompanied Gong Lan merged with it, causing the tree's vitality to surge in this key moment. "Protect this world, Cha Ming," she said. "Because I won't be able to accompany you on this last leg."

He felt a shiver as much of the golden energy in Gong Lan's soul surged into his, leaving only a transparent phantom to float back down to her cross-legged body below.

Life and death went full circle. The sun rose in the morning and set at night. Swords dulled after countless blows, only to be sharpened again on the next day. The characters seemed to materialize like barren earth, split apart from oceans at the time of creation. Motion started then, yet so did stillness. The world broke as the continents hardened.

Everything clicked then, and Cha Ming finally saw twisted black characters coated in corrupted crimson. It burned to watch them, as they were loathsome, and the story they told was devastatingly horrible. He rose and took out the Clear Sky Brush and painted. The first character shot above the Devil-Sealing and Spirit-Banishing Pillars, forcing them down into the transparent shield. He then drew the second, forcing them even further, and the shield lurched as it was about to give in.

Three more characters remained. Names didn't take long to paint. It was less about the strokes in the characters and more about their essence. As he painted the third, the shield shattered, only to be stopped by a crimson chain barrier.

"You're finished," Cha Ming said to Zhou Li, who looked up indifferently.

"I am," Zhou Li admitted as the fourth character firmed up. The crimson mesh strained and groaned as the pillars sought to break free of their obstructions. "You won the game after all. Only one of us can live. It's too bad for you that I never planned on winning that game. Only one outcome mattered."

As Cha Ming hurried the fifth character, Zhou Li withered as he poured his soul force, life-force, and qi into the black fireball. It grew to a hundred and eight feet in diameter before he hurled it toward the World Tree. At that moment, the pillars fully activated, fully powered by his name. They fell down to the earth, and the white and black pillars slammed down on Zhou Li, sealing his mind, body, and soul. He was completely helpless, but Cha Ming ignored him and rushed toward the fireball he'd just unleashed.

It was fast, faster than he could travel, but not faster than combat sigils. He summoned a half-step-rune-carving combat formation that mimicked the Myriad Truths Diagram. Its five colors, its black-white-and-gray core, appeared as a resplendent net before the World Tree. Cha Ming infused his pseudo-domain, somehow feeding five different elements into the net in a mad moment of inspiration.

Such a feat was beyond him, but necessity had removed his inner limitations, striking him with a dreadful backlash in exchange for this massive burst of power.

The fireball stopped for a moment, and time seemed to stand still. He threw five of his most powerful remaining talismans to reinforce the barrier. The fireball shrank, yet as it did, Cha Ming's eyes narrowed. It was shrinking for a reason, and Zhou Li had counted on his intervention. The fireball shrank, but as it did, the density of its power intensified. Then, as quickly as it had stopped, it tore through the net, breaking it apart. Cha Ming collapsed to the ground beside Zhou Li as his sigils fell.

"No!" he yelled.

Gong Lan, who'd been sitting cross-legged, screamed as black flames consumed the World Tree. Its bark, its branches, and its many leaves. Its blossoms and the spot of green vitality that had burned in its center thanks to the spirit of the Bodhi Seed. They all burned with disgusting black sin flames. And in that moment, they all felt something. Moreover, Cha Ming *saw* something.

The threads of karma on the plane shifted at that moment. These were threads that bound every living thing and guided their destiny. Normally, they would be invisible, but now that Cha Ming was watching with his Eyes of Truth, he could see them.

Every life, no matter how small on this plane, was connected by the tree to goodness. Normally, there was a balance, but that balance had been skewed by the tree's planting long ago.

With its death, all these connections were severed. The balance was slowly returning to normal and would soon usher in an era where devils were as normal as angels.

"You saw this too, didn't you?" Cha Ming asked softly.

"I saw possibilities, dreams of what could be," Zhou Li said, hacking as he coughed up a mouthful of black blood. "I wouldn't have lasted more than a few lifetimes anyway. My soul couldn't handle the forceful reincarnations or the memories. This was my last chance. I planned to die."

Despite their victory, the allied forces couldn't help but weep as they saw the peaceful tree burn. It was only now that it was gone that they appreciated what it had done for them. They sensed an almost maternal connection from it. Its death wrenched out their hearts as though their own mother had passed away.

"End this," Zhou Li said. "It is done. Though I pray that you're strong enough to preserve the world I've created."

Cha Ming gritted his teeth and lifted himself up. He summoned the Clear Sky Staff in gray pillar form and directed it to float above Zhou Li. "Zhou Li, you'll never bother this plane, or any other plane, again. What doesn't die cannot be reincarnated, and what is sealed can never be recovered. This wasn't just one of your many lives in the cycle of reincarnation. It was your last one."

He motioned downward, and the pillar slammed down on Zhou Li's body, consuming it as it transformed into gray mist. There were no angels or devils in this sealed dimension, no evil spirits or buddhas. It was a return to nothingness from which everything was created, a small bit of entropy created to make the world a better place. Zhou Li was dead. And though the passing of the monstrous man who'd led the Southern forces was a relief to many, Cha Ming felt no satisfaction in his disappearance.

"It's gone," Gong Lan whimpered as she cried on her knees. Cha Ming was back to the normal world, and the game board had disappeared along with Zhou Li. "The World Tree is gone."

The few monks who had survived kneeled down beside her and bowed in worship as the last of the black flames died out, leaving behind a burnt trunk with no branches. With his eyes, Cha Ming could see all the way down to its roots. They were blackened and scorched and completely devoid of life.

"Feng Ming," Cha Ming said as his friend flew over. Wang Jun was there too, holding a hand to a wound to his gut. "I'm worried."

"We're all sad," Feng Ming said. "We felt it the moment it happened."

"Not sad, worried," Cha Ming said, grasping his shoulders. "The last thing he said was he prayed I could save the world he'd created. What did he mean by that?" In his experience, Zhou Li might be annoying, but there was often intent behind what he said.

Feng Ming's expression darkened as he pulled out a jade tablet. "Seven hells," he said. "I can't believe it." He summoned five jade slips—each one was broken.

"Whose jade slips are those?" Cha Ming asked, though he already knew the answer.

"They belong to the transcendents that were in charge of delaying the Taotie's advance," Feng Ming said. "According to the messages I've received, it attacked our army, and they were forced to fight it before it killed everyone."

"Five transcendents?" Cha Ming said. "You're saying that we have both a Taotie and the Southern army running loose near the Evergreen Kingdom and five transcendents are dead?"

"No," Feng Ming said. "Far worse than that." He gulped. "Before the Taotie attacked their troops, it completely destroyed the Southern army. It started by devouring the transcendent that was keeping it, then broke through to half-step initiation by condensing a mark so dark no one could see it. Within ten seconds, half the troops we'd stationed there were gone. The last message I have is one announcing that they were going with the fourth contingency."

"Which is?" Cha Ming asked.

"Self-detonation," Feng Ming said. "And judging by Zhou Li's words, they weren't successful."

"You assumed right," Wang Jun said, bringing up a projection of the entire continent. He moved his fingers and zoomed in on a familiar location: the land between True North Country and the Great Redwood Forest. There, they saw a dark pit rapidly advancing toward the forest, so teeming with life. "It seems to have located the plane's Leyline of Wood."

Cha Ming's heart sank. Before the Taotie had broken through, they could barely contain it. Now, it was a full half realm higher. Five transcendents had died like they were ants. Zhou Li destroying the World Tree was now just an afterthought. If they didn't do something, anything, what remained of the world would die alongside it.

Huxian struck a proud pose as his body floated in the blackness of space. The Candle Dragon's Time-Torching Eyes channeled their power of time into a bright white symbol in the air above. The Void Phoenix's Moon-Eclipsing Wings, four pairs of glasslike wings that floated above his back, poured dark spatial power into a black symbol beside the white one. The symbols danced around each other in a feeble attempt to destroy the balance. But it was the chase that enforced the stalemate, the eternal struggle between opposing forces.

Both the Candle Dragon and the Void Phoenix floated beside Huxian, using their respective powers to stabilize the mark. The power they contained was inconceivable for a single beast to handle. Yet this small fox had somehow completed both their trials with full marks. That was unheard of in demonic circles—full marks could usually only be achieved with bonus marks, pity points, or direct instruction to one's descendant, not someone of an entirely different lineage.

He's holding, the Candle Dragon said. *But something's not quite right.*

Agreed, the Void Phoenix said. *The marks are stable, but it's like they're trying to expand, and he's not containing them but encouraging them.*

Let them, a voice said to both of them. It was Bagua Hushao's voice. Huxian's ancestor was hidden in another dimension, far away from the prying eyes of his nosy descendant.

But if we don't stabilize them, he won't be able to control their power, the Candle Dragon protested.

If he can't control them, he doesn't deserve them, Bagua Hushao said.

Both the Candle Dragon and the Void Phoenix exchanged glances before ultimately letting it go. The black and white marks orbited around each other above the fox, and black and white lines began extending.

At first, they seemed like nonsense, forming a simple frame around the two parts to keep them together. But then, they noticed something familiar.

Is that... the Void Phoenix said.

Yes, Bagua Hushao replied. The black and white lines merged into gray, condensing the purest power of space-time. Then it expanded in eight directions. Broken and unbroken lines formed at the same time until each of the eight sides had three sets of lines. *It is the power of the bagua. He is using his bloodline to control both of your powers and condense them into something greater.*

Both the dragon and phoenix stood slack-jawed as the symbol shrank and melded into the fox's forehead. The fox grew another three feet to a total of 333. He let out a howl that shook space and time alike. Light and darkness danced at his command.

His three tails flailed behind him. They yearned for the fourth to appear, and that was only a step away. With but a thought, Huxian would be able to break through that boundary and begin his initiation, calling forth heavenly tribulation.

His eyes burned gold and red, projecting time as it affected all things. They caused the sun to rise. They caused the sun to set. They caused it to shine brightly at noon, all the while superimposing all of it.

Meanwhile, the glassy wings on his back flapped wildly. They pierced space and cut it. They separated it, and they shattered it. The Moon-Eclipsing Wings were a chilling representation of lethality and fear, a tool that very few in the universe possessed.

And it was all contained in one package, a Godbeast above Godbeasts. Regardless of what eventually happened, both of them would remember Bagua Huxian for the remainder of the long lives.

With this mark, do you think he can do it? the Candle Dragon asked.

I don't know, Bagua Hushao replied. *We've always culled worlds to destroy Taotie, or destroyed the creatures after they've left into the void of space. No mortal has ever slain one. It's only...* He shook his head. *If they can't do it, no mortal can. Remember, it's not just us that have interfered. Buddha, the Jade Emperor, the Demon-Subduing Emperor, and Fuxi have all had a hand in this conflict. If that doesn't cut it, I'm afraid nothing will.*

The world seemed strange to Huxian as the black and white light faded, leaving him on one of the red platforms. He could see many fluctuations in the space-time matrix that permeated the entire area. With but a thought, he appeared on another platform. With a single stare, a platform evaporated before his eyes. There were no living things in this realm. It contained nothing but space-time power connected by law fragments.

Time to go back, he thought. He didn't summon a portal but walked forward through space. The air flashed gray as he walked out of the demi-plane and into the Silverwing Mountain Range.

All was quiet.

He took in his surroundings and noticed that not a single demon above the purification realm remained.

Where the hell are they? he thought, expanding his senses. *There.* He took another step and appeared beside Cha Ming. Eight pillars had been shoved into the ground, and he, Feng Ming, and Wang Jun wore grim expressions.

Gong Lan was an outlier. She was kneeling on the ground, crying. And for good reason. Huxian recognized the tree at a glance. It was one of the thousand thousands of trees Siddhartha Buddha had scattered all around the mortal planes to preserve their good alignment.

All that remained of it was a burned-out husk. He could sense no karma flowing to and from it, and no vital energy coursing through its wooden flesh.

Brother? he said, nudging Cha Ming's leg.

Cha Ming looked back and smiled. "You made it. You condensed your mark."

It's no big deal, Huxian said. *You usually don't look so glum after winning.*

"Perspective does that to a person," Cha Ming said. His eyes were gray now, he noticed. Huxian had been worried that he'd do something stupid and blind himself, but all that worrying had been for nothing. His brother had grown up, gotten swanky-looking gray eyes, a new toy, and broken through to half-step rune carving and half-step blood awakening. Not bad.

The Taotie? Huxian asked. *How strong is it?* If it wasn't any stronger than the peak of core formation, he could definitely trounce it.

"Half-step initiation," Cha Ming said grimly. "Think you can handle it?"

Huxian gulped. *We can only try.*

"My thoughts exactly," Cha Ming said. He held out his hand, and the eight pillars in the ground fused into a gray one before disappearing. "Gong Lan?" he said. She didn't move. "Gong Lan?" he repeated.

She looked up.

"Come," Cha Ming said. "You might be injured, but we need all hands on deck for this. Same with the wounded transcendents. There'll be plenty of time to grieve later." She nodded and wiped her face. "Disciples? Vice chancellor? Headmistress?" he called out alongside other names. The leaders of the remaining forces flew out. "I know we're all mourning. I know it hurts deeply. But right now, we have a Taotie on the loose, and I'm sure you've all heard news of how dangerous it is."

We're going to go kill it! Huxian said, hopping on his shoulder.

They all stared at him, not knowing what to make of him. Silly humans. Couldn't they feel his power?

"He said it," Cha Ming said. "Let's go kill ourselves a world-ending calamity." To drive home the message, Huxian's eyes glowed gold and red, and his tails flailed as he summoned his Moon-Eclipsing Wings. He revealed his initiation mark, and Gua and friends, who'd run back after learning of his arrival, cowered in its presence. It was an oppressive might that even Cha Ming had trouble withstanding.

His brother might be good at formations. He might even be good at talking and making friends. But in times like these, he was lacking.

In times of war, motivation was everything.

Chapter 26: Gathering

Cha Ming flew much faster than he'd ever thought possible as he made his way to Gold Leaf City with Gong Lan in tow. Space and time warped as he traveled. Just like the small fox could summon the five elements alongside creation and destruction, he, too, could summon a trickle of space and time and its lesser elements, light and darkness. Minute control eluded him, but fine-tuning wasn't required to tear through the simple spatial restrictions of the mortal realm.

Wang Jun and Feng Ming had gone to recruit what manpower they could, while Huxian and his friends had gone to bully some hidden demons on the continent. Zi Long had gone to Haijing, while Yue Bing, Ling Dong, and Jin Huang were collaborating to heal as many transcendents and half-step transcendents as possible.

"And here we are, Gold Leaf City," Cha Ming said cheerfully as they appeared in Gold Leaf Square. "It's a lot cleaner than I remember it being."

"But much filthier than I remember it," Gong Lan said, noticing the light-red stains on the square's concrete that hadn't yet been washed out. "When I came to visit the chancellors and the monks stationed here, it was in pristine condition. There were golden leaves here as well, as the name implies there should be."

"Details, details," Cha Ming said. "The cultists are gone, and the Spirit Temple is no more." Indeed, what used to be a massive cathedral of darkness was little more than a pile of rubble. The smoke had cleared, and whatever valuables were left had long been picked away by the army. Sinful treasures had undoubtedly been destroyed by the clergy. "I still don't understand why you wanted to tag along."

"I hear the Greenwind Pavilion can answer questions for a fee," Gong Lan said. "Alas, I've abandoned all mortal wealth to attain monkhood. It's fortunate that I have a wealthy friend who's willing to foot the bill."

Cha Ming coughed lightly. "Hardly wealthy anymore." Indeed, he'd used up most of his liquified elemental essence and spirit stones. If not for the massive casualties in their most recent battle, he'd have had difficulty scrounging up a large-enough sum to satisfy the avaricious Elder Zhong.

They entered the complex through the front gate. Unsurprisingly, there was no one there to greet them. An attendant let out a surprised yelp when he opened the door. Confused at their presence amid the hurried packing she'd been doing, she walked over to greet them."

"I'm sorry, sir, but we're closed for business," the attendant said. "We're in a hurry."

Cha Ming smiled. "Don't worry. I won't take up your time. Could you please get your manager to lead us to the sixth floor?" Her eyes widened at the mention of the secret floor in their five-floor building.

"I'll lead you there immediately," a grizzled man said, walking up to them. He was, unsurprisingly, a peak-core-formation cultivator. As one of the Greenwind Pavilion's central branches, it was important for them to maintain the appearance of a powerful organization.

They followed the man up the stairs, and at the end of them, another set of stairs appeared. They climbed it, and in the final room, a gray formation glowed, revealing a white-haired old man with green-and-silver robes.

"Greetings, Elder Zhong," Cha Ming said. He bowed lightly with hands clasped, and Gong Lan did the same.

"Hurry up. I don't have all day," Elder Zhong said gruffly. Gone was his usual cheerful demeanor.

"It seems like everyone is packing up," Cha Ming said. "Are you leaving?"

"Me and any mortal who's got half a brain is leaving," Elder Zhong said. "I happen to own the last and most stable spatial passageway leading out of this plane."

"Access to which I'm sure you sell at a premium," Cha Ming said.

"I do sell at a premium, yes," Elder Zhong said. "And I'm willing to offer you a dozen slots. Discount pricing. Call it a preferred customer's bonus."

"I'm afraid I'll have to pass," Cha Ming said. "I suppose that means I only have half a brain."

"No, it means you think with your heart instead of the organ that's meant for it," Elder Zhong said. "Well?" He held out his hand expectantly. Cha Ming could only roll his eyes and give him a pouch—a retainer of sorts. As they were short on time, he expected none of the precious weapons or spirit stones back.

"We were wondering if you or any of the transcendents or half-step transcendents who report to you would be willing to fight," Cha Ming said. "I know that you employ many for information-gathering purposes. Could such services be extended to fighting?"

"Not for any money in the world," Elder Zhong said. "It's not that I'm against hiring them out. They're not the strongest fighters, but some people want their discretion or other abilities from time to time. But this is suicide, and I don't send my employees on suicide missions."

"A pity," Cha Ming said. He'd expected as much. "Then tell me, are there any tools you can think of, any sealing formations or weapons or defensive barriers—anything at all that can help us fight this thing?"

Elder Zhong shook his head and sighed. "Look, lad, let me be straight with you. You have a fancy new pair of eyes. What do you see with them?"

Cha Ming frowned but looked the man over. He'd seen many transcendents before, but he had to admit that this man was an anomaly. His energy was completely reserved, and he appeared like little more than a mortal. But that couldn't possibly be true. Above his head floated a name, but its characters were completely obscured by a gray mist. And around that name danced many characters on a script. The script seemed inviolable, almost primal.

"You're not a normal transcendent, are you?" Cha Ming asked.

"I'm not a transcendent at all, kid," Elder Zhong said. "I'm an immortal, and a powerful one at that. Believe me when I say there are no tools to fight this thing, only raw power. An immortal could do it—I could do it, since it's still an infant—but doing so would damage the universe irreparably. It is a last resort, like a doctor amputating a limb to save the body. In this case, the entire plane would have to be amputated."

"Do you mind if I ask some questions?" Gong Lan said.

"It's his money," Elder Zhong said, looking to Cha Ming, who nodded.

"Is there a way to channel the plane's will or draw its attention to our cause?" Gong Lan asked. "It's clearly in its own self-interest to defend itself, but it refuses to do so."

"This is a common reaction to a Taotie," Elder Zhong said. "There are hundreds of documented cases. It seems that their laws exceed that of the plane's. Also, any probing by the plane or any energy emissions are devoured by it, rendering it a silent killer. A plane isn't like a normal being—instead, it's like a sleeping child that never wakes. Its responses are akin to a body's immune system to a deadly virus, which as you know, can kill the body while trying to rid it of infection.

"More broadly, there are hundreds of thousands of data points related to channeling a plane's will. Many people have tried to damage planes, and so many people have tried to invoke its will or channel it. In all those cases, very few have succeeded. In all those cases, it was because someone had bonded the plane's core—which is usually impossible unless the plane is a remnant of your ancestor—with a piece of a god, an immortal, or a demon. In this case, the plane is the remnant of a demon. Even if you did manage to find its descendant, there are 176 documented cases of success on mortal planes, and

10,171 attempts at replicating this effect through scientific study have ended in failure."

Cha Ming was impressed at the thoroughness of the answer. He decided to ask some questions of his own. "You said its laws were on a higher level than the plane's will," Cha Ming said. "Do you have examples of laws that are on a higher level?"

"Sure, there are many," Elder Zhong said. "As it stands, the Taotie's laws aren't exactly laws, per se—they are fragmentary manifestations, just high-level ones. It makes it difficult for lower-level fragments to kill it. A peak transcendent's laws could kill it, but such things are so powerful they would destroy the plane. If we were to tone down the power to, say, a lower transcendent's power, it would take stronger law fragments to deal with it."

"Like?" Cha Ming asked.

"You have a few that are on the same level," Elder Zhong said. "Creation and destruction laws are on the same level as void annihilation. Space and time laws are as well. Grandmist laws trump it, but good luck finding anyone who can use those. Before you get too excited, that technique you've been using, Origin Strike, doesn't count. It's at best a precursor of what it could be."

Cha Ming frowned. "Nothing else?"

"I mean, it's worth giving it a shot with everything you have," Elder Zhong said. "If you're going to fight it, go all out. I know for a fact that at least four immortal emperors left inheritances on this plane. They weren't really powerful inheritances, but maybe they'll do the trick. There are also a few god-level inheritances—that new Sea God Emissary isn't bad. Still, as far as I know, this is all spitting in the wind." He shrugged, then looked to Gong Lan.

"You mentioned trying to request the plane's help is futile," Gong Lan said. "Then tell me, what of the inverse? Is it possible to avoid the plane's punishment?"

"That, my dear, is nearly impossible," Elder Zhong said. "I can do it. Immortal Obscurus can do it. Maybe a few dozen others. Planes have a sixth sense for this sort of thing, and when you do something that upsets it, it's like a wake-up call for a grumpy, exhausted factory worker. It draws its attention, and any interference with its judgment adds the perpetrator to the hit list. That's why no one can help you defend against an ascension calamity. The tribulation you face will increase in power due to the outside intervention." He shook his head. "At most, such things can be a crutch. Seniors sometimes give treasures to juniors to skirt the rules, but they can only do so much." He shook his head sadly.

"I thank you for your kind help," Gong Lan said.

"I don't have any other questions," Cha Ming said. "Can I liquidate these treasures?" Another few pouches and storage rings appeared. These were treasures of the fallen, quickly allocated after the battle.

"It's a fire sale, but I'll give you a good price," Elder Zhong said. "Half of list price." It wasn't an unreasonable sum. In fact, he'd been offered the same before as a quick settlement for the crystalized gold evanescence from before. It almost seemed like the greedy old man was actually being nice for a change.

The man tossed the items on the array, which flashed twice before a ring appeared. It contained small mountains of spirit stones and lakes of liquified elemental essence and its evanescence equivalents. Cha Ming took them all into the Clear Sky World, and Elder Zhong gave him a meaningful look.

"I'll be leaving now," Elder Zhong said. "But keep in touch." He threw a silver-green card to Cha Ming, and though it seemed to be made of cardboard, Cha Ming had never seen so tough a material in his life. "If you ever get to the transcendent realms, go to any Greenwind Pavilion. I'll give you a free consultation. Consider it my condolences for a world I couldn't help you save."

Cha Ming took a deep breath. "I'm afraid if you see me, there'll be no need for condolences," he said.

"Then it'll be a congratulatory gift," Elder Zhong said. "Because if you succeed, you'll be the first."

Then, the man faded. The entire room faded. And soon, Cha Ming and Gong Lan found themselves standing on an empty plot of land in Gold Leaf Square.

"Well, that was a bit of a waste of time," Cha Ming said. "And a bit of a downer."

"Perhaps," Gong Lan said. "I, for one, found his answers quite insightful."

"Oh?" Cha Ming said, looking at her in surprise.

"He clarified that we can't beg the plane for help," Gong Lan said. "And that breakthroughs attract its attention no matter what. I think that's something we can work with."

"How?" Cha Ming asked.

"That depends," Gong Lan said. "Tell me more about your relationship with Huxian."

Well, are you coming or not? Huxian said in an overbearing tone, causing the walls and cliffs to shake. The Shattered Lands, a network of cliffs and shifting tectonic plates, had been ripped apart by Mr. Mountain to allow them passage.

The Life-Leaching Monarch, a dreadful spider that had terrorized the Southern Lands for generations, lay on the ground convulsing. One of its legs had been ripped off, and its thousands of eyes trembled in fear as they looked up at Huxian and his entourage.

This is impossible, the Life-Leaching Monarch said. *Such power is impossible. You're a mortal. A mortal!*

A mortal that can beat you within an inch of your life, Huxian said. *And if you're not careful, he could steal the Leyline of Gold you've been feeding on for millennia. So, are you coming, or are you going to make me make you regret it?*

I'm coming! the spider yelled, cowering as the purple mist that was Mr. Mountain floated above. *You're all a bunch of freaks. Unnatural freaks!*

Huxian took no issue with those comments. He knew compliments when he heard them.

Mr. Mountain, help her condense her mark, Huxian said. The violet mist grunted and floated toward the Leyline of Gold, coaxing its powers out with affiliated mountainous energy. Earth yielded metal, after all. Purified golden energy surged out, forming a complex matrix with the runes engraved on the walls. The power sought to escape, but Huxian growled, forcing it to cower in obedience. The energy then flew into its most ideal recipient—the Life-Leaching Monarch. The marking process began, and Huxian activated Time-Torching Eyes: Sunrise to speed up the process.

Minutes passed before the monarch surged with energy. Fortunately, she'd been working on shoring up her compatibility with the mark for millennia. With anyone else, it would have taken hours at least.

Thank you, my lords, the Life-Leaching Monarch said, giving a light bow.

Where to next? Lei Jiang asked, appearing beside him. He'd already relieved his anger at the spiders by knocking a few thousand of them senseless. Like any other decent demon, he loathed spiders with a passion.

Next? Huxian said. *Next, we go to the Leyline of Fire near Huoshan.* There weren't many areas on the plane that could condense initiation marks, and most of them were centered on leylines. Those that Huxian's friends had condensed were exceptions—though Mr. Mountain's mountain mark had drawn at least some of its power from the unoccupied Leyline of Earth.

The Leyline of Water was near Haijing, and he had no doubt that it wasn't demons that occupied it but godkin. The Leyline of Wood would be their next stop after Huoshan. No doubt its inhabitant would be overjoyed with their presence and all too eager to defend its source of power.

Let's go, Huxian said. Crystalline wings of spatial energy appeared on his back and tore into the air. The eight appendages cut a portal from their underground chamber directly to the fiery mountains of Huoshan. Huxian, his friends, and a giant spider walked a short distance and appeared above a large volcano.

Wake up, you stupid lout! Lei Jiang yelled when they arrived.

Huxian flinched. He should have warned the little rodent. A giant tail flew out of the magma and smashed into the tiny demon, who crashed through two consecutive mountain peaks before finally stopping.

Hello, esteemed Magma Serpent Initiate, Huxian said. *My associates and I wish to discuss a business proposition.* Magma serpents were actually descendants of fire dragons, and they were happy to discuss anything to do with money.

Go on, the serpent said. Huxian nodded to Silverwing, who began to talk about potential plunder and resource allocation, as well as a deal with local governments to expand demonic territory. It was for show, of course, but the serpent didn't need to know that. And if they managed to survive this crazy suicide mission, he'd definitely make sure that snake was well compensated for his efforts.

"The honorable Feng Ming and his attendant Wang Jun seek an audience with the Ancestor," a woman called out, announcing their arrival. They'd already traveled to many places in a short amount of time thanks to Wang Jun's wondrous abilities. This was the final—and perhaps the most important—stop in the Northern Alliance.

They weren't in the royal palace of the Phoenix Cry Empire, but rather a smaller palace meant for vacationing in the mountain range near the Phoenix Burial Battlefield. It was a fortified building made of red and white stone and covered in golden patterns. It had suffered no damage during the invasion, where they'd narrowly rebuffed the enemy forces with the aid of the mountain's demonic inhabitants, though the cost had been a heavy one. Only two half-step transcendents and their ancestor remained. And now they were going to ask them to go on a suicide mission.

As per the customs of the Phoenix Cry Empire, they kept their heads bowed and their gazes averted as they entered the main audience room. They avoided staring at the Phoenix Cry Ancestor—a dazzling beauty, according to eyewitnesses—and looked at her feet, which were bare save for ruby sandals that complemented her red-painted toenails. And her feet were beautiful.

"Do not avert your gazes," a melodious voice said. "You are not like most who visit here."

Feng Ming gulped and did as instructed. A fire lit up in his heart as he saw the Phoenix Cry Ancestor's bewitching appearance. She wore a red qipao with golden patterns, and her hair was tied back with red-and-gold ornaments. Though the costume was similar to what the Red Dust Headmistress wore, the charm it exuded was regal instead of bedazzling. Her bearing was every bit a queen as the late monarch who had just died for her kingdom.

"We have come to request—" Feng Ming started.

"I know why you're here," the Phoenix Cry Ancestor interrupted. "You wish for us to help you fight the unkillable. You wish for us to help you in a futile errand while most of those on my level have either fled the plane or are holing up to take advantage of the situation should you succeed. Am I right?"

"One hundred percent correct," Wang Jun said. "We realize it's a big ask, which is why we've come prepared."

"Oh?" the Phoenix Cry Ancestor said. "The overbearing young master of the Wang family has come here to negotiate? Charming."

"I can hardly buy your services, as I don't have a spirit stone to my name," Wang Jun said. "But my family is still influential. We could arrange many trade contracts or give more favorable terms for future business."

"Interesting," the Phoenix Cry Ancestor said. She stood up from her chair and walked over to Feng Ming and pressed her finger on his chest. Though the gesture seemed innocent enough, and he wasn't armed, he felt a lethal power accumulating at the tip that could end him should she wish it. "And what of you, dear Marshal Feng? What do you offer in return?"

"I offer the two Southern Alliance kingdoms south of yours

when we eventually go down there to claim them," Feng Ming said. "And two more of your choosing. If you would be so kind as to help us."

"How generous," the Phoenix Cry Ancestor said. "Far more generous than those ungrateful louts that wouldn't help defend our kingdoms when the South was invading. Unfortunately, I'll still have to decline."

Feng Ming's brow furrowed. "It isn't in your best interest to let the Taotie rampage and destroy the plane. What do you have to lose by fighting?"

The Phoenix Cry Ancestor laughed lightly. "Naïve little boy. Just because the viziers are defeated, you think the war is over? You think those remaining transcendents in the South won't act up should I fall in battle? The risk is too great."

"I could improve on my original offer," Wang Jun pointed out.

"Which would be fantastic, if this weren't about more than just money," the Phoenix Cry Ancestor said. "In this war, we lost our queen and seventeen princesses. Only two senior princesses remain, and both of them were the least worthy of the lot and very unlikely to be able to replace me. That means that I'll have to start over from scratch in raising an inheritor."

"I see," Feng Ming said. "If you die, your kingdom dies."

"If I die, my kingdom dies," the Phoenix Cry Ancestor repeated. "I'm sorry for wasting your time."

"It's not much different than most places we visited," Feng Ming admitted. During their recruitment run, they'd only found a dozen half-step transcendents and three transcendents willing to fight. On top of the half dozen transcendents they had left, who were now on the mend thanks to Yue Bing and her remaining blood doctors, they had nine transcendents and maybe twice as many half-step transcendents. It was a far cry from what they needed but much better than he had expected. "Thank you for entertaining us," he said, bowing and turning to walk to toward the door.

"So it's about commitment," Wang Jun said suddenly. "You won't commit unless enough of your enemies are willing to participate? If they were, would you be willing to discuss further?"

The woman tapped her fingers on her chin and looked at him thoughtfully. "I would think about it," she said. "I'd at least hear you out."

"Thank you," Wang Jun said, bowing and following Feng Ming.

"What was that about?" Feng Ming said as they passed the attendants. The palace was understaffed compared to most, probably because the transcendent enjoyed her privacy.

"I just had an idea," Wang Jun said. "A risky but wonderful idea."

He opened a portal of shadows, and Feng Ming followed him into it. They walked out in a desolate place, a harsh land Feng Ming had never seen before. Built on it was a bustling city that had strange customs he'd never witnessed.

"This is the first of many stops," Wang Jun continued. "Our results here will likely dictate what we can accomplish."

"Where are we?" Feng Ming asked. He'd never known this place existed.

"Welcome to the Southern Alliance," Wang Jun said. "Are you ready to fight a transcendent?"

"I'm not so sure," Feng Ming said, paling. "Sounds risky."

"The South is losing, and we can offer these people a tasty carrot," Wang Jun said. "A peace settlement in exchange for fighting a creature of destruction incarnate."

"Then why talk about fighting?" Feng Ming said, though he was intrigued by the prospect. Many of the people they'd talked to thus far had reservations because of the few transcendents south of the border. If they could recruit them, didn't that mean they had a potential second chance? Wang Jun's quick traveling ability might give them enough time to pull it off.

"In my experience," Wang Jun said dryly, "bad men respond well to carrots but need a stick to help keep them in line." Feng Ming couldn't refute that knowledge, but he had very little experience in this matter. "I've dealt with unsavory men like this before. Just shut up and follow my lead."

Ah, Feng Ming thought. It seemed the rumors were true. Wang

Jun hadn't fought his way to the top of the Wang family only through legitimate business practices. A few months back, mysterious assassins had shown up all around the Northern Alliance at around the same time. Most people had thought it was the Spirit Temple. Who else could rally so many strong fighters excelling in stealth in such a short amount of time?

Now, Feng Ming knew different. Wang Jun might be a good person, but he definitely had a darker side. Moreover, he could think of no one else with an uncanny ability to travel the continent and set up shadow portals. It wasn't the Spirit Temple that had murdered, threatened, and blackmailed all those people. It was Wang Jun himself. And those skills he'd practiced would finally be used for a higher purpose: saving the plane and all life on it.

Nostalgia nearly overwhelmed Zi Long as he walked through the streets of Haijing. The underwater city, stricken by civil war just a few years prior, was a buzzing hive of activity. It was business as usual in this advanced metropolis ruled by the descendants of the Sea God. What happened on the continent was of no import to them, and they had no desire to get involved. They would leave the land dwellers to their petty fighting and allow them to ruin themselves and build up from scratch like they always did.

"Halt!" a guard yelled as he walked close to the Sea God Clock Tower in Clock Tower Square. It was an ancient white building covered in gold and blue runes that protected Haijing but was also the Sea God Emissary's personal treasure.

Zi Long smiled and held out a bottle containing a gray pill. "My teacher, who made this, requested that I speak with the Sea God Emissary about an important matter."

The two guards shifted uncomfortably as they looked at the item. They were familiar with Grandmist seals, which would only appear on the mysterious pills his master had made over a year prior. Even now, these pills floated on the unofficial market at record values.

"Please wait a few minutes," one the guards said. He caught the bottle Zi Long offered and walked inside. As he waited, Zi Long admired the city's timeless architecture.

It didn't take long for the guard to come back out. "Right this way," he said, leading Zi Long inside. Even though he was a peak-core-formation cultivator, the guards showed him very little respect. Perhaps that was because even simple guardsmen like them were middle-marrow-refining cultivators, and anyone with a sufficiently dense bloodline could easily reach the peak of the mortal realm.

They walked through the independent space in the clock tower, passing through the gardens outside the palace proper. Several double doors later, they reached a short lineup leading to the audience hall's main door.

"Wait in line for your turn," the guard said, turning to return to his station.

Though time was of the essence, patience was a virtue when dealing with the powerful. Zi Long walked to the back of the queue where he was greeted with strange glances from the other supplicants, who were mostly Haijing nobles.

Hours passed before he finally entered the audience hall. Gong Shuren, a white-skinned beauty covered in blue runes, wore a golden grown. Golden scales and a golden shell lay on a table beside her. To Zi Long's surprise, the proud ex-emperor of the Sea God Empire lay kneeling on the floor. Judging by the dust that had settled around him and his calm demeanor, this had been going on for quite some time. Yet the empress didn't seem to notice him, and neither did the other supplicants. They cast the man no curious looks, nor did they laugh or jeer.

"You may address the Sea God's Emissary," a crier announced.

Zi Long stepped forward and bowed deeply. "I send greetings from my master, Du Cha Ming," Zi Long said. "He brings grave news from the continent."

"Does he now?" Gong Shuren said. Her expression was

unreadable. "I do recall telling him that I wouldn't interfere in the continent's affairs. Your wars are none of our concern."

"He understands this perfectly well," Zi Long said. "And he considers your position admirable and aloof. This urgent news concerns the South to some extent but does not involve fighting with them."

"I see," Gong Shuren said. "Continue."

Zi Long swallowed and looked up. The pressure she emanated was considerable, but he was able to keep himself composed enough to speak. "It is the creature," Zi Long said. "The Taotie."

"We are aware of the creature," Gong Shuren said. "And I am happy to announce that I've heard back from the Sea God Plane. They have assured us that they will have a seal ready within a week. They have accepted that neither angels or devils are capable of keeping it constrained and saving the plane and will be footing the bill for this great expense."

"That is good news," Zi Long said. "Yet I must still beg for aid on behalf of my master. The creature is wreaking havoc and must be contained."

"Use your transcendents to contain it," Gong Shuren said. "We are paying a significant price to seal it. It is only fair that you keep it busy."

Zi Long clenched his teeth and breathed in and out to calm himself. "Pardon my rudeness, but with what army?" he said. "The war is over, but the cost was terrible. The World Tree has been destroyed, and there's maybe a half dozen transcendents left, and all of them injured."

"A half dozen should be plenty enough to contain it," Gong Shuren said.

"That would have been the case three days ago," Zi Long said. "Unfortunately, it has broken through. It has killed five transcendents and is currently making its way to the Leyline of Wood."

These words seemed to give her pause. She thought for a moment before replying.

"What realm has the creature reached?" she asked.

"Half-step initiation," Zi Long said. "I'm afraid we don't have the resources to fight it. And if it consumes the Leyline of Wood… well, I'm sure you understand what this would mean for the underpinnings of this mortal plane. Perhaps the Leyline of Earth would be next, or maybe the Leyline of Gold. But I'm afraid it won't be long until the plane is too damaged to continue operating."

The Sea God Emissary tapped her fingers. The hall was so silent that Zi Long could hear Gong Xuandi, who was still kneeling, breathing. His fists were clenched, and he was staring up at her with a glare that said: *I told you so.*

"Very well," Gong Shuren said. "You've convinced me." Then she looked down to Gong Xuandi. "Rise. You have convinced me also. Marshal Ling?"

"Yes, Emissary?" said a large man, a half-step-marrow-refining cultivator.

"Congratulations, you've been promoted to grand marshal," Gong Shuren said. She flicked her hand, and the Sea God Shell on the table flew toward him, instantly glowing blue with the light of attunement. Minister Hao?" She continued, flicking her wrist and sending the scales over. "You've been promoted to prime minister."

"Yes, my queen," Prime Minister Hao said, bowing as he accepted the blue scales.

"Not queen," Gong Shuren said. "Emissary." She stared and Gong Xuandi long and hard before sighing and taking the crown off her head. "You foresaw this. You acted accordingly. You obeyed Feng Ming's commands unfailingly. Now that you know how to follow, you may now lead again. That is assuming we all survive."

The crown landed on Gong Xuandi's head and glowed blue. His aura, which was tyrannical even before donning the crown, grew even stronger.

"It's time to gather Haijing's forces," Gong Shuren said. "Our ancestral homeland is in danger, and someone has to save it."

Chapter 27: Calamity

It was noon when Huxian arrived with three demons in tow. Cha Ming cracked an eye and smiled at his brother's success. "I hope you didn't bully them too bad," he said, standing up from his cross-legged pose. He'd been thinking about the next steps in his cultivation.

Only one of them, Huxian said. *The other two were quite reasonable.* He glared at the Life-Leaching Monarch. The metallic spider, now significantly stronger than before, shot an imploring look at Cha Ming, who resolved to put in a good word.

Cha Ming coughed lightly. "Did you get my message earlier?"

Huxian nodded. *Sounds reasonable. We're up for it.*

"You're sure?" Cha Ming asked. "Because the idea was far from reasonable, and very dangerous."

Well, we're already fighting a world-ending calamity set on destroying us body and soul, Huxian said. *How much worse could it get?*

"Good point," Cha Ming said. They were at the edge of the Redwood Forest, with its brown-red bark and lush green leaves. The village he'd visited before with Jun Xiezi was still some ways away, completely oblivious to the upcoming battle. Hopefully, they were far enough away. At the very edge of the horizon, they could see the Taotie. It wouldn't be long before it arrived.

Any word on Feng Ming and the others? Huxian asked.

"They'll be here any minute now," Cha Ming said. As he spoke, a portal of darkness appeared. Wang Jun and Feng Ming walked out looking quite pleased. "How did it go?"

Wang Jun replied by summoning another portal. Then a second. Then a third. Many dozens of portals of shadow filled the meadow, and from each one came a few powerful figures. There were six transcendents as well as a few dozen half-step transcendents. Most of them were unknown to Cha Ming, though he recognized several from Bastion in the Southern Alliance.

"It took a lot of convincing, and ultimately, what sealed the deal was an offer of peace for participating kingdoms," Feng Ming said. "Among other promises."

"You can hardly blame us for pushing you," a woman in red said. Cha Ming deduced from her presence and appearance that she was the ancestor of the Phoenix Cry Empire. "The future of our descendants is at stake."

"You won't regret your decision," Cha Ming said. He looked to the east where another group of men and women appeared. The Red Dust Pavilion's headmistress and vice heads were there, along with the remaining vice chancellor of the Church of Justice and a few higher-ranking chaplains. Judging by their unstable auras, they'd just broken through in their cultivation. The power they gained in the short term would come at a great cost, likely forever stunting their growth. It was the smaller of many sacrifices those here would make today.

"Is this everyone?" Feng Ming asked. "What about Zi Long?"

"He sent word through core-transmission jade," Cha Ming replied. "They're on their way with reinforcements, but it will take a bit of time for them to arrive."

"We don't have much time," Feng Ming said grimly, staring at the advancing Taotie, who was running at an alarming, steady pace. "What's the plan? We go all out?" He looked to Cha Ming, who'd been in charge of gathering information.

Cha Ming, in turn, looked to Gong Lan. She was the strongest remaining monk from the World Tree Monastery, one of the few survivors. Though her injuries were great, her wisdom was respected by many.

"With everyone here at their current strength, it is unlikely that we can defeat the creature," Gong Lan said. "At most, we can delay it. Attacks by transcendents don't seem to damage it. But by delaying it, we can buy precious minutes."

"And what does stalling gain us?" the Phoenix Cry Ancestor asked. "Forgive me for being blunt, but I must consider this before charging into battle."

"Understandable," Gong Lan said. "It buys us time for two things. For one, we can stall for reinforcements from Haijing. Though they have no transcendents, they have half-step transcendents and transcendent treasures aplenty. They are also body cultivators, which are especially suited to prolonged battles."

"And the second?" the Phoenix Cry Ancestor asked. It seemed that a few transcendents were still on the fence, and her decision would likely dictate their course of action.

"Huxian, his friends, and I will all transcend," Cha Ming said. "At the same time, right away."

This attracted a few frowns. Now was probably not the best time for quick breakthroughs, and the odds of dying during an ascension calamity was fifty-fifty, and each of their deaths would mean a great loss in manpower.

"I thought you said transcendents couldn't hurt this thing," Feng Ming said doubtfully. "I take it there's a reason for the sudden breakthrough?"

"There is," Gong Lan said. "While we're bleeding and dying to stall for time, they will be transcending. This part isn't what's most dangerous. The calamity that follows is the true test. You are right that transcendents normally can't do much to this creature, but that's not what we're relying on. Instead, they will be summoning their ascension calamity at the same time. As they are bound together by brotherhood and friendship, that is within their rights. They will fight it together."

"That's madness," the Phoenix Cry Ancestor said bluntly. "Not just one calamity, but six? You realize that the tribulation will be amplified several times over? This isn't just addition. It's multiplication."

"They understand this," Gong Lan said. "But even that is not the risky part. After summoning the tribulation, they will proceed to attack the Taotie."

This silenced any criticisms.

"The Taotie's nature allows it to elude the plane's will. The plane is akin to a sleeping child. It knows not what it wants, but when someone makes too much noise, it awakens. By transcending, they will invoke a heavenly tribulation. And when the heavens' eyes are upon them, they will attack the Taotie, dragging it into battle with the plane itself. The theory is that this won't just amplify the tribulation but make the plane's will aware of the risk the Taotie poses. With any luck, it will divert energy away from those breaking through and actively attack the Taotie, weakening it or destroying it."

No one spoke. A man and five demons breaking through at the same time was ludicrous, but this was sheer madness. Fighting *during* a tribulation? It was unheard of.

"How sure are you that this will work?" Feng Ming asked.

"We're not," Cha Ming said. "It's a big gamble. But as a worst-case scenario, we're reasonably confident that we can drag the Taotie into our tribulation. The clouds never ignore outsiders interfering. With the tribulation amplified manifold, even if we die, there's no way the Taotie will survive as a half-step-initiation-realm fiend. If we die, it dies with us. If we're lucky, and the plane sides with us, then we might just survive."

It was the ultimate sacrifice. Six of the best talents the plane had ever seen, gambling their very lives against the creature that sought to destroy them. And though technically speaking, they could break their word and overcome their tribulations to leave the plane without fighting, Cha Ming's reputation was solid throughout the North, and even the South had a grudging respect for him. Of course, they knew nothing of his exploits in Bastion, but now was not the time to bring that up. The Phoenix Cry Ancestor agreed to the plan, and they began making their battle preparations.

A few minutes passed, and finally, the Taotie roared.

"How complicated is transcending for you?" Cha Ming asked Huxian, who stood guard for him. He was focused on his core and the pattern he would carve.

"Not difficult at all," Huxian said. "The mark is a key. Once I turn it, nature will do the rest."

"Then I'd better get started," Cha Ming said. He looked inside his Dantian at his core, which he had painted with the Myriad Truths Diagram. The diagram had served as an excellent pre-carving, amplifying his qi and giving him multiple pseudo-domains. With his angelic endowment, he was far more powerful than he had a right to be.

But not powerful enough. Not to face this creature. "Are you sure you want to do this?" the Monkey King said, popping outside of the Clear Sky World.

"It's a gamble, but we need to win," Cha Ming said. He took a breath, then waved his hand. The Clear Sky Brush appeared above his core and retracted the ink it had painted. The core's transcendent glow faded as his cultivation dropped from half-step rune carving to the peak of core formation. Only his eight-colored core remained, with its five-element swirl and lines of black, white, and gray. "Let's do this."

He took another breath, and the world went dark. A projection of his soul appeared outside his core. Grandmist Essence from the universe began to swirl and form a sharp carving knife. He didn't force it to coalesce, however. Instead, he summoned the Grandmist energy in his own core from the time Yu Gen's mother had fed them their special soup.

The plane sang in praise as the Grandmist energy appeared. There had been a resistance to the process before, but with the energy supplied, much of the Grandmist disappeared. A quarter of it joined his own supply, and it seemed malleable, very accommodating to his will.

"Why make my own knife when I already have the best crafting tool available?" Cha Ming wondered aloud. He summoned the Clear Sky Brush, and it shifted, becoming a carving knife like he used when carving runes on weapons. It was a large knife, but in comparison to the gigantic core beside his soul, it was actually quite small. As expected, the Clear Sky Carving Knife drank in the Grandmist energy greedily. It glowed with a soft gray light that gave it the power to carve not just words on his core, but concepts.

Strictly speaking, Cha Ming shouldn't have had to banish the pre-carving of the Myriad Truths Diagram. He could have carved the same pattern all over again, and it wouldn't have taken as much time or energy as starting from scratch. Unfortunately, what he wanted to carve was very different from that all-encompassing pattern. And he didn't have enough time to pre-paint before carving it.

He took in a slow, deep breath as he recalled the first of the five elements and its foremost aspect, flow. The Clear Sky Carving Knife became a fluid projection that resounded like crashing waves upon contacting his core.

The ocean cares not for drowning children;
Man is a slave to the sea of fate.
Flowing down from high to low;
Never questioning his direction.

This was also the emotion he was most familiar with. The helplessness, the resistance. It was what had driven him to seek a better life after reincarnating. Life had gotten in his way many times, starting with his crippling in Crystal Falls and the corresponding enslavement. Even after mending his meridians and gaining freedom, he'd had to overcome many roadblocks to heal his core. Building up momentum to fight through these obstacles was now his defining character trait.

Where there's a will, there's a way. He felt it every time he drew the Flow Talisman. And now that he'd condensed his angelic wings, this familiarity had deepened. The concept was now part of his very soul. And it would be part of his core as well.

He carved each character with intricate precision, pouring his thoughts and memories into every cut. A thin line of Grandmist remained in the grooves. Unlike a painting, these cuts could never be erased.

It was a gamble. According to Sun Wukong, no one had ever done it. Standard runic patterns were used to carve cores, as they represented the deepest laws. But heavens be damned if he'd let that stop him. He had faith in his talismans and faith in his emotions. They'd grown alongside him and given him power when he needed it. And their power was great. They far exceeded the runes he used in formations. If he would transcend, he would do it grandly. He wouldn't just increase his realm; he'd regain control of his life and destiny.

Hold! Feng Ming sent as the Taotie advanced. *Hold!* The dozens of cultivators present were taut bowstrings itching to be released. *Now!*

A battle formation activated, joining three groups of twelve half-step-rune-carving cultivators, covering them in a protective bubble as they launched their attack.

The Taotie swung out a horned fist. It crashed into the pseudo-domain-reinforced chains that sought to restrain it. One of the cultivators, a halberd-wielding old man with long gray hair, unleashed a technique that summoned the projection of a golden otter. It cut into one of the Taotie's many appendages, severing it for a few seconds before it rejoined the writhing mass of darkness.

The creature roared soundlessly, shaking them to their very cores. Feng Ming yelled again, and another party attacked from the rear while a pair of transcendents collided with it. The heavens rumbled in anger at their defiance and struck at them with lightning as they unleashed their domains, but the man and woman didn't care, ignoring its scorching heat as they unleashed a barrage of wooden stakes and serpentine whips of watery transcendent energy. And unlike before, what it destroyed didn't reattach so easily. The pieces of Taotie wandered around, confused by their transcendent might.

"It's working!" Feng Ming cried out. "Attack from the ground!" They'd waited for the beast to come to this place for a reason. The earth erupted in a rush of green vines, and red bark grew around the creature, forming a natural cage to trap its perverted nature. The creature's horns and tentacles tried to suck out their energy, but the vines resisted. They were controlled by a half-step initiate who was one with the Great Redwood Forest and supported by the Leyline of Wood.

"Swords!" Feng Ming yelled, prompting two transcendents and four half-step transcendents to appear above the Taotie. Gold was a popular path, and swords were just an abbreviation for their power—cutting, slicing, and stabbing. Gold was incisive and sharp, and those who cultivated it specialized in offense. They poured power into their swords, sabers, and spears—mostly transcendent treasures—and sent them into the creature's body where they could wreak havoc.

Pieces fell to the ground, pieces of writhing darkness, but these pieces took much less time to reattach themselves than before. The creature was learning.

"Retreat!" Feng Ming ordered.

Too little too late.

A whiplike tentacle moved faster than they anticipated, and a half-step transcendent disintegrated on contact, his life-force absorbed by the fierce creature.

"We're going to lose a lot of men if this goes on," Wang Jun, who stood beside him, said. "Do you have a plan?"

"Sort of," Feng Ming said. "It's going swimmingly."

Wang Jun raised an eyebrow. "I sense a breakthrough."

"Someone might as well try it out first," Feng Ming said. "To know if it'll work."

Wang Jun looked at him thoughtfully. As they observed the battle, Feng Ming directed a Grandmist knife within his core to make quick strokes based on the pattern of the Good Fortune Scripture. Though his cultivation was a very effective one, it relied a little too much on the urgings of fate. Who knew if it was the right time for him to break through, or if fate would tell him no, not this time, not ever?

The cultivators fought, and the Taotie killed. Every few minutes, either the cultivators or the demons would suffer a blow. And more often than not, it was a lethal one. Not only did these losses directly feed the Taotie, but their strikes were growing increasingly futile. With each blow the creature received, its energy seemed to spike, granting it a resistance similar types of energy. The Taotie was not only unkillable, but adaptive. It was a walking self-improvement book, taking whatever life threw at it to become a better, stronger monster.

"Well, if you're going to take forever to do this, I might as well try something," Wang Jun said. He disappeared and reappeared above the creature, his black scythe cutting down. It roared in pain as its arm was lopped off and used its other arm to counterattack. Feng Ming expected Wang Jun to dodge but was surprised to see a dark barrier come up. It pulsed with inviolable energy, and the heavens rumbled in defiance.

What the hell? Feng Ming sent. *When did you break through? How?* He'd seen no calamity or lightning, no unnatural storms seeking to destroy him.

Those of my lineage don't carve their cores, Wang Jun explained. *Instead, they obscure it. The heavens couldn't sense my ascension.* Wang Jun disappeared and reappeared, supporting the transcendents and their helpers. Soon, the creature was forced to acknowledge the threat he posed and stop its advance toward the Leyline.

Come on, Feng Ming thought, his hands itching. *There!* The process had taken no time at all, as luckily, his quick strikes had been flawless. "Evacuate!" he yelled to the fighters, who immediately retreated. He hefted his spear and lunged at the creature as dark clouds appeared overhead. They weren't the normal clouds that the heavens sent to punish transcendents, but clouds punishing a new ascension, not here to chastise him for disobeying, but here to destroy him.

The transcendents and their helpers cleared the battlefield as Feng Ming charged in, dodging and weaving. His domain erupted, its transcendent might granting him what he was best at—unparalleled luck. Now that the energy of the plane was under his control, he felt no more itching and tugging. Instead, he saw strands of fate woven in an intricate pattern. He simply had to follow them in fighting the creature. He stabbed, thrust, and cut with his lucky spear and was surprised to see Wang Jun still fighting alongside him, scythe in hand.

"Get the hell out of here!" Feng Ming yelled. He dodged a bolt of lightning, which happened to strike the Taotie. Another bolt of lightning struck it, this one more aggressive, burning a hole through its body that caused it to roar in pain. "It's working!" he said, laughing as he looked to Wang Jun, only to realize the man wasn't there. Instead, he was still atop the creature, slashing at an open wound where black blood oozed from its body. The lightning seemed to ignore him altogether, choosing to focus on the Taotie first and Feng Ming second, completely ignoring Wang Jun in the process..

Maybe they wouldn't need Cha Ming's ascension. Maybe they could finish it off right here and now. He knew it was a foolish thought, but every fool could hope. The heavens charged up for a second attack, which he dodged easily, cutting a deep gash into the creature. And though it howled in pain from both his cut and the lightning's stronger strike, Feng Ming could see that the damage was minimal, and it was infuriated at the inconvenience.

"Stop daydreaming," Wang Jun said, appearing beside Feng Ming and grabbing his wrist. They disappeared into a world of shadows and reappeared a short distance later, where Wang Jun slashed out with his scythe, creating a wide gash that Feng Ming stuck his spear into. Lightning followed, searing the exposed flesh.

Cha Ming's core chipped and cracked as the Clear Sky Carving Knife cut crude and rough strokes that perfectly manifested the words in his heart.

> *The weight of the world crumbles countless dreams;*
> *Man's foundation is ever brittle.*
> *Hardening through countless ages;*
> *Never questioning his resolve.*

The Matter Talisman came to him easily as he recounted his past experiences. He was a rock, shaped through trial after trial that broke him repeatedly. Time pressed on his many layers, creating stronger strata that resisted before breaking once again. It was an endless cycle, much like the shifting tectonic plates of earth, or the tremors of the Shattered Lands as the leyline tore them asunder.

In the distance, the earth broke as well. The familiar Life-Leaching Monarch was, in a twist of irony, fighting alongside him again. His core let off a soft brown glow as the last of the words were carved, and a portion of Grandmist energy left the Clear Sky Carving Knife to etch them.

It was time to move on to the next talisman, the Shape Talisman. Everything in the world had a shape, whether it was a droplet of water or a complex human being. Metal could be sharpened or could grow dull with use, and skills could be cultivated or be forgotten. Practice made perfect, and lack of practice did the opposite. Every man could gain hope through constant work, by refining himself like a metal in a blacksmith's forge. The knife became a golden scalpel as it precisely wrote his innermost feelings.

> *Countless swords leave not a mark;*
> *Man's edge is dulled by the passing of ages.*
> *Honing his worth through endless practice;*
> *Never questioning his skill.*

It was a motto to live by, and an irreplaceable part of his being. This self-improvement, this repeated process, was what made weapons last and cultivators stronger. Even mortals, with their limited skills, had to constantly sharpen their minds and tone their muscles.

As the knife cut the first character, the story of Cha Ming's life, past and present, flashed before his eyes. He needed to hurry, that he had no doubt of. But carving his core was more than just an art. He wasn't just carving character. With the Clear Sky Carving Knife, he was shaping his ideal self.

The earth broke apart as the seventh bolt struck. It more resembled a dragon than a natural phenomenon, a projection of transcendent displeasure. It barely grazed Feng Ming's thigh before shooting into the Taotie, joining a much larger bolt in burning it. He winced in pain as he simultaneously dodged a tentacle while severing another with his lucky spear.

By now, the Taotie was covered in scorch marks, and its movements were sluggish and unwieldy. Yet the force it wielded showed that these wounds were superficial, and the stabs Feng Ming landed mere delays. All around them, the ground was covered in burnt blood. The transcendents and half-step-rune-carving cultivators who had fought the creature were nearby, regenerating their energy. If this failed, they, too, would join the battle, fighting a creature that was stronger than ever, tempered by lightning from the heavens.

An eighth bolt crackled in the skies, this one as dark as midnight. The lightning dragon came, and for the first time, Feng Ming wasn't lucky enough to fully dodge it. He summoned a fiery sandstorm domain around himself and drew on the Good Fortune Scripture as he bellowed, striking out at the heavens and disintegrating the lightning dragon with ease.

The heavens paused. They seemed to rumble in anger at his lackadaisical approach. The Taotie writhed under his own bolt and began attacking, using the moment of respite to begin a second offensive. Wang Jun was beaten back one strike at a time, and Feng Ming's spear, which was about to strike one of the creature's many limbs, struck bone. It was an impenetrable black plate that had suddenly appeared on the Taotie's body.

Damn it, damn it, damn it, Feng Ming thought. Their plan had backfired, it seemed. The Taotie wasn't just building an immunity to lightning; it was strengthening every part of its body. As the heavens sent out one last bolt, this one gray, Feng Ming ducked beneath the beast. The lightning could only pass through it. It struck the creature in the back alongside its sister bolt, splitting the creature in two, revealing a large black gem.

"Destroy it!" Feng Ming bellowed, prompting the transcendents standing by to action. The calamity was over, and the storm clouds retreating. They were replaced by lighter cloud cover as transcendent domains erupted, smashing against the creature's marked core. The fire serpent from Huoshan and the Life-Leaching Monarch joined in as well.

The Taotie's body twitched as transcendent weapons struck against its only weakness. Fortunately for it, their beatings clanked off with no effect. Feng Ming wondered why the creature had ceased moving if their blows posed no threat.

"It's a trap!" he realized. But it was too late. The two halves of the beast joined together, quick as lightning, trapping three unfortunate souls inside its mouth of a body. The remainder scrambled to clear the area, but whipping tentacles and spiky bones erupted everywhere, slaying yet another one of their few transcendents and five more half-step-rune-carving cultivators.

Feng Ming himself was struck by one of those blows, and it had reduced his treasured marshal's cape to little more than ashes, forcing him to discard it. Others were not so fortunate; they didn't possess such treasures or such luck. The creature roared once more as black plates like he'd struck earlier appeared all over its body, armor black as midnight, impenetrable to mere transcendent weapons.

Hurry up, you fool, he thought, looking back to the cross-legged Cha Ming. They'd proved the concept, at least, but it was clear that just one calamity wouldn't cut it.

Kindling and dousing. The embodiment of energy. Carving this poem hurt Cha Ming's heart like no other. The searing-hot knife didn't so much cut as melt its way through his solid core.

> *Disappointment douses the hearts of the needy;*
> *Man is left wanting and ever-yearning.*
> *Kindling the flames of love and caring;*
> *Never questioning his devotion.*

He'd loved and lost. He'd been disappointed beyond comprehension. Yet it was that loss that kept him going, that fueled his ambition toward the summit of power. A man without a goal was like a sailboat without a strong wind. He could only float aimlessly on a calm lake, waiting for the currents to take him.

But a man with a goal, a man with desires? That was something else entirely. Energy, not just in terms of raw power but motivation and willingness to bleed for a cause. It was a key component of faith, for what faithful man could keep on going without a fiery passion that burned brightly in his heart, melting away ice that tried to cool it?

The carving was completed without a hitch. Around it blossomed a beautiful red pattern unlike any other. He proceeded to the last of the five, living and dying in samsara. A green knife coated in poison but brimming with life touched his core, and creeping vines grew out from it to write the last of the five poetic talismans.

> *Dying leaves carpet the forest floor;*
> *Man is left pondering his demise.*
> *Living life to its fullest potential;*
> *Never questioning his struggle.*

In a sense, energy and samsara were related. His goal was to get powerful enough to find Yu Wen and recover her memories from the river of time. Everyone who was born would eventually die, but some lives were too short, and some suffering too miserable. Life was a struggle, a struggle that should be embraced. But in the end, it all led back to one place, and that place was Diyu.

He let these feelings wash over him as he carved, and with the carving came a deep understanding that in the end, he, too, would die. Many would think this made life meaningless, but he thought differently. It was the trying that mattered. The journey. The fight.

It was slaughter unlike any she'd ever seen. Though Gong Lan had spilled her share of blood, including during the battle on the mountain, there was something about this fight that was much more horrifying and primal than the tens of thousands of men who had died before.

These transcendents were stronger than the plane could tolerate, and the dozens of half-step transcendents weren't far off. But they seemed like little more than children to this creature who sought to devour them to fill the endless void within it. The others couldn't see it, but she could. It was growing stronger by the minute, in body, mind, and soul.

Alas, she had barely energy left. Perhaps enough for one or two interventions to save someone important from dying. Medicinal pills alone couldn't change that. She'd been fundamentally damaged when the World Tree died and the Bodhi Seed along with it. Her soul was withering, and soon it would be nothing more than a mindless ghost heading toward the Yellow River. But Cha Ming was right—this was her duty. She would defend her home until her very last breath.

Though there were many transcendents fighting, Feng Ming and Wang Jun were the stars of the show. Their teamwork was impeccable, but frighteningly enough, the beast seemed to know it. Each and every move they made was met by the cunning fiend. The terrible thing wasn't just a monster; it was a thinking being.

There, Gong Lan thought as one of the spiked tentacles finally found its mark. It slammed into Feng Ming, forcing him to the ground. Gong Lan glowed with a golden light as Feng Ming fell. "I have walked the path of solitude for many lifetimes, but little did I know I would find a companion," Mantra evoked, golden words floated around her and Feng Ming. They were joined through a tether that she pulled, yanking him outside of the beast's attack range.

"Thanks," Feng Ming said, wiping the blood from the corner of his mouth. But Gong Lan screamed, forcing him to turn around and face a horrible claw that had appeared out of nowhere. He brought up his spear to deflect it, and the artifact faltered. Thousands of hairline cracks appeared all over the lucky spear as he and Gong Lan were forced back.

Meanwhile, on another side of the beast, six claws appeared around Wang Jun. He tried to vanish and avoid it, but the trap of darkness pulled him away from his portal, exposing him to a dark fist that struck him, sending him crashing into the mountains.

Was he all right? Gong Lan wasn't sure. Though she could sense souls better than anyone else, Wang Jun was an enigma. Besides, it didn't matter. They were losing, as evidenced by another transcendent dying alongside his capable assistants.

"It's over," she muttered, laughing in despair.

"It's never over," Feng Ming said, holding out his cracked spear. He prepared himself to charge back in, when on the horizon, a wonderful sight appeared. Hundreds of ships and giant creatures of the sea—whales, sharks, and giant sea turtles. Atop them rode white-and-blue-skinned figures with runes glowing on their chests. A group of scholars was also there, led by a purple-robed man Gong Lan recognized as Cha Ming's disciple. They'd managed to stall long enough for reinforcements to get here.

Feng Ming sat down cross-legged as the army and the creature clashed, swallowing too many pills to be prudent given his current condition. Yue Bing, who had been standing by with medics, rushed in to help and heal who she could with her blood vitality.

Meanwhile, Gong Lan took one of the pills Cha Ming had given her. It was a rare soul-replenishing pill, something useful even for someone who cultivated the Buddhist way. She had maybe one or two more strikes left. And then, darkness would take her.

Cha Ming breathed out a sigh of relief as his core glowed with five-colored light. He'd successfully carved his core with all five poetic talismans, and he could feel a fundamental change washing over him. The runes had been accepted, and he would finally get to transcend.

A pity, he thought, looking at the gray carving knife. It still had energy left. Was there something that he was missing? Something more that he could carve? He frowned as he scoured his mind, searching for answers to an unconventional puzzle.

There were five poems, five elements. But something called out from his heart and words came to his lips.

Many became three and three became two;
All of existence, a fog of gray.

No one knew what came first, creation or destruction. Grandmist was the origin of all, but to obtain it, destruction was necessary. It was also a quintessential part of what he was identifying more and more as his Dao, faith. If nothing was ever destroyed, what sense was there in believing? It was striving against adversity that made the journey worth it. Destruction was the embodiment of slowing and dulling, of breaking and dying, and of course, dousing.

These two lines linked all of destruction, leaving behind only a small portion of what came before to kindle a new fire. From a stagnant pond, a river could flow and a dull knife could be sharpened, broken land hardened. Living things could sprout from a dying land, sowing a prosperous field.

Two made three and three made many.
Who made this clear sky?

He carved quickly and heartfully, and an unfathomable energy began surging out from inside him. And when the last word was carved, the two lines glowed as white as the white circle that had once linked the pillars in his Dantian. Yet there was something missing, something connecting it all. It suddenly clicked.

Tender heartstrings tug on the wandering mind;
Right and wrong are cast aside, with only faith to guide the way.

This time, he didn't carve the words but spoke them, and his core took on a violet hue as the power of emotions grew strong within it. The words appeared as a soft violet mist that flowed around the sphere, amplifying the power of the runes just like it would any poetic talisman. This was the power of heart and feelings. He'd imbued emotions into each of his talismans, and these same emotions fueled another carving.

But there was one more, he was sure of that. He took the carving knife in his hands, but just as the words were about to touch his lips, they drifted away, unreachable.

No, that can't be it, he thought. He struggled to latch on to the thought, wrestled to contain it. But it wouldn't come no matter how hard he tried.

He opened his eyes and realized why that was. The knife, which he'd been carving with this whole time, had grown dull. There was no Grandmist available, and he had a feeling this carving would take far more mist than any of the others before it.

"Such is life," Cha Ming muttered. Perfection was difficult to achieve. He gazed suspiciously at the five flaws remaining in his core and guessed that they were the likely cause of his failure. These imperfections had resulted in a loss of Grandmist throughout the carving process. Unfortunately, there was no turning back time. He would have to be satisfied with eight carvings, the five elements, creation, destruction, and heart.

The Clear Sky Carving Knife disappeared, and he disappeared from the space outside his core. His core began to glow with eight-colored light, manifesting in a domain. It expanded out to one hundred feet, and he knew with certainty that anything inside it was under his control. Heaven and earth energy would obey his commands, as elements of the domain he manifested. And unlike the other domains he'd seen, this one was prismatic—its colors shifted as he willed it. They would never overlap, but where there was gold, he could manifest gold, and where there was water, he could manifest water. Creation, destruction, and heart, however, seemed outside of his reach. He couldn't manifest them as domains, yet something tugged inside him.

He became aware of three new abilities granted to him by the Clear Sky Brush. Words of Creation, Words of Destruction, and Thirty-Six Heavenly Transformations. He paled as he realized what the abilities could do and the frightening manifesting price he would need to pay for them.

His rune carving complete, there was one more thing to take

care of. Cha Ming looked within his body at the interspersed divinity in his veins. He willed it to move to one central location, and like a spark igniting a giant fire, divinity was kindled. He condensed his first drop of divine blood and entered the Blood Awakening Realm. The earth seemed to tremble and bow before him in a display of respect. And like when he broke into rune carving and gained his domain and abilities, he became aware of a divine power, granted to him by the heavens.

It was Five-Element Affinity, a passive ability that seemed extremely useful to Cha Ming. Not only did he gain high resistances to all five elements, but he could now fully manipulate his physical force, converting it to any single one of them. Now, instead of beating someone with the Clear Sky Staff, he could beat them with a literal pillar of transcendent fire not unlike the domain he projected.

It was an earth-shattering transformation. His body was as strong as an early-blood-awakening cultivator's, a full level higher than his initial-blood-awakening cultivation. He wasn't just restricted to a million jin of strength, but two million, assuming the plane would cooperate. And it wasn't only his body strength that was a step higher, but the power of his qi and domain as well. He could display early-rune-carving strength despite only being an initial-rune-carving cultivator. The strength was overwhelming, but it came with a storm in the skies.

You did it? Huxian called out.

"I did it," Cha Ming said.

Finally, Silverwing said. Above him, a mark made of wind appeared. It broke apart into motes of azure light that rained down and blessed him. The same happened to Gua and his mark of swamp, Lei Jiang with his mark of lightning, and Mr. Mountain and his mark of mountain. They glowed in four colors as Huxian's mark appeared. It was the mark of the Bagua, though in the center, a white dragon and a black phoenix were fighting. It glowed with the potent power of space-time, and when it broke apart, it became a gray rain that bathed him like a baptism from above.

Clouds gathered. Winds blew. And as they did, the five beasts transformed. The demons had already shrunk down to manageable sizes, but now they became even smaller, Mr. Mountain included. Huxian's foxy fur melted into pale skin, and his fur into shoulder-length hair half black and half white, with fox ears poking out. And though his features seemed mostly like a human teenager's, there was something bestial in his amber eyes. His precious tails—a fourth had sprouted along with his baptism—had merged together and become a large shuriken half the size of his body. Its black and white edges were unbelievably sharp and radiated the power of time and space.

Like Huxian, Silverwing also transformed. He became a tall young man with white hair and eagle eyes. Feathers sprouted from his hair just behind the ears, and though he had human hands, they had sharp claws at the tips that could break metal and armor. His prized wings, which could cut through anything with gusts of wind, became twin longswords he wore at his waist.

Next came Lei Jiang. He was even younger than Huxian, less a teenager and more a child. He was no longer a fat mouse but a deadly boy with gray hair and violet eyes. Lightning danced around him, threatening to consume all who came near. The only feature that gave away his demonic heritage was a slender whiplike tail. His paws had melted away into hands, and the claws formed two weapons, assassins' claws, and even his boots—the demons had manifested clothes—had a pair of assassins' claws for climbing and slashing.

"Am I beautiful? Am I gorgeous?"

They looked to Gua, who was now a middle-aged man with a shaved head. He wore pink lipstick, and near his right eye there was a large wart that no one could avoid seeing. He wore an ill-fitting assortment of clothes—a suit jacket with jeans and shoes one would wear for sports. All things considered, they went very well together, even though they didn't match the time or the place. And like the others, he had also manifested a tool, an ugly olive-colored gourd, which he wore on his back. A hissing mixture threatened to overflow, filling the area with a poisonous miasma.

"You're quite literally the ugliest human I've ever seen," Huxian said, stretching his human arms. "Not at all handsome like Silverwing and me."

"Thank you, boss," Silverwing said, bowing his head elegantly. They looked to Mr. Mountain, who hadn't yet said a word. But what words needed to be said? He was now a muscular man with violet eyes, wielding a giant hammer. The bare-chested man's arms were so large they made Cha Ming, an initial-blood-awakening cultivator, feel inadequate.

"I am Mr. Mountain," Mr. Mountain said. "Pleased to make your acquaintance."

It was more words than the demon had ever said in his illusory form, save maybe when he'd condensed his mark. With his Eyes of Truth, Cha Ming could tell that he wasn't fully corporeal, but could dissociate and reassociate at will alongside his hammer.

"So what next?" Cha Ming asked, looking up at the heavens. He'd long since known they would be able to assume a human form, though the weapons intrigued him. Clouds were gathering, but not the type that he was used to seeing.

"I may have forgotten a crucial detail," Huxian said.

"Crucial?" Cha Ming asked hesitantly. "How crucial?"

"You know how we were planning on fighting a single calamity, superimposed six times?" Huxian said. "Well, I forgot that for this one, it's a double whammy. We're fighting two at the same time. Consider it a shit sandwich from the universe itself trying to destroy me."

"That's not a bad thing," Cha Ming said, looking at the parting clouds. Six specters of six mountains appeared, and the heavens urged them to move apart, to scatter, to face them alone, but they stood together defiantly, and the mountain merged and grew. The winds howled fiercely, and the transcendents who were fighting the Taotie scrambled away.

"We're here to destroy a Taotie," Cha Ming said to Huxian. "Surviving is great, but defeating it is our primary objective." The foxy teenager gulped and nodded.

Their transformation complete, Cha Ming, Huxian, and friends flew into the sky. The windy mountain calamity, something he'd never heard of before, grew increasingly close.

"Get back!" Cha Ming shouted, causing the Sea God's forces to retreat. They grabbed their wounded, pulling them miles away from what would undoubtedly be a wasteland after they were done. "First things first, let's deplete its energy stores."

Huxian and his friends nodded. While Huxian and Cha Ming flew above the Taotie, who stared at them hungrily, his friends went to four corners of the abomination in something resembling a formation.

"Cool weapon," Cha Ming said, looking at the massive four-pointed shuriken Huxian held.

"Thanks," Huxian said with a toothy grin. "It's a perk of being a demon. When we get human forms, we get a weapon. We can't be having a defenseless demon representing an element, can we?"

Cha Ming supposed not. Given the warlike and militaristic nature of demons, their weapon was the least surprising of developments. The human speech was great, though, as there was something off about mental communication. It would be nice to finally get to sit down and have a nice conversation over tea.

They approached the Taotie, and soon they breached an invisible perimeter. The wide mass of writhing tentacles, of stabbing horns, of eyes and mouths stretching across an indistinct body, shivered as the mountain in the sky expanded twofold. The Taotie, which had taken a severe beating from the lightning before, trembled as it prepared itself for the unusual trial it couldn't escape.

Wham!

The mountain suddenly came down on them, forcing them to the ground as gravity increased by several orders of magnitude.

Blades of wind appeared and began cutting into them, and the pain was dreadful and unavoidable. Wherever they looked, the wind cut. Fortunately, Cha Ming was an initial-blood-awakening cultivator who could punch above his level, so this was nothing for him, and he simply grunted and adjusted his posture. Huxian was a Godbeast, so he, too, was fine.

Gua, Silverwing, and Lei Jiang were flung downward, however, knocking them off balance just as the creature was winding up to hit them. Only Mr. Mountain resisted, but that was natural, wasn't it? Mountains were strong and steady, not influenced in the slightest by mere gravity. Only the wind blades struck him, though they bounced off his strong chest. Silverwing seemed to have an immunity to those; in fact, he devoured them and made them his own.

"We can't afford to stand by and do nothing," Cha Ming said. The creature had also been affected and seemed to attract the majority of the plane's wrath. Its many horns, claws, and tentacles struggled to move, buying them precious time to maneuver. Cha Ming led the charge, running across the now rocky ground under the effects of the suppression. He struck out with Splitting Heaven and Earth, and his staff cleaved through bony tentacle and solid horn, breaking them off the main body like fragile but expensive porcelain. The energy was still the Taotie's, but Cha Ming could feel through his domain that the transcendent energy he projected had disrupted the creature's attachment.

"Attack!" Huxian yelled. He took up his shuriken and ran with frightening speed. Whether it was space he pierced through or time that folded around him, Cha Ming could barely see the lanky teenager. He grinned as he stabbed the object in the beast's main body, cutting out a large chunk beside where a mouth was. It oozed black blood onto the ground, the first of many that would soon join together in a massive ocean.

Silverwing, Gua, and Lei Jiang joined the battle. So did Mr. Mountain. They began breaking the creature apart, but not faster than it could re-form. Then, when they reached a sort of equilibrium, the mountain above them glowed. The suppression doubled, throwing

Cha Ming and the others off balance. The Taotie was also affected.

It became difficult to breathe. The air Cha Ming managed to take in rampaged within his lungs. The calamity of wind cut him from the inside, depleting his precious energy stores. His body bled, and so did Huxian's. Even his tough skin could not protect him from the wind's devastating damage. Only Silverwing was immune, but the mountain's suppression was more than enough for the silver-haired demon.

Cha Ming ran forward and threw out his hand. His domains materialized as an amorphous blob of flame. He plundered energy directly from heaven and earth, using his superior control over his environment. And with another thought, it expanded into runic lines, though these lines shuddered then broke as he realized they were insufficient to contain the transcendent energy. His runes were of the mortal realm and therefore useless in the current situation.

So instead of wasting the energy, he breathed in then blew out, using the wind around him as a fuel. Fire burst into a cone that seared the Taotie's alien flesh, burning its defenses to a crisp before Cha Ming whipped out his staff, elongated it, and gouged out a chunk of charged black flesh. The Taotie, outraged that an ant could sting it so painfully, sent out seven tentacles. But it was too late—the third stage of the calamity struck. The suppression doubled again, causing all seven tentacles and Cha Ming to sink to the ground.

This is getting difficult, Cha Ming thought. His bones creaked under the weight of the mountain. He looked around and realized that the demons were having no trouble at all. Mr. Mountain stood strong, and Silverwing still flew, his dual swords biting deep into the fiend, shearing off chunks that now fell to the floor as flattened pieces of black goop. Lei Jiang was still as fast as ever, lightning trailing behind him as he scratched and shocked the creature, giving it no time to rest. Even Gua seemed calm and composed; he used the swamp in the gourd on his back to both protect himself and encase the Taotie, limiting its movements to protect his friends.

Just what are they doing that I'm not? Cha Ming thought. If he didn't act quickly, he'd soon die under the pressure. In fact, even the

Taotie seemed to be adapting, making him, who could barely move, a sitting duck. He used his Eyes of Truth to stare around the demons, and he soon realized the crux of the matter. They had... domains? No. It wasn't the same. His domain plundered elemental energy and converted it, while theirs seemed to be using ambient natural energy to reinforce themselves and vice versa. Lei Jiang drew on the power of lightning clouds that still hung thick in the air, while the wind from the calamity was easily controlled by Silverwing. In fact, he was greatly reducing its lethality to them. Only Mr. Mountain seemed not to use this area of effect, this dominion, to his advantage. He resisted out of sheer stubbornness and strength inherent to the mountain that he was.

It dawned on Cha Ming that to get past this trial, he would need to use the strength of his domain and divinity. So he took a deep breath and focused on his qi, retracting his domain to ten meters around himself from the original hundred. This small and concentrated, he could see tethers of karmic obligation. Energy sank into him from his surroundings, waiting obediently to be used. Then, a thought struck him. The demon dominions seemed to ally with their surroundings, but what were immortals? What were gods? Immortals controlled, and gods were revered. The lessons Ancestor Wang had beat into him finally sank in.

Taking in a deep breath, Cha Ming expanded his prismatic domain again, sensing the energy that was crushing him toward the ground. The fourth stage of the calamity came, and the pressure doubled. The wind blades cut deep into his bones. He ignored the effects and focused on the powers controlling it behind the scenes. Then, sensing them, he attacked them. This was his domain, not Heaven's.

There was a resistance, an intense tug of war. The heavens were strong, but he didn't need to match them; he just had to wrestle control away from their sphere of influence. The fifth stage came, and he coughed up blood. His viscera were crushed, and his body had trouble regenerating. Yet little by little, the pressure receded, and within him glowed a heavenly light—the light of divinity. It glowed softly, recognizing and resisting the elements. For what was wind but the cycle of creation, the cycle of the five elements? What was a mountain but a projection of earth and metal, and the waters that flowed, and the forests that covered it? The mountain grew clearer in his mind, and as it did, he was able to regain motion, just in time to stop a weakly flailing tentacle.

"Took you long enough," Huxian said. They nodded to each other and rushed out at the Taotie. As they did, Cha Ming's body became attuned to metal. It glowed with a soft golden light, and his Clear Sky Staff became translucent and sharp. His domain expanded, granting a bladelike extension to the staff, which he stuck into the creature, which was still struggling against the calamity's gravity.

As he did so, he noticed that Huxian had thrown his shuriken. It spun and bit into the creature as his eyes shone with a gold time-torching light and glasslike wings appeared on his back, then struck at the fiend, digging out large chunks from its body. These wings weren't like Cha Ming's white angel wings, which were mostly ornamental and boosted his affinity with the elements. Instead, they were weapons of specialized destruction, a scalpel meant to surgically remove threats. Each chunk that fell to the ground burned with golden light. It lay there, inert. They were damaging it, though whether it was enough, only time would tell.

As Huxian eviscerated, Cha Ming struck out. Blade after blade of golden domain projections cut into the creature. And with each strike, Cha Ming's familiarity with his domain and the control it gave him grew deeper. He worked in the might of his body, converting his physical strikes to gold-aligned ones. As his affinity grew, it lessened the strain of the windy mountain on his body just in time to prevent a fatal backlash from the doubling of the mountain's pressure yet again. It was the sixth stage, and the mountain grew clearer, throwing the wind out of his lungs and the lungs of all the others. Even Silverwing felt it, and the fighting paused momentarily. The creature was wounded, but they could barely act against it.

"God, I hate the universe," Huxian said with a grunt. "If I hadn't condensed a space-time mark, I wouldn't have even considered your stupid plan."

"Tell me about it," Cha Ming said. He had no doubt that his superior body cultivation method, his poetic core, and his angelic wings were the only reason why he was still alive. Effectively, he didn't wield the power of an initial-rune-carving cultivator but an early-rune-carving cultivator, and a powerful one at that. The divine ability didn't hurt either.

Just as they were recovering from the increased strain of the sixth stage, the mountain glowed with a white light, and the wind intensified a thousandfold. Blades of wind became gales that ripped into Cha Ming's flesh, and he had to use everything in his power to hold his body together, whether it was by using his domain to disrupt the wind blades before they struck or his vitality stores to regenerate the damage. He manipulated his domain to form a cutting shield, but the moment he did, the winds shifted, attacking him in the direction where he was most vulnerable. And that was only the wind—the mountain was worse. It crushed down on them with the power of creation, making his bones crunch and crackle under the pressure.

The Taotie was no exception. It was essentially flat on the ground, its body unable to resist the cutting blades and the mountain's devastation. After all, it wasn't even a transcendent, but a half-step transcendent with unimaginable strength. And the plane, now knowing full well what threat it posed, seemed to exert several multiples of its power on it, ravaging it from the inside out and sparing Cha Ming and the others the brunt of the joint calamity. Even the energy the Taotie had plundered and attuned to itself was breaking off and rejoining heaven and earth as the storm raged all around.

Then, the eighth stage arrived. The mountain turned black, and all around them was nothing but sharp emptiness. Cha Ming's skin split under the pressure, and the bones that were cracked shattered. He could barely hold them in place as they were reduced to splinters by the heavy mountain. The gales became destructive whirlwinds that lopped off limbs with every single pass. The demons weren't immune to it either, though fortunately, like him, they could regenerate. Their vitality stores seemed like endless reservoirs granted to them by the land itself.

"Everyone, get ready!" Huxian yelled. "Give it all you've got!"

Cha Ming did just that, unleashing not just his domain and his divine ability, but activating the one and only ability of the Thirty-Six Heavenly Transformations. By carving his emotions into his core, he'd gained access to a unique soul path which he could use in emergencies. Currently, with his transcendent angelic soul, his power was passively boosted by half a level. Now that he activated it, however, he literally burned away at his soul power, wounding himself to overdraw on this emotional strength. His power shot up yet again, and now he felt he could match a middle-rune-carving cultivator.

Of course, such great power didn't come without a price. It would only last a minute, and any longer would damage his soul permanently. But a minute was all he needed. Because at that moment, the mountain glowed gray, and everything around them transformed to mist. The mountain became mist. The wind became mist. The flesh the winds hacked away became mist that sought to consume them.

The mist bored into his flesh, his blood, and his bones, baptizing him with origin energy. His vitality stores struggled, and he wasn't alone in this predicament; Huxian and friends were linked up in their Greater Friendship Circle, sharing energy as required. Gua and Lei Jiang seemed particularly affected at this point. They were supported by Silverwing and his calming power of wind and Mr. Mountain and the stable strength of a mountain. Huxian anchored them all, feeding them raw power and a shield of light and darkness. Space and time extended around the five. He didn't extend his shield to Cha Ming, but Cha Ming could tell why in an instant; it creaked and groaned despite its small size, and growing any further would render it unstable. And unlike Cha Ming, who seemed to be able to resist the rampaging Grandmist energies, the demons could do no such thing. Every bit that made contact with them eroded their life essence.

It was the single-most excruciating moment in his entire life. His body had been destroyed many times, and he'd even carved himself new meridians and broken through with a shattered core, but all those things felt like nothing as the Grandmist bored into his very existence. If not for the fact that the Taotie seemed to be taking far more punishment than they were, he'd be crying. The creature shrank as the Grandmist ate it, devouring ever larger amounts of its black flesh. It moaned as the amount grew and eventually reached a full half of its mass before finally relenting.

Then, as quickly as it came, the mountain left, leaving Cha Ming and the others exhausted. They panted heavily and stared at the Taotie, whose tentacles were just now beginning to twitch. It wouldn't be long before it started attacking.

"Time!" Cha Ming gasped. "We need time!" His body was broken, and so were the demons'. The first stage was over, depleting the enemy, but if they didn't recover before fighting, the plane's wrath would surely kill them.

As Cha Ming and the others went down on one knee, the Sea God's army charged with Gong Xuandi and Gong Shuren at the forefront. They cut into the creature, preventing its regeneration, though it seemed like too little too late as one after another, horns and tentacles re-formed. And at one point, one of the tentacles was about to hit Gong Xuandi when Feng Ming charged out, pulling him back and clashing against it.

It was all or nothing now. Transcendents and half-step transcendents joined, dealing what little damage they could, buying Cha Ming and the others precious time to recover. A transcendent fell, and another was stabbed. The new prime minister, wielding gray scales and the power of space, was struck by a horny protrusion, ending his life in an instant despite being a half-step-blood-awakening cultivator wielding one of the Sea God's precious treasures. In fact, the Taotie seemed like it was about to devour the scales, but Gong Shuren flicked her sleeve, and they appeared beside her, supplementing a small projection of the Sea God Clock Tower, which tolled incessantly, its rhythmic noise damaging the creature with vibrations.

"Huxian," Cha Ming said. The foxy teenager appeared beside him.

"What's the matter?" Huxian asked, pouring what vital energy he could into Cha Ming's recovering body.

"I can't see its name," Cha Ming said as he looked in the air around the creature. Usually, his Eyes of Truth could see something, but this time, not even blurry characters could be seen. As much as he focused, and as weak as the creature was, he couldn't discover its identity, a key component in boosting the Tri-Sealing Pillars.

"You won't find it," Gong Lan said, landing a short distance away. She looked pale as a sheet, like a stiff breeze could blow her over. "It is a creature of void and devouring. Its name is not known to the heavens; it is known only to itself."

"Great," Cha Ming said. They'd just have to do without it.

But as he thought this, Wang Jun appeared from out of nowhere, scythe in hand. He skipped past tentacles that flailed around the creature and struck deep into the creature's heart with his scythe, hacking away at god knew what. Then, to everyone's surprise, he used his bare fist coated in a dark domain and plunged it into the beast, extracting *something*. He threw out the object just in time for a newly arrived fist to hit him with a sickening crunch. His mangled body was flung miles away from their perception, and though Cha Ming wanted to save him, he needed to keep calm.

He looked up to what Wang Jun had thrown: It was a dark orb encapsulating something even darker. What Wang Jun had captured was a writhing mass of blood seeking to rejoin its owner. It rampaged within its impromptu prison, which looked like it could break at any moment. Cha Ming frowned, then an idea struck him. He took out the Space-Time Camera and took a picture of the item. The picture cut off the connection of the blood with its master, and the blood stopped writhing and struggling.

"Why blood?" Gong Lan asked with a frown.

"I understand now," Cha Ming said. "Sometimes, names were unknown. Devil sealers couldn't always procure a name, so the blood of demons was used." Without hesitating, he summoned the Clear Sky Brush, then dipped it in the blood. It drank the blood in greedily, though it shivered as it did. Alien characters of black energy appeared on its sides.

"Now we're ready." He unleashed his body cultivation and his qi, which he'd kept sealed to recover from his wounds. And though it hurt to do so, and lightning appeared around them, the lightning seemed far less aggressive than it should be—in fact, it seemed almost understanding. It tickled him lightly, but more as a gentle warning. It wouldn't fight him, at least not until the Taotie, which it now recognized, was gone.

Emboldened by the leniency of the heavens, Cha Ming, Huxian, and friends flew up into the sky. The transcendents, who were on their last legs, mostly cleared out, leaving only Feng Ming, Gong Xuandi, and Gong Shuren.

"Will it work?" Feng Ming asked.

Cha Ming shrugged. "If it doesn't, we're all dead." He spread out his arms, and eight pillars appeared. One for each of the five elements, one for heart, one for creation, and one for destruction. They slammed down around the beast, which was still weak from the tribulation. Runic lines began to take shape. Then Cha Ming took out the last sealing pillar. It wasn't like the others, plain and unadorned. This pillar was gray and bore black characters representing the Taotie's true name.

"Here goes nothing," he said. He flew up and used every ounce of his strength to slam the gray pillar down onto the Taotie's center.

"Manifestations!" Huxian yelled. Demon initiates received a few boons along with their human forms, Huxian had once told him. Their ultimate attack was a manifestation of their aspect. It would take the shape of a phantom in the sky. The five demons glowed, and suddenly, six massive figures of them stood above Huxian, who was at the center of their formation.

A purple mountain appeared above Mr. Mountain; it weighed

down on them with a power not unlike the calamity that had just befallen them. In fact, the power seemed identical, like the mountain had stolen it from the heavens and brought it down to their battle.

And above Silverwing, a giant roc appeared, a massive bird with enormous wings. It flapped, sending blades of wind onto the Taotie, unleashing the unbridled fury of nature onto its defenseless body.

Gua's and Lei Jiang's powers didn't lose out to either of them. They, too, had been enhanced by their respective tribulations. Lei Jiang's projection was not that of a mouse but of a giant mouse-shaped lightning storm that struck every inch of his corner. In Gua's corner, a massive spotted frog appeared. A poisonous bog had taken up the entire area, entrapping many horns and tentacles in sticky resistance. Purple lines of poisonous corruption coursed through the Taotie's dark-energy pathways.

These four calamities were joined at the center by two more manifestations, a dragon and a phoenix. The dragon's eyes glowed brightly with time-torching power. The sun rose, the sun set, and high noon shone simultaneously. They burned the creature with the power of time while stifling its power. At the same time, the time-torching power doubled the strength of everything, including Cha Ming's pillar, which sank a little deeper.

The dark phoenix spread its eight wings. There was a moon behind it, but that moon was hidden behind shards of glass that suddenly erupted as space broke all around the Taotie, stabbing and slashing its still-weak body. The pillar sank further as Cha Ming mustered everything he had—angelic power, demigod power, and transcendent power—and poured it into the gray pillar.

But it wasn't enough. Still not enough. At that moment, Feng Ming appeared. He wielded a now-cracked spear, which he stabbed into one of the creature's many mouths, and to everyone's surprise, detonated it. Shards of transcendent metal exploded and bit into the creature, and as they did, Cha Ming felt his fortunes change. Feng Ming had used the last of his strength and sacrificed his lucky weapon, and then he'd blessed him, granting him whatever luck he could.

At the same time, the Sea God Emperor wielded the power of his crown. His body grew tenfold, and he took out his trident and stabbed it into the Taotie, who bellowed in pain. Beside him, Gong Shuren's white skin glowed blue with runic light. A giant clock tower appeared and slammed down atop the pillar, forcing it further down into the Taotie and freezing time for the beast as everything else around it still flowed, harming the creature.

But it could only hold so long. The Taotie roared and flailed, lashing out, and finally broke the time containment, sending Gong Shuren and Gong Xuandi flying. Feng Ming, who'd retreated earlier, rescued them. As they retreated, they heard an angry cry. A projection of a fiery phoenix appeared. The ancestor of the Phoenix Cry Empire burned her bloodline, summoning an avatar of her ancestor. And though the damage to her cultivation wouldn't be permanent, her lifespan would be greatly reduced. The phoenix flew into the Taotie, burning the freshly regrown flesh where Gong Xuandi and Feng Ming had stabbed.

It's still not enough, Cha Ming thought. *We need more.* As he thought this, he saw a golden flash. Gong Lan appeared, burning bright golden sunlight. Her soul was no longer resplendent—it was transcendent. *What the hell is she thinking, breaking through when she's so weak?*

The heavens roared in protest, summoning calamity lightning to fight her like it did the shepherd that he'd fought in Bastion.

But in the face of certain death, she simply smiled. "Nine-Story Sealing Pagoda," she said. A golden building appeared, smashing atop the Clear Sky Pillar, shoving it downward. Unfortunately, this left her defenseless. A single bolt of lightning struck her, reducing her body to ashes, leaving a golden soul to be whisked away by the Yellow River.

"Damn it all," Cha Ming said, clenching his teeth. Another friend, gone. Breathing deeply, he activated Thirty-Six Heavenly Transformations one more time. His soul burned under the pressure, but he ignored it as he forced the pillar further down, and it touched something solid. It was the core of the Taotie's being that had been exposed by Feng Ming and the others.

Helpless, his soul screamed as he activated yet another taxing ability, Words of Creation, which he'd learned upon transcending. It overdrew on his wounded soul and drew on his depleted qi stores; it drew on his liquified elemental essence and elemental evanescence. Words of Creation was just like it sounded: it allowed him to create things he knew instantly, as long as he had the soul force, creation qi, and raw materials he required.

Five talismans materialized—Energy, Matter, Shape, Flow, and Samsara. They flew out to their respective pillars, which glowed with elemental runes as they were strengthened. For a few precious seconds, the elements bent themselves even further to his will, a much more powerful interaction than his domain would normally allow. The pillar sank again, and though the core resisted them, Cha Ming could sense cracks forming on it.

"Huxian!" Cha Ming yelled. "Is that all you've got, you wimp?"

"I just wanted you to use your trump card first," Huxian yelled as he floated in the skies, controlling the phoenix and dragon manifestations.

"Together?" Cha Ming asked, mentally preparing himself for the inevitable excruciating pain he would feel.

"Fine. Together!" Huxian yelled. "Manifestation: Space-Time Devouring!"

"First Word of Destruction: Ruin!" Cha Ming yelled.

The black portion of his prismatic domain came to life, and the dark qi in his Dantian rushed outside his body. It ruined his body and soul as it exited, reducing what it touched to ashes. It didn't create a character; instead, it became a sound. But the sound called Ruin made the Taotie fall apart, just as his own body and soul were eroding. He'd used four abilities that overtaxed his soul, something unthinkable in normal circumstances, never mind while fighting a Taotie after first overcoming a tribulation.

As the word of destruction struck the Taotie's body, a gray light appeared as a maelstrom, revealing a giant projection of a fox. The burning white dragon and the dark phoenix cried as they became nothing more than shadows in the fox's eyes. The fox opened its mouth, and little by little, bits and pieces of the Taotie flew inside. He was somehow consuming devouring incarnate.

As pieces flew off, Cha Ming's Grandmist Pillar sank deeper, and then he heard a loud crack. Cha Ming lifted the pillar and slammed it down with the strongest Origin Strike he'd ever manifested. He poured in domain strength from all five elements, which congealed into a single gray misty point at the tip of the pillar and slammed down onto the Taotie's fiend core, which shattered.

A gray mist expanded there, and it struggled with Huxian's space-time devouring ability. Both of them raced to consume as much of the Taotie as possible. As they did so, the manifestations of the four others gave out. The four demons collapsed to the ground, which was now free of tentacles and bones, as they'd been completely consumed or eradicated.

Cha Ming, who was still weak and sweaty from the battle, still held on to the massive pillar, which stood atop shattered pieces of the fiendish core and a black swirl he now knew was its soul. The black fragments and the mist swirled into the gray pillar, and the black characters finally disappeared as the Taotie's soul joined Zhou Li's. It sealed its power—or what was left of it—and the heavens crackled lightly in triumph. The transcendents released their powers out of reflex, but the gray clouds of lightning didn't dissipate. Instead, they poured a healing rain.

Within the nearest few miles, there was nothing but desolation. The Great Redwood Forest, or at least half of it, had been reduced to smoldering ashes. So, too, had many of their companions. Only a handful of transcendents were left, and most of them were maimed beyond recognition.

It was the end of an era, but also the beginning of another. They would rebuild a new world from the ashes. With that thought, Cha Ming fell unconscious. Darkness took him as the wounds on his body and soul took their due. Would he ever wake? It was difficult to say. No matter what happened, he had no regrets.

Chapter 28:
Mourning

Rise and shine, sleepyhead," a voice said, waking Cha Ming from the deepest sleep he'd had in years. A curtain was flung open, filling the room with a soft yellow light. He wanted nothing to do with that light. He pulled his blankets closer, but they were pulled off. By human hands, not foxy paws like he expected.

Right. Huxian had a human form now. That would take getting used to.

Cha Ming reluctantly opened his eyes as he probed his body, looking for residual injuries. To his surprise, however, he found none. He looked around and realized why. Yue Bing was sitting at the foot of his bed, exhausted.

"Although you're healed, Master, you'd best not do anything strenuous for the next day," she said. "You've been out for—"

"One day, seven hours, forty-seven minutes, and six seconds," Cha Ming said, surprising himself.

Huxian, still holding his blanket—though he'd somehow had time to fold it—grinned. It seemed that since Huxian's breakthrough, his ability to sense time had improved to the point he could keep track of it without even being conscious. A useful ability.

"He's made of tough stuff, little niece," Huxian said, tossing the blanket on a short table beside the bed.

Yue Bing sniffed. "He may be my master and you his brother, but

I'll be damned if I call a teenager 'uncle.'"

"How—how dare you!" Huxian said, looking to Cha Ming. "Cha Ming, please teach your disciples some manners."

To which Cha Ming rolled his eyes and stepped out of bed. He stretched his body from side to side, testing his reknit flesh. Now that the battle was over, the massive strength he had access to was gone. His body reflexively hid it within, shielding it from the plane's watchful eyes. And though technically, he could unleash it whenever he wanted to, he sensed that strange shackles would appear to restrain him should he choose to do so. It was for that reason that he'd been able to defeat the blood master in Bastion and the Wang family's ancestor. He hadn't been fighting full transcendents, but transcendents with weights attached to their arms and legs. It was a humbling revelation.

"My body's all right," Cha Ming said. "Though my qi will need some work." He thought for a moment before summoning a wisp of his domain-infused creation qi. In response, the heavens rumbled. They didn't appreciate his meddling.

"Stop that this instant, you dummy!" Sun Wukong said, appearing outside the brush. Only Cha Ming could see the man, but he quickly heeded his advice. "The plane won't play nice with you from now on," the Monkey King continued. "And it won't just harm your body and qi, but also your soul. Which, might I add, is badly damaged."

Cha Ming looked within his spiritual sea and found Sun Wukong's prognosis to be accurate. His transcendent soul, which he could technically send out of his body whenever he wished, was much dimmer than usual. Before, it had been almost corporeal, but now, it looked like a wet bedsheet held out in the sun, barely able to stop light from crossing through its thin surface.

"All right, then," Cha Ming said. "Thank you so much for your care, Yue Bing."

"It's no problem, Master," Yue Bing said. "This is my calling, and you're not the only one I've been caring for."

Cha Ming nodded. He sensed a few other strong presences here, though none of them were from the South. He recognized one of them as Feng Ming, and another as the Long Clan ancestor. The last remaining one was a craftsman who looked over the Huoshan Kingdom. Though he wasn't technically affiliated with anyone, most people knew not to test his patience and attack the place.

"Let's go for a walk," Cha Ming said.

Huxian, who was fiddling with his hands nervously—probably unsure of what to do with them—followed him as he walked out of the house.

"You're going to need to stop all that fidgeting eventually."

Huxian pouted. "Human forms are great for some things and inconvenient for others. No one judges you when you scratch, shake, or shiver in demon form."

Cha Ming chuckled. "So why did you take on a human form, anyway?"

"It's not exactly a secret," Huxian said. "Our true forms become a little inefficient when we transcend, both inside and outside of combat. That, and we're huge. Our energy density is a little low, so we need to compress it. That's why our ancestors came up with the great idea of mimicking humans. By condensing a human body and splitting our power between the new body and our weapon, we can increase our battle prowess by several multiples."

"And what about those manifestations I saw?" Cha Ming asked. "Is that your true body?"

"Naw," Huxian said. "That's something we call our Authority. As initiates, we're granted a dominion, and that dominion grants us power over nature. Specifically, it lets us rally our element. Or bolster it. For some demons, that makes them quite weak in some settings, but since my element is space-time, I'm literally strong everywhere. It's overpowered."

"Good to know," Cha Ming said. They left the makeshift house, which was one of a few in a larger encampment filled with tents and campfires. The soil, which had been rich and plentiful, was now covered in a thin layer of dust. Any redwoods that had been present in the nearest ten miles were gone. "Taotie are terrible things, aren't they?"

"Tell me about it," Feng Ming said, walking out from another building. He held out his hand, and Cha Ming clasped it. "Good to see you up and about so fast."

"Same to you," Cha Ming said. "I'm sorry for your loss." The man's lucky spear had been very dear to him. He'd only gotten it back for less than a week before having to sacrifice it in battle.

"Bah," Feng Ming said. "Others have lost far more. Who am I to complain with what happened to Gong Lan?"

"True," Cha Ming said. He remembered her last brilliant moment, striking out against the darkness before the heavens consumed her. She'd sacrificed everything to defend the plane.

The trio walked toward a crater in the distance. It was surrounded by nine circles—one for each of the Tri-Sealing Pillars, and one for each of Huxian's friends. The four other pillars had been in the center, right atop the Taotie.

"How bad were the losses?" Cha Ming asked, dreading the answer.

"We lost all our transcendents but three, including myself," Feng Ming said. "I'm not counting the Phoenix Cry Ancestor, who suffered wounds so terrible she decided to undergo Phoenix Nirvana, reverting back to the form of a mortal infant. Only a single transcendent from the South survived. He fled as soon as the battle was over, as he was suspicious that we wouldn't honor our word and would attack him."

"Typical," Cha Ming said. They hadn't signed a contract, and anything not enforced by a contract was suspect in the South. "Half-step transcendents?"

"A dozen," Feng Ming said. "Two Northern ones for every Southern one. They fled along with their transcendent, likely to carve up what they could south of the wall while we're busy recovering."

"A smart move," Cha Ming said. "I doubt the North will be in any position to deal with external threats or retaliation for at least fifty years."

"Maybe even a hundred," Feng Ming admitted. "Every powerhouse is precious, and no one would dare risk them fighting for territory. Better to preserve what you can. On the bright side, this will make achieving peace in the North so much easier. Let's see who dares squabble in meetings while I'm lurking in the shadows."

Cha Ming chuckled, then his expression fell. "You said three including yourself."

Feng Ming grimaced. "I'm sorry. We didn't find Wang Jun. What remains of the Wang family is rallying behind the influential Wang Bing. Though their funds are completely depleted, they still have a lot of business and logistical knowhow. The North needs them, so I'm sure it won't be long before they're back in power."

Cha Ming had been hoping the young master had survived, but he'd seen how vicious the Taotie's strike had been. Even if he'd survived the impact, every bone in his body would have been broken, not to mention the devouring power that would have accompanied it.

"Let's hope he turns up," Cha Ming said. They both understood searching for him was meaningless. Too many things had been destroyed by the Taotie, and very few of them had left behind any remnants.

"The remaining elites from our battle near the World Tree have returned to their kingdoms to stabilize the situation, stamp out devil cults, stem rebellions, and aid the civilian militia," Feng Ming continued. "Even if Wang Jun has fallen, he changed the continent. His legacy will live on."

Thanks to his cultivation-endowment investment, the North had entered a new industrial age. And the best part about it was it would take no time at all for them to get back to work. Every single person, no matter how weak, could contribute to the recovery of their nation. What he'd seen in Quicksilver was only a precursor. Soon, billions of innovative minds would shape the fate of the continent.

"It's too bad not everyone can see it," Cha Ming said.

Hong Xin, though she'd lost her cultivation, had been relatively lucky. Gong Lan and Wang Jun hadn't made it. Out of their original group, only Cha Ming and Feng Ming had come out relatively unscathed, though Feng Ming had lost his weapon. This was the price of war; they'd walked into it knowingly. He could only wish the karma they earned would give them a better life in the next one. As for Zhou Li and the nameless fiend whisperer, they were no longer a problem. Only the enemy general might show up in the future, though Wang Jun's assurances that he'd "handled" him implied he wouldn't. It would be up to Feng Ming to search for him, and if he found him, constrain him.

They left the crater behind them and flew toward what remained of the Great Redwood Forest. At the edge of the tree line, Silverwing, Gua, and Lei Jiang were basking in the sunlight. They weren't fond of human encampments, despite their human forms and human clothes, preferring the thick demonic energy that still pervaded the area. Beside them was an old gray-haired man.

"Jun Xiezi," Cha Ming said as he landed. The man turned around and smiled. He only had one arm, Cha Ming noticed, the other having been cut off between his shoulder and his elbow. "You've seen better days."

"This?" Jun Xiezi said, looking at the stump dismissively. "I'll get it healed eventually. It's not a big deal to find an alchemist—or a blood doctor, for that matter—who can heal me. I put it off, though. Many other people need the help more than I do. Besides, it's an interesting experience, wandering the world, itching to paint but reaching for air."

"You fared better than the forest," Cha Ming said, looking down at the ashen ground. The forest ended abruptly, and many large red tree trunks had been cut in half. A small mercy was that Jun Xiezi's village had been spared. Two miles of forest still stood between them and the edge of the cataclysm that had consumed the rest of the greenery.

"You've changed, you know," Jun Xiezi said, bending over. He used his left hand to dig a pit out of the dust, ignoring the qi he could normally access. "But in some ways, you're still the same. Didn't I tell you that the trees support each other?" He dug down a full foot before finding a root. To Cha Ming's surprise, a green sprout was already growing upward. "Give it a few days, and this entire wasteland will be crawling with tiny seedlings. The demons will move back, and the demonic energy will feed the forest. Nothing short of destroying this entire woodland, its guardian half-initiate, and the Leyline of Wood would cause its destruction."

Cha Ming chuckled as he bent over and uncovered another sapling. "Life is so wonderful and mysterious. Even in death, it springs up anew."

"*Especially* in death," Jun Xiezi said. He pushed the pile of soil he'd dug out back onto the sapling. "The dust might seem lifeless, but it contains everything the sapling needs. One might say that without the forest's destruction, this sapling would never have grown. Just as destruction leads to creation, death inevitably leads to life."

"And that's the circle called samsara," Cha Ming said.

"Exactly," Jun Xiezi said. "You're young, but not as young as you used to be. It seems you did a fair bit of living in the past year."

"You could say that," Cha Ming said. He looked back up to Feng Ming, who was staring southeast. Toward the Song Kingdom and its capital, Songjing. "Is your wife all right?"

"She's doing well, as are our children," Feng Ming said. "I'd like to see them right away, but there're still a few matters to take care of. For one, I need to organize allied forces in pushing the Southerners back. For another, there's still a funeral to preside over."

"When and where?" Cha Ming asked.

"Where the World Tree used to be," Feng Ming said. "I hear all the Northern leaders will be there, and the Sea God Emissary and the Sea God Emperor will also be going. We're making it a funeral for all the fallen. There're just too many dead without leaving a body."

"I'll be there," Cha Ming said.

Feng Ming stayed a while, then excused himself, leaving Cha Ming with Huxian, his friends, and Jun Xiezi. Exhausted and emotionally traumatized by the whole experience, he took out a canvas and joined the older man. While he tried to paint his feelings, his friend took a stab at painting left-handed. The results were atrocious, but the laughter was priceless.

"When will you leave?" Jun Xiezi asked.

Cha Ming knew he wasn't talking about leaving the forest.

"Soon," Cha Ming said. "After I tie up a few loose ends. Speaking of which, when I've healed a bit, I'll make you those talismans I promised."

"No need," Jun Xiezi said, waving his good arm. "I hardly need your pitiful insights on living and dying. And besides, it's not worth it for you to suffer the plane's punishment to give them to me."

"Thanks," Cha Ming said. Having tasted the plane's punishment firsthand, he agreed with the man.

Three days passed as they sat there, drinking and painting. Three wonderful days filled with comedic entertainment. Huxian and his friends, careful to contain their power as much as possible, sparred daily to get used to their human forms. They also played games to practice dexterity and agility. Mr. Mountain was the obvious loser of these exchanges, but it wasn't Huxian who won most of them. Rather, Lei Jiang and Silverwing were tied, and it took a lot of convincing by Huxian and the others to not let them come to serious blows and attract heavenly tribulation.

At the end of the third night, a few hours before dawn, Feng Ming came to visit again. "Are you ready?" he asked.

"Let's go," Cha Ming said. They flew southeast as a group toward what was left of the World Tree Monastery.

The sun had not yet risen when they arrived at the mountain. They skipped the formerly enchanted steps that used to lead to the peak, as those had been torn up in the assault on the World Tree. Though blood still stained the mountain, the corpses had been cleaned up and buried.

The monk quarters and the temple, formerly in pristine condition given all the sweeping the monks tended to do, were broken remnants. Monks still lived there, however, as evidenced by wet robes that hung outside the doors to dry, and bed mats that could be seen through broken walls. The monks were standing in orderly ranks before the burnt husk of the World Tree. Not a trace of life remained within it, nor could Cha Ming sense anything several hundred feet down thanks to his affinity for wood.

The crowd here wasn't large. Most men didn't have the time to spare to attend. But representatives from every country in the North were present, including many monarchs. Even Song Guo was here representing the Song Kingdom. Feng Ming flew to her and embraced her, leaving Cha Ming with Huxian and his misfit friends.

They waited for an hour for others to arrive. They came in pairs or fours, but never more than that, as space on the plateau was limited. There were people from trade associations—Cha Ming recognized many from Quicksilver and his short time in the Evergreen Empire. And when it seemed like no one else would come, representatives from Haijing came, which included Gong Xuandi, their new Sea God Emperor, and Gong Shuren, the Sea God Emissary. They came with a procession of several dozen important royals and scholars, which was only fitting given the devastating losses they'd suffered fighting the Taotie.

Unsure of where they fit in with all the guests, Gong Xuandi and Gong Shuren made their way to Cha Ming and Huxian, who had gathered the few demons who cared about the life and death of their comrades. Though demons were usually indifferent to such things, it was honorable to remember the fallen. Gong Lan's brother was also near them, sitting beside monks he'd befriended many years ago.

"I'm glad you could make it," Cha Ming said, bowing lightly.

"I'm glad all of us could make it," Gong Shuren said, returning the bow. "It was a close call for everyone on the plane." The battle with the Taotie had forced them out of hiding, for fighting such an atrocity didn't break their rule of non-interference. Survival was paramount.

Discussions continued for several minutes until suddenly, a chime sounded. A monk—a middle-resplendent soul cultivator who wasn't too impressive—walked up to a dais with the oddest of companions: a chaplain of the Church of Justice. As a result of this war, there were no more chancellors or vice chancellors. Those were transcendent positions, and all their transcendents had perished.

"Amituofo," the monk said.

"Greetings from the goddess of light," the chaplain said.

"It is unusual for such a ceremony to take place," the monk continued. "We monks hold vigils for deceased members and extended ceremonies for our leaders, but it has been thousands of years since so many have died."

"Indeed, I have never done anything with a monk, but everything from here on must be done in the spirit of cooperation," the chaplain said. "Truth and propriety are important, but doing good comes before all else. Closure is important for us to move forward with rebuilding our nations, our religions, and in many cases, our families."

"Though I've never had a family in the usual sense," the monk said, "I can also relate with this great loss. My family—the monks I grew up with, my parents, the leaders of our order—is dead. Only a few scattered relatives remain. Though it saddens me to only make their acquaintance in difficult circumstances, I am glad they are there when I most need them."

"Family can also be extended to those outside your order," the chaplain said. "For example, I can count this monk, Tou He, as a brother. We are supporting each other in difficult times and giving each other the strength we need. We've lost much, bled much. Relatives can help you in ways others can't."

He paused for a moment, allowing everyone to soak in what he'd said. Then he held out his hand to the blackened husk behind him. "I never knew of the World Tree growing up. I was raised in a religious family, and I'd always been told that goodness sprang from truth and passion, and both were necessary to make the world a better place. It was only after being made a chaplain that I learned of this tree's influence—the influence everyone here was made aware of the moment it was destroyed. It had a karmic attachment to all of us—blessing us with a predisposition for good despite our ability to choose either light or darkness."

"Though it did not give a preference to the monk's unfettered path," Tou He said, "it is as Chaplain Tong says. Good people are more likely to see value in alleviating suffering. This, in combination with our reclusive lifestyle, made us ideal guardians for the World Tree and its peaceful aura. Ironically, when the World Tree left us, we were most acutely aware of its influence and karma. It was a tree of life, and a tree of peace. It kept the world unified."

"Peace is something we must strive for even now," Chaplain Tong said. "For while vengeance might seem appealing, peace and stability are what the common people need. It is for them that we must rebuild, instead of giving in to the avariciousness of expansion."

"For the wielder of a sword cuts twice," Tou He said. "Once his opponent, and another himself. Violence can only cause loss, while plowing a field can only lead to gain."

"But enough of the future," Chaplain Tong said. "Let us turn to the remnants of the World Tree. We grieve for it, yes, but more so, we grieve for our loved ones. There are too many to count, and too many to gather. Let the tree stand in for the fallen so that we may respect them. Everyone, light your incense sticks."

They did so, Cha Ming using a minute amount of flame qi to light his up, and many others did the same for their neighbors. Thousands of trailing wisps of smoke floated into the air. They gathered around the World Tree's dead trunk, which seemed to drink in their prayers.

May the world become a better place, Cha Ming thought. *Though I won't be around to see it. I hope the heavens have mercy and bless my disciples, Feng Ming, and everyone else as they rebuild.* He infused this prayer into the incense smoke with his soul. It wandered to the World Tree like the others, clinging to its blackened bark.

They spent an incense time in silence, waiting five minutes for the last of the sticks to end their slow, fragrant burn. When they finished, they dropped to their knees, mimicking the chaplain and the monk.

"We kowtow once to remember our first meeting," Chaplain Tong said, smacking his forehead to the ground.

Cha Ming kowtowed, and as he did, he thought of his first match with Gong Lan, where he'd thrown her out of the ring. He thought of the time when Wang Jun woke Cha Ming at dawn, introducing himself as a new roommate and treating him to supper that same night. Though over a hundred years had passed for Cha Ming, these memories were still fresh in his mind. They fed the sadness in his heart, which was only amplified by the strange faces that came to mind, those rapid acquaintances in the heat of battle just before they died.

"We kowtow a second time to remember all they did for us," Tou He said, slapping his head to the ground. The others followed, and Cha Ming was lost in deep thought. In only a few seconds, he recalled an entire lifetime of knowing them. For Wang Jun, he remembered the man giving up ten years of his life to bless Huxian. Then, when Cha Ming fell off the Greatwood Bridge, he posted a bounty and came running the moment he resurfaced. Later, in Songjing, he saved Cha Ming from Zhou Li's curse by taking him to the Church of Justice, the place where he was least welcome on the continent.

Many years passed before they saw each other again, and when they did, they drank. They remembered their mutual losses together and their disappointment with what life had taken from them. Much time passed again, and this time, he wasn't sure if Wang Jun was an enemy or ally. He chose to believe in their friendship, and together, they ended the Wang family's rebellion.

During the war, they had been comrades. It was the same with Gong Lan. Though Cha Ming hadn't spent much time with her, what little time they had spent together had been spent fighting. That was ironic, given her occupation as monk. Together, they'd fought back the corruption invading the Song Kingdom's Seal of Pure Jade. Then, after much time apart, they'd fought against the tide of Southerners hell bent on destroying the World Tree. Despite her wounds, she'd continued on, fighting to the bitter end against the Taotie. She'd sacrificed herself to land just one more blow against the creature, to spit in the eye of destruction in case it tilted the scales in their favor.

Though she'd lived a sinful life early on, she'd more than made up for it with her later actions. Gong Lan was the most selfless person he'd ever known. He only wished such a tragic ending hadn't befallen her, and so shortly after seeing the World Tree she guarded burn down and the monks she led die by the thousands.

"We kowtow a third time... to say goodbye," Tou He and Chaplain Tong said together, smacking their heads on the rocky platform. Their foreheads were bleeding and raw, a testament to their sincerity. And though Cha Ming wished he could do the same, the plane wouldn't tolerate him generating enough force to wound himself.

His forehead hit the soft ground, and he pictured his two dearly departed friends. One was wreathed in shadows, smiling despite the sad story of his life, and the other was wreathed in the golden light of redemption and atonement for what she'd done. Both were imperfect. Both weren't saints. But they'd done what they could in the end, giving it all up for the chance of a better future.

One day, if I die, Cha Ming thought, *I'll die the same way. Fighting for what I believe in, making the world a better place.* With this thought came great pain. He remembered another loss—the loss of Yu Wen, who had sacrificed herself to fight the Curse Sovereign. He also remembered the loss of Hong Xin's cultivation, yet her willingness to throw herself in harm's way to protect those she loved.

Sacrifice and faith; they were both intertwined. One did not sacrifice himself with certainty, for by dying, you gave up all control over the situation. It was only hope for a better future and hope for others that could drive someone to lay it all down. Sacrifice was the ultimate gamble, and the ultimate freedom.

With this thought, a glow appeared on his white wings—the transparent wings no one could see unless he wished it. It was the Thirty-Six Heavenly Transformations, his new soul-cultivation method. He no longer advanced through normal means, but through personal experience and realization. Through this change in outlook, his soul broke through to the second stage of the lower transcendent soul realm. Each stage was divided into four, and each set of four corresponded to a full cultivation realm. This soul cultivation would develop his wings.

This new breakthrough in his soul connected him to his surroundings like never before. He felt each individual soul gathered mourning, and their intentions, as they wafted toward the World Tree. They mingled before diving into its dying husk of a trunk, which seemed to accept their faith as an offering, sending them down to the plane's core where they would be well received.

But why? Cha Ming thought, realizing the oddity. He opened his eyes, frowning as he glanced up to the trunk. He felt around with his soul, but it only traveled a mile down before stopping. Was there something deeper he hadn't noticed? Ignoring the frightened crowds, he flew to the World Tree and placed his hand on the trunk, interrupting the ceremony.

"Sir, I know you are grieving, but—" Chaplain Wu said.

"Quiet," Cha Ming said. He closed his eyes and listened. All around him, hearts were beating beneath the soft chatter he had caused by flying over. The trembling winds caused the stubby broken branches on the trunk to sway. "Huxian, some help?"

His fox brother and his four friends appeared around the trunk. Using Huxian as a medium, they poured the strength of their souls into Cha Ming.

Empowered by their support, Cha Ming's soul delved deeper, reaching three miles down. It was said that the roots of the World Tree traveled as deep as the world's core, and Cha Ming was starting to believe it.

He embraced his wood domain, unleashing his qi, and above him, lightning crackled and stuck him, wounding his body and soul. Lei Jiang was able to mitigate some of the damage, but he could only do so much. The lightning hurt, but Cha Ming ignored it as he searched for a softer sound: a light pulsing sound that drew in the hope-filled incense smoke.

His qi and soul force traveled down the charred trunk, not seeing a speck of life in the process. By the time they reached six miles deep, he was about to give up before Huxian spoke.

"I smell something," he whispered. This encouraged Cha Ming, who continued downward. Seven miles. Eight miles. Then finally, nine miles. At the nine-mile mark, he finally saw what he was looking for: a crystalline core that shone with a power far beyond him. It was connected to many natural energy lines, one of which Cha Ming recognized as the Leyline of Gold.

Yet it wasn't these mystical natural objects that baffled him—it was the single green speck he saw at the very end of the World Tree's longest root. It was a spark of life, so carefully hidden that even karma-destroying sin flames hadn't destroyed it. It had taken refuge on the plane's core itself. Which made sense, Cha Ming realized. It had implanted itself in the world's most fertile place.

"Feng Ming, transcendents, anyone above core formation!" Cha Ming yelled. "Come here!"

His voice carried authority no one dared question. Even Gong Shuren, the apathetic Sea God Emissary followed his lead. As lightning raged above him, he invoked words of creation. Five talismans appeared around him, all transcendent, drawing the plane's ire. He shielded them with his transcendent power, personally absorbing the damage.

"Everyone, lend me your strength!" he said. They didn't question him and poured it into him unconditionally. Cha Ming used the five talismans to pour in the vast amounts of energy, and as it traveled, it destroyed the trunk and roots of the ancient tree. By the time the first trickle of energy reached the seed, all of the old wood had vanished, becoming only the purest nutrients for the new sapling.

He poured and poured until nothing was left, and poured more still, ignoring the lightning that beat down on him, charring his flesh and soul. He only stopped when the last of those linked were drained, and Huxian and friends collapsed to the ground, unable to move.

Cha Ming kneeled, then nodded to Gong Shuren. He hadn't drawn her power on purpose. Realizing his intention, she summoned the Sea God Clock Tower, which appeared above the mountain in blue-gold perfection. It radiated a soft aura of time, which she didn't project outward in a bubble, but downward. Time compressed all the way down to the world's core, and though Cha Ming couldn't see it happening, he was filled with anticipation.

One minute. Two minutes. Three minutes passed. Then, suddenly, the ground erupted, and gnarled branches jutted out, full of vitality. An aura of peace and prosperity filled the air as karmic tethers that had been cut days ago reestablished themselves. The World Tree grew at an accelerated rate until it reached half its original height, halting for a moment before budding. Pink and purple flowers bloomed for only a few seconds before covering the entire mountain peak with a beautiful carpet. And once the last of the flowers had fallen, it grew thin foliage that rapidly thickened, blocking out the bright noon sun and covering all of them in its plentiful shade.

Then, and only then, did they know true peace. Acceptance washed over them. A willingness to move on filled them. And every man and woman, without exception, began to weep.

Many things might have gone wrong. They'd lost so many. But this momentous miracle, this nirvana rebirth, gave them all a new lease on life. It was a turning point for everyone, a beacon of hope that could see them through any struggle. It was a clarion call for battle, leading the charge toward a new beginning.

The Taotie and the South had damaged so much, but from the ashes rose new life. It was like the Phoenix Cry Ancestor undergoing nirvana rebirth. It was like the Great Redwood Forest nurturing new saplings in the ashes of devastation. There was no need for an aura of glum hopelessness. Everything would be all right in the end.

No one said a word as they said their own silent prayers and trickled off the plateau one after another. Even Cha Ming's disciples went their separate ways without greeting their master, careful not to waste a single moment of this new inspiration the tree had given them.

"Goodbye, Gong Lan," Cha Ming said. "Goodbye, Wang Jun." He turned his back to the World Tree, and together with Huxian and friends, he flew southward.

"Where to next?" Huxian asked. He was controlling himself, but Cha Ming could see pent-up frustration at the plane's restrictions.

"To tie up loose ends," Cha Ming said. "I won't take long, I promise."

Epilogue

Dying wasn't at all like Gong Lan expected. Yes, Gong Lan. That was her name, wasn't it? She remembered the burst of lightning that had ended her life but very little before or after that. Here, she was but one of many souls floating peacefully through the Yellow River.

She didn't struggle as the yellow waters enveloped her pure white soul, its guardians mostly ignoring her as they focused their attention on more tarnished individuals. The judges that gnawed away at the sin of yellow souls seemed to know everything about her, like it was all written down on some sort of ledger. It was these deeds that would decide her future fate and reincarnation.

What would win out, she wondered? Would it be the bloodthirsty warmonger who slaughtered men at the drop of a hat? Or would it be the calm Buddhist monk who'd done her all to protect her realm? Likely, a balance would be struck, a middle ground that gave her a chance at redemption through a fresh start in different circumstances. Repetition led to eventual progress on the eternal journey toward salvation.

The river dragged her along, and in the distance, Gong Lan saw a large bridge. It was the Bridge of Forgetfulness, where employees tossed down tea leaves, a final hurdle to cross before her eventual reincarnation. She dreaded the thought of forgetting, but she knew it was inevitable, so she braced herself, closing her eyes, not opening them until the feeling of hard land awakened her.

Where am I? she thought, looking around. She was still several hundred meters away from the bridge but had somehow washed up on a beach near a large tree. The tree had tall, gnarled branches and coffee-colored bark, and its leaves were of the purest emerald. Beneath that tree sat a golden figure, a bald man wearing pristine white robes. His eyes were closed, and all around him, ghosts sat, meditating peacefully. Not knowing what to do, she sat before him, closing her eyes and calming herself as well.

Years seemed to pass, and perhaps years did. One after another, those beside her disappeared. It wasn't until only she was left that the man finally opened his eyes. He smiled a gentle, almost paternal smile. "You have done well," the man said. "Congratulations on making it this far, child."

Gong Lan's soul shivered. "Are you Siddhartha Buddha?" she asked.

"I am, and I am not," the man replied. "Being and not being, they intersect. Much like karma connects us and at the same time frees us. Everyone is connected, so we are everyone at the same time."

"I'm afraid I don't understand," Gong Lan said. "Isn't being unfettered what Buddhism is all about?"

"Perhaps," the man said. "But it is also about salvation. About ending suffering. Is not great karma incurred when fighting against evil men?"

Gong Lan thought to argue against him, but who was she to speak? She'd done just what he was saying, sown karma with an entire plane in order to save it. "Why am I here instead of in the river, passing under the Bridge of Forgetfulness?" she asked.

The man took his time to answer. "You are here because you have a choice to make," he said after some time. "You have severed enough karma through atonement, making it possible for you to escape the cycle of reincarnation. If you so choose, you may follow me. I will deliver you to a place, safe and sound, free from all suffering."

Gong Lan frowned. She hadn't thought this was a possibility.

Didn't she have a long way to go before that was allowed? "You said a choice. What is the other option?" she asked cautiously.

The man gave her a knowing smile. He extended his hand, summoning a projection of the Yellow River. One branch led to emptiness, and another to a large pool surrounded by six others. "You may choose to reenter the cycle of reincarnation. The path of the Buddha is one way, but the path of the bodhisattva is another."

"A vow to never to become a Buddha, until the last soul is saved," Gong Lan whispered.

The man smiled and nodded, leaving her to her thoughts. She longed for that unfettered feeling that she had tasted for a brief moment as she meditated beneath the Bodhi Tree's tall branches. But did she truly deserve it? Was there still more she could accomplish? "Will I remember anything? My purpose? My mission?"

"No," the man said. "That is the risk you take. Endless lifetimes before realizing your entrapment, only coming to realize your true purpose after an undetermined amount of time, where you can only do your best to save a few helpless souls. It is a thankless mission, one which will take an eternity to accomplish. Even I do not see how it ends."

She could hardly fault the man for his honesty. "So it's my choice? My decision?"

The man nodded.

She took a deep breath. "I choose to reincarnate."

"Very well," the man said, glancing at the river. "You must reenter the river yourself. You have refused once. You will have to do so twice again."

Gong Lan nodded and stood up. She bowed to the man and walked over to the river, throwing herself into the current. There, she became acutely aware of the other souls, which had been flayed to rid them of their sin, floating down the river toward the bridge. Just beside that bridge, she saw a river branch. A bypass she knew she could take. She firmly refused it.

As she passed the bridge, tea leaves floated around her and dimmed her memories, casting her in a haze of forgetfulness. As her mind faded, she saw a light in the distance. She refused that light, that third chance, pushing it away, and finally, she let her soul forget as it made its way to the pool of reincarnation, where it would wait a sixty-year cycle before once again reincarnating.

"Phew," Yama said, standing up from beneath the tree. He banished the golden halo and summoned his black reaper robes. "That was a close one. You never know what they'll choose." Dealing with Buddhists was tricky, especially after they transcended. They weren't like normal people, who you could just push around like domesticated sheep. They could leave the river if they wanted, joining Diyu in their spirit form, completely subverting his fine-tuned system and stealing a precious soul from the universe's circulation.

In the past, Siddhartha had roamed these coasts, poaching souls by the dozens. Yama had been forced to put a stop to it, but for the sake of the stability of the universe, he'd struck up a bargain. Each individual would be left a choice, whether to join the Buddha in eternity or reenter the cycle. The truth of the matter was much more brutal. By accepting the Buddha's proposal, they'd join Siddhartha in Diyu where they would preach for all eternity. The injustice often drove monks mad, eventually corrupting them into evil spirits, further destabilizing the situation. Pangu, he hated that man.

"Another bullet dodged," he said, fading into his surroundings and reappearing in a much more important location: the front of City Hall, where ballots were being counted. Millions of ghost volunteers were hard at work. Numbers went up and down as the ballots were processed through an octuple check to avoid mistakes, the carefully crafted algorithm rooting out "accidental" miscounts through robust checks and balances against each counter's personality.

"It's going to be a close one," Usama said.

"Yeah, for the wrong people," Judah grumbled. He was currently second to last in the polling, having gathered only fifteen percent of the votes.

"It's not over till it's over," Yama said. Still, he sweated. He'd hoped Judah could gather at least twenty percent of the votes in the first round. Hours passed, and soon all the ballots were counted. Judah was now fifth among eight final contenders, four of them clear front-runners.

"There you have it," Judah said. "My goose is cooked."

"Patience," Yama said. "This isn't first past the post. We're civilized here." Which was lucky, because Ragthor the Bloodied was winning. He wasn't sure what he'd do if the barbarian won—he'd come close in many elections—but he was sure that the result would indeed be bloody, whether for the citizens of Diyu or their newly elected leader.

The official counts, which were floating in the air above City Hall, suddenly blurred as one of the names was dropped. Elsa of the Hive Mind jumped past Ragthor, and to Judah's surprise, his own standing increased by one place.

"It's preferential ballot," Yama explained. "It eliminates the weakest contenders one after another until there is a clear majority. You went up because you were a popular second choice. So was Elsa. A lot of people don't like the thought of getting slaughtered in war."

"But Elsa wants to control minds!" Judah exclaimed.

"Only ten percent at first," Yama said. "And living in mind-slavery is much better than dying to a lot of people."

As he said this, another name disappeared, leaving them with six. Judah climbed up again to third, displacing Galahad the Brave. Ragthor the Bloodied took back his lead and was sitting at a cozy thirty-five percent. Judah had inched his way up to thirty-one percent, while Elsa of the Hive Mind was at thirty-four percent.

The votes danced up and down, staying more or less the same with the next drop. Finally, Galahad's votes caused a large jump. Judah went up to second with thirty-four percent of the vote, and Ragthor went up to forty percent. Elsa of the Hive Mind dropped to twenty-six percent.

"What the hell?" Judah said. "Are you kidding me? How can so many people in Galahad's camp support Ragthor the Bloodied?"

"They're very practical," Yama said. "Rather than seeing people incapable of committing sin, they'd rather take matters into their own hands and kill as many evildoers as possible in the bicentennial wars."

"That's crazy," Judah said.

"We already established that they're all crazy," said Mary, one of his councillors.

"Wish me luck," Judah said, crossing his fingers.

Yama crossed his own fingers as well. He hoped his careful gerrymandering, his attack ads, and his coercion would bear fruit. The third and last name to be eliminated faded, and everyone let out a boo of indifference.

"Yes!" Yama yelled, contrary to the obvious disappointment of the crowds. "It worked! We did it!"

"I really don't feel like I won," Judah said, frowning as the crowd packed up and left instead of cheering like he expected.

"Our campaign wasn't centered around energizing a base," Mary said. "It was about abusing the system and making you the clear second-best choice to as many voters as possible. We thought it was highly likely that Ragthor, who draws great crowds, would come out as a strong contender, so we appealed to Elsa's followers, showing them how boring you were and how their lives would change very little. That pleased them, and as a result, everyone is displeased about the election but not as angry as they could be."

"I don't know what to say," Judah said, clearly disheartened.

"Don't say anything," Yama said, popping the cork off a bottle of champagne. He poured a tall glass for Judah and all the councillors present, giving a wink to many, as well as mental assurances that what they asked for would be given. The people didn't vote for mayors directly, after all, but for councillors who represented them.

Soon he would be flooded with phone calls and requests for interviews. The cycle of reincarnation would be saved, and the universe would continue. And his company would get back much of its lost talent, much to the detriment of Heaven and Hell.

He grinned as he pulled out his phone and sent a message to their respective leaders and chuckled as he pressed send. Then he added an emoji of him laughing.

"You lose!" it said. It was a good day to be alive in the land of the dead.

Two weeks had passed since Cha Ming had last visited, but already, the devastated city of Bastion was showing signs of activity. The Life-Leaching Monarch had already returned, but by now she'd been so intimidated by Huxian and his friends that she didn't dare crawl out of the Shattered Lands and cause any trouble. The Ji royal family, nearly devoid of powerhouses now that the war was over, tread a careful line between different political factions, keeping everyone happy at great cost to their near-empty treasury.

Many had died, but many still lived. They were slowly rebuilding from the bottom up. Which was good news for a certain thriving smithy and the attached weapon shop. Cha Ming observed every customer as they came and went, screening them for signs of trouble. He did so while eating at a familiar restaurant with three good friends.

"So, what will you do now that you're free?" Cha Ming asked as he ate his bowl of red curry noodles. The soup was both sweet and spicy, and somehow creamy despite the absence of dairy.

"Go home," He Yin said decisively. "And work myself to the bone making life better for them, I suppose. They'll need some powerhouse or another to stop some a local warlord from trying to take it over." Like the other two, he'd been imprisoned soon after the Breaker's failure. Fortunately, the three craftsmen were too valuable to just execute.

"Fair enough," Cha Ming said, looking to Shao Qiang. "What about you?"

"I'm not sure," Shao Qiang said. "I have no family left, and very few friends. But I've always wanted to go traveling."

"Do you want to go north of the wall?" Cha Ming asked. By now, they knew his real identity. He'd revealed it to force the few half-step transcendents there to release them.

"I don't think so," Shao Qiang said, shaking his head. "There's much of the South to explore, and I've always longed to go back to Haijing. Perhaps I'll find a way to make a breakthrough there before I die."

"And you?" Cha Ming asked Pan Su, who was busy eating the restaurant out of house and home. Apparently, she'd hated prison food and had refused to eat during her entire imprisonment. Though she didn't need to eat as a cultivator, she talked as though she'd been inches from death the entire time.

"No point in going anywhere," Pan Su said. "It's a well-kept secret, Pai Xiao—I mean Cha Ming—or whoever you are, but I'm *old*. Four hundred and seventy-six to be exact."

"But you behave like a young lady," He Yin protested. "You don't look a shade past three hundred."

"Thank you," Pan Su said. "And people say you can't talk to women."

They laughed.

"Well, I can't say my protection will last forever, but I'm pretty sure I scared all the nobles and powerhouses in the city by coming here," Cha Ming said. "And I may have dropped some not-so-subtle hints that I know the Life-Leaching Monarch. They won't bother you during your stay."

"Much obliged," Pan Su said. "I'll need the peace and quiet for when I start my last seclusion."

Last seclusion was a polite term referring to a cultivator's last-ditch effort. Either they would break through to the next realm, increasing their life span, or they would die trying. By then, the cultivator's fires of life burned too low, and they rarely succeeded.

"I don't know how much it will help, but here you are," Cha Ming said. He placed three bottles on the table, each containing a Grandmist rune-carving pill. After much trial and error, he'd discovered that crafting things inside the Clear Sky World did not incur the plane's wrath. In addition, his breakthrough had expanded and strengthened the mystical dimension. The space there was much more stable now, though it lacked something he could put his finger on to advance. "One for each of you. As an apology for lying."

"You didn't lie," Pan Su said, palming one of them. "You just didn't tell us the full truth. Who you really were still came through in our conversations and our dinners together."

"I won't say no to a free pill," He Yin said, coughing lightly.

Shao Qiang accepted his as well. Though these pills wouldn't guarantee their ascension, they'd double their chances of successfully carving their core, as small as it was. The tribulation would be up to them.

"When are you leaving?" Pan Su asked. "People usually give gifts like these at the end."

"I have one more person to visit in this city," Cha Ming said. "She's a well-kept secret."

They continued eating and drinking until night fell and the shop closed. Only then did Cha Ming excuse himself and walk out of the restaurant, crossing the street and entering the closed shop. He walked past the smiths working throughout the night and went up the stairs unnoticed.

He was greeted by cooking smells on the second floor. He sniffed and recognized the dish—barbecued bamboo shoots with a familiar sauce. It was the dish he'd cooked for Mo Ling that first night after rescuing her from the Blood Master Monastery. She hadn't forgotten it, despite having lost her memories.

Instead of introducing himself directly, Cha Ming walked past the dining room and into a side room, where a baby slept. The baby opened its eyes and blinked as it looked at him.

"Shh," he said, using his soul to soothe the baby and send him back to sleep. Then he took out a small white pill and shoved it into the baby's mouth. It became a small stream of energy that entered his still nascent qi pathways, nourishing them along with his Dantian so that eventually, he would gain exceptional cultivation talent.

"Who are you?" a voice said.

Cha Ming turned around and smiled at the woman holding a kitchen knife at him.

"Someone you know," Cha Ming said. "In case you're wondering, I gave a medicine to your baby. He'll grow strong and healthy. He'll become a cultivator, and a strong one at that."

"I said, who are you?" Mo Ling repeated, anger dripping from her voice but worry coming from her eyes as she looked toward her baby.

Cha Ming got out of the way and let her pick up the weak child, waking him to ensure nothing was wrong. Then, after probing him with her spiritual force, she placed him back in the crib.

"To what do I owe the pleasure of a visit from someone so powerful?" she said, motioning for Cha Ming to come. He followed, and to his surprise, she had him sit down and served up two plates.

"Just like that, you'll feed me?" Cha Ming asked, curious.

"I clearly can't do anything to you, can I? So I might as well charm you by feeding you," Mo Ling said.

"Clever," Cha Ming said, smiling wistfully. "You were always clever back in Ashes."

She frowned. "Do I know you?"

He chuckled and ran his hand across his face, revealing the gentle smith, Pai Xiao.

"Pai Xiao, what are you doing here?" she said harshly. "Get down!" she hissed, urging him to duck. "There are wanted posters for you all over the city!"

"Oh, I doubt they'll be up much longer," Cha Ming said. He'd seen to that when he'd revealed himself. "It's an interesting choice of dish, by the way," he commented, taking a bite of a bamboo shoot.

"I tried my best to replicate it," Mo Ling said, shaking her head. "It was hard to tell what it could have tasted like, as the man who cooked it accidentally burnt it."

"You need to apply the sauce in layers," Cha Ming said. "Three, to be exact. I missed the third when the bandits came."

Mo Ling dropped her fork, then looked up. "It can't be…" she said, her eyes reddening.

"It can," Cha Ming said, changing his face again. It was an appearance that only existed in her memories, one he'd inserted when tampering with them. "I'm sorry, Mo Ling, but it was out of necessity. I did it to protect yo—"

She leaped from her chair and hugged him. She sniffled and began to cry, and he hugged her as she did so. "Do you miss your home?" he asked between her cries.

"Every day," she sobbed. "But I was too scared to return."

"I did some digging before coming here," Cha Ming said. "Your family was removed from power after the incident, and they were forced to travel to a city called Nanjing. I also let them know of your survival and your address. You can expect a letter shortly."

"Thank you," she said, wiping away tears from her red eyes.

"I wish I could do more," Cha Ming said. "But there's only so much I can give you before attracting thieves and thugs." He pulled out five talismans from the Clear Sky World. They were poetic talismans at half-step-core grade. Powerful enough to be a deterrent but not so powerful that the treasure halo would be blinding to those who could sense it. "Stay safe, Mo Ling, and keep your son safe."

"Where will you go?" Mo Ling asked as she stored the talismans without question. No mother would refuse something that could help her protect her child.

"To another world," Cha Ming said, summoning a sliver of power. Lighting crackled above them, a single bolt striking down within the room without breaking through the roof. "The plane doesn't want me here. I'm an unwelcome guest. It's time for me to go."

"Will I ever see you again?" she asked, the tears coming back.

"I'm afraid not, my little niece," Cha Ming said. He glanced over to the crib. "But I might see your son if he makes enough progress. What did you name him?" He hadn't stayed long enough to hear it.

"Mo Xiao," Mo Ling said.

"I'll remember it." Though the little boy would have a strong talent for cultivation, there were many variables to consider. It was unlikely he would ever make it past the peak of the plane.

"Goodbye, Mo Ling," Cha Ming said. He suppressed his own tears and disappeared from Mo Ling's home. Then, he left the Southern Lands for good.

"Is tying up loose ends always so heartbreaking?" Cha Ming asked.

Sun Wukong appeared beside him and nodded. "Every time," Sun Wukong said. "Every world, every place. You'll have many homes in your lifetime, and many friends that live much shorter lives than you will."

"It's better than the alternative, I suppose," Cha Ming said. Losing everyone one at a time was much preferable to not knowing anyone. Then again, he had little experience in this regard. His time on this plane had been so short, and he'd only lost two close friends and very few meaningful acquaintances. Rather than bemoan the difficulty of the situation, he should count his blessings.

They were in Songjing City now, walking through the city streets and smelling the blooming greenery. Cha Ming recognized many places, whether it was the lackluster Talisman Artist Guild or the many noble houses he'd visited to lay energy-gathering formations. The Jade Bamboo Pavilion was, to his surprise, still operational. But instead of the usual business traffic, it seemed to be dealing in bulk shipments and logistics for rebuilding. Time was money, after all, and opportunity waited for no one. Even with the modest sums they would make in such endeavours, the amount of orders they received would be massive.

It didn't take long for them to reach the royal palace. The guards let him enter unhindered. Who would dare try to stop a well-known transcendent? He passed the gardens where he'd given a lecture many years ago. To his knowledge, many of those he'd taught had advanced and become key contributors to the war effort.

"Ancestor Cha Ming, may I help you?" one of the court's high-ranking eunuchs said as he entered the palace doors. The form of address nearly made him cough up blood. *Ancestor? Who's your ancestor?* Cha Ming wasn't even a hundred and fifty, forget the hundreds of years those relics had on him.

He stifled the urge to punch the man and smiled lightly. That was how ancestors behaved, right? "Is Li Yin around?"

"As a matter a fact, he's in his office in the west wing," the eunuch said. "Shall I take you there?"

"No need," Cha Ming said, disappearing and reappearing beside Li Yin's office. He'd never liked eunuchs, as he found it difficult to trust a man who chose to amputate his manhood. Cha Ming knocked three times, then waited. A few seconds later, the door was opened by a man looking much older than he remembered.

"Cha Ming, my boy," Li Yin said. "Have a seat. Have a seat."

Cha Ming entered the room, but instead of taking a seat right away, he walked over to a teapot on the side and began brewing for them. Despite their vast difference in cultivation—Li Yin wasn't even a qi cultivator—the man was still his teacher. Li Yin didn't refuse him and accepted the cup. He'd never been one to care about cultivation.

"I see you've done well for yourself here as chief medical officer," Cha Ming said. "You not only have the king's respect, but you've somehow gotten on the Spirit Doctor Association's good side." A commemorative plaque hung above his desk, an honorary spirit doctor certification, granting him as much authority as a spirit doctor at the core level.

"More like *they* somehow got on *my* good side," Li Yin said with a grunt. "The bastards finally started listening to my advice. The fact that you could level their headquarters definitely helps, I'll admit, but saving the king did have its benefits."

"I'm happy everything is going well for you," Cha Ming said. He noticed the man's medical research shelf had grown substantially. It was all in paper, of course. Li Yin had insufficient soul force to use information jades. For now.

Cha Ming placed a Grandmist seal pill on the table.

"What's this?" Li Yin asked, putting on his spectacles and looking into the bottle. "What a curious alchemical pill. A gray seal. Never seen anything like it." He pulled off the stopper and smelled it, noticing that it didn't let off any medicinal scent. "Good power retention too. Very high quality." Most mortals would think the opposite way and discard it as garbage. It was this scientific way of looking at the world that had served the doctor so well in his profession.

"The pill is for you," Cha Ming said. "It will heal your shattered qi pathways, enhance them, and increase your cultivation talent, all while nourishing your soul. Though I don't guarantee that you'll ever reach core formation, reaching foundation establishment before the end of your life span and doubling it shouldn't be a problem."

Li Yin frowned. He shook his head and pushed the vial back. "It's too late for me, Cha Ming. No need to trouble yourself. Something so valuable should be reserved for the gravely injured. And we have many of those around here."

Though the Southern army hadn't done much to Songjing, defending the city had still taken its toll. Less than half of the original powerhouses that had defended it remained.

"I insist," Cha Ming said. "You've helped me so much. This is one of the few things I can do to ease a knot in my heart."

"If I took this pill, I'd feel dreadful," Li Yin said. "I don't want to concern myself with childhood dreams." The man had always yearned to become a spirit doctor, only to have the opportunity snatched away from him by misfortune. The world had been cruel to the man, who'd wanted nothing more than to help.

"Then you're forcing my hand," Cha Ming said. He wouldn't let the man's stubbornness get in the way. With a wave of his hand, Li Yin froze. With another, the pill forced its way inside his mouth. The pill was incredibly mild and gentle, and Li Yin felt not a bit of pain as his pathways mended and many of his internal injuries and old-age afflictions healed.

"It's not polite to force medicine down your elder's throat," Li Yin growled as he sat back down, a pink flush coming to his cheeks.

"But as you showed me many times in Crystal Falls, some older patients need more aggressive convincing to take their medicine," Cha Ming said with a smile. "Don't you agree? Besides, with another hundred years and some cultivation, think about all the research you can perform. Think of the jade slips you'll finally be able to read."

Li Yin's expression brightened at that. "I don't suppose you have a few more of those pills? I wasn't lying when there were a lot of severe wounds to treat."

Cha Ming placed a dozen bottles of similar pills—general healing pills in this case—on the small table between them, each containing detailed instructions on use. "These pills are hard to come by, as only I can make them. There won't be any more for a long time, I'm afraid."

Li Yin nodded. "When are you leaving?"

News of Cha Ming's ascension was common knowledge by now. Those who transcended would either choose to leave or stay. Most ended up leaving.

"Soon," Cha Ming said. "I just couldn't bear to leave without helping you. My mentor. My friend."

Li Yin's eyes reddened. "Good lad. You have a good head on your shoulders and a good heart. I wish you the best of luck on your journey."

"And I yours," Cha Ming said. He placed two scrolls on the table, one with a two-colored seal and one with a three-colored one. "I tested your abilities a while back. You're quite gifted, with a triple affinity for water, wood, and fire. Though you only need to cultivate water and wood to be a spirit doctor, you might like to add fire to be able to craft pills and reagents."

"I'll have to think about it," Li Yin said.

"Don't think too long," Cha Ming said. "I don't want you dying of old age before you make a decision."

Li Yin scowled at that. Cha Ming laughed and raised his cup of freshly poured tea. "To your health."

"To *our* health," Li Yin said, toasting and drinking his.

"This is where I say goodbye, my friend," Cha Ming said, getting up. He gave Li Yin a deep, heartfelt hug and turned to leave. He was halfway out the door when Li Yin called out.

"Be careful out there," Li Yin said. "It's not all fun and games in the cultivation world."

"Trust me, I know," Cha Ming said. He closed the door and walked several tens of feet before speaking. "You can come out now."

Feng Ming appeared from behind a pillar. "Am I that obvious?" Feng Ming said.

"Not at all," Cha Ming said. "It was a lucky guess."

Feng Ming chuckled. "You didn't bother hiding yourself, and the eunuchs made sure I knew as soon as you set foot in the palace."

They walked outside to a garden where Feng Ming had, when they were children, alienated his current wife. The beautiful woman was laughing in the park, playing with their two young children. One was around a year old, having been born just before the Taotie attacked the Westvale Wall.

"I take it you're staying," Cha Ming asked, watching the children play.

"It's not right for a father to leave his children," Feng Ming said. "Or his grandchildren, or their children, if he can help it. Besides, the North needs stability. I can give that to them by staying."

"You'll have to be careful," Cha Ming said. "The plane's will really has it in for me." Whenever he tried to summon the least bit of power, it struck down on him with increasing ferocity. It seemed there was a penalty for repeat offenders.

"Well, you're a lot stronger than many transcendents before you," Feng Ming said. "You're a bit overpowered, and the transcendents who stayed barely advanced after their ascension."

"True," Cha Ming said. He felt that increasing his cultivation would be impossible here. And worse, if it did, the results would be disastrous. "Here, I found you something." He summoned a weapon from the Clear Sky World. It was a rust-colored sword he'd pilfered from one of the Southern transcendents.

"I'll have to shamelessly accept," Feng Ming said, grinning. "It's no spear, but a transcendent can't fight properly without a transcendent weapon, can he?"

"My thoughts exactly," Cha Ming said. "Besides, I noticed what you did, distributing all those weapons to all those kingdoms."

"Strong kingdoms need strong leaders, so I don't regret that," Feng Ming said. "Besides, none of them were fire aligned for some reason. It was rotten luck."

"Or maybe luck just found a way for me to say thank you for all you've done for me," Cha Ming said.

"When will you leave?" Feng Ming asked, just as the others all had.

"Soon," Cha Ming said. "After the party. You'll be there, right?"

"I wouldn't miss it for the world," Feng Ming said. They clasped arms and pressed foreheads.

"See you soon," Cha Ming said, then flew off toward the Quicksilver Empire and his next appointment.

Crystal Falls was very different from how Cha Ming remembered it. Li Yin's missing medical clinic aside, the town now had well-maintained roads that led through the center and connected it to others. Before, cultivation was a rare talent. Now, it was commonplace. Many of the villagers made a living gathering herbs in the Spirit Woods. Outsiders also came to enjoy the peace and quiet granted by the perpetual mists.

The mist did nothing to impede Cha Ming's transcendent eyesight. Many of the children he'd treated had grown, and many of the elders from before were no longer there. War, mercifully, had spared this village. Perhaps this was a twist of good fortune, a recompense for what they'd suffered previously.

"Teacher!" Yue Bing said, landing just outside the village. Her three apprentice brothers landed beside her. Zi Long also had another person accompanying him, a familiar blind woman Cha Ming had come to know in his time in Quicksilver.

"Luo Xuehua, I'm glad you could make it," Cha Ming said, nodding.

She bowed lightly with the others, likely due to her relationship with Zi Long. Though he and Luo Xuehua were friends, Zi Long was his disciple. It put her in an awkward position, though his identity as a transcendent angel likely made her decision easier.

They entered the village, drawing stares from everyone as they did so. There were no guards at the entrance to the village, as it was a peaceful town with little crime. The villagers had no idea who they were or where they'd come from, but the aura surrounding Cha Ming and the others made it so they didn't dare approach.

"I spent many months here," Cha Ming said, holding out his hand. "This village is my shame, but it is also my redemption. It was here that I washed up after suffering a tribulation before foundation establishment. I was crippled, unable to cultivate, and close to dying. It was Li Yin who saved me and gave me inspiration, so whatever you do, make sure to help the old man whenever he needs it."

They walked for a short while, passing an abandoned shack that had been burnt to the ground. It was the ruins of the abandoned bandit warehouse. The slave pens were nowhere to be seen. They walked a while longer until they approached steps that led behind the waterfall.

"What, no secret cave?" Zi Long asked as they reached the top of the steps. "I would have thought…"

"It suits the cliché, doesn't it?" Cha Ming said with a smile. "If you look carefully, you'll notice the stone is slightly incongruent. I backfilled it after mining out everything here. You see, I was enslaved here as a miner, as were many others in this village. It happened because I made a bad decision, saving an evil man I should have let die. I deserved every ounce of punishment I received, though these villagers suffered much for it. Because that's always the way it is with cultivators. Your every action will affect all those around you, both positively and negatively. You need to weigh the consequences every time you act. Regardless of how careful you are, you'll be left with regrets."

Cha Ming pressed his hand to the stone wall, and it melted away, slipping inside the Clear Sky World. He ignored the old mining passageways and took a more direct route to the large pit in the darkness, where he stood remembering the suicidal attempt at escaping that drove him to jump down into the chasm.

"Though I don't advise doing this, sometimes jumping down holes to certain death can lead to unexpected gains," Cha Ming said.

He hadn't told them why they were coming. They floated down the chasm until a speck of blue light appeared. The speck grew until it became a giant building of glowing blue stone with white runes. They landed before it and walked toward the front wall with no visible door. A gate appeared as they neared, and they were welcomed by a familiar middle-aged custodian.

"Cha Ming," the Custodian said. "It is nice to see you. And you've come with friends. Come in, come in."

The man led them inside, and just like before, he gave them water to drink and qi-derived pellets. They ate them out of courtesy and sat beside the Custodian at a small table.

"These are my disciples," Cha Ming said. "Zi Long, Yue Bing, Ling Dong, and Jin Huang. And this is Luo Xuehua. I take it they meet your satisfaction?"

The Custodian's eyes twinkled. "Thick merit halo, potential for future angelic endowment. I can't complain."

"This place is Fuxi's Library," Cha Ming explained. "It's where I learned most of my runework and sigilcraft. I obtained the jade slips I taught you here. Every ten years—though perhaps this can be accelerated with enough resources—a single person can inherit the library's contents, learning runes and sigils through a medium that directly conveys primal truths. The ones who learn them will have karmic obligations to teach others what they've learned. The only requirement is merit glow."

"I'll have to stop you right there," the Custodian said. "Back then, you were alone, so I could only take one. I can actually accept ten every ten years, and the process can't be accelerated."

"I stand corrected," Cha Ming said. "Is there anything else we need to know?"

"Yes, it is ideal if those who come here are at least initial-foundation-establishment cultivators, but no higher than middle foundation establishment," the Custodian said. "Initial-foundation-establishment cultivators are ideal. There's only so much qi-condensation cultivators can learn about the truths of the universe."

Cha Ming coughed. "I didn't exactly pass with flying colors."

"Five-element cultivation is best," the Custodian continued, "as others won't be able to absorb the full complexity of what is presented. For those with differing elements, however, the library will offer an alternate rune set. I highly recommend those with space affinity to be sent here."

"This is one of the final tools I give you to stabilize the forces of good on this plane," Cha Ming said. "Not the library—I can't give that to anyone—but the knowledge of its location. Guard it closely."

"We will," Zi Long said. The others echoed the statement.

"Come with me," Cha Ming said. He bowed to the Custodian, who smiled and bowed back. They flew back the way they came and moved outside the waterfall. Then they flew higher until they were atop the mists that shone with prismatic colors, giving the falls their names.

"I'm leaving soon," Cha Ming said, landing atop the cliff overlooking the village. "I wish I had more time to spend with you, but I can't do much more around here. You've also learned everything I can teach you."

Down in the valley, the villagers went about their daily lives. Just like his disciples would, they had already forgotten his influence.

Cha Ming turned around as he heard a smacking sound. "That is unnecessary," he said, looking at the broken rocks on the ground.

"We kowtow once to remember our first meeting," Zi Long said. "We all had nothing when we met you, except maybe Jin Huang, of course, though he wasn't far off."

The youngest disciple had been a promise fulfilled, a boy he'd noticed with ample karma in the Song Kingdom.

They slammed their foreheads down again. This time, Yue Bing spoke. "We kowtow a second time to remember all you did for us. You taught us, never asking for anything in return."

Memories flowed through Cha Ming's mind. He had educated them, yes, but they'd fought for everything they had. He remembered the stark change in their dispositions before and after he'd left for Jade Moon Planet. He'd seen their efforts firsthand in Haijing, and he remembered Yue Bing's agony at his disapproval.

"We kowtow a third time to say goodbye," Ling Dong said as they smacked their foreheads down.

"It's a tradition, so it's definitely necessary," Jin Huang said, grinning.

"Get up," Cha Ming said with a light smile. "Who's to say we'll never see each other again?"

His disciples glanced at each other, then shook their heads. "Brother Zi Long won't be leaving if he eventually transcends, and it doesn't feel right to leave him here," Yue Bing said. "We've decided to stay and guard the Ling Nan Plane with him. It's very unlikely that we'll meet again."

"I respect your decision," Cha Ming said. They were just like Feng Ming, unable to move forward because of very human attachments. They didn't have greater goals like he did, a desire for immortality that couldn't be ignored. Not only did he want to meet Yu Wen again, but Huxian's tribulations would keep coming. He also had a promise to Sun Wukong to fulfill—a new body to replace his old one and grant him freedom from the Clear Sky Brush.

"Here, let me give you one last gift. You know everything I can teach you already, but you didn't get a lot of treasures."

Only a few transcendent treasures had been left on the battlefield. Lu Tianhao had left his sword behind for Luo Xuehua, but many of the others had detonated them, using the burst of power to kill their opponents and eliminate the risk that their enemies might wield them. Many more had also been lost in the fight against the Taotie. Their transcendent metals simply weren't enough to resist the void calamity and the tribulation Cha Ming and Huxian had summoned.

Four treasures floated in the air—a greatsword, two staves, and a pair of boots.

He'd bartered with the other transcendents to obtain these, just like he had for Feng Ming's sword. The greatsword would go to Ling Dong, and though it wasn't ideal given his demonic nature, it would be useful for now. The staves were for Zi Long and Yue Bing. Though Yue Bing had her mystical ankh, it wasn't a full transcendent treasure. It needed the power of a staff as a base. Jin Huang, on the other hand, had no need of weapons. What he needed was speed. These treasures were the last he had. He wasn't sure how valuable they'd be where he was going.

His disciples were used to gifts by now. They simply accepted them and bowed in thanks.

"You're all close to angelic enlightenment," Cha Ming said. "You can't force your way there. What it takes is an epiphany, the realization of an ideal. Don't focus on your weaknesses. Ling Dong, you'll never be the kindest man. But your resilience and tenacity are admirable, and they suit you well. As for the rest of you, I won't dwell on the specifics. It will come or it won't. If it does, a whole new world will open to you, a whole new level of power."

With that, he turned around and flew off the cliff and into the mist. He left his disciples with Luo Xuehua, knowing full well he'd never see them again.

He had one last thing to do before he left. It was a long time coming.

It was night in Green Leaf City. The stone streets in the residential area were well lit. Cha Ming approached one of the many mall houses, hesitating before he knocked. He'd been to mansions and palaces but had never felt the trepidation he now felt. Endless moments passed as he waited for the eventual footsteps, the unbolting of the lock, and that final twist of a doorknob before the door opened, revealing a familiar face.

It was Hong Jin who opened the door. His black hair, grown to shoulder length, as was popular these days, had many streaks of gray now.

"How can I help you?" he said.

It took some time for Cha Ming to muster up the courage to reply. "I'm sorry for waiting so long to come see you," Cha Ming said. "I suppose I was too ashamed to show my face after what I did to your family."

Hong Jin frowned for a moment, then his eyes widened. "Cha Ming? Is that really you?"

"It's me," Cha Ming said. He glanced into the house—no one was here yet, just as planned. "May I come in?"

"Please," Hong Jin said, recovering from his shock. "My love, a guest has arrived! Why don't you cook dinner?"

"That won't be necessary," Cha Ming said, following Hong Jin inside. A shocked Madame Xu ran up to him and held his face, shaking her head.

"You're growing too old too fast," Madame Xu said, concerned.

"No need to worry yourself," Cha Ming said. "Come, I've brought you tea from a faraway place." He summoned a teapot and hot water and began brewing for them.

A few minutes later, they were all drinking a cup around the table. No one had said much of anything.

"It has a metallic taste," Madame Xu said to break the ice.

Cha Ming nodded. "It's from far to the south, where the power of gold is very concentrated. Everything that grows there tastes metallic, a light rusty flavor that complements this red tea's taste."

"You have a friend who likes tea, I remember," Hong Jin said stiffly. "How is he?"

"He's dead," Cha Ming replied.

"I'm sorry," Hong Jin said, flushing with embarrassment.

"You couldn't have known," Cha Ming said with a sigh. "Much

has changed over the years. I see Green Leaf City didn't escape the war unscathed."

"Half the city guard died fighting cultists," Hong Jin grunted. "I got promoted to vice leader of the city guard as a result."

"And I'm sure you'd rather you'd never gotten the promotion," Cha Ming said. "That's war, unfortunately. I lost friends and acquaintances, but I'm much better off than many others I know." There was no need to go into specifics. Hong Jin and Madame Xu were weaker cultivators. They lived in a backwater town with very little information. Even if they'd heard his name, Cha Ming, they'd never imagine he'd been one of the peak fighters. Coincidence was much easier to believe than the alternative.

"There's someone at the door," Cha Ming said, nodding toward it.

Hong Jin frowned. His senses were inferior, but it was usually enough to sense the average guest. His skepticism only lasted until the knock came. He walked over to the door and opened it, dropping his cup when he saw who it was.

"Love?" Madame Xu called out, rushing toward him. He walked past her, leaving her alone with the guests at the door. It was Hong Ling and a beautiful woman. To Cha Ming's surprise, she'd already reached the peak of foundation establishment.

"I don't want him in here. I don't want to see him," Hong Jin said, before charging through the kitchen door.

"Just give him some time," Madame Xu whispered. "Come in, come in."

The two awkward guests were ushered into the living room where Cha Ming waited. He poured them each an extra cup, then poured a few more as other guests walk in.

"Mother, Father should really hear him out," Hong Xun said, letting himself in. He still lived in Green Leaf City, but he'd moved out of his parents' house. His wife followed him, as did their three children.

"Perhaps he needs a moment," Cha Ming said. "It's a lot to take in all at once."

"I'm surprised you came back after all this time," Hong Xun said with none of the resentment his father clearly had. "I had to double-check your message, checking the writing with some of your old homework that was lying about."

"Here I am," Cha Ming said. "And your brother is back. It's a thing to celebrate, is it not?" He summoned a bottle of baijiu and poured some. They drank three cups before a huffing Hong Jin walked out of the kitchen, flanked by his insistent wife. He didn't speak to his estranged son right away. Instead, he addressed the woman beside him.

"When did you get married?" he asked, nodding to her jade ring.

"Three years ago," the woman said. "Please call me Xiao Li. I've heard so much about you."

"Any kids?" Hong Jin asked.

She shook her head. "We're working on it, but we've been terribly busy. The war didn't make things any easier."

Hong Jin nodded and accepted a cup of baijiu from Cha Ming. He grimaced when he downed it, then frowned at Cha Ming, who was drinking it like water.

"I'm sorry for not writing, Father," Hong Ling said. "And I'm sorry for not inviting you to our wedding. And for not visiting. I've been unfilial, though I suppose I did it because I didn't want to tear old wounds open."

Hong Jin took a deep breath, and at Madame Xu's nod, he let out a deep sigh. "Everyone's been through so much. So many have died. Since the war is over, it's time for a new beginning." He held up a cup of baijiu, and the others raised one with him. "To new beginnings!"

They drank their single shots, and Cha Ming poured them another from a bottle that never seemed to run out of the tasty wine.

"All three of you showing up here at the same time can't be a coincidence," Hong Jin said. "What happened? What aren't you saying?"

"It'll become obvious soon enough," Cha Ming said, pouring him another glass. "There's another guest at the door. Better open it, or the door will find a way to get him inside."

The exasperated Hong Jin ran up to the door again. This time, it revealed a young man in a military uniform, though his usual marshal's cape had been replaced by a coat officers often wore to avoid showing off their rank.

"Mr. Hong, I'm pleased to finally make your acquaintance," Feng Ming said. "Please accept this gift." It was a fine bottle of baijiu from Quicksilver, one of the best brands known in every household.

"It's too expensive," Hong Jin said, pushing it back, but in doing so, the bottle slipped out of his hands. Somehow, however, Feng Ming's coat brushed up against it as he walked in, pushing it back into place once again. Hong Jin frowned and decided to heed Cha Ming's warning and let the man in. He placed the bottle on the table as he got back to his seat, only to curse at himself for forgetting to place it on the table nearest the door.

"Feng Ming!" Hong Xun said. "Long time no see!"

"It's definitely been a while," Feng Ming said. "And look at you, a foundation-establishment cultivator. Nice!"

"We're not all like you," Hong Xun grumbled. "You're richer than half the town. You could get any cultivation pills you wanted from your father."

Feng Ming's expression flickered for a moment, and Hong Xun looked at him, suddenly understanding. "I'm sorry. I didn't realize."

"We've all lost people in this war," Feng Ming said. "I lost my father over ten years ago."

"To the fallen," Hong Jin said, raising a glass and drinking it back. His face was now flushed from all the drinking.

"To the fallen," the others said solemnly, drinking back their cups.

"You shouldn't drink so much," Cha Ming said. "You want to be sober for the surprise."

"Surprise?" Hong Jin said, groaning. "You're just stacking up one misery on another. No offense."

"None taken," said Feng Ming, whom he had addressed.

They continued drinking, and finally, Cha Ming shot Hong Jin another glance. The man sighed and walked toward the door in resignation. He opened it before the new guest knocked, only to drop his glass yet again.

"Love?" Hong Jin said softly. "Come to the door. Tell me if I'm drunk or dreaming."

Madame Xu ran to the door and yelped. She rushed out the doorway into the rain and hugged Hong Xin, who stood beneath an umbrella her friend Bai Ling held for her. "My daughter!" she wailed as she cried uncontrollably. "We thought we'd lost you."

Hong Xin hugged her back tightly. "Father," she said, looking to Hong Jin. "May I come in?"

The red-eyed man didn't know how to react to the question. He simply stood there, stunned as Hong Xun came to greet his sister and bring her inside. Bai Ling followed, not wearing any of the usual attire befitting her station as the Red Dust Mistress. Instead, she wore a light-blue qipao that matched her umbrella.

"My name is Bai Ling," she said. "I'm one of Hong Xin's good friends. We met under unusual circumstances. She was lost, so I took her in."

"Thank you," Madame Xu said. "I don't know how I could ever repay you."

"No need," Bai Ling said. "Your daughter is safe and sound."

As they spoke, Hong Jin still couldn't believe it. He touched Hong Xin's face with his wet hands, not daring to believe his eyes. Then he hugged her tightly, only opening his eyes to glare at Cha Ming.

"You'd use this as a surprise for this old man?" Hong Jin said. "I should beat you to death for daring to keep her away from me for a few more minutes. When did you lose all your respect for the elderly?"

"Noted," Cha Ming said, laughing, pouring another cup for everyone. They spoke for a while longer, and soon, food arrived. They'd placed a special order beforehand from Songjing City, express-delivered by a core-formation cultivator. They didn't tell the Hong family any of that, however. They just simply refused to share where they'd purchased the meal, laughing off any offers to pay for it.

It was a situation unlike any other Cha Ming had ever witnessed.

Some of the most powerful people on the continent feasted with mortals, completely hiding their talent. He'd heard stories of capricious immortals, tricking men and women into believing they were ordinary. He'd always wondered why they'd ever do such a thing, but now he understood.

The simple life of a mortal was enviable. It gave no great freedom, but it compensated for that with peace. Even craftsmen cultivators couldn't avoid death and destruction. Power came at a price, and there was no turning back once you started.

As they spoke, the ice in Hong Jin's voice toward Hong Ling faded. His bitterness toward Cha Ming disappeared. It was that bitterness that had frightened Cha Ming in the first place and made it impossible for him to set foot in this household where kind people had taken him in on the first leg of his journey, only for him to repay them with sadness and lost and estranged family members.

The night grew dark, and there wasn't only laughter. There was also sadness when Hong Jin expressed his condolences for Wang Jun. Hong Xin cried, and her father cried with her. How could he have known that the man he'd grown to hate had died to save her? In truth, Wang Jun was a far greater hero. He'd died to save all of them, and that was a secret the Hong family would never know.

The mortal Hong Xin, who could no longer cultivate, had returned home. As they'd discussed before bringing her here, she'd never mention she was crippled, because the truth would simply devastate her parents. Bai Ling would come visit often, as would Hong Ling. They both had people posted to protect her in case escaped members of the Spirit Temple came looking for vengeance.

"So," Feng Ming said, chugging the last of the baijiu. "Tonight?" Everyone else had passed out, as the liquor was too strong for them. Only Feng Ming and Cha Ming, with their excellent constitutions, remained awake. Even Bai Ling had fallen asleep.

"In the morning," Cha Ming said. "In the Silverwing Mountain Range. I'll be leaving right away."

"Makes sense," Feng Ming said. "Don't worry about everyone. I'll take care of them."

"Then you have my thanks," Cha Ming said, getting up and clasping arms with him. He hugged the man this time. They'd likely never see each other again.

"Godspeed," Feng Ming said.

"Good luck," Cha Ming replied. Then he vanished, disappearing from the place where it all began. His journey on this plane had come full circle, and it was time for it to come to an end. He reappeared in an alley now far away, and on a whim, he kowtowed three times. Once to remember their first meeting. Once to remember all they'd done for him. And once to leave it all behind.

"You won't see them? Talk to them? Let them know you're safe?" Daoist Obscurus asked from across a dining table at a restaurant a few streets over. Though they were some distance away and transcendents were there, they could see and hear everything in this town like it was whispered in their ear.

"No," Wang Jun said, sighing deeply as he drank a cup of tea. "They're better off not knowing. I'm a cursed existence, Master. Everything around me goes wrong no matter how much I try."

"And now you see why I left it all behind," Daoist Obscurus said. "Secluding myself in research, separating myself from the rest of the world."

"And how did that go?" Wang Jun said. "The research you've been talking about all these years?"

"A failure," Daoist Obscurus said with a silent sigh. He held up his hand in a signal to a waitress, who took his wordless order and brought it to the kitchen. "Needs tweaking, but I got good data. Can't complain, I suppose."

"And you didn't think it was a good idea to stop the Taotie while it was rampaging?" Wang Jun asked.

"I thought about it," Daoist Obscurus said. "Though I'll have you know that the slightest leak of an immortal's power could lead to planar devastation. Everything you knew and loved would be destroyed. I thought it safer to let the young ones handle it. Make sense?"

"Makes sense," Wang Jun said, ignoring the plate of food the waitress dropped off. He drank tea while watching a sleeping girl, knowing full well it would be the last he saw of her. "Why does the universe have to be so unfair, Master? Why does it love some people and hate others?"

Daoist Obscurus shrugged. "It's the Painter's fault, I suppose. I wasn't born then, but they say he painted the world in black and white, a beautiful matrix full of competing existences. With it came karma, stringing us all together. Now we dance like mere puppets, performers to the greater spectator."

"Can it be changed?" Wang Jun wondered. "Can people like us truly walk in the light again?"

"I think so," Daoist Obscurus said, biting into a new dish called a "hamburger," a piece of pork shoved between two pieces of round bread. "It's what I've been working on for countless aeons, and I must say, the results are encouraging. It's too bad neither side has any interest in my solution to end all this karma and violence."

"Figures," Wang Jun said. Good and evil were always that way. They fought tooth and nail to kill one another, always ignoring the countless lives they trampled in the process. "Where to next?"

"I was wondering when you'd ask," Daoist Obscurus said. "To the Plane of Eternal Darkness, where you'll train for the next long while. It's difficult to master the Dao of Void Encompassing, but I think you have a talent for it. You also have the drive and a motive for advancement. The data I got in my time here was all right, but you, my boy, take the cake. If you don't become an immortal, I'll eat my hat." It was a nice hat, a top hat of sorts that was only a foot tall and was completely flat on top.

"Let's go, then," Wang Jun said. "I've had enough of this. If I wait any longer, I'll change my mind and stay." He looked one last time to the beauty sleeping inside her home. At long last, Hong Xin was safe. He wouldn't stay to weigh her down and water down her happiness. To have loved and lost was cruel, but the closure was far better than staring across Gold Leaf Square, never sure when they could be together.

"You coming?" Daoist Obscurus said. He was standing, and the dishes he'd ordered were finished. A pile of spirit stones lay on the table, a generous tip for a generous restaurant owner, who'd let them stay as long as they wished.

A portal of darkness opened in the air. It led outside the plane into an unknown world filled with powerful enemies and lucky chances. Wang Jun looked to Hong Xin and Feng Ming, to Hong Ling and Xiao Li. He'd miss every one of them and the precious moments they'd shared. Especially Hong Xin, who'd taken his heart. He wasn't sure if he could ever love again, knowing that he was leaving her alone on this mortal plane. Finally, he looked to Cha Ming who was slowly walking out of the city. Like him, Cha Ming was also leaving. And they were headed in opposite directions.

Would they ever meet again? Who knew? They were both destined to become immortals on their separate paths. Sighing one last time, Wang Jun walked through the portal behind his master. The world shook as realities connected. He emerged in a world of darkness.

"Finally," Huxian said, brushing the dirt off himself as he got up off the ground. Cha Ming raised an eyebrow as he eyed each of the demons—they were scratched and bruised and covered in filth.

"I'm glad I didn't stay away too long," Cha Ming said. He kept a healthy distance from the five demons. "You might have destroyed the mountain range by then."

The desolate trees that were normally present at the center of the mountain range lay broken in piles. Surprisingly, there were young saplings growing everywhere. With the Pure Jade Defensive Formation gone, along with the primary formation that he'd used to form his Tri-Sealing Pillars, the demonic energy in the mountains had returned to normal. The small shrine he'd noticed before was also gone, and not a single trace of it remained.

It was just before dawn, and a thick mist hung in the air, hiding the small red light peeking from between two mountains. It was rapidly disappearing to make way for the light of day. "Dawn is very poetic time to leave, don't you think?"

"It was a tossup between dawn and sunset," Huxian said. "Sunset represents a good ending."

"But it's not an ending, is it?" Cha Ming said. "Every good story has three parts. This was just the opening act to a long and fulfilling journey."

"Do you think you'll find her?" Huxian asked, walking up beside him to watch the sunrise.

"I can only try," Cha Ming said. "It's all anyone can do, really. Teacher, are you sure we'll find something to make you a body in the next realm?"

"Barring a complete disaster," Sun Wukong said. His spirit body appeared before Cha Ming and the demons. By now, they already knew of his existence. "The main thing is getting a hold of my teacher, or one of Mother's disciples."

"Mother?" Cha Ming asked. "Weren't you born from a rock?"

"I was," Sun Wukong said. "But what does that have to do with anything?"

Cha Ming shrugged. They watched the sun as it rose, and finally, when it was all the way over the mountain ridges, and the pink in the clouds was finally disappearing, Cha Ming sent a message to the plane's will. The moment he did, a portal opened. It was a large gray circle leading into the endless unknown. All transcendents had a single chance to leave the mortal realm, and if they took it, it was extremely difficult to get back. Stepping through that gateway was a one-way ticket to a brand-new place.

"You ready?" Cha Ming said, biting his lip.

"Born ready!" Huxian said.

"Born fierce!" Silverwing said.

"Born powerful!" Lei Jiang said.

"Born beautiful!" Gua shouted, prompting glares from all his companions.

"Born a mountain!" Mr. Mountain said.

Cha Ming slapped his forehead.

"Well," Huxian said awkwardly. "Together?"

"Together," Cha Ming said. They inched up to the portal, and as a unit, they took a single step. Their bodies vanished, and the world flashed before their eyes. The entirety of the cosmos appeared, its entire contents spinning inside a crystal ball. On the inside was reality, and on the outside, oblivion. They saw warring angels and devils, spread across the universe like pieces on a Weiqi board. A large yellow river wove between them, splitting the board in half and drawing a careful balance. And as they saw all this, a world approached. It was a world of water and rain that let out painful moans, like a dying man waiting to be put out of his misery.

There was another flash, and Cha Ming felt his bond with Huxian grow distant. They split off into separate directions before shooting down onto six large continents much larger than the plane they'd come from. At the center of the largest continent was a single ocean, blacker than the deepest night. Another flash, and all that vanished. Cha Ming appeared on a runic circle that tethered him to this reality.

"What is your Dao name?" a deep voice asked.

Though it was in a different language, the residual power leading him to this plane poured knowledge of it into his mind, giving him instant understanding. Dao name? He'd never thought about it. In ancient tales of immortals, Daoists put aside their original name, introducing themselves with something that reflected their Dao or nature.

"What is your Dao name?" the voice asked again with not a hint of impatience.

"Clear Sky," Cha Ming said. "You may call me Daoist Clear Sky."

– End Book 9 –
– End of Arc 1, Angels and Devils –

A Note to Readers

If you've enjoyed this book, I would greatly appreciate it if you left a rating and/or review on the site where you purchased it. Ratings lead to credibility in this competitive marketplace, and by leaving one, you signal to the world that this book is worth reading.

I send out updates to readers from time to time, such as writing progress, release announcements, and the like. If you're interested in receiving these updates, subscribe to the Painting the Mists newsletter at:

http://eepurl.com/dymvO1

You can also find a link to the newsletter at www.paintingthemists. com. Also, if you check out the new website, you'll find that there are nifty progress bars keeping you up to date on what I'm working on.

You can also get updates from me on social media:

Facebook: https://www.facebook.com/PatrickGLaplante/
Twitter: @PatGLaplante

The Cultivation Systems

This record is a summary of the cultivation systems on the Ling Nan Plane. Note that cultivation systems can change depending on the type of plane or the stability of the plane.

Qi Cultivation (Human)

Some humans are talented in harvesting the ambient energies of heaven and earth. They cultivate qi, enabling them to perform fierce magics by bending the elements themselves. Angelic cultivators gravitate toward this powerful but complex path.

Qi Condensation – Cultivators start their cultivation journey by condensing qi from their surroundings into their Dantian. They can circulate this qi in their qi pathways, executing qi techniques by expending it. A cultivator's qi pool expands and deepens as they cultivate. Many schools separate each step of the process into grades.

Foundation Establishment – After forming a sufficiently large qi pool, cultivators solidify it into solid pillars known as a foundation. Their foundation grows from the bottom of their Dantian and eventually grows tall enough to reach the top. Their qi thickens, and the amount of thickened qi they control depends on the height of their foundation. Foundation-establishment cultivators can fly a short distance from the ground using treasures like flying swords or special boots.

Core Formation – When their pillars reach their maximum height, cultivators melt them into a core, the most efficient way to store qi. Qi now takes the form of a fluid that travels in and out of their core. The core grows until it reaches its maximum size. At this point, cultivators are able to use their potent qi to fly unaided.

Rune Carving – By carving runes onto their core, mortal humans can transcend. Not much is known about this realm, but legends say rune carving cultivators can generate a "domain."

Body Cultivation (Human)

Let's face it, some people aren't as smart as they are strong. For those people, body cultivation is the preferred way to get ahead. Devilish cultivators and descendants of deities are drawn toward this brutal, straightforward path. Body cultivation makes one physically stronger, tougher, and nearly unkillable at higher cultivation levels.

Body Strengthening – Body cultivators start off by performing a basic strengthening of their body, purifying it in the process. Typically, the body is nourished with qi and then refined with an opposing qi, removing any impurities.

Bone Forging – After sufficiently strengthening their body, body cultivators must forge their bones to further support their growth. Bones are the basis of strength and durability. They traditionally subject their bones to intense quantities of qi, strengthening and tempering them in the process. They become akin to magic treasures, making it extremely difficult to shatter them using strength of an equivalent realm. Bone-forging cultivators gain the ability to manipulate their weight by using voids that are formed in their bones, making it easier to wield heavy weapons and use their immense strength to their advantage.

Marrow Refining – Once the bones are strong enough, it is necessary for cultivators to refine their marrow. Marrow is the basis of their blood, which feeds the remainder of their body in turn. Marrow-refining cultivators gain powerful regeneration abilities stemming from the deep pool of vitality hidden within their marrow and the voids in their bones.

Blood Awakening – To transcend, body cultivators must awaken the divinity within their blood. How this is done is uncertain, though descendants of a god have a much easier time in doing so.

Soul Cultivation (Human)

The foundation of a cultivator is their soul. Sufficient soul force is necessary to become a professional, such as an alchemist or spiritual blacksmith. In some cases, a sufficiently strong soul is required to advance in cultivation. Buddhists and evil spirits often lean toward soul cultivation.

Innate Soul – Cultivators are born with an innate soul, and it grows as the cultivator advances in qi condensation. Eventually, with sufficient cultivation, the soul will make a rapid breakthrough into incandescence.

Incandescent Soul – In the incandescent realm, the soul begins to shine with incandescent light. Advanced soul manipulation of objects and mental communication is then possible.

Resplendent Soul – Once the soul is sufficiently incandescent, it becomes resplendent. A wrapping appears around the soul, which is called a resplendent vestment. It embellishes the soul and prepares it to transcend. Long-range scanning is possible at this realm.

Transcendent Soul – A transcendent soul grows sufficiently large and gains the ability to move. Since it has broken free from its shackles, it can then leave the mortal body and operate independently from it.

Demonic Cultivation

Humans aren't the only ones who can cultivate. Demons, manifestations of natural forces in the material world, take a different path. They are incapable of cultivating their qi, body, and soul separately. For demons, these three components are part of a complete cultivation system. Demon bodies can grow to massive sizes.

Demonification – Spirit beasts are products of nature. By gaining demonic qi from their natural surroundings, they grow in power. If their bloodline is sufficiently potent, they can break through and become demon beasts.

Purification – Bloodline purity is essential for a demon's advancement. Demons in the purification realm continuously purify their bloodline with demonic energy they gain by either consuming other demons, humans, or natural treasures. They can also do this by living on a demonic mountain, but the process is much slower. Demons who possess sufficiently pure and potent bloodlines can awaken ancestral memories.

Core Formation – When a demon's bloodline is sufficiently pure, it can be crystalized into a demonic core. By feeding this core with demonic energy, a demon grows stronger. Core-formation demons can fly.

Initiation – To reach the initiation realm, demons must first gain approval of the land. They condense demonic energy into an initiation mark that anoints them as initiates.

About the Author

Patrick Georges Laplante was born in a small town in the Canadian prairies in 1987. He began publishing Painting the Mists online under the pseudonym RedMirage in January 2018.

An engineer by trade, he graduated from the University of Alberta in 2009 and completed his master's degree in 2011. While writing and engineering have little in common, he actively utilizes his experiences and attention to detail in fleshing out a vivid world and answering the "whys," which are often left unanswered in xianxia fiction.

As an avid vegan, he aims to prompt internal reflection in his readers through various themes like non-violence, choice, and begging the question: Is personhood restricted to humanity? And what is proper conduct, morality, and love?

His work is inspired by a combination of Western fiction, *Dungeons and Dragons*, Chinese web novels, and various Japanese, Korean, and Chinese comics and illustrated novels.

www.ingramcontent.com/pod-product-compliance
Lightning Source LLC
Chambersburg PA
CBHW051536250626
47157CB00001B/75